BRIDE
of a
DISTANT
ISLE

A NOVEL

SANDRA BYRD

HOWARD BOOKS
AN IMPRINT OF SIMON & SCHUSTER, INC.

NEW YORK   NASHVILLE   LONDON   TORONTO   SYDNEY   NEW DELHI

Howard Books
An Imprint of Simon & Schuster, Inc.
1230 Avenue of the Americas
New York, NY 10020

First Howard Books trade paperback edition March 2016

HOWARD and colophon are trademarks of Simon & Schuster, Inc.

For information about special discounts for bulk purchases, please contact Simon & Schuster Special Sales at 1-866-506-1949 or business@simonandschuster.com.

The Simon & Schuster Speakers Bureau can bring authors to your live event. For more information or to book an event, contact the Simon & Schuster Speakers Bureau at 1-866-248-3049 or visit our website at www.simonspeakers.com.

Interior design by Jaime Putorti

Manufactured in the United States of America

10 9 8 7 6 5 4 3 2

Library of Congress Cataloging-in-Publication Data

Byrd, Sandra. Bride of a distant isle / Sandra Byrd—First Howard Books trade paperback edition.
        pages ; cm. (Daughters of Hampshire ; Book 2)
1. Young women—Fiction. 2. Inheritance and succession—Fiction. 3. Great Britain History—Victoria, 1837–1901—Fiction. I. Title.
PS3552.Y678B75 2016
813'.54—dc23
        2015026541

ISBN 978-1-4767-1789-0
ISBN 978-1-4767-1791-3 (ebook)

BRIDE
of a
DISTANT
ISLE

CHAPTER ONE

NEAR MILFORD ON SEA, HAMPSHIRE, ENGLAND
MAY, 1851

I had no warning before evil befell me.

Edward had abruptly recalled me to Highcliffe, but why now? It was not as if we'd often holidayed together, or enjoyed one another's companionship. In fact, over the course of our adult years I'd been home infrequently and we'd been mostly separated, at school, years before that. Grandfather was long dead, as were Edward's parents. Pretense could be done away with. Perhaps he'd had a sudden, inexplicable longing for family now we two were all that remained.

Unlikely.

The day after I arrived, I walked from the house, which was now crumbling, across the green lawn, now thinning, toward the Edge of the World, to gather my thoughts. I'd forgotten how the sea around Highcliffe relentlessly pounds the land, undermining it so fiercely that the earth quickens, churns, and slips; the breakers smother all sound, throwing off thickly salted mist that clouds vision like a cataract. For this reason, I had no signal that someone was approaching. Instead, I suddenly felt his breath curdling in my ear.

The whispering started.

"It was many and many a year ago," came the murmur, *"in a kingdom by the sea, that a maiden there lived whom you may know by the name of Annabel Lee; and this maiden she lived with no other thought than to love and be loved by me."*

"Mr. Morgan," I acknowledged, then hard-swallowed my bile and turned round to see his face. I knew by the familiar warped timbre of his voice that it was my cousin Edward's childhood friend and current associate. Their fathers had been friends, too, and their dubious dealings together extended back to that time. "I am taking my leave of you, returning to the house."

"Take your leave? No, indeed. I've long prepared to read Mr. Poe's poem aloud to you, Annabel. I purchased the book at great expense. Surely you'll give me the respect of listening attentively to the complete recitation."

"Please do not call me by my Christian name." I turned to face him. "It's forward." He wore finely spun black trousers and highly polished boots, but his girth was poorly restrained by a red silk waistcoat. Nearby stood a young woman, her face flat-planed and impassive.

"My sister," Mr. Morgan said at my glance. "Mrs. Wemberly. A widow." The gaps between Morgan's teeth had been charming as a child but now reminded me of the widening cracks in his soul, like a cobblestone path long left unattended, mortar washing away, extending the spaces as the years passed.

He placed himself between me and the worn walking trail, most often used by the sheep. I looked for a way around him, but there was none to be had without risking a fall. By the look of

Widow Wemberly, she must have been a child bride. "I do not recall you having a sister."

"My father had many children." He grinned. "Not all of them born, as they say, on the proper side of the blanket. I do not hold that against a person, especially a beautiful woman, though many others have and undeniably still do." He held my gaze. "Surely that is something you well understand, Miss Ashton. I've always kept *you* in my greatest admiration and esteem."

I flushed deeply, and he delighted in my discomfort. He closed the costly gilt-edged book from which he'd read and handed it toward me. "A gift. You can read it as we travel to London."

"Thank you." I twisted the cameo ring on my first finger, as I often did when discomfited. "You will accompany us?"

He nodded. "Perhaps it would be better put to say that you'll finally be coming with me." He suddenly seemed to tire of the effort required for false cheer and let his face take its natural course, falling into expressive displeasure: mouth turned down, skin dropping in folds round ruddy jowls that remained half hidden by unruly, hedge-like side-whiskers.

"Good day, Mr. Morgan, Mrs. Wemberly." I moved past them, walking toward the house.

Once in my room, I unwrapped myself from my light outer garments, using a corner of my shawl to scour the film of his words from my ear. I sat by the fireplace in my small room, though a fire had not been lit against the morning chill—to economize. I tentatively opened the volume and scanned a passage of Mr. Poe's poem.

And neither the angels in Heaven above
Nor the demons down under the sea

Can ever dissever my soul from the soul
Of the beautiful Annabel Lee;
For the moon never beams, without bringing me dreams
Of the beautiful Annabel Lee.

I closed the book and then closed my eyes to banish my grow-ing apprehension. *Perhaps*, he'd said, *it would be better put to say that you'll finally be coming with me.*

An hour later I made my way down to the kitchens. As a rule, the family did not venture below stairs, but I was different, not truly holding the same status as Edward and the others. Instead, I was caught between two worlds: born highly enough to be a lady, but with circumstances that dictated my lower position. It was an awkward and uncertain place to hold.

"Miss Annabel, how happy we are to see you!" Cook, a larg-ish matron, crushed me into her substantial bosom, which smelt of flour and the eye-watering pinch of bargain-priced violet perfume. I melted into her for a moment until Chef came. He made a small bow before turning to shout an order at a scul-lery maid. Chef still conducted himself with vigor, but his step had slowed.

None of them had been employed here in many years; most, I believed, had retired from service. I knew the reason they'd all re-turned to Highcliffe for one last season: to honor the memory of my late grandfather, whom they'd faithfully served for many years before Edward's father had taken over. Edward, living in London, had leased the country house to others for years, hoping his fi-nances would turn around. They had not.

Now, Highcliffe was to be sold. The old house was being

packed. The rooms were ghostly, furniture packed or covered with parchment-colored dust sheets like loosely draped shroud cloths. Only current living areas were to be left untouched, for now.

Chef bowed politely, and then led me into the stillroom, a place I'd often visited and had even hidden in when I was a young child. It had been a refuge for me, a quiet corner away from Edward's taunting.

"You'll need the *bonbons, non*? For the long journey?" Chef handed a small box to me, neatly wrapped in ribbon, and I opened it.

Perfectly square-cut fruit jellies shimmered in a dust of sugar, releasing the perfume of blackberry summer. Candied orange peels rested like a bundle of kindling against one side of the box while puffy pink pastilles, lips pursed to kiss, rested on the other.

"I shall need *les bonbons* for any journey, long or short, or even for simply indulging while visiting home. Thank you very much. I'm afraid I've boasted of them so often that my friends at school have asked me to stop speaking of them. When I return to teach, I shall keep quiet about this gift lest I incite further hostilities."

The room grew silent; unexpectedly, Chef looked with concern toward Mrs. Watts, temporary housekeeper, whose face grew sad. The others scurried away, none of them meeting my eye. Why the sudden change in their demeanor?

I stealthily returned up the back stairs to the second floor, the air dead and stale as it often is in houses long abandoned. I passed a new hall boy as I did. He, perhaps ten years younger than my four and twenty, nodded in surprise but didn't speak, which was to be expected as I should rightly have taken the main staircase. I nodded and smiled in return.

Strangely, the door to my small room was open, and although Maud had not yet arrived, the room looked to have been readied. My small trunk was neatly packed with the few belongings I had brought with me from Winchester. My vanity was prepared: a porcelain salver of water for washing, a silver powder jar of lemon chalk powder. *Horses sweat, men perspire, but women merely glow*, I recalled.

Clementine's lady's maid, older than most, with a face pungent as ripe cheese, soon arrived and we nodded to one another. "Well, then, Miss Annabel, if you're ready, I'll just help you into your dress, do your hair, and then I must return to Mrs. Everedge and her trunks."

"Of course, Maud, and I do appreciate your assistance." I was painfully aware that the few minutes granted me with Maud were a generosity Edward's wife, Clementine, spared as I would, of course, have no lady's maid of my own. I did not need one. I, and the other teachers at the Rogers Day School for Young Ladies, looked after ourselves.

Maud laced me tightly, prettily but firmly, as Chef might truss a chicken prepared to impress and then be served, and I sat down again, balancing on the edge of the dressing chair in front of the mirror.

She reached around me, and the longish necklace in her hands dropped in front of my dress while she clasped it from behind. I could see it in the mirror. I did not recognize it.

"This is new?"

"Surely you would be better put to answer that than I," she said. "'Tis yours, after all."

"I am quite sure it is not mine." I looked down. The chain was of finely polished gold, heavy and of the brightest quality. Dangling from the loop at the end of it was a silver fish with a gold ring in its mouth. "I would remember something so unique. I've never seen anything like this."

"Nor I. It was in with your other jewelry, miss." She held up the trinket box, and yes, I recognized everything else within it. Her voice lowered and was edged with a suspicious tone. "Perhaps you simply forgot, though it would be difficult to forget something as valuable and unusual as this."

I owned very few pieces of fine jewelry and would not have forgotten this, or any, one. Maud looked at me, still, an uneasy expression stealing across her face. I recognized that look; I had seen it many times before and was well practiced at discerning its implication. *Your mother was mad and died in an asylum. Are you quite sane yourself?* An off comment, a tired day, an unusual observation—any of these would have been casually overlooked in another woman. But not in me. Never in me.

I pushed away the panic that particular implication always aroused and applied my most soothing voice, also well practiced, like a warm, gentle hand on a goose-fleshed arm. "I'll bring it up with Clementine."

Maud exhaled and her face relaxed. She finished with me and returned to Clementine, with whom I hoped she would not share the strange necklace appearance. I stared at it again, both in my hand and in the mirror's reflection. From where had it come? I was certain it had not been there earlier in the day—nor ever. Had it been misplaced?

An unwelcome thought: had Mr. Morgan somehow acquired it and brought it with him this very afternoon, another odd gift? I grew light-headed with the thought and wished I were back in my small, safe room in Winchester.

I fingered the chain and then the fish. Touching it made me discomfited and wistful; it dredged up something murky and painful and anxious that I could not clearly place.

Stop being childish, Annabel. I pushed the feelings away and hoped whatever had been stirred up would soon settle once more to the bottom, allowing the emotional clarity and control I so carefully kept to return.

I walked down the hallway, where Clementine was finishing her travel preparations with Mrs. Watts.

"Yes?" Clementine asked impatiently.

"This necklace." I held it out. "Did you place it in my room?"

A strange look crept across her face. "Why . . . no. It's not yours?"

I did not know what to answer. "I thought it might have been misplaced."

She shook her head.

"It may just be that I don't remember it," I offered. "I do not wear much jewelry when I am teaching," I finished honestly, if perhaps a bit feebly.

She nodded. "You do not remember your own jewelry? You have so much, then? Or is your memory so unreliable for a woman your age? Of course, I do not know where you could have obtained the resources to purchase such an item. It looks quite valuable."

I said nothing. The hallway remained silent and still but the implication that the necklace had been stolen was nearly palpable, though unspoken.

"Yes, I must have forgotten it," I said, taking control of the conversation. "I'll continue my preparations and leave you to yours."

They each nodded slowly, but did not return to their conversation till I'd turned my back and retreated down the hallway. I heard Clementine's hushed, concerned voice whisper, *"Her mother."*

I certainly could not remove the necklace now without calling attention to our awkward conversation and all that it might imply. I would wear it for a week and then put it away.

CHAPTER TWO

Edward sent the young lad to fetch my bags. We were leaving for London.

I waited in the drawing room; it was papered in faded light blue silk, slightly torn here and there, that reflected both the waning afternoon light and the better days of my family's fortunes. It reminded me of my mother. I had a faint memory of the two of us in the drawing room together, singing. It made me smile.

Clementine and Maud were nowhere to be found, and I understood that the few servants would stay in place to continue packing the house; Edward had staff in London. We were to travel by train, spend some days, and then return to Highcliffe before I went on to Winchester. For now, it was just Edward and me in the room together, as it had occasionally been throughout our lives.

"I understand Mr. Morgan will be traveling with us?" I hoped the tremble in my voice and the dryness of my mouth did not betray my deep concerns and, yes, fear.

"He was to have accompanied us, but his sister suddenly took ill, and they departed about an hour ago. He'll meet us. I've invited him along for very specific reasons."

"What are those reasons, if I may ask? Forgive my misunder-standing, but I thought this was to be a family holiday to the Great Exhibition. That was what Clementine's letter relayed." The Great Exhibition, held in Hyde Park, London, was the favored project of Queen Victoria's husband, Prince Albert, as a showcase for the nations of the world to celebrate modern industrial technology and design. Prince Albert hoped to develop ties of commerce and investment among all nations—and, of course, claim pride of place for Britain. I looked forward to seeing what newfangled items might be displayed, and then sharing my finds with my students.

"It is, indeed," Edward reassured, his voice kind, always a warning and one I'd often failed to heed. He drew near. "I don't mind telling you, Annabel, now the staff are not nearby, that the family has fallen on somewhat challenging times."

I stepped back. "Which is why you've decided to sell High-cliffe."

He nodded and drew close again. "I'm retaining the house in London. I cannot maintain both."

There was no room for me, I knew, at the townhouse. It was fashionable but smaller than sprawling, crumbling Highcliffe. "I'll be in Winchester, so I won't impose upon you."

Notably, he did not acknowledge that.

"The family has always accommodated your schooling," he began instead.

"Yes, it is my family, too." He nodded, but we both knew our circumstances were dissimilar; Edward, as heir, held the purse strings, no matter how light in hand the purse had become.

"I consistently supplemented your insufficient stipend as a teacher of fine arts to young ladies. The family would benefit from your assistance now," he said. "I need your help." His voice, normally commanding, was strangely pleading. It softened me. I shouldn't have let my guard down, but I did.

"Of course, whatever I may do to assist," I replied after a brief prelude of hesitation.

Relief softened his features. "We knew we could count on you."

We?

He continued. "I have in mind two things. First, I'd like you to make small conversation, offer companionship and other social pleasantries, with someone whose family shipping operations could greatly enhance our position. Make him comfortable. And . . . learn what you can for me, especially if he is disposed to work together, or if he is making arrangements with others, instead. His name is Dell'Acqua."

"*His* name?" It would be most irregular to suggest I entertain a man. I could not imagine his suggesting this to Clementine, nor her approval on my behalf, frankly.

"In good and plenteous company," Edward said. "He's Maltese. "

"I see." And I did. Normally, my "mongrel" heritage, as Edward usually referred to it, was an impediment. But now it was to be used to show Mr. Dell'Acqua how open-minded and affable we were. And, in the process, learn his secrets and take his money.

"It is his first visit to England."

I sighed. A young lad, then—that explained all. It could not prove too difficult a task. I, of course, would be present for only a few weeks, but if I could smooth the path for Edward during that time it seemed little enough to request.

"You have more in common with him than Malta," he continued absentmindedly.

I waited for him to explain, but he did not.

"If the arrangements prove profitable enough, I may be able to save Highcliffe."

My heart leapt. There, perhaps, was motivation enough for me. "And the second way I might assist the family?"

"Excuse me, sir." Watts, the butler, stepped into the room. "All the cases are on board and the footman is ready to assist the ladies into the carriage."

"Annabel, after you." Edward held his arm out so that I might pass by, and Clementine and Maud stood nearby.

It had not escaped me that Edward had neatly circumvented several questions.

The carriage was heavily loaded, and we creaked our way down the long drive, toward the train station in nearby Brockenhurst. The lawn to either side was overgrown but still sharply green, dotted with white clover, over which hovered the fat honeybees our property was once known for. My mother would have inherited Highcliffe had her unwise choices not intervened. It tethered me to her; it was the only place we'd lived together. When it was gone I should be adrift.

I had been encouraged to forget all about my mother, to not think of her or speak her name, for fear of reminding others of her condition and setting them wondering if madness was to be my legacy.

But still, I remembered her. Being at Highcliffe once again, after so many years away, provoked those happy memories even more strongly. A young girl, no more than twelve, ran in the field, a shepherdess gathering her cloudlike sheep, their nubby little tails flapping up and down, before night fell. What would come of her upon the house's sale? Would she, too, be adrift?

Before we came to the end of the long entrance, which was rutted and muddy with neglect, the driver pulled over to let a cart pass. Who could be coming just when we were leaving? The cart held none but the driver and two heavy trunks. As it passed, I could clearly see that they were not just *any* trunks. Alarm flooded me and I swiftly turned back to Edward, sitting beside me.

"Those are *my* trunks. From the Rogers school. What is the meaning of this? I shall need my things when I return to teach two weeks hence."

Clementine looked out the window; Maud peered at her stained gloves. Edward met my eyes straight on, smiling a frozen little smile.

"You shall not be returning to Winchester, Annabel."

CHAPTER THREE

LONDON, ENGLAND
MAY, 1851

The next morning in London we ladies prepared ourselves, with Maud's help, to visit the Great Exhibition. I stayed in the room that was normally young Albert's, as he had remained at home at Highcliffe with his nanny. I'd not slept well, turning this way and that, listening to the outside night noises of cats crying and rats scurrying, the singsong pleas of early-morning pie and egg vendors, and worrying about what Edward had planned for me and why he had refused to say more. Highcliffe would soon be sold, the townhouse was small, and I had nowhere else to go. Where would I be sent?

And with whom? niggled at the back of my mind, which continued to present only one possibility. Edward had made an arrangement for me with Mr. Morgan. The Lord God promises His children that He has plans for them that will bring good, and not disaster.

In my experience, Edward worked in completely the opposite manner.

I closed my eyes for prayer and when I looked up, found that Clementine had entered the room and was looking wistfully at her young son's furnishings. She stepped to the clock and wound it; winding the clocks was normally Edward's exclusive domain but he would not enter the room while I was dressing, of course.

"Do you miss Albert already?" I asked. "I'm certain he misses you." In the years after my mother was taken, I felt her loss keenly, like an amputated limb.

Clementine nodded. "We are not often separated. I have but a few more years until he will leave for school." She drew herself up and asked, "Are you ready to depart?"

I nodded and followed her downstairs; our wide gowns squashed between the side walls and then popped into fullness again, like umbrellas expanding, once we were in the main hall. The carriage was brought round from the mews, and we were off.

The city bustled and bristled; wind had whisked away the London fog for the moment, and as we were not near the river it would not collect again for some hours. As we drove from Mayfair to Knightsbridge, caustic black flakes of coal still clung to the moist foliage that lined our route. We were let off near the south entrance to Hyde Park, and Clementine and I, arm in arm, made our way up the path. The smooth lane was lined on each side with trees, politely bobbing their slim green tops to all who passed. Constables on horseback patrolled, and there were hundreds of people from all over Great Britain wandering toward the Exhibition Hall, which beckoned in the distance. Prince Albert's triumph.

Yes, a crystal palace, I thought, *built completely of glass, like the world's solarium*; several stories high, it was a shimmering wedding cake with a vast atrium that resembled nothing so much as a spread lady's fan.

"There are rather a lot of foreigners," Clementine noted, looking around.

"That's the reason for the worldwide exhibition, is it not?" I gently rebuked.

She ignored that. "We're to meet Edward at the Maltese stand." Clementine checked the finely wrought gold watch she always wore round her neck; it had belonged to her mother and was very dear to her. Her father, I understood, was a clock collector, as was Edward. They'd met when Edward was a guest at their home in Dorset at an event for clock fanciers and then, rather unexpectedly, he and Clementine married.

"It won't do to be late." Her eye twitched. Far from being wrapped in the gauze of connubial bliss, I suspected she was nearly as uneasy as I was with Edward, who could be warm or cool, friendly or not, as the situation warranted—for his benefit, that was. We walked in through the south entrance, as we'd been instructed, and up the transept. Crowds of people milled about: couples with chaperones, youngsters sporting cheerful sailor hats with long ribbon tails, mothers firmly holding children's hands in their own gloved ones.

We had not walked far when I spied the Maltese flag. Malta's stand was wedged between India's and Ceylon's, strangely, rather than across the hallway with Italy, its nearest neighbor. I'd often thought of Malta, a tiny island in the middle of the Mediterranean, as being much like myself. Isolated. An amalgam of cultures, but with the purity of none. I smiled broadly with the anticipatory pleasure of meeting other Maltese.

"Please be temperate," Clementine admonished, her seriousness far advanced for someone of her youth. I hid my smile. My heart swelled again as we approached the Maltese stand with its beautiful fine art, sculptures and urns welcoming at the front, striking paintings hung on the walls behind.

I had never felt proud of my Maltese half. I hadn't been al-lowed to, really. But now, something kindled.

My father. Who was he? Why hadn't he wanted me or my mother? Why had he left her in the worst possible circumstances? She had, I believed, died of a broken heart. I could never forgive him that, whoever he was, nor the desperate straits his uncharita-ble lack of chivalry and attention had left me in.

I shook the thoughts off as I spied Edward standing among a group of men. I quickly looked the group over; Mr. Morgan was not present. I exhaled a bubble of relief.

"Yes, yes, here she is." Edward reached his hand out toward me, entirely ignoring Clementine, who bristled but quickly hid the affront. "My cousin, Miss Annabel Ashton."

The men were all shy of thirty years, rugged but well dressed, several with dark hair, clearly Maltese. One man, who seemed to be in charge, was English, or looked it, and had been staring in-tently at me. His hair was wheaten and pulled back into a sailor's queue, his jawline square with a hint of a beard, as if it had been caressed in sand; it looked nothing like the carefully landscaped, sometimes bushy faces of most of the men I knew. Unlike the others, this man did not wear a top hat.

I caught and held his unwavering gaze; his eyes were unex-pectedly deepest brown. Clementine, from behind me, cleared her throat, and I looked away.

"Miss Ashton," the blond man bowed. "I am Captain Marco Antonio Dell'Acqua."

What? He looked English. This was the young Maltese Dell'Acqua? "You are a man, not a lad," I burst out, immediately wishing I could reclaim those words, but I could not. I felt Clem-entine glaring behind me. *Be temperate* indeed!

The men, save Edward, burst out in pleasant laughter. "I'm

most gratified that you noticed," Dell'Acqua said teasingly, his English dashingly accented by a baritone, Italianate roll.

I blushed and corrected myself. "How do you do," I said. "My cousin has spoken well of you."

Edward smiled at me then, and I hoped I had regained my balance after an initial stumble. We made small talk for a moment, and then Captain Dell'Acqua's colleagues returned to the back of the stand. Edward insisted that he'd just remembered he had arranged a meeting and asked Dell'Acqua if he would show me, and Clementine, of course, around the exhibition.

"*Ecco*, I would be delighted," the captain said in his lightly accented English, which, I admit, I found enchanting.

"Now, and whilst he is in England, learn what you can about his plans and affairs through pleasant enquiries, and make him comfortable with England, and us in particular," Edward whispered to me. "And then convey to me anything you learn."

I frowned but did not reply. I could certainly be courteous. I could help where it was appropriate. But I was not going to spy. Why should I?

I reached around for Clementine to take my left arm, the captain on my right, but instead, she trailed a few feet behind us.

Very irregular.

"Perhaps with the right investment arrangements, Highcliffe might be saved."

I looked at him, and he winked. He knew that I'd want to help save our home.

As we left Edward, he pulled a packet of ginger chews from within his trouser pocket and put one in his mouth; they soothed his touchy digestion.

We strolled toward the flamboyantly decorated ceiling displays, all swirls of baroque, which caught Clementine's eye. As she spoke with the artisans, Captain Dell'Acqua made small talk with me.

"Your name, Miss Ashton, it does not sound Maltese, and yet your cousin said you were Maltese?"

Oh dear. Had we to begin here? First minutes of the conversation? For some peculiar reason, I did not want this man to view me or my mother negatively, as he surely would once he knew the circumstances.

"Ashton was my dear mother's surname," I said. "I never met my Maltese father."

He blushed deeply, and I was glad of the sensitivity that showed. "I apologize on behalf of the men of Malta," he said. "And for my ungallant question."

"No apology required," I answered quietly. Clementine had moved on to look at draperies across the aisle.

"My father is an Englishman," the captain confided in return, perhaps in penance at having raised my shame. "And *I* have never met *him*. He came to Malta on a Grand Tour, where he met, wooed, won, and then left my beloved mother. He did not return." His voice took on an edge of resentment.

I looked up wonderingly. "Truly?"

"Truly."

This, then, must be what Edward meant when he'd said Dell'Acqua and I had more in common than Malta. I quickly changed the subject as Clementine rejoined us. "Edward says this is your first visit to England."

He nodded. "I normally sail in warmer waters."

Was he referring to the bitterness with which he held his English father?

"But I could not pass up the unique opportunity to meet with other men of commerce from all over the world. I understand *Signora's* husband has similar sentiments." He nodded toward Clementine. She did not disagree. "It is an age of exploration," he continued, "and your Prince Albert believes that world trade might bring peace and prosperity to all nations. I hope so, too, as does your husband, I believe, *Signora.*" He looked at Clementine. "That's why we've come from Malta and these others," he spread his arm to indicate the other nations' exhibits, "from their homelands."

"Tell me of Malta," I implored as we walked. "No one will speak of it with me—well, no one but a nun I once knew in Winchester, she being Maltese."

"I should be very happy to do so. Let's take a seat." We made our way to a refreshment area, and after buying Mr. Schweppe's effervescent ginger beer and soft Bath buns studded with chewy sultanas, we sat down.

I took a sip, and my eyes opened wide.

"You are quite well?" the captain asked.

"Yes," I said. "Delighted. It's just that it bubbles up the nose and down the throat at the same time." I took another drink and giggled.

Clementine's frown declared her dissatisfaction at my forthright comments if not at my swigging and giggling, but Dell'Acqua grinned.

"Malta is a small island, wholly surrounded by blue," he said, his gaze searching my face, "perhaps the very color of your eyes. Our homes and buildings are sculpted from butter-yellow stone and are hung with black lanterns so each can find his way in the dark."

"What a beautiful sentiment," I said, thinking of it well beyond surface meaning.

He smiled. "Each home has a porch that invites both fresh air and meddlesome neighbors into loud family arguments. Often those neighbors come unsolicited to offer an opinion on the matter at hand."

Even Clementine smiled at that.

"We have many churches, perhaps a hundred, perhaps more. But our churches are Roman Catholic. As are we."

"As am I." I pinched off a bite of my bun before catching the look of revulsion that flitted across Clementine's face at my admission.

Dell'Acqua's face, on the other hand, reflected astonishment. "*È vero?*" he asked, reflecting my earlier question, but slipping into Italian. "You are Catholic?"

"*È vero,*" I answered in return. "Truly. But in England, Captain, perhaps we should speak English."

"Ah, the lady is correct." He regained his composure. We spoke of the Chinese exhibit as we bought tea. China had declined to come to London, still angry over the British taking of Hong Kong, but someone had ensured there was a lovely display of Chinese porcelain, textiles, jade, lacquer and silk paintings, medicine roots, and, of course, tea. Clementine took two lumps of sugar; I stirred honey into mine.

"Did you know that Malta is famous for our honey, which is made from thyme-fed bees? I shall have to see if I can find some for you. Come, let's visit the Greece exhibit—perhaps they have some, though it is certain to be of poorer quality than Malta's."

"Of course it is." I laughed.

"Greeks are more famous for their 'crazy honey' than for their herbed honey." He held one arm out to me and the other to Clementine.

"Surely you jest, 'crazy honey'?" *Please, please, let's not discuss my mother's shame today as well as my father's.*

"I do not jest, Miss Ashton. Ancient Greeks fed it to young women who would then be inspired to tell the truth, among other things—if they did not imbibe too much, that is." He continued speaking of Malta and its people as we made our way to the Greek stand and admired their wares, but no matter how he charmed, he could not convince them to give some of their displayed golden honey to me. This was, after all, the Great Exhibition, not the Great Sale.

We then walked upstairs to the area in which there were toys displayed. Clementine found a drum she thought Albert would adore and Captain Dell'Acqua tried to acquire it, again cajoling and pleading with no luck.

"I am sorry, I failed. I am disgraced." He looked chastened, and I liked him all the more for it. I suspected he was a man used to getting his way.

"You've been a very kind host," Clementine reassured him as we returned to where we'd begun.

"I could not have asked for a better afternoon," I offered. "I have somehow found something I was longing for but didn't know until you began to speak."

"And that would be . . . ?" He left the sentence dangling and grinned, having reclaimed, I saw, his swagger.

"Malta, of course, Malta." I playfully returned the volley. "What else?"

Clementine looked askance at me, and honestly, I was rather surprised at myself. What was it about this captain that made me intemperate and impulsive? Perhaps it was not him at all, but the freedom of London. All of it was rather intoxicating. I found that I did not, just then, miss the safety of the day school.

"We shall see you tomorrow evening." Clementine nodded toward him, and the captain bowed toward each of us. He then took my hand in his own for a long moment. I did not wish for the moment to expire, but it did. I looked away from him to see Mr. Morgan in the distance, staring at the extended exchange between Captain Dell'Acqua and myself.

While we waited for Edward to collect us, Clementine studied a marble urn; I edged my way a bit farther into the booth. Dell'Acqua had left, but some of his sailors remained. The stand was not large, and two of them spoke in low voices, guttural, in a language difficult for many to penetrate and untangle.

"He is not taken with her. I do not care what you think you see," the bald one, who wore the rank of lieutenant, answered the other. "Marco is here for two reasons alone: to try to meet his father and to gain investment for Malta. That's all. If he breaks an English girl's heart to avenge his poor mother along the way, why, so much the better. He'd say so himself."

The second man nodded his agreement. "But did you see how he looked at her? Kept her hand? That is not like him."

"Of course it is," the lieutenant answered. "He's the consummate flirt. Eh? You've seen him. And Everedge can help him achieve both of his objectives. In the end, that is what Marco cares about most. Passing time with a pretty girl will help him attain what he wants."

"Won't Everedge be enraged when he finds out his cousin's heart was wooed and discarded?"

"Everedge only cares that she may be of assistance to him. Then?" He made a motion like tossing a handkerchief behind him. "The English, they are not like us. And Marco?" The lieutenant switched from Maltese to Italian. "*Chi vuol pigliare uccelli non deve trar loro dietro randelli.*" Deal gently with the bird you mean to catch.

"She's educated, and likely to speak Italian," the other said softly, looking at me. He smiled, and I smiled back, and then turned away, ears still tuned toward them.

He shrugged. "She understood nothing. She does not speak Maltese."

I moved away, slowly, pretending to look at the paintings on the wall, meeting no gaze, nor indicating that I had overhead.

Oh, but I do speak Maltese, Lieutenant. Yes, I understood you. Completely.

CHAPTER FOUR

The next morning Clementine told me to be ready to visit some shops just after breakfast. Normally the seamstress came to visit, but on this occasion Clementine wanted to visit the dressmaker herself. "They have ready-made items in shops run by milliners and other tradeswomen of quality," she added, comfortingly. "Edward says you need some new attire."

I set my teacup down near my plated egg. "Edward wants me to buy dresses? I had thought we were to economize."

She nodded. "We are. But you must be appropriately attired for our station. He looks at the improvements as an investment." She glanced at my fish necklace, her face scrunching, but said nothing about it, for which I was glad. What should I answer if she asked me how I'd come to own such an unusual object? I willed her gaze away, and saints be praised, it worked. Clementine dregged her tea and stood up. "Be ready on the hour."

She excused herself whilst I finished, and as I did, I took in the richness of the room. It had been expensively papered and the floors furnished with plush carpets that our family had imported from Turkey, one component of the family investments that yet flourished. We'd been importing and exporting for a century or more, I knew. Around the room were many fine examples of Grandfather's sterling collection: table bells and candlesticks, even silver ostrich egg cups, some fashioned to look like coconut shells. I recalled our confectioner serving coconut ices in them at Highcliffe when Edward and I had been children. *Edward's pilfered all the best bits from Highcliffe, scavenging the fleet as it were before he abandoned it.*

I met Clementine by the front door; as the weather was mild we decided to walk, which I greatly enjoyed. We nodded at other women as they, too, walked along the promenade and made our way toward the shop Clementine had in mind.

"I'm still confused at why I am not returning to Winchester." I hoped the truth would be easier to pry from her than from Edward.

"Resources. You cannot stay there without a supplement to your stipend, and we can no longer afford it. Clearly, Annabel, you see that. We are selling Highcliffe."

"Will there not be sufficient funds for my needs then, after the sale?"

Clementine looked at me as though I were a child, and not, in actuality, a year older than she. "What is 'sufficient,' Annabel?"

"A rightful portion. Where has the money gone?"

"Revenue Acts," she said quietly. "Taxes are lowered. Times have changed. There are debts."

It still made no sense to me. What had revenue collection to do with the family's importing and exporting concerns? "What will happen to me? Shall I move to London with you?"

She shook her head and just then we arrived at the dress shop. We spent an hour or more there; she bought several dresses for me, day wear and evening wear, which would be delivered that very day, including a lovely midnight-blue gown that set off my eyes. I delighted in it until she commented, "Perhaps the darkness of the dress will bring out the paleness of your skin and minimize your freckles."

Crestfallen, I said, "I hadn't thought they were conspicuous. Perhaps I should employ rose cream and try to lighten them."

"Don't bother. Apparently Mr. Morgan finds them charming. Distinctive. His opinion is what matters."

"It is?" I asked, but she kept looking ahead, walking briskly. A chill swept over me though there was no wind. Had Morgan made so personal, so evaluating a comment about me to Clementine? And was I now to please him? At what cost to myself, and for what reason? I felt ill and though normally spry, in need of a rest.

Edward will ensure you come to no harm, I tried to reassure myself. He was a merciless teaser, he was selfish, yes, but we were cousins. Siblings, almost, at least in my eyes. Perhaps I just very much wanted to convince myself that I could trust him.

As we walked toward the townhouse we passed what looked to be a Catholic church; as there were few left in England, I couldn't be certain. "I should like to attend before we leave, if I may," I said, tentatively. "It will have been a week and as you know, there is no Catholic church in Lymington."

I had felt spiritually at home during my years in Winchester, at St. Peter's on St. Peter's Street. Where would I now attend Mass? Who would hear my confession?

To my great surprise, Clementine said, "You may attend if it brings you comfort."

"Thank you!" I gently squeezed her arm.

After a few moments, she asked, "Why did you become Catholic?"

She had been married to Edward for but a few years, and most of that time I had been in Winchester. I did not know what she had been told of my background.

"My mother, Julianna Ashton, was the older sister of Edward's mother, Judith," I began.

"Oh, the sainted Mrs. Judith Ashton Everedge," she exclaimed, bitterness filling in the edges of her voice. "Of whom one might never imply wrongdoing, or even the clay feet of mere humanity. Edward's petulant that I have inherited her things."

I had few memories of my mother's sister; she had not wanted me around, so many of my holidays were spent with governesses or at school, and when I'd been home she'd had little to do with me. In truth, she'd had little to do with Edward.

"Carry on, Annabel." Clementine waved her fan at me. "Continue."

"When they were young ladies they took a Grand Tour, spending an especial amount of time in Malta because of the rich art history. My mother became a Catholic while there, and, I assume, fell in love with a Maltese man. When trouble began brewing with Greek independence, Grandfather sent for them to come home. He was ill. They returned, and, well, Judith married Edward's father."

I'd heard that Grandfather had first intended Edward's father for my mother. "My mother soon bore me. She died a few years hence."

In an asylum, gone mad, having had a child out of wedlock. Then there was the strain of having been abandoned. Papist. Raving. I did not speak this, of course. There was always vigorous concern for the children of the insane, that they, too, might carry a tainted strain that would suddenly manifest itself. It was best not brought up, even to oneself, because there were moments when I realized how different I was from the others around me and wondered, *I, too?*

This thought inevitably provoked internal panic: Would I also be locked away in an insane asylum, listening to the shrieking, raving cries of those around me? My own shrieking, raving cries? Imprisoned. Frightened. Terrified and alone and forgotten. And then dead.

I'd spent years imagining and then pushing away the dread thoughts I'd conjured up about my sweet mother's last years. I'd carefully ensured that I did or said nothing that might lead to her terrifying fate, and I'd spend the rest of my life doing so, if need be.

It was my greatest fear. I shivered in the sunlight.

"Are you quite all right?" Clementine asked.

I took my handkerchief out and dabbed my forehead, then nodded and continued. "In any case, I was, er, naturally born, which meant I was ineligible to inherit Highcliffe and Grandfather's other interests and estates when my mother passed away. It all went to Judith, and then to Edward."

Clementine nodded.

"Despite the circumstances, I wanted to learn something about my parents, so I began with what I knew, and that was their faith. Along the way, I discovered and committed myself to its truth." I did not tell her that a kind elderly woman I met in church, whom I assumed to be a nun as she wore a habit and called herself Sister Rita, had taught me Maltese, carefully, patiently, week by week.

Clementine said nothing further for a long moment until we rounded the corner to the block where our townhouse was.

"I wish I had something to lean on, to cherish and bring comfort."

"Your faith?" I knew she attended an Anglican church each week with the rest of the family and staff. To not have done so would be to call her very decency into question.

But no. She shook her head.

"Then faith in Edward, and Albert?"

"Albert. Yes, Albert," she said, sounding weary. She looked me in the eye. "Do you want children, Annabel?"

No one had ever asked me that, the kind of question a good friend might ask. Why the sudden interest in my life? I supposed it was a natural enough question, having just thought of Albert.

"If it were possible," I said, giving voice to a longing I'd quelled. "Marriage to a good man, and children. If not, then teaching brings me pleasure and satisfaction."

Second best is always less, my old governess used to say.

Clementine held my gaze for a bit longer. "Marriage would do you good. It can certainly be arranged, and quickly." As we rounded the steps to the townhouse, I thought, *It hasn't seemed to have done you good.* Was the arranging, indeed, already underway?

"Quickly does not seem wise to me," I said.

"Edward and I were married quickly," she said.

Yes, I remembered the circumstance, and a quote from Mr. Congreve came to mind. *Thus grief still treads upon the heels of pleasure: married in haste, we may repent at leisure.*

Jack Watts, Edward's steward and the son of Mr. and Mrs. Watts at Highcliffe, opened the door. His face, so young, so eager, reflected his absolute contentment at having found a situation for himself in London, not easy for a young man from Lymington.

"Welcome home, Mrs. Everedge, Miss Annabel," he said.

Clementine barely acknowledged him. "Packages will be delivered this afternoon," she said. "Please let Maud know when they arrive."

Later, I sat on my bed, thinking about the day. It had been a kindness of Clementine to allow me to attend Mass, to take me to purchase clothing, to share Maud for a moment or two each day. I wanted to repay her favor.

I had an idea and sat down to sketch Albert, in his curls still, from memory. I took it and tentatively knocked on her door. There was no answer, and I was just about to leave when she opened the door slightly.

"Yes?"

I faced the door's crack. "I've drawn something for you. To thank you for your kindnesses."

She opened the door a bit more and took the paper from me; her hair was disheveled, and I smelt something strange, like licorice, or spirits, or both. The vacancy in her eyes alarmed me, as did the sorrow. She closed the door without a word.

I then took afternoon tea in the drawing room, as was my habit, the particular Chinese blend that had been a family standard for years. When I returned to my room to prepare for the evening, I found all of my clothing had been removed and replaced by the new items Clementine and I had purchased. I sought out Maud to question her.

"Did you remove my things?" I asked.

She nodded. "Mrs. Everedge said it was for the best."

"Without asking me?" I felt naked, violated. She shrugged. We both knew whose whistle she must answer to. Later, as she dressed me in my new garments, it felt as though I were dressing for a part rather than enjoying the blessing of new and beautiful clothing.

Perhaps I shall *dress for a part*, I suddenly thought. *One of compliance, while I seek occasion to turn things my way. I shall find a way.*

CHAPTER FIVE

There was not a bare inch of space in Nigel Morgan's foyer. The very walls suffocated with objets d'art, most of them curious, frightening. The surfaces were papered in bloodred velvet, and though most homes had progressed to using lamps, gas or oil, Morgan's home was ablaze with hundreds of ivory candles that seemed to wink malevolently. Clementine and I reluctantly yielded our wraps; perhaps she, too, felt the need to insulate herself from the oddities. Edward seemed more comfortable; I assumed he had been in Morgan's home many times before.

We were led into the drawing room, where crystal glasses rested on a silver tray with flasks of spirits, which I politely declined.

"You'll not join Mrs. Everedge in enjoying the green fairy?" Morgan pressed. He drew uncomfortably near and smelled of the Turkish hookah smoke that sometimes clung to Edward; hookah was fashionable at men's clubs, and I knew it was part of our family's imports.

"I'm not familiar with green fairies," I answered politely. *And they suspect* me *of madness!*

"Absinthe, my dear," Edward said. He looked disapprovingly as

Morgan poured water through a sugar cube and into a small glass that held the verdant liquor. Immediately, the area filled with the sweet tang of licorice.

"This particular blend is stronger than most—it's the wormwood, you see. It will free your mind," Mr. Morgan added.

And the tongue and perhaps restraint, I thought. *A pleasant boon to you, I'm certain.* "Thank you, but no." I could not afford to act in any way that was not completely self-composed. Clementine took hers immediately.

"Tea with honey," I said. "If you have it."

The drawing room was as strange as the foyer, perhaps even more so. A hundred or more busts of men had been placed on pillars and hearths around the room: lifeless, white, flat eyes everywhere, following us, plaster visages staring, silent, but listening. No matter which way I turned my head I was met with a dead gape. The only way to escape would be to close my own eyes, which, of course, I could not do. "This is an interesting collection," I noted, politely.

"Men I admire," Morgan said. "Men of letters and music, commerce, industry, self-made men."

"I'm in debt to such as well," Edward said casually.

"You're in debt to many, aren't you, Everedge?" Morgan spoke too bluntly for polite company or even for a friend among gentlemen. "Including to me. Though we shall take care of that soon." He turned to me and grinned. "Shan't we?" The mordant stink of a hundred burning wicks mingled with the floral-scented candle wax, oversweet, like the stench of a decaying but not yet dried rose.

I hard-swallowed.

"And the cameos," Clementine said. "They are . . . ?" She referred to a wall papered in deep pink silk, upon which were hung several dozen plaster cameos of women's profiles, all framed in antique gold.

"Conquests, of course," Morgan said, and Clementine gasped while my eyes grew wide.

"See here!" Edward interrupted indignantly.

"I but jest," Morgan stepped in. "My apologies, ladies. I spend far too much time in the cruder company of my own sex and I forget myself. They represent ladies I have known and admired—such as my mother, my nanny, a governess, my sister-in-law, and women throughout the ages whose beauty I appreciate and whose likenesses I have commissioned to be reproduced."

I quickly scanned the wall. I did not see a cameo that resembled the widowed Mrs. Wemberly.

Morgan continued. "I appreciate fine art and, with no disrespect to the fairer members of my own nation, prefer something different from the typical bland English rose. You'll notice the center of the wall, pride of place, remains empty." He looked firmly in my direction. "For now."

I cast my gaze aside. Edward spoke up, changing the subject. "What time are Dell'Acqua and his company anticipated?"

There was a longish pause before Morgan answered. "They will not be coming."

I hoped I hid my disappointment. I thought back to Mr. Morgan staring at the captain and me at the Great Exhibition. Had he subsequently disinvited them?

Edward looked puzzled. "I thought the idea was to build on our common investment interests. We're exhausting the other alternatives."

"He'll rejoin us on the coast," Morgan said as his butler came to announce dinner. "We've months to complete negotiations before summer ends." Mr. Morgan then stood, offered his arm to me, and led the way into the dining room.

Clementine and Edward, Morgan and me. An awkward foursome. I wondered if Edward was truly surprised by this change in dinner guests; he seemed to be.

We sat down at the table, also blazing with candles, and I looked around. There were pictures of exotic animals as well as some real animals, killed and stuffed, all gazing down upon us. As the turtle soup was served, I became aware, in particular, of a monkey on the wall, its face stretched into a permanent scream.

"I grew fond of monkeys after seeing some at the Saint Bartholomew Faire," Morgan said, following my interest.

I murmured something about how interesting his collection was, which seemed to satisfy him, but I wondered if this was the manner in which he treated those of whom he was, temporarily at least, fond. I no longer had an appetite. He pressed a second helping on me anyway.

"Cook can be instructed to prepare whatever you like to eat," he said. "She's versatile. You'll get on quite well."

"I hardly think that will be required," I responded.

The dinner conversation revolved around the Exhibition and contacts made there, of which the most promising were the Maltese, as they were strategically located in the center of the Mediterranean Sea and, therefore, critical for victualing and restocking all sides. I couldn't have been certain and they'd not admit to it, but the implication was that Edward and Morgan, along with their contemporaries, would be happy to supply and arm both Great Britain and whomever we might fight against, for profit.

Horrifying. Did the Maltese also operate thusly?

After dinner, the gentlemen retired to the library to smoke cigars and Clementine excused herself from the company to tend to personal needs. The men assumed I accompanied her. I did not.

Instead, I quietly sought out the housekeeper I'd seen floating like an apparition around the edges of the house.

"Excuse me," I began, once I had trapped her in a corner. "I'm just wondering, is Mrs. Wemberly well? I knew she'd been taken ill a few days ago."

The ferret-like housekeeper looked confused. "Who, miss?"

"Mrs. Wemberly. Mr. Morgan's sister." I had a quick look around to make sure neither the men nor Clementine were coming to find me.

She shook her head. "Mr. Morgan does not have a sister, miss."

"She is about my age, perhaps a few years younger, with reddish hair and a dimple"—I touched my chin—"here."

At that, a veil dropped over her countenance, and I knew what she was going to say before she said it. My breath quickened.

"Never seen anyone like that," she said, but her darting eyes betrayed her. "I must be about my duties, now. Good evening, Miss."

I had suspected Mrs. Wemberly had not been his sister. More likely he had tipped his own hand earlier . . . she'd been a conquest, a woman held lightly.

This was the man Edward had, by all indications, destined for me.

The next day was to be our last at the Exhibition. Edward and Clementine, and Mr. Morgan and I, walked through the transept. I had always been fascinated by India and wanted to spend some time at their booth. I looked at the lovely lace, made by Indian hands but using British methods. Mr. Morgan was most eager that we visit the jewel, literally, of the Indian offerings.

He led us to the Koh-I-Noor, the great diamond, 186 carats uncut, and guarded in a cage that had been topped by a crown.

"No one can steal her, then," he said. I thought it would be hard to lug such an item away, and while I murmured politely, as did Clementine, in truth I found it a bit vulgar.

"Do you like it, Miss Ashton?" he asked me, his voice pleading for any affection, which I could not give. The few times I'd met him as a child and young lady, he'd been likewise beseeching and clingy.

"It's a lovely bit of colonial culture," I replied. He took my arm in an overly familiar manner and grinned widely, the smile of a man who had been given permission.

Permission to me, of course.

CHAPTER SIX

꩜

HIGHCLIFFE HALL, PENNINGTON PARK
EARLY JUNE, 1851

We returned to Highcliffe, I still wondering when someone would speak aloud what was already eddying in the unspoken currents: what my future held. I, however, did not want to speak first and suggest something that might not yet be determined. The house was still being packed. Edward continued making arrangements. One morning, I repaired to the nursery with Lillian, Albert's nanny, as the chambermaids made up our rooms.

"Mrs. Watts herself is preparing the guest rooms," Lillian chattered freely to me as she wiped Albert's face after his morning toast.

"Indeed! Unusual, is it?" I invited the conversation to continue.

She nodded. "If you can imagine that, though she's not worked here for twenty years, I've heard. She's come to help Watts, of course, and to keep them all happy with her son Jack, who is Mr. Everedge's valet but remains in London to run the house this summer as the mister is more often there. The house-maids work hard. Six and a half days a week, one day off per month, blacking beneath their nails, out of work completely when the family moves, and for what, I ask you?"

"I'm sure I don't know," I answered politely, and played patty-cake with Albert, who shouted in delight.

"I'm sure you don't, not that I mean it unkindly," Lillian answered forthrightly, which pleased me very much. She took my smile as permission to finish her thought.

"It's working for the rich, married to a man they like or not, or the workhouse. Them's the options for the likes of us. The house is meant to be sold by end of summer, and then they'll all have to find new positions."

My stomach clutched. End of summer. I had perhaps two months to find a situation that would allow me to escape Morgan. I knew Edward's intentions, though they'd remained unstated.

Lillian spoke up again as I ran my hand affectionately over young Albert's hair. "I love the boy, but I shan't remain in service. I already raised my mum's whole brood after she died giving birth to the last. I can read and do sums quite well. I intend to become a shopgirl."

"A shopgirl?" I asked. "In Lymington?" I was not aware of any female shop help nearby.

"No, miss, in London," Lillian said. "And if I cannot be a shop-girl then I shall marry a shop owner and be in charge that way." She fastened a loose button on a pair of Albert's trousers before setting them aside. "I will be mistress of my destiny."

"Right after you put a stitch in Albert's clothing," I said. She looked at my face and saw I was teasing, and smiled herself.

"Yes, Miss Ashton, it may not be now. But it will come."

"I've no doubt it will," I said, taking courage from her own. I, too, had decided to take action of some sort this week. Several ideas had presented themselves and I would put my mind to them simultaneously and soon, very soon indeed . . . just after I greeted Captain Dell'Acqua, that was.

He was due to arrive that day.

By late afternoon, I heard a carriage drive up, and then soon enough a commotion of deep voices assembled in the foyer. I'd thought that perhaps at the last moment he would have his invitation withdrawn, as had happened at Mr. Morgan's. But no. He had come.

Clementine and I were taking tea in the solarium, the one room of cheer in a dim home being shuttered and packed. Its glass allowed a flood of sun in year round, and while it was especially pleasant in the winter, it must have been too warm just then because I felt my face flush.

"My dear." Edward held out his hand, and Clementine rose to meet him and greet their guests. Captain Dell'Acqua caught my eye but allowed his gaze to linger on me for only the briefest moment; it would not do to be inattentive to his host's wife, and he warmly greeted Clementine. I was not called over, so I did not stand, but I could hear and watch them.

The captain smiled warmly at Clementine and took her hand in his own, kissing the back of it, never letting his eyes wander. I watched her soften and lean toward him in a way I had not noted before—not even with Edward.

He gently released her hand but did not move away from her. Nor did she from him. "I have something for the young Albert." The captain held out a beautifully wrapped square box.

"How delightful, Captain Dell'Acqua. You shouldn't have."

Clementine then called for Lillian, who brought the young

ruffian downstairs. The captain presented Albert with the box, which he tore open with great hunger and little decorum.

"A dwum, a dwum, a dwum!" Albert shouted and then banged the sticks against it, causing a glee-filled hullabaloo. His spaniel ran under one of the sofas and remained there. The men burst out laughing, and one of them pretended to reach for the drum that Albert firmly tucked under his arm.

I felt a pang of love for him, and then an unexpected pang of desire for a child of my own.

"Lillian shan't thank you for that noise, but I do," Clementine said softly. "How very kind of you to remember."

"I saw, at the Exhibition, how important that drum was to you. At that moment, it became important to me. It is a pleasure to indulge the son of a . . . friend." *Very astute, Captain Dell'Acqua. You have at least one ally at Highcliffe now.* To please Albert was to win Clementine. To please Clementine was to please Edward.

Could the captain find Clementine attractive? He certainly exuded charm toward her, and she had clearly responded. Maybe it was just convenient flirting to assist him in achieving his goals, as his friends had suggested he was given to.

Watts said that he would show the rest of the party to their quarters; the guest wing was a floor above the family's rooms. "If I may speak with Miss Ashton for a moment," Dell'Acqua said. Watts looked at Edward, who nodded.

"I shall be rearranging some volumes in the library," Clementine said, smiling at me. She could see into the solarium from the library, chaperoning, though from a distance.

I sat on the sofa, trying to keep my face placid and wondering, as I did, why this man even stirred my interest. Simply because he was different? *For shame, Annabel.* Hadn't I rebelled against that peculiar kind of novelty when it had been directed toward me? Because he was Maltese? Maybe. Because he made me smile? I did smile, then. Yes, that.

"You're smiling." He sat on the chair across from the palm tree–fabric-lined sofa upon which I perched. I appreciated his manners; he did not sit next to me, which would have been uncomfortably forward.

"Am I?"

"You are," he said, his tone playful. "Maybe because I have brought a gift for you. I hope that Everedge, or you, do not mind."

I looked in his hand then and saw a much smaller package, also carefully wrapped, which must have been hidden behind Albert's larger one.

"You needn't have . . ." I began. What would Edward think? Probably little, if the familiarity brought him the arrangement he sought. *I shan't be as easily won over as Albert.*

"I wanted to." Dell'Acqua held the package out to me, and I took it and carefully pulled the ribbon wrapped around it, which dropped to the floor. I lifted the lid of the box, and nestled inside was a glass jar filled with amber liquid.

"Thyme honey. From Malta." The captain's face was suddenly boyish and seeking my approval. I offered it freely in response.

"I'm delighted! I believe this is the first time in my life that someone has purchased a gift for me, thinking and remembering something that would perfectly suit."

"I was sorry I could not acquire it at the Exhibition, but I did not give up. If I'm not interested in something"—he snapped his fingers—"I forget about it immediately. But if there is something I truly want, I go after it until it's mine." His voice took on an arch tone, which I did not acknowledge.

"How industrious," I said demurely while reaching over to pour a fresh cup of tea for myself. "Henceforth, I shall only sweeten my tea, which I drink without fail every afternoon, with Maltese honey, whilst the supply holds. Thank you kindly, Captain Dell'Acqua. I shall store it in the silver honey pot my grandfather treasured."

"You're most welcome," he said. "And I shall replenish it as often as need be while I am still in England, having it delivered to your cook." I offered to pour a cup of tea for him, and he accepted.

"Honey?" I held the new jar toward him.

"No, thank you," he said. "I do not take a sweetener. But if I did, I know what I should choose. Your Mr. Fielding said that love and scandal are the best tea sweeteners of all." His eyes twinkled, and I remembered what his friends had said about his being a flirt.

"You shan't find much of either here, I'm afraid," I parried, with a twinkle of my own, thinking of how little love was offered to anyone save Albert.

"No?" he said, not turning away, his voice lowered, and he held my gaze. "Are you certain?"

I caught my breath but did not look away before answering, "One can never be certain, Captain. Sometimes one leads to the other." I set the teapot down. "Since you've quoted an Englishman, I'll quote an Italian. *'Non si può aver il miele senza la pecchie.* Honey is sweet, but then the bees sting.' Perhaps you'll tell me that Maltese bees do not sting." *Nor their men,* I left unsaid. *I know firsthand, through my father, that they do.*

He laughed aloud at that and with ease, and I maneuvered the conversation to appropriate small talk. He commented on our tea and I mentioned it had come from China, directly, through a family investment concern.

"I understand you intend to be in England for some months." I sipped my tea, which did, indeed, taste herbal and divine with the addition of his honey.

"Until the Exhibition closes in October. I have no desire to sail upon winter waters if I am not required to. I have many things to attend to, but should be able to conclude my affairs by then, and my mother will worry if I'm home late." He winked at me.

"Malta is home? With your mother?"

"I have my own palazzo, a small one," he said. "But no true home." He sounded wistful. "A port in any storm, as they say."

"Do you have any other ambitions while you're in England?" I pressed, thinking of what his companions in London had said. And then I worried that perhaps I was doing exactly what Edward hoped I'd do—probe for useful information. I did not wish to be a go-between, for either man. But I had no choice. And it might save Highcliffe.

"Perhaps to meet my father," he admitted. "I have not yet decided." *Ah!* So his shipmates had been telling the truth about that. And therefore, maybe, about everything else. Clementine signaled to me from the edge of the door.

"I look forward to seeing you at dinner this evening." As I stood, my necklace disentangled itself from the buttons on the front of my dress and dropped heavily, calling attention to itself. Captain Dell'Acqua looked at it, and then at me, wonderingly. "Until dinner," he said, then turned and left.

. . .

Chef had prepared a feast to impress, and we sat at the dining table that nearly spanned the length of the room. Our best silver and best artwork were still showcased in the dining room as that was where Edward was most likely to entertain, and therefore impress. Mr. Morgan, sadly, was in attendance, and he came round to pull out my chair, brazenly brushing against me as he did.

All along the length of the table the first spring peonies flaunted their round, ruffle-covered pink crinolines in tiny silver vases, set alongside cruets, saltcellars, and sweating bottles of water. Watts and his entourage poured and served; the pleasant hum of conversation married with the delightful tastes and smells brought forth by one dish after another. First we had hare soup and lobster patties, a family favorite. Then, the first remove and the table was cleared. Next came saddle of mutton and stewed sea kale. I noticed that Clementine had another glass of wine before the second remove. The third course was longer in coming, and as we waited, one of the Maltese men spoke up.

"You are engaged to be married, then, *signorina*?" He looked directly at me.

"No, I'm not engaged to be married, Lieutenant," I said. Captain Dell'Acqua was looking at me intently as his friend pressed the point.

"But I was certain you were. The necklace, you see . . ." He pointed to my fish necklace. Suddenly, all eyes were on me. Watts hovered in the background with the Cherry Cabinet Pudding and Chef's *jaune mange*, the yellow milky sweet that had been an especial favorite of mine when I was a child. The atmosphere was tense; no one moved until Edward indicated that the food should be served.

"The necklace, you say?" Edward's voice grew pointed.

"Yes," the man continued confidently. "In Malta, the parents, the brother, the man of the family will sometimes choose a woman's husband."

"That is our custom, too," Morgan spoke up, smugly twirling a renegade mustache hair back into compliance.

"Sometimes," I added. "Please, sir, continue."

"When a girl's father decides that the time is right for her to marry, he puts a pot of sweets out on the family's porch to indicate young men may begin wooing. A loving father only chooses a man who will love and cherish his daughter."

Dell'Acqua looked in my direction, but I kept my gaze steadily upon his junior officer. The pudding was set in front of me and I took a slice to convey that I felt all was normal.

I did not.

The room was heavy, and my uncomfortable feelings about the necklace began to surface again.

"If a suitor desires to marry the young woman, he finds an older man to act as a go-between, and if the lady and the father agree then a dowry is agreed upon. Once all parties have given consent the man delivers a fish—we are a seafaring nation, after all, much like England—to the girl's family. In the fish's mouth is a gold ring, signifying a marriage. Gold is expensive. It is only given upon a commitment to marriage. Whoever wears a necklace like yours indicates she's married, or soon will be."

"What a lovely story," I said. "But I am most certainly not married."

"Yet," Morgan said before digging into his sweet course, "perhaps this is an omen, a happy one at that. Let's not allow the puddings to go unappreciated, shall we?"

Clementine carried the conversation along in another direction, cheerfully distracting from the emotional undertow, but I saw a moment's bewildering fear crawl across Edward's face before he banished it.

They continued to talk, but their voices grew distant and then ran together as I focused only on the thoughts gathering clarity and momentum in my head. It was unlikely the necklace would have come from outside the household. My memory then beckoned forth the hazy recollection of seeing it before, swinging in front of me as someone bent and took me in her arms. I flooded with momentary warmth.

A head bent low, near mine, blond hair, soft to the touch, brushing lightly against my cheek.

"What is it, Mama?" I took the chain in hand; at the end of it was a silver fish with a ring of gold in its mouth.

"It's yours now, my sweetness and light." She laughed, low, but behind the laugh I heard a quick catch in her throat, like trapping a sob before it escaped. Her hair was scented with herbed wash water, the scent of summer gardens, and I closed my eyes and inhaled deeply. "I do not think they will let me keep it." She clasped it on me, then tucked the necklace under my dress. "Keep it here, close to your heart, and I will keep you here," she touched her chest, "close to mine."

I wrapped my arms tightly about her neck. "Don't leave, Mama."

"I must," she said. The sun streamed through a stained-glass window, lighting it up. Jesus. Angels.

"Come back soon, Mama," I pleaded, tears coursing down my cheek. She didn't answer, just buried her head in my hair, kissed my cheeks over and over again, and then let her own tears make their way, too.

I exhaled slowly, knowing that I'd been given a blessing, but a mixed one. A memory of my mother as she was to leave, to be taken away to the asylum. Anxiety rippled through me. It was, I believed, the last time I'd seen her.

I returned to the conversation at the table, grateful that the evening was drawing to a close.

Later that night I took the necklace off and stared at it. Could it have been my mother's—and did it indicate she was married? If I truly remembered it and had not imagined my mother having given it to me, where had it been these many years?

CHAPTER SEVEN

The following days found the men away from Highcliffe, mostly attending to their common interests. The Maltese sailed from Lymington, where they'd been anchored, to meet with other Englishmen. While I was sorry to lose the company of Captain Dell'Acqua—I told myself I was simply eager to learn more of Malta during his stay in England—I did not miss the hovering menace of Mr. Morgan. He had departed quickly and without comment to me. Very unexpected.

One morning Edward sent Mrs. Watts to request I meet him downstairs.

"He'd like to see you right away, miss."

"I'll be down presently," I said as pleasantly as I could. Mrs. Watts had a bit of a French lilt in her voice. She was always perfectly polite to me, but perfectly correct as well, so we did not have occasion for discussion. Not like Chef. He encouraged my sweets-pinching and chattering manner, then and now. I fancied that I was one reason he'd returned for the summer. It felt lovely to imagine someone wished for my company.

I smiled at that and to my surprise, Mrs. Watts smiled back at me. "Did you meet my son, Jack, in London?"

"Oh yes. He was running the household like a man twice his age but with the energy of a man of his years. I'm certain he does Edward a great service."

"Indeed," she agreed, and cheerfully plumped my pillows before taking her leave. Shortly thereafter, I met Edward in the library, which was graced with a priceless long-case clock, its polished oak case inlaid with mahogany and satinwood. He'd said once, teasingly, I hoped, that the only reason he'd agreed to marry Clementine is her father had added the clock to the deal. Edward set his newspaper down and popped a ginger chew into his mouth.

"You had a brief occasion to speak with Dell'Acqua," he said. "Did you learn anything useful?"

His pleasant disposition toward anyone, including me, depended upon their usefulness to him. "He did say that once he decides upon something—perhaps an investment arrangement—he pursues it until it is his." Being helpful to Edward would allow things, perhaps, to remain inconclusive with Mr. Morgan till I could figure a way out. I'd had an idea.

"He enjoys your company and opens up to you." Edward smiled. "Excellent." He glanced down at the front of my gown.

"That necklace . . ." he began. "You're not wearing it any longer."

I was wearing it, of course; it may have been my mother's, treasure of treasures, an unexpected grace! I had tucked it beneath my chemise and dress.

"I don't want to give the wrong impression," I answered. "That I'm married."

He nodded. "Where did you come by it?"

"It was in my jewelry box. Perhaps it had long been there; I don't know."

He stared at me for a moment, and then said, "I know your faith would preclude you from speaking mistruths."

Was that a question? "I take my faith very seriously," I responded.

"Maud said you were shocked to see it." Had he thought that I was plotting against him somehow before Maud had spoken up? Had he interrogated her or had she freely offered information about our strange discussion? "Do you know who may have placed it in your jewelry box or when?"

"No. But it shall cause no further troubles." It had been my life's habit to comply and cause no trouble. Perhaps, I'd thought, by acting perfectly in every situation I could reclaim some of my mother's honor for her. For me.

He nodded his approval and Watts slipped into the back of the room, signaling to Edward, so I knew our time would be short. One of the maids came in to dust and Cook refilled the hot water in the teapot. I heard Albert fussing in the vestibule, and Lillian shushing him lest Edward become annoyed. Where was Clementine? We were to ride together that afternoon. And where was Morgan?

"Mr. Morgan has taken his leave?" I asked.

"You miss his company. I understand. He's attending some unexpected complications while I sort through matters close to home. He's, well, he has better-established connections with the firms under discussion."

They preferred Mr. Morgan to Edward? For a brief moment I wondered if Morgan was double-dealing my cousin.

"He'll return soon, and at that time, he and I must conclude important matters that I will then share with you."

"Why not now?"

He waved a hand in dismissal. "Soon. Now, I must visit Winchester for the day, to tend to my affairs, and call upon my solicitor." It sounded as though he were consoling himself. I saw an opening and slipped into it.

"Would that be the same solicitor that Grandfather had?"

"Why do you ask?" He abruptly stopped winding his watch. I did not want to alarm him further after the affair with the necklace, so probable reasons raced through my mind. I settled on one.

"I thought that as you have recalled me from Winchester I may need my dowry, and perhaps this may be an opportune time to speak with him. I will need the dowry, isn't that correct? Or why else would you insist I come home?"

His face relaxed then, and he stood up. Perhaps he thought my question implied compliance with his plans.

"I have only recently engaged this solicitor."

"So who, then, was Grandfather's solicitor?"

"I cannot recall Grandfather's solicitor's name," Edward said, too smoothly.

His faith, apparently, did not preclude *him* from lying. Nor did he mention my dowry. I did not bring that up again just then. I did not want to suggest something he may not have thought of. Instead, I pressed forth another concern.

"You mentioned my faith," I began. "I should like to seek a Catholic chapel nearby. Do you know of one?"

"No," he responded. "Why would I know of some papist gathering? You've no need." He waved his hand condescendingly. "Burn a candle or pray a rosary in your room if you must."

"Clementine gave me permission to attend in London."

"Clementine acted out of turn. I won't nurture idolatry in my household."

I rolled my eyes and as I did, glanced at the large portrait of his mother. I wondered that it had not yet been packed away in the attic, as so much of the artwork already was. It had been rather strange to observe our rooms with nothing hung on the walls, the wallpaper bright in areas where it had been hidden, dark where the sun had discolored it over time.

I then realized that there was no portrait of his father at High-cliffe. Or at the London townhouse, either. Suddenly a memory wended its way back to my heart: a holiday at home, I upstairs near a speaking tube, Edward's father beating him for poor academic performance and having joined the cricket club instead, where he'd shined. Shaming us all, his father had said as Edward sobbed that he would, from then on, obey.

"And now I must be off." Watts handed Edward's hat and gloves to him, briefing him on what the day ahead held as they walked to the door.

I remained in the lonely library for some time. Its walls had once been painted a deep gold to better reflect the burnished leather tones of the books. I bathed in the river of morning sun coursing through the unclean high windows as I sipped a cup of tea. I then chose a volume or two of reading to take to my rooms—something, anything, to replace that odious Poe. I climbed the ladder and plucked a book of saints and angels from the shelves. It was coated in dust and very old. What was a Catholic book doing in our household?

I took it and climbed back down the ladder, then returned to my rooms, where I spent the afternoon reading.

Two days later, after breakfast, I returned to my room to pick up the book again, as well as my sketchbook, to take outside and enjoy the pleasant weather, when I noticed a slip of paper sticking from the top of the book; it had not been there when I selected the book. I slid the paper out.

In nondescript handwriting, freshly inked, was written, JACOB LILLYWHITE, ESQ., LYMINGTON.

Who is Mr. Lillywhite?

. . .

The next morning, Clementine sent a note that she was unwell and would not be able to ride with me. I saw my chance. I pulled on my walking boots and tucked my sketchbook in a satchel so I'd have an excuse should someone stop me. Then I began the trek to Lymington. I passed through our property, hoping not to call any attention to myself, and I didn't, except to the young shepherdess in the near distance. I waved to her, making sure to flaunt my sketchbook so that if asked she could say she'd seen me go walking with my art case. She waved in return and then turned back to her charges. I made my way down the neglected drive, more dirt than gravel, and onto the path that would lead me to town after a bit more than an hour's walk.

I crossed the green expanse of lawn, and then passed the small pond that seemed out of place, dwarfed, on a property that bordered the sea. In the middle of the pond stood an elaborate fountain, chipped and stained, the gargoyles stock-still and dry, their mouths open; in better years the pumps drove water through them. Pumps were costly to maintain and had been abandoned. Instead, their mouths remained open but mute, gasping as though they were dying of thirst, crying to me for help. I shook the worrisome thought from my head and tried to replace it with sensible observations, instead.

Did others have worrisome, fanciful thoughts? Or just I . . . perhaps, like my mother.

My skin grew tight with the salt mist as I approached the town and the sea. The grasses of summer grew on one side, and I had a care not to allow the nettles to latch onto me. To the other side were the tide flats, shallow pools of water that still held partly sunken ancient salterns, which since Roman times had been used to gather salt. The flats were outlined by patches of marsh and bog that smelt of rotting fish. Birds cried and cawed in the background, but other than them, and the steady hum of insects, I heard nothing.

I grew suddenly aware that I was a young woman alone on the trail.

Could I come to harm? The thought had not occurred to me before, but there was always a possibility that ruffians may lie waiting; I stepped up my pace and to distract myself I composed, in my head, letters to my friends in Winchester, whom I had unwillingly and abruptly left behind. They were mostly like myself, in somewhat constrained circumstances. I could not expect a visit from them.

I soon arrived at the outskirts of the town. It was built up from the harbor as most sea communities were, anchored by the yacht club and centered on the spine of the High Street. As I stepped onto the street near the yacht club, a fine carriage began to exit the drive. As it passed, an older woman peered out of the window at me from beneath her tight bonnet. She held my gaze as if she were someone I should have known.

But I did not know her.

I smiled politely and bowed my head, and she nodded back at me and then her carriage was gone. I sauntered up the street and asked a kindly looking man where I might find Jacob Lillywhite.

"Oh, miss, he's in his office rarely these days. Him being old and all that. What's today? Wednesday?" He shook his head and clucked. "Head up toward Christchurch Road, and you may find him."

"And where might I post a letter?"

He looked at me oddly. My dress, station, and accent clearly marked me as a lady, but here I was, unattended and unchaperoned.

"Mr. Galpine has a circulating library, which acts also as a post office," he said. "Say . . ."

I bowed slightly. "Thank you, I shall be on my way."

I turned onto Christchurch Road and halfway up found a narrow doorway tightly leveraged between two other buildings.

SHUT, a sign on the door said. IN ATTENDANCE ON THURSDAYS.

My heart fell. I did not even know why I was here, and now Mr. Lillywhite was not present. I had no idea if I would be able to make my way to town again, alone, the next day. But I knew I must try to find out why I'd been pointed to him and hope that it would somehow lead me to freedom.

I returned home, wrote letters to my friends, and blew the lamp out early, then extinguished the lone candle in my room. Its smoke rose and curled, wended and wound like wispy white specters. The house was still but for weak crying in the distance, though I could not tell from whom. I prayed with all my might that I would be able to slip away again on the morrow.

My prayers were favorably answered.

Clementine was feeling well again and had decided to do her calling on Thursday morning and early afternoon. This was a double boon as she would not only be out of the way, but her lady friends would be taking callers, too, which meant none of them would see me in town. I slipped out of the door, but Watts saw me, as did the young hall boy.

"Can I help you with something, miss?" he asked earnestly. As for many boys, this was probably the only work situation that offered him any hope. Those salterns that had kept the young boys and men working had gone quiet; salt was now cheaply harvested in Liverpool.

"I'm going to sketch," I said, and then promised myself I actually would so I was not fibbing. "But thank you . . ."

"Oliver," he said. "My name is Oliver, and I'm at your service."

I grinned at him. I hastened to the office of Mr. Lillywhite and was overjoyed to see that he was in. I tried to open the door, the wood of which had swelled with age; I pushed forcefully and as I did, it flew open. I nearly fell into the arms of the old man on the other side.

"Please forgive me." I pulled myself up. "The door . . ."

"It's my fault entirely," he said, "Mrs. . . ."

"Miss Ashton," I corrected him, and he looked behind me for a chaperone.

"I'm quite alone," I admitted.

He nodded. "Ashton!" he suddenly burst out. "Arthur Ashton's granddaughter."

I smiled. He was, as I'd hoped, Grandfather's solicitor. Who had placed that slip of paper in my reading to tip me off? I could not ask anyone for fear of informing the wrong party.

I nodded. "Yes, I am his granddaughter, though I cannot recall him. He died when I was very young."

"Julianna's daughter," he said softly. "You have her gentle smile. Your grandfather had great expectations for her." He may have realized that line of thought might be hurtful, and changed it. "I was given to understand you were in Winchester, rather permanently until you were to come home and marry."

Marry? "I have been in Winchester, but things changed." I clasped my hands in my lap to steady them from trembling. "I am hoping you may be in a position to help me."

"I am not Everedge's solicitor."

I tilted my head. "His solicitor is . . ."

"In Winchester," was all he would say. "How may I assist?"

Lillywhite's wife arrived and hovered nearby, listening.

"I'm wondering . . . I'm wondering about my dowry. I was certain that at one time I'd been told there was a dowry set aside for me. There are a number of ladies of good station that I teach with, former governesses and the like, who had hoped to start a day school in Lymington. Some of them have saved funds or inherited. I thought, perhaps, the terms of my grandfather's will would allow my dowry to be used, immediately, to join them."

I had to access those funds before Edward gave them to Mr. Morgan.

Lillywhite inhaled deeply, coughed, and then finally spoke. "The terms would have, Miss Ashton. And he'd left a fine sum for you. But Mr. Everedge, not your cousin but his father, accessed and depleted it years ago."

I stood up, opened my mouth, and then sat down again. "He did? Could he do that within the law?"

He nodded. "They'd been paying for your schooling, and the dowry was left to be used at the discretion of your guardian, who was, after your mother's death, Mr. Everedge."

"Why would he have needed my dowry sums? I understood that there were plenty of resources, the properties, the incomes . . ."

"There were. But times have changed for us in the past decades. There used to be quite some profit for your family in, er, secretly exporting wool out and importing spices, liquor, and rich fabrics in, but that money is coming to an abrupt end with the change in revenue structure; duties have been relaxed."

Secretly exporting and importing, all right. Smuggling! I recalled the piney, bitter smell and puckering taste of the hundreds of barrels in the abandoned abbey properties behind Highcliffe. Edward had dared me to take a sip when he did. Gin.

"The trails behind Highcliffe, which lead to the Keyhole," I said. Naturally hidden, easily accessed from our land, but not from anywhere else.

"Indeed." He answered all without saying anything.

"I see. If I may return to my grandfather's will. May I know the terms?"

"There was little else that involved you," he said. "And Everedge's solicitor, if you could even get to him, owes his fiduciary duty to him, not you."

"My mother?"

"The will disallowed the insane, the illegitimate, and anyone who married a French person from inheriting."

I laughed loudly at that, and both the aged Lillywhites stared at me with alarm. I composed myself. "I'm sorry, it's the shock."

They nodded warily but said nothing. Mrs. Lillywhite moved a step back from me.

"Catholics were not precluded, then?"

"No," Lillywhite answered. "Just the French."

"Why?"

"The wars, one presumes," he said. "Also, Ashton had a distinct distaste for Republicans, mainly because he had a firm view on what was proper, which meant monarchy."

"And legitimacy," I offered, and he nodded his agreement.

Invalidating me.

"And mental soundness." Invalidating my mother.

"I'm afraid so." He looked hard at me, suspicious of my mind, perhaps. Others sometimes were. My familiar fear caught and held my breath, but I forced it aside and spoke.

"Who was it that had my mother committed to the lunatic asylum?" I asked. "Mr. Everedge?" As the male head of household, that would have been most likely.

"Not at all," Lillywhite disagreed. "It was her sister, Judith.

Your mother was accused of—I'm so sorry to have to say this—moral madness after she returned home from Malta *enceinte*. She continued to insist that she was married, would not waver from that in spite of all proof to the contrary."

I sat back, shocked. I had never been told that my mother had claimed to be married.

Mr. Lillywhite continued. "When her father died, she descended into a final spiral of grief. Her sister tried everything, I'm told, including hiring nurses, but nothing forestalled the fits. When young Edward was born, his safety was paramount."

My heart clutched within me. Was I ever to be paramount to anyone? I had so few memories of my mother, but those few I treasured were happy and pleasant. How she'd suffered! Would I share her fate? Some had implied I would, that it ran in families. It frightened me: madness and the asylum, and most of all, death within its walls.

"When your mother died, you being, ah, naturally born, you were left *filia nullius*," Mr. Lillywhite proceeded. "The daughter of no one."

After a long silence, I whispered, "I am not the daughter of no one. I am the daughter of . . ." I had no father's name to offer. To remind them of my mother was perhaps not in my best interest. "I am the child of God," I finished. At that, Mrs. Lillywhite came forward again and rested a hand on my shoulder, as her husband spoke one last time.

"Then you should implore God to come to your assistance with all speed," he said. "For there seems to be no one else who can or will."

CHAPTER EIGHT

*T*here *was no one who would or could assist me.* Mr. Lillywhite, who knew so little about me, seemed to understand so much. A light rain pattered on my parasol then stopped, the very essence of a summer shower, as I walked down the High Street toward Mr. Galpine's lending library to post letters.

I stepped into his small shop, which smelt of lemon wax, the tickling dust of newspaper, and the tang of fresh leather-bound books.

"One moment, if you please." A tall man hardly older than myself raised a finger to me while he finished helping another man, taller yet, in a black top hat. The hatted man spoke about placing an advertisement to hire a secretary.

"Just have the responses sent round, then," he said, finishing and paying. Galpine nodded and then beckoned me forward.

"How may I assist you, ma'am?"

"My name is Miss Annabel Ashton," I said.

"Oh!" He smiled. "Of Highcliffe." His face dimmed. "I'm sorry to hear about the old house."

I nodded. "You know it's to be sold."

"I've handled several letters of enquiry. Unfortunate matter. And what can I do for you?"

I'm in desperate straits, I thought, but of course did not give voice to those worrisome musings. *I must find the means to support myself before the end of the summer—barely two months away.* "I'd like to post letters to Winchester if I may." I looked at the advertisement, just written, on the oak countertop in front of me and spoke nearly as fast as the idea appeared so I would not lose heart. If I had no resources to form a school for young ladies, I would go to the students, and their paying parents, instead. "And place an advertisement in the local papers."

"Certainly." I dictated a short piece, seeking a position as a governess, quickly outlining my qualifications. I need not remain a governess forever, but it would allow immediate independence from Edward.

He nodded his agreement and I left. This was an answer! It was only a matter of time before a suitable arrangement presented itself. I knew from my time teaching that qualified governesses, trained in art, Italian, and literature, were in short supply. It would be lonelier than teaching at school, but no supplement to my stipend would be required. I should simply have to make myself indispensable to Edward until a governess arrangement appeared. He could certainly not disapprove. I would be financially self-sustaining, which is what they wanted.

Wasn't it?

I thought of the quiet mention of Edward's owed debts, by Clementine, Mr. Morgan, and Edward, and wondered if they meant financial obligations or personal ones. How did Edward intend to pay the last type?

Through me? I did not think I would mention my ad until an enquiry arrived.

I headed home, stopping near Highcliffe to sketch the sea at a spot not far from where Mr. Morgan had trapped me only one month earlier. How long did I have until he returned? I shivered, though it was warm, and then sat down on a stump before pulling out my sketchbook and a stick of charcoal from my satchel. I began drawing the Edge of the World, as we'd called it when we were children, in the distance, where the land seemed to drop straight into the sea. The sheep gamboled nearby, and I waved again at the young lass tending them.

Within a few minutes, the young shepherdess came running toward me, brown, beribboned plaits bobbing behind her.

"Hello, my name is Miss Annabel Ashton," I said. "I don't recognize you. What is your name?"

She shook her head and made a motion of pursing her lips, then shook her head again. I tilted my head toward her.

"You don't speak, then? You're mute?"

She nodded, and hurriedly pointed to a sheep that had wandered near the ledge. She made motions to indicate she was going to fetch the sheep, and could I take her staff and not allow the other sheep to wander?

"Shall I fetch the sheep for you, instead?" I offered. "I don't mind."

She vigorously shook her head no. I agreed, reluctantly. It didn't seem right letting a child take the risk, but she was certainly more sure-footed and knowledgeable of the trails than I was.

She made her way to the bleating, confused little lamb and knelt. She did not send her dog, which perhaps would have startled the young lamb over the edge. Just went by herself, low and beckoning. And the sheep, which well knew her, came her way to safety. She was wise; the sheep certainly would not have come to me.

She returned to me, and the little lamb ran to the summoning bleat of its mother.

"Well done," I commended. I quickly sketched a picture of her into the field of sheep I'd already drawn. I titled it *The Lost Lamb and Her Courageous Rescuer*, and read that aloud as I did not know if she could read. I tore it out of my notebook and handed it over. She grinned at me and nodded, then relieved me of her staff and went on her way.

As I made my way back to the house, a sudden and unsettling, even ominous, feeling overtook me. I looked at the sky, a bolt of lightning splitting a black cloud hovering over the water in a summer squall. An omen? *Come now, Annabel*, I reasoned with myself. Mr. Morgan and his talk of omens had tainted my mind. *There is nothing to be concerned about. You've made some fine arrangements and shall soon hear back from your advertisement.* But the shadows persisted, dogging me.

Perhaps it was because the young girl and the sheep had been so close to danger. Perhaps the situation only reminded me of Mr. Morgan, trapping me nearby some weeks before. I tried to shake off the gloom, so unworthy of a summer day, but found I could not; it clung to me like my clothes, moist with the day's humidity.

I walked up the steps, opened the door to the foyer, and put down my case. I spied Edward in the library not far off, home again, his voice carrying, but happily. Clementine was with him. I stepped toward them; she did not look at or greet me, which was odd. Maybe they'd had a row.

Edward summoned me. I went into the room and stood before him; his wife had abruptly stopped talking as I had appeared.

"I've had a letter from Captain Dell'Acqua," he said, holding it in his hand. "Oliver delivered it just now. He said that his second line of enquiry had proved unsatisfactory, and although he has a few more to consider, he's leaning toward joining with Morgan and me. He set out to help the Maltese." He glanced at the letter. "And perhaps, he thinks, that may mean you, too. Or your family, anyway, meaning me. Nicely done, Annabel! He'll return shortly and be with us, on and off, throughout the summer."

I smiled. "I'm here to help in any manner."

He smiled warmly. "I knew you would be."

I turned to go but he gently took my arm. "Annabel. I don't know why you need to remain in the small room Clementine insisted you be placed in."

"I did not . . ." Clementine started, but Edward silenced her with a look.

"Your stay will be a bit longer than anticipated. Perhaps you'd like to take the rooms that belonged to your mother? I could ask Mrs. Watts to prepare them for you."

"Edward! Yes, thank you. What a lovely idea."

"I'll ask Mrs. Watts to do so. You may find them more comfortable . . . and perhaps comforting, at least for a time."

"Thank you again, Edward. It means so much to me." The fog surrounding me lightened, if only a little.

"Very happy to help," he said, and then returned to the letter, and as I headed to the door to ring for Mrs. Watts, Clementine picked up her conversation again even as Edward steadily ignored her.

"She came when we were out. And she herself came; she did not send a servant."

He spoke up then. "How do you know? And why ever would she be calling on us now, after all these years? We're rarely here, and she's not bothered to stop by when we are."

"I cannot say. They're most often at their lands in the north, I believe. But she left her card with the corner turned, so I know her visit was in person. We can't afford to snub the Somerfords, Edward. She said she'll return tomorrow."

I moved into the rooms that had been my mother's. The staff seemed to have done as much as they could to warm the empty space again, adding pillows and counterpanes, waxing the wardrobe, and bringing the porcelain pitcher in from my other room. I sat in the chairs, which had been covered in sea foam–colored velvet with pineapple designs stamped into it. On the mantel was a clock. I reached up and touched it; it was made of lacquered wood and Chinese symbols marked the hours. Had she touched it, wound it, too?

These rooms overlooked the front of the house, which I rather enjoyed, as I could see who was approaching when I was by the window, as well as the fat geese waddling their way across the lawns. My breath caught when I recognized the fine carriage that pulled up the drive the next morning.

It was the one I had seen just outside of the yacht club the first day I'd visited Lymington! I pulled back from the window, just a little, so I could see who alighted from the carriage.

It was the older woman who had caught my attention in the street. *Oh dear!*

I dropped the faded drape and sat down at my mother's writing desk. I was thankful I did not have to receive callers. What if she recognized me and mentioned seeing me in Lymington?

A short while later, a knock sounded upon my door.

"Yes?" I called out. Maud entered the room and shut the door again before speaking.

"It's Mrs. Everedge, miss," she said. "She wants you to come down and greet her visitor, the Countess of Somerford."

I glanced at my dress, which, while serviceable, was hardly the kind of thing I'd want to wear to be introduced to someone from the aristocracy. "Can you offer regrets?"

Maud shook her head. "No, miss. She insisted." She came a bit farther into the room. "Lady Somerford is now greeting the *staff*! One by one, in their areas, in the kitchen, even downstairs. It's said she knew many of them from the days when your grandparents were alive."

Well, then, I did not feel as concerned. She simply wanted to greet everyone present, and that included me. Lady Somerford must be the caller about whom Clementine had been so exercised.

Had she known my mother?

Maud wound my hair into its normal roll, pulling some tendrils to hang prettily, and I smoothed my gown, then twisted the cameo on my finger to hide the raw patch underneath it. I walked downstairs.

Lady Somerford must have finished greeting the staff, as I saw them round the corner toward the drawing room, itself a dame past her prime, returning just as I approached the foot of the stairs. Clementine looked positively unwell. I hoped she hadn't been visiting with the green fairies that morning ahead of calling hours. I was a few steps behind the two of them, heading into the drawing room. As I arrived, Clementine stood and beckoned to me.

"Miss Annabel Ashton, Charlotte, the Countess of Somerford, of Pennington Park, our near neighbors."

To my surprise, Lady Somerford patted the sofa near her. "Do take a seat here, dear," she said. "How lovely to learn you've come back to Highcliffe."

A trickle of perspiration slid down my spine. Lady Somerford grinned at me, and at that moment I knew she would not disclose my secret visit to Lymington.

"My husband and I have donated land for the school run by the Benedictine Sisters. They keep in touch from time to time and they had noted that a teacher they'd made the acquaintance with, you, had recently returned to her family home."

I smiled. "You're Catholic, then!"

She smiled back. "Yes. As are you?"

I nodded.

"The sisters had related as much. I've come to invite you to attend divine service with us each week, and as often as you feel you may need to visit a priest. We have a private chapel and welcome every Catholic of any social station to Pennington, even when we are in the north as we mostly are. Your mother worshiped with us. Father Gregory serves the parish here."

Clementine shook her head. "How kind, Lady Somerford. But I'm afraid . . ."

Lady Somerford snapped her fan shut, all the while keeping a pleasant but firm look on her face. "I know, you're worried about her being chaperoned. Understandable. I shall look after her myself."

I held back my delight. Clementine could hardly refuse the Countess of Somerford!

Clementine spoke up. "That's so very kind. But Edward . . ."

"Yes, he'll want to see for himself that all is well. So. I'm hosting a large dinner and musical evening shortly. My husband has grown weary, he says, of long seasons in London, and so we've recreated some here. Of course, you'll attend. I'll have the details sent."

"Regrettably, we shall have visitors staying with us off and on all summer; Mr. Everedge's associates come and go, arranging their investment matters." Clementine tried once more not to offend the most powerful family in the area while simultaneously keeping Edward's injunction that I not attend a Catholic church.

"Bring them!" Lady Somerford said. "All the merrier. Summer in the country is a round of house visitors coming and going, neighbors all attending social occasions. In the meantime, I shall expect to call for Miss Ashton each Sunday starting with the next."

We spent the best part of another thirty minutes talking about Lady Somerford's recently married daughter, and young Albert, the possibility that Highcliffe might be sold, and the blessing of French chefs. Then Lady Somerford stood, and Clementine capitulated.

"Thank you, Lady Somerford. We shall look forward to your musical evening with great anticipation."

"As shall I," I said, and hoped my joy shone through my demeanor. I believed that it did, and Lady Somerford returned my humor with a glint in her eye.

"I shall enjoy becoming better acquainted, young lady." She snapped her fan at Watts, who called for the lady's carriage driver, and they were off.

I returned to my rooms, sat at my dressing table, and patted powder on my face. In spite of the happy ending, the encounter had been rather taxing.

Something red glinted in the setting summer sun. I reached over to the open India box in which I kept my hair combs. My plain ones had been added to!

After the fuss over the necklace, I could hardly ask Clementine, Mrs. Watts, or Maud.

I plucked out the first pair; they had long, sharp teeth made of costly jet. These were set with rubies and what looked to be diamonds. I had never owned anything so fine. But I did seem to recognize them from somewhere. Clementine? Had Clementine worn them and then had them delivered to me, in keeping with our newly prominent station?

The second new set was encrusted with high-quality clear crystals. I did not recognize it.

As I mulled it over, I thought I remembered where I had seen them.

In a portrait.

Late that night, after I was certain that the household was asleep, the fires all cooled, and no one would see me, I pulled on my dressing gown, blew out my lamp, and slipped down the stairs. I quietly tiptoed to the ground floor, hoping the creaking would not give me away. It was nearly the end of the month, and there was a new moon, which meant scarce light found its way through the windows. *Thank you*, I thought, *for little graces.*

I turned right down the long vestibule that led to the ball-room, now mostly packed. Perhaps it would need to be unpacked; now that the Somerfords had invited us to a social event, Edward would have to reciprocate. The doors were shut, and I opened one quietly, then pulled it closed behind me. Nothing. Silence.

And then . . . a noise.

CHAPTER NINE

I stood statue still, but no further sounds aroused my concern. In the dark, I passed the shrouded game tables and the piano, which had long been closed; Clementine did not play well. The thick dust covers on the furniture rustled against my dressing gown, the rough fabric catching on the smooth, like hands clawing at me each time I tried to pull loose. I shook off the sensation with a shiver and turned toward the window. I pulled back the curtains, stirring up a frenzy of dust, and coughed once, twice. But it had done what I needed it to do. It let in sufficient starlight so that I could clearly see the very thing I thought I'd remembered and now sought.

Hung near a sea-facing window was a portrait of the Ashton daughters: my mother, Julianna, and Edward's mother, Judith. They were formally gowned, facing each other in profile. My mother's blond hair was swept back and rolled up, then held by combs studded with rubies, the very combs I now held in my hands.

My mother. Her hair had been rolled and teased exactly as I wore my own. Had I adopted that unconsciously, after having seen the portrait? Or was it simply a style that flattered me? I recalled a moment, long ago.

I reached up and patted her hair that looked like nothing so much as sunlit strands wrapped into a spool anchored by jewels. "So pretty, Mama, so pretty."

She reached out and traced the outline of my face. "So pretty, sweetness, so pretty." We both giggled, and she carried me down the hallway.

A creaking noise brought me back to the present. I stilled myself, but then there was nothing more. I reached under the collar of my nightgown. Yes, the necklace was still there; I gripped it like a holy relic. What was happening? How were all of these items being returned to me, and by whom, and why now?

Perhaps they had been there all along, as Maud suggested. In that case, I feared for myself, for my mind.

I let the heavy curtain fall and stealthily walked back to the door. I heard a noise behind it. Shoes, footsteps. I heard breathing on the other side and held my own. The breathing accelerated to panting and my limbs iced.

If I made noise enough to jar the door open, I was certain to wake staff or family—or fall into the grasp of whoever was just outside. But I had to escape. After ten frantic seconds looking about, I remembered a concealed door hidden behind a portrait of some long-dead relation so that staff could come and serve and then leave unobtrusively. Edward and I had eavesdropped on social doings from behind that door, on one of the rare occasions when we were partners, and friends. Now I tiptoed over to it and then jiggled the clasp that held it shut, pushed the door, and turned into a hallway that led to the back stairs, closing the concealed door to the ballroom, and not a moment too soon. As I did,

I heard the door I'd first come through, which had just been blocked, open.

I quickly and quietly fled to my rooms and, after having arrived, closed and bolted the door behind me before collapsing onto my bed. My palm bled; I'd pressed the teeth of the comb too firmly into it as I fled.

Someone had been bracing the ballroom door against me. I could not imagine who it could have been, who even might have known that I'd gone downstairs unless they had been observing me in secret. The thought sent a scared chill through me.

Could I have imagined that scenario? Had darkness and fear gotten a hold of me, grasping me as that rough fabric had the smooth? I turned my mind away from the temptation of those ruminations and back to the hair combs. If I wore them, Edward would be sure to notice. Who had put them in my India box? There had been an opportunity for any servant or any family member, except for Clementine and me. Even Clementine could have given them to, perhaps, Maud, to place in my room as we took Lady Somerford's call. Maud would do whatever she asked.

I got up out of my bed and stared out across the dark lawn. Even through the panes of glass I could hear the ocean churning, wearing down the land by means of gentle persistence. Why should Clementine have secretly offered the combs to me? Pity, perhaps. Maybe she had inherited them from Judith's things. She had no love for her former mother-in-law—that was certain.

Perhaps Lady Somerford had brought them and left instructions with one of the staff. I should like to wear them Sunday next. I would ask Lady Somerford about them then, and all might become clear.

· · ·

$\mathbb{N}$ext morning, I was shocked to find Mr. Nigel Morgan at the slightly worn breakfast table, dining with Edward.

"Mr. Morgan. I . . . I had not expected to see you," I said. "I was not aware that you had returned."

"Is that delight in your eyes?" Morgan asked. I do not know if he jested or if he had completely duped himself over the state of my feelings. I looked at Edward, who continued to read his papers. I pushed away my egg and sipped my tea, hoping those choices would settle my stomach.

"I'm glad you met with no harm on your journey." I could say that, at least, with sincerity.

"You look lovely this morning," Morgan spoke up. "Those jeweled combs in your hair are exquisite."

"Where did you come by those?" Edward tossed his paper down and looked intently at my hair.

"They were my mother's." I sipped my tea and willed my hand not to shake. "Surely you remember that."

"I do not recall ever seeing them on you," he replied.

"You do not?" I opened my eyes wide like others did when they were politely questioning my mental well-being.

"Oh, but I think they are her mother's," Mr. Morgan spoke up, coming to my rescue. My mouth was agape. How could he have known this?

"You never met her mother," Edward insisted. "It's not likely you'd know."

"I do remember seeing them once." Morgan stroked his beard and looked at the ceiling, where porcelain cherubs floated ethereally. "Ah, yes. In a portrait of the sisters, in the ballroom."

I looked at Morgan, fear coursing through me. He smiled and winked.

He had been following me, stalking me like the prey he'd had mounted in his townhome.

Edward got up and made his way down the vestibule—leaving me alone and unchaperoned with Mr. Morgan!

"I should like to have your portrait painted," Morgan said. "What shall you wear?"

"You shall not have my portrait painted," I answered.

"We'll start with a cameo, then." He bit into his egg, and I heard a doorway open in the distance, and then close again. Edward made his way back and said nothing further, though he gave me a hard look.

CHAPTER TEN

HIGHCLIFFE HALL, PENNINGTON PARK

JULY, 1851

True to her word, as I knew she would be, Lady Somerford arrived on Sunday to fetch me, unusually, herself, so that I might attend Mass at Pennington. Her footman helped me, and I sat opposite her for the short ride. Although the driveway was uneven, this ride was smooth because of their expensively appointed carriage.

"I cannot thank you enough," I said. "I was in despair over losing the comfort and guidance of my faith. I prayed, and magically you showed up with a solution."

"Not magically, my dear." She reached across the aisle and squeezed my gloved hand in hers but for a moment. "Divinely. And I've been looking forward to your company."

"I, too." The carriage rolled down the drive and onto the now smooth, better-tended road that led us west. "I'm delighted to learn you've provided the property for the Benedictine school. Your name had never been mentioned."

"My husband does not like it to be trumpeted about," she said, and then quoted Holy Scripture. "'But when thou doest alms, let not thy left hand know what thy right hand doeth.'"

I nodded. "I felt such comfort there."

"The sisters are wonderful, godly women," she agreed. "Not all are called to take solemn vows. But we can each assist those who are."

In saying that, Lady Somerford teased forth a thought that had been but a wisp when I'd lived in Winchester and had steadily spun into a sturdier thread in the past weeks. I should have to ask Father Gregory about my idea.

The carriage soon pulled up in front of Pennington, an imposing estate perhaps twice the size of Highcliffe. It was centered by a three-story column, two-story wings extending to the right and left. It seemed to me that those wings were arms flung wide open, and as soon as I entered through the heart and into the grand hall I felt embraced.

The chapel was a large room; perhaps it had once been an additional study that was repurposed for the sake of worship. Until only a few decades earlier, and since the English Reformation some three hundred years past, Catholic worship had either been outlawed, forbidden, or, if one was highly enough placed and well-to-do, frowned upon and overlooked. Some large towns, like Winchester, had actual churches. But in the country, it was mostly house chapels.

Lord Somerford had thoughtfully provided pews with padded kneelers, and he knelt contritely. I spied several others who were well dressed, and some tradesmen, and finally low-born servants. In this household, at least, all were equal in the presence of God.

Lady Somerford arranged for my confession to be heard and afterward for me to speak with Father Gregory. His vestments were neat and carefully fitted, his body slender and his warm eyes the middling brown of autumn leaves; all round them his skin was crinkled with age, just like those leaves. His smile, though, his smile! It conveyed his genuineness and made me feel at ease in his company. We spoke for a few moments, me telling him how much I'd craved attending service again, how thankful I was for his good words and presence. He welcomed me to return anytime, and then quietly got to the point.

"What troubles you, daughter?"

I told him that I had just learned that I had no dowry, and that my cousin would not care for me much longer, and that it was possible that he would marry me to a man who seemed unusual and perhaps cruel. "I do not wish to take the vow of the sacrament of marriage with a man who will not uphold it . . . I have been considering making solemn vows and becoming a nun."

He did not ridicule or dismiss me, for which I was grateful. But he did speak. "Living in this world can be difficult, but interceding for this world is just as difficult if not more so. It should not be undertaken by those who are not certain they are called to do so."

I nodded but remained unconvinced. "I'd even pray for the souls of Edward and Mr. Morgan if I were allowed to make vows."

Father Gregory laughed and took my hand in his own. When he did, I did not need to twist my ring to gain comfort; it came through Father's hand, which though it shook with age was the steadiest thing I'd held on to for a long time.

"It's honorable and holy that you do not want to undertake the sacrament of marriage without a true and willing commitment," he continued. "Similarly, you will not want to make the solemn vows of a nun without God's calling. Promise me you will make no vow without speaking with me first."

"Of course, Father, I promise," I said. I then walked back to

Lady Somerford, who was to return me to Highcliffe herself so Edward could have no protest.

All the way home I thought about vows: solemn and marriage. When I considered marriage, though, it was not fear of Mr. Morgan that dominated my thoughts but, extraordinarily enough, the persistent image of the compelling Maltese captain who would soon return to Highcliffe. Perhaps he would ill use me, as had been implied. But . . . perhaps he would not. I chided myself, *Do not continue drifting dreamily like a foolish schoolgirl.* It was no use.

My heart and thoughts had begun to settle upon Captain Dell'Acqua.

A week later our guests were shortly to arrive. I waited in the vestibule as a young maid finished sweeping damp tea leaves off the Turkish carpets, trying to coax away the musty smell of an unattended house. Oliver, the hall boy, stood near the speaking tube, waiting to be called into duty, polishing a stair rail with his shirt-sleeve. I walked up to him. He was so often up and down the back stairs; perhaps I could ask him if he'd noticed anyone near my rooms.

"That young lass," I pointed to the departing maid, "reminds me of the shepherdess who tends the flocks. Do you know the shepherdess?"

Oliver smiled. "Of course I do, miss. She's my sister, Emmeline."

"Ah," I said. I sat on the bench next to him, which seemed to make him uncomfortable, so I stood again, and he relaxed.

"I did not know her name. I asked her, but she indicated that she was mute."

He nodded. "Yes, miss. She is, so she cannot be a maid like the one you pointed out, that one that just left. We all have to work, you see, cleaning boots, shoveling coal, taking rubbish out, taking post to and from town. Someday, I hope to be an under-footman!"

"I'm certain you shall be," I said, though I did not know who would employ him once Highcliffe was sold. Perhaps the new owners. The other staff would not require or desire new positions, I thought; they were older and had only come back for this short season. But what about the young ones?

"Emmeline, well, tending the flocks with the dogs was something she can do," he finished.

"She does it very well," I said, pleased by the proud look that came upon him at my praise. "Has she always been mute?"

A troubled look came over him, and he seemed pulled into a memory. "Mr. Everedge—the big man, not Mr. Edward—used to be here. Before he died. There was a lot of men coming and going near our house," he said, as much to himself as anyone. "On the trails."

"The sheep trails outside Highcliffe?" I asked. "That lead to the sea?"

He nodded and continued. "We were just young ones, then, out amusing ourselves. How were we to know what was happening? We all hid and followed them, and one of the men started begging and such and Mr. Everedge put him in that smuggling cave with the bees, he did. We heard him scream, and then when he came out he was crying and swollen and his mates took him to the apothecary. A grown man crying! We ran away good."

I'd stopped breathing, I realized. Such cruelty numbed a person like ice on the tongue. I took a deep breath and encouraged Oliver to continue.

"My brother told my father, he did, and Father switched him

and told him to say nothing if he didn't want to be put in with the bees next. My brother didn't snitch on us that we were with him. But after that, Emmeline didn't talk again. Doesn't need to. Safer to say nothing about what we see. And . . . I sometimes have frightening dreams."

"I'm so very sorry, Oliver," I said, my heart breaking. "That is a terrible thing for a young lad and lass to witness."

"You shan't say anything, shall you?" His lips grew white. "I shouldn't have told what we saw!"

"I shan't," I said. "But you may call upon me if you ever have a need of help and I will help you. I promise."

He nodded, and ten seconds passed. "Is there some way I can assist you, miss?" he asked. His whole face had gone bluish white now; I knew he was anxious he'd said too much. Family did not usually linger in vestibules gossiping with servants.

I could not now, in good conscience, ask what I'd intended: if he had seen anyone entering or leaving my rooms. Oliver's words of warning ran in my head. *Safer to say nothing, one way or another, about what we see.*

"Do you like sweets, Oliver? Does Emmeline?"

His voice grew bright and cracked; in spite of his bravado his voice had not yet broken into manhood. "I think we do, miss, not having had them often."

"Wait here."

I made my way down to the stillroom and filled two small boxes with soft sweets and hard caramels. I returned and held them out to Oliver. "One for you, and one for your sister."

"Are you sure, miss? I wouldn't want anyone angry."

"They shan't be," I promised. "And there will be more in future. I'd rather you think of my family sweetly than with bad dreams."

The next week, Clementine and I took tea in the drawing room on a day when callers were not expected. It was warm, being mid-July, and I had asked to be served cool rosewater in addition to my tea. Chef willingly obliged; I think he rather enjoyed serving something unusual as well as the opportunity to utilize the still-room. While she browsed her lady's periodicals, I paged through Edward's *Hampshire Chronicle*, which drew an arched brow from Clementine. Advertisements for dental surgery, wet nurses, cottages for let, estate sales, and yes! Governess.

No, this was not mine. It began with, *A Young Lady of the Established Church, desirous of forming an immediate engagement in a clergyman's or gentleman's family.*

I could not say I was of the established church, and clearly that was important enough to be placed at the top of the solicitation. Where was my enquiry? What was I to do? I must find a situation—and quickly! Midway through the hour, Watts announced the arrival of the Maltese men. I did not have time to continue looking.

Clementine rose to greet them and advised Watts to bring their things to the guest quarters.

"Thank you, kind Mrs. Everedge, but we shall quarter on my ship, the *Poseidon*. It will be easier for me to discuss my ventures that way, too," Dell'Acqua said.

Ah. Perhaps he had matters to conduct that he did not want Edward to know of.

"I'm sorry my husband isn't here to greet you just now," Clementine said. "May I offer you refreshment in his absence?"

Dell'Acqua shook his head no and then caught my eye. Had he not seen me earlier? *Oh, Annabel,* I reproached myself. *You are*

*perhaps nothing more to him than a means to an end, as he is in-
tended, by Edward, to be for you.*

"I should very much like to take tea with you and Miss
Ashton," Dell'Acqua said. Two other men accompanied him, and
the three of them, plus Clementine, joined me in the drawing
room. Whether it was intentional or not, Dell'Acqua took the seat
Clementine had been sitting in, the one directly across the small
table from where I sat. That left the others to be seated near the
window, a little ways away from the two of us.

Unaccountably, my spirits rose.

"May I pour tea for you, Captain?" I asked. "My grandfather's
tea set, from Malta, I believe. He was a great collector of fine
silver. I like to think I get my artistic interests from him, and from
my mother."

The captain smiled. "And we are renowned for our silver-
smiths. Our artists, really." He smiled at me. "Perhaps your father
was an artist."

"I have no father," I gently rebuked. "I am, in English law, *filia
nullius.* However, sometime I shall have to show you the art of
Highcliffe," I said. "Before it's sold off or carried away to London."

"I am most interested in the art of Miss Ashton," he said,
not mentioning my father again. He looked at the teapot. "Yes,
I do believe that is Maltese. Is this the only Maltese teapot you
have?"

"No, there are others, of course." I set down the pot and
handed the cup to him. "Grandfather once had a teapot in the
shape of a mermaid, which then came down through the family,
and Edward and I would giggle endlessly over it. Someone, some
years ago, got rid of it. I think perhaps Edward's governess, not
wanting to taint the child."

He laughed. "I keep an eye out for mermaids as well."

"Do you believe in them?" I repressed a grin as I observed Clementine trying to calmly entertain the noisy "foreigners" across the room.

"No. But there are many sailors who do, and some captains who have them carved into the mastheads of their ships."

"You do not?" I sipped my rosewater and fanned myself.

He shook his head. "Quite simply, the lads cannot be distracted by images of beautiful women while sailing or they're useless to me. I shall not be wrecked on the reefs by the distractions of any siren, no matter how charming or beautiful she may be." He gave me a firm look. *What did that mean?*

"I keep my mind on the business at hand. The ship is my bride, as it were, and as has been said, the sea is a cruel mistress. They are enough to manage."

"I see." His voice seemed more withdrawn somehow than it had at our last conversation. Why? He had, after all, wanted to share tea and had chosen to sit next to me. Perhaps it was for the best. There was no good cause for the crestfallen feeling spreading within me.

"Your cousin . . . has he had any further interest in Mediterranean partnerships?" he asked.

Now he probes.

"I believe so." I remained loyal to Edward, but was starting to waver. "He has much to offer. He's been away quite often these past weeks, in Winchester as well as London. Like you, I am certain he hopes for a successful conclusion of whatever arrangements may help the family as soon as possible."

But not, please God, before I have arranged for a governess position. As long as the matters with Dell'Acqua remained unresolved, Edward needed me.

"I thought you may like to know that the Somerfords of Pennington Park hold Mass in a Catholic chapel for all who would come each Sunday," I said. "I don't know if you have found some-where to worship whilst here, or have a chaplain aboard . . ."

He shook his head. "No. Priests aplenty at home. One of my brothers is a priest, and one sister is preparing to become a nun. They pray for me."

"Well, you must feel well protected, then," I said, only partially teasing. "I have always wished for a brother or sister."

"Half-brothers, half-sisters," he reminded me. "But good people. I love them."

"I do not have a sister who is a nun," I said, thinking about those vows again, "but I do know some wonderful Benedictine sisters at the school in Winchester. I've grown close to them over the years. They've sheltered me in so many ways. Did you know," I added, "they educated the natural daughter of the Duke of Wellington?"

"I did not know," he said.

Oh, Annabel! How could he have known? He's not ever been to England. So many mistakes. Something in our conversation had thrown me, had taken away my confidence. His coolness, perhaps.

"I am rather fond of those who are naturally born," he said, rescuing me. Of course, he meant himself, but it was a circum-stance we two shared, and when I spoke of it to him it seemed to bind rather than to shame.

"I am, too," I said with delight.

"I should very much like to celebrate Mass." His voice grew softer, and so did his face. "It was very considerate of you to think of us."

Us. Not "me."

"No trouble at all," I said. Clementine stood, signaling the clo-sure of refreshments, and we said good-bye to our guests near the door. Watts showed them out.

"I need something to steady me," she said, and I didn't have to wonder what she meant.

"It did not go well?" I asked.

"Oh, as well as could be expected," she said. "I understood them with difficulty."

"English is one of Malta's official languages!" I protested. "They speak it perfectly. And with a charming accent."

She gave me a sharp look then. "Still. For Edward, yes, we'll carry on for Edward. And for Highcliffe. They're to join us at the Somerfords' a few days hence for dinner and the soirée."

I kept my face placid though my heart swelled. "You needn't have invited them, as they aren't staying with us . . ." I offered, only suggesting it to win her confidence because I knew she could not retract the invitation.

"It'll do Edward good for them to see we mingle with the best sort," she said, and then made her way to her rooms.

I made my way to mine, too, to carefully consider what I would wear to the soirée. *I may soon be a nun or a governess. In either station, it would be fitting to dress plainly.* For now, though, I was my own woman, and I wished to find a gown that would set my mother's combs, and yes, me, to best advantage.

CHAPTER ELEVEN

"You look lovely, Miss Annabel."

I turned around to make sure that it was Maud speaking to me, and not an apparition that had taken her form. Maud had never offered me the slightest compliment.

"Thank you, Maud," I said. "It means much to me, as a lady's maid sees women in finery all the time."

She smiled, and when she did, her face smoothed and she looked decades younger. "I've been a lady's maid for quite some time. Days gone by I served Miss Judith."

"I did not know that!"

"It's true," she said. "There was a French lady's maid close at hand, in need of a new position, that most women would have preferred. But not Miss Judith . . ." She shrugged. "That lady's maid married soon after, anyway. After Miss Judith died I left the household, but recently Mrs. Everedge—the new one—took me on."

"Mrs. Everedge must have thought you'd do a fine job," I said. "And so do I."

She grinned. "Yes, miss, and thank you. Look what I found for you." She shook a few drops of something from a small bottle in her hands and then ran it through my hair. "Neroli oil," she said. "Chef said you'd asked after it from the stillroom."

"I had. I have never had the resources for cologne."

"This is better." She smoothed it over my hair until it shone. "I know a few tricks, you see, having served ladies over many years. For example, when I was young, we learned to help the young ladies hide what they did not want to be made public."

I tilted my head. "How interesting. What sorts of things did you hide?"

Maud smiled at the memory. "Love letters, notes, trinkets given by young men of whom they did not want their fathers to learn. We women wear many layers, have many layers within and without, and there is much we can keep hidden."

"That is a most wonderful insight," I said, and it was. Rich, and multifaceted. I would view her with new eyes. It was not only *others* prejudging *me* without knowledge of my character; it seemed I had also fallen into like habit.

She began to roll my hair into an elegant knot at the back, with two coils at the sides, just over my ears. I'd placed the ruby combs on the porcelain dressing table top, as they would match the silver gown I'd chosen to accent my black hair. The dress was off the shoulder but held up by thin straps that ran near the collarbone, to either side of my neck, and a fine bodice that conformed to my figure. After being cinched in at the waist, the silver silk cascaded over my corset like a waterfall, in wavy ruffles, to the floor.

It was delightful and would most certainly do.

She left me to help Clementine with her considerably more demanding toilette, and soon we all met in the foyer and Watts had the carriage brought round. Within thirty minutes we arrived at Pennington, which was ablaze with garden torches outside though the night was not yet dim. The grand entrance hall proclaimed generation after generation of Lord Somerford's family with stoic, richly painted portraits. All were centered around a commanding likeness of James II, last Catholic monarch of England.

The decor softened as we made our way toward the large but warm dining room, which was enriched with vases overflowing with summer roses. Lady Somerford was a perfect hostess, though she looked, I thought, a little wan. I was seated next to the Maltese first lieutenant, Bosco.

"So how does a man who is named 'from the woods' become the lieutenant of a ship?" I teased as we finished spooning our lemon ice from frozen silver lemon cups.

"Lieutenant of *many* ships!" he said. "The Dell'Acquas—better named for the venture, I might add—have a large fleet. Which is why"—he pointed to the captain, who was in animated conversation with one of the Somerfords' acquaintances—"he is in such demand."

I thought back to his comment about Dell'Acqua being a flirt. In demand on nearly every front, it seemed.

"Tell me of Malta," I said, and he regaled me with stories of the calmest, the purest sea.

"If the water is so calm, how is it that Saint Paul became shipwrecked off of its shores?" I teased.

He shrugged. "He was not Maltese, of course, and therefore not a good sailor!" I laughed, which caught the captain's attention. Did he look the tiniest bit envious?

The lieutenant continued to amuse me with tales of their most beautiful women and, by far, the most gallant men in the world. "Our art is second to none," he promised.

"I shall have to judge that for myself."

"Come, come. There are many who would take you in, embrace you as their own. My family, even." He slipped into Maltese with that last phrase, and I caught myself just before answering it.

"I hope to visit," I said as Lord Somerford rose, indicating that we would withdraw to the ballroom for music and dancing. "I truly hope to." *Unlikely*, I thought sadly, *on a governess's stipend.*

I danced several times with men of our area, and with Edward, who seemed to enjoy himself; I even awkwardly partnered with the young Somerford lad, who faltered rather charmingly, like a new calf. It was a delight.

At the end of one dance, I sat in a chair next to a large silver urn that held long-stemmed red roses in it. Their fragrance was heady, exhilarating. Or perhaps it was just that Captain Dell'Acqua decided to join me. He sat down in the adjoining chair.

"You're the most beautiful woman here," he said, and the bold simplicity of his audacious admission, not prefaced in any way, took my breath away. "When I said that the Maltese were artisans of silver, I never imagined something like you"—he waved his hand toward my silver gown—"in this."

A thrill ran through me. "Thank you, Captain Dell'Acqua. I believe you to be mistaken, but I appreciate your sentiment."

"We shall have to work on freeing the Maltese woman dormant inside you," he teased. "My youngest sister would have responded, 'Yes, but of course, and if you hadn't pointed it out I would have been required to question your vision!'"

I laughed. "She sounds delightful."

"She is," he said. His blond hair was roughly pulled back but one strand had escaped, and I resisted the urge to reach up and tuck it back in. His casual grooming was in direct contrast to the fine quality of his clothing. I noted, as I had before, that he had an embroidered red rooster on his waistcoat.

"Would you care to dance?" he asked.

I toyed with the idea of letting my Maltese half answer, *I have been waiting an hour or more for you to propose this very thing*, but my English heritage won. "I would be delighted." I touched the velvety roses in the vase as we stood. "Red roses are my favorite flower."

He led me to the dance floor as the orchestra began to play. "Why red roses?"

I smirked. Some playfulness must be allowed, after all. "A lady must keep some things secret."

"A challenge, Miss Ashcroft, and one I gladly accept!" One hand reached round my back and the other led the dance. I'd enjoyed dancing with some of the other men, even young Somerford, but each had seemed, in some way, an effort. Not this time. I wanted to close my eyes and hoped for the music never to end. He brought his head close to mine, closer, perhaps, than was necessarily required for the dance, and as he did I could smell a trace of salt—due to the sea or to the heat?—as well as a light suggestion of musky, Arabian oil.

It intoxicated me as even the roses had not, nor ever could.

As the dance wound to a close, he said, "You are at ease nearly everywhere. Teacher, country house, London, Winchester, kitchens, dancing, with the Maltese and with the English."

He drew back as the music stopped, and I answered softly, honestly.

"If I fit everywhere, Captain Dell'Acqua, it's because I truly belong nowhere."

He kissed the back of my hand, and the impression lingered long after he made his way back to the associates who had been looking eagerly in his direction. I watched, with an unjustified pang of envy, as he danced, so comfortably, so charmingly, with another young woman. She, too, seemed smitten. And why not?

We returned to Highcliffe some hours later, just after Edward promised all in attendance that they were welcome for an afternoon's sport, playing a game lately from Ireland called croquet, the following week to celebrate St. James's Day. Clementine had not mentioned this event; that meant she had been taken by surprise. She'd have fewer than seven days and a minimal staff to entertain two dozen or more people in high style. It would be followed by a night's entertainment, sponsored by Mr. Morgan.

As I walked up the stairs to my room, I heard Albert whimper and Lillian soothe him. 'Twould be a shame when she left; he would miss her. I commended her desire to be a shopgirl and mistress of her destiny.

I slipped into my bedroom and locked it fast. *Could I be mistress of my destiny?* The thought thrilled me. It had been expected that I would teach at a school, or become a governess, or marry whomever Edward chose.

But maybe I did not have to walk the path someone— Edward—set before me. Perhaps I could choose my way after all. My mother had.

To horrible consequence, perhaps. But she'd given life to me. And as I was learning, I did not know the entire truth of the matter.

In the stone silence, I could admit to myself, and to God, that I did not truly want to be a governess instead of a wife. And that I wanted to know what had happened to my mother and set her honor to right, if possible.

The memory of a dance floated through my mind, and I captured it and played it over and again.

I was also growing quite certain I did not want to take the solemn vows of a nun.

The next morning Maud did not arrive to assist me, which did not trouble me at all. Clementine most probably needed additional attention after the late evening, and I was well prepared to take care of myself, as always. I opened my wardrobe to look for a dress for the day, which was to be at home with the family.

What was this? I liberated something small and white, pressed between two cotton dresses.

A white lace bonnet, a cap. I held it. I'd not seen it before, and I had carefully gone through my dresses just one morning earlier after they'd been returned from being laundered. Mrs. Watts had hired an additional laundress for the summer, someone new and unknown, to assist with the number of guests come to stay. My clothing had been freshly tended to.

Who was the new laundress? Could she have placed it here?

I sat before the mirror and slipped the lace bonnet, almost more like a veil, on my head. It was finely wrought, thousands of tiny stitches, the cap beautiful, and different and . . . foreign-looking somehow.

I sat down at my dressing table, where my ruby combs rested from the night before. I pulled the mysterious fish necklace from under my dressing gown. And now, the odd cap. A third clandestine gift, an unexpected appearance.

I pulled on my cotton stockings and attached them with the usual garters, and then, using the same clips, I also fastened the light lace cap with the clasp.

Maud's trick, recently shared, was very welcome indeed.

I should not mention the cap just yet. But I would seek to find out what it meant, if anything.

That night at dinner, it was just Clementine, me, and Edward. We sat close to one another at one end of the extended table, and Watts had placed a small bowl of gilt fruit nearby, for decoration.

Edward grinned. "Do you recall, Annabel, when you and I bit into gilt pears as children, home on holiday, thinking them to be edible?"

I laughed. "Yes. We had gold lips and teeth for days after that and your parents were most displeased. We looked like Roman statues."

"We did!" He laughed, and we shared a genuine smile along with the memory. It was that occasional happy memory, I suppose, that kept me hoping that a kind of family relationship might be resurrected, or perhaps, truly constructed for the first time.

Clementine smiled pleasantly but had little to add. I asked about the croquet picnic, knowing she was a good hostess, drawing her in, and then they nattered on about the plans for the celebration of St. James's Day and what gain Edward and Mr. Morgan—who would soon return from London—could be expected to acquire from the event. I took by the drift of the conversation that Captain Dell'Acqua still favored Edward and that the captain had, somehow, invited an associate of Lord Somerford's to consider joining with them.

"What do you hope can be arranged?" Clementine asked as the saddle of veal was served in pools of muddy brown gravy. I was very glad she'd asked, as I had been wondering that very thing myself.

"Dell'Acqua's thinking of the ropewalks," Edward said.

"The factories in which the ropes are made?" Clementine asked.

Edward nodded. "Everything is in place here—they would not need to be built, just reconditioned and re-roofed, as Lymington had active structures some time ago. Materials are cheap and plenty, as is labor."

I noticed one of the footmen serving us bristle at that remark.

"Is rope still in high demand?" I asked. "I thought with the commencement of steamships . . ."

Edward smiled benevolently at me as if he were my father and not my one-year-younger cousin. "Coal-powered steam costs money, my dear Annabel. Wind costs nothing. It will be some time before ships that sail on Mother Nature's boundless, *gratis* energy are done away with. Rope is in high demand. Many ships require twenty miles or more of it to operate. Much potential for investment in a world covered by seas."

Yes. Much potential. "The ropewalks being local," I continued. "Would that mean we could save Highcliffe?" Perhaps we could make enough legally to maintain the family home, and the enterprise would need to be overseen from nearby.

Clementine turned to me. "Yes, it would, Annabel. I'm certain you could visit often." She glanced at Edward, who shook his head, so she said no more of that, but the next words from her mouth betrayed what she'd been thinking. "Mr. Morgan arrives again tomorrow. He'll be here for St. James's."

So the celebration was to be ruined, and maybe my life as well. But perhaps . . . perhaps there was hope. Nothing had been clearly spoken of, committed to, after all. If I should find a governess position, I was free to take it with or without Edward's permission. Watts and his men removed the final dishes, with the assistance of a housemaid who had replaced the disgruntled footman.

The maid wore a white cap. All maids did. Not lace caps, it

was true, but still white caps. Could the cap I found have been one for servants? A laundress, perhaps? No, too costly.

"Whatever are you staring at?" Clementine asked me.

"Her cap," I answered honestly and absentmindedly. "The maid's white cap."

Edward glanced at Clementine, who looked worriedly back at him. "That's a rather unusual focal point." I knew he was waiting for an explanation.

"Oh, it's only that I've been wondering about white caps," I said. "Nothing to concern yourselves over." Could I have forgotten that we'd had the bonnet since London? It may have been among my things, and now I just could not clearly remember. I was shaken. It was, after all, unlikely that things would keep turning up without account. But women of my station did not wear caps such as this. I simply could not puzzle it out.

Edward quickly excused us from dinner. It was clear by her surprise that Clementine had had nothing to do with the lace cap, in any case. It was also clear that Edward thought my mind was tainted.

Perhaps it was.

CHAPTER TWELVE

The morning of the St. James's celebration, I quickly paged through the newspaper, licking my fingers in a most unladylike manner to keep the pages flipping quickly—nothing again! What could have transpired?—and then marched down the back stairs to the kitchen. Chef was huffing, and so were his stoves; Cook groaned as she freed pans from the ovens; a young girl carried in baskets of shells.

"Oysters?" I said. Chef smiled but was too busy to welcome me, I knew.

"Yes, miss," the girl said. "And scallops." Ah yes. I'd smelled the garlic-infused butter when I first came into the kitchens.

"Coquilles St. Jacques." St. James's shells. I closed my eyes, and when I opened them, Chef was nodding toward me.

"*Mais oui!* It would not be just to celebrate the feast of Saint James without his shells, *n'est-ce pas?*"

"Indeed not," I said. I hurried on with my question, as I knew he had much to attend. "There are two young children I know . . . they work for Highcliffe. I was wondering, well, if perhaps you had made two extra ice creams?"

We typically enjoyed molded, frozen sweet creams on St. James's Day, often with the season's last strawberries, at least when we were all at Highcliffe. It had been a family tradition, and though I was not certain if Edward was keen to keep those traditions, I thought perhaps Chef was, as I understood my grandfather certainly had been.

"I am so sorry," Chef said. "But if I give one to the children, there shall not be enough for you to enjoy one."

"Oh." I grew a little disconsolate, as I perhaps would not have another year here to enjoy them. "That is perfectly fine by me."

He then let a grin break out across his face. "What? I make a feast for dozens of guests and would not have extra ice creams?"

I laughed. "Of course you would." He motioned for me to follow him to the cold pantry, blocked with ice from the icehouse dug into the ground near the old abbey. I'd always felt vaguely uneasy entering the pantry but could not pinpoint why.

He moved some ice creams behind old butter churns. "I will place them here, *n'est-ce pas*? And after the guests leave, you can come back down and deliver them to the children."

"Thank you." My hands chilled as I touched the brass molds, seams lightly greased with lard so the treats would easily pop out, but my heart warmed throughout.

He did not answer me as he hurried back to the copper din of the kitchen shouting, *"Vite, vite!"* Hurry, hurry!

I must hurry, too. Our guests would soon arrive.

Within the hour, I waited on the lawn with Clementine as her guests were dropped off in carriages, fine and not so fine. Highcliffe's front façade had been quickly repaired, though the new stones hastily installed to replace a dozen or two crumbling old ones rather made the old girl look as though she'd been overtaken with spots.

Mr. Morgan pulled up and around to the carriage house. His driver parked inside, as Morgan would be staying for a few days. A second, more tawdry carriage followed them, and a cart. Was he bringing additional guests? That would be most irregular. In any case, I did not wish to appear to be awaiting his arrival, so I turned and aimed for the green expanse in front of the estate, which Clementine had had beautifully prepared. I assisted as she greeted guests . . . including the Maltese sailors.

The long lawn leading toward the sea had been made to look rather like a seascape, though there was no beachhead accessible for a half mile or more. Sand had been hauled up, and the ruin of several skiffs had been reclaimed from somewhere on the property and repurposed to become serving tables. Rope coils served as stands that held the croquet mallets. A nice touch, as Edward was cultivating the ropewalk investments. It would certainly bring that to mind for all involved. I'd overheard him berating poor Clementine for her "jolly country ways" that could not keep up with the sophistication that his associates expected of him, his circle, and indeed, his family. I thought she'd done rather well.

Edward initiated the croquet matches, and I watched as Captain Dell'Acqua and his lieutenant were partnered with two lovely ladies. One, with thick-coiled auburn hair, seemed to hold the captain's rapt attention, and I found myself growing a little envious at the easy camaraderie and laughing rapport between them. The captain seemed solicitous; in fact, I had not seen him this solicitous since he was delivering the drum to Albert, and winning over Clementine in the process.

Who was this young woman? She had a bright smile, and her laugh was musical. I took the mallet that Clementine's brother Harry, who was visiting as well, held out to me and partnered with him. He was pleasant company and rather fond of puns, which I quite enjoyed. After our round I made my way, surreptitiously I hoped, toward the red-haired woman.

"Ah, Miss Ashton." Captain Dell'Acqua held out his hand toward me. "I was wondering when you'd make your way over to say hello."

I glared at him from under lowered eyelashes; he seemed to understand my displeasure at having been called out, and his smile told me he relished it. But that smile held no malice, and he introduced me to his companion.

"Miss Annabel Ashton, Elizabeth, Viscountess Leahy. Lady Leahy is the daughter of Lady Somerford."

I nodded. "How do you do." I smiled, and she smiled back, warmly, with real affection. "Ah yes!" I suddenly remembered. "You're recently married."

She nodded. "Indeed, and have been in London with Lord Leahy. But my mother has been taken ill, and I've come back for a time to help attend to her."

"Oh dear, I hope it's nothing serious." I'd noticed that she was not in attendance, which was unusual.

"I hope that as well," Lady Leahy said. "She's sent me in her stead. She's asked me to collect you on Sunday . . . I do hope that will be all right?"

"Certainly, and I thank you for taking time to think of me." From the distance, her father motioned toward her; he was standing with Edward, who looked pleased.

"I look forward to reconvening with you later," she said. "For now, Papa calls." She turned toward Dell'Acqua. "I know he holds you in high esteem, and hopes you may arrange investments together. I shall tell him how I've enjoyed passing the hour with you."

The captain bowed gallantly and flashed one more somewhat

intimate smile. It troubled me, a little, but I was stuck on a word she'd said so casually.

Papa. I could not envision calling anyone by that tender term of endearment, but that did not mean that I didn't mourn the lost opportunity and the security that it held.

"Come, Miss Ashton." Captain Dell'Acqua took my arm. "Let's walk around the lovely grounds of Highcliffe, shall we?"

I nodded, cheerful again. Some still played croquet; some drank champagne that Watts's men circulated on polished silver trays. Many stood by the skiff filled with ice, and with shellfish.

"I've eaten too many oysters," I admitted. "You know it's been said that whoever eats them on Saint James's Day shall never want. At this moment, I feel I shall never want of another oyster."

He laughed and led me toward an arrangement of chairs near the Edge of the World, where we could best see the horizon, the cloud-pebbled sky as it married the bright water. I did not look down, though, where quicksand waited to catch whoever fell into its malevolent arms.

"You are so partial to oysters, then?"

"No," I admitted. "Though I can better tolerate the ones doused in garlic and butter."

"Why so many, then?" He waited for me to settle down, comfortably, on the best of the small group of seats assembled.

"Pearls, Captain Dell'Acqua. Chef has told me one must open at least one hundred oysters to find a pearl. Every year I try to find one."

His beautifully lashed eyes opened wide and, against my will, drew me. He did not turn away but held my gaze with increasing intensity. The nature of the very air changed, as it does just before a storm approaches. It was thick and charged, heavy, and the world around us faded away.

"Did you find your pearl today, then?" he asked softly. "I've never found one, myself. Until, perhaps, today."

He held my gaze and I knew what he meant. I felt it, too. Yes. Perhaps there was someone for me. Perhaps *this* could be the kind of man for me. *Maltese. English. Charming. Kind. Engaging.* I realized I'd been holding my breath, and exhaled so I might answer. "No. I could not eat more than ten, no matter how dedicated to the quest."

He laughed again, which broke the spell but brought joy and intimacy of another kind. "We eat them raw, in Malta."

"I would do that," I said, "if I could be assured of a pearl."

He smiled and drew his chair closer. "There are so few pearls in Malta." His voice grew somber. "This is the very reason I am here. There is little for our people."

By *our*, was he including me, or simply meaning the Maltese? I rather liked being included but did not wish to interrupt him.

"Malta is desperately poor, and my family's firm can help the people. We are deprived and barefoot; although everyone in the world uses us as a way station, we do not profit from it. If the business of the world is trade or war, then I will find a manner for our people to eat during both or either and not simply be used. I care deeply about their welfare. Now, I have discovered that perhaps there is a way to gain the investment of the English, arrange for investment for all concerned, and provide for my countrymen. I simply need to ensure I arrange the right partnership whilst here. At home, that might finally . . ." He stumbled a little and then lowered his voice: "Finally prove to everyone that I am Maltese, fully and completely one of them in spite of my father and"—he tugged his blond queue—"this."

I touched the back of his hand. "I understand. Perhaps like no one else could."

He nodded and looked uncharacteristically anxious. "Has your cousin . . . has he had any further dealings?"

Inwardly, I sighed. Of the three men triangularly rotating in my life, Edward and Captain Dell'Acqua seemed to be interested in me for what I could bring to their arrangements. Only dreadful Mr. Morgan was honest with his intentions. Could I blame Dell'Acqua, though, when I had set out with the same purpose, though bid by Edward? Perhaps the captain counted my affections as strictly family loyalty, and commercial as well.

Affections. 'Twas the first time I'd acknowledged it that way. "I believe he has made some progress with Lord Somerford," I answered honestly. "But I am certain he is interested in Malta. Very certain indeed."

Dell'Acqua nodded and relaxed. It was clear this situation was as important to him as it was to Edward, though neither would tip his hand. There was no harm in that. I wanted to help my family and my nation, and the captain, his.

"And then, once securing the arrangement for Malta, you will return home." I stated it, but there was an implicit question left lying should he care to pick it up.

"I would like to find my father, and wish to learn that he did not know he left my mother stranded. I hope that he loves and will be proud of me. And then I will return to my family."

His vulnerable, honest answer stole my breath once again. He'd had no *papa*, either. I knew he'd entrusted me with something dear. "Your family will surely be happy to see you arrive."

And I will be sorry to see you leave.

"My mother has an irrational fear that I will marry someone in a distant port and not return," he answered with a wink. "Lots of sailors' mothers and even their wives fear such! I've promised her I shall not."

The day, which had taken on the warm luster of the inner shell of an oyster, had now turned to dull, flat white like that shell's exterior.

"Tell me about that." I pointed to the rooster on his waistcoat to change the subject. "An Englishman would have to be rather daring to wear that as an emblem. It might convey a certain, oh, boastfulness," I teased. "I cannot imagine that's your intent. I've noticed you have them on all of your . . ." I stopped myself. Now he'd know that I had been examining him carefully each time we'd met. *Temperance, Annabel!*

He was a perfect gentleman and did not prod me. "Ah yes, the *serduq*," he said. This time, I was prepared. I did not let on that I knew what the Maltese word meant. Instead, I tilted my head.

"Rooster," he said. He pulled back his jacket so I could see it better. I saw a flash of his white linen shirt, too. It had been well tailored to mold perfectly to his body under the waistcoat; he was trim and taut. I convinced myself that I admired him from an artistic point of view, but other models had not stolen my breath.

"I am not afraid to boast when it is called for." He took my teasing in good spirit. "But in this case it reminds me, each day, of Saint Peter." I felt very bad then, for entertaining more worldly thoughts when he was thinking of his faith. I firmly redirected my thoughts to the conversation at hand and away from his attire and physicality.

Across the lawn, I spotted Mr. Morgan, who was looking in my direction with a glum, and perhaps angry, visage.

"It reminds me of Saint Peter—the rooster does—the time when Peter denied Christ as the cock crowed," he continued. "I do not want to fail those who depend on me when it matters most, and so I wear that as a reminder."

Whispers of his father's betrayal again. Did he even know his father's name?

"I have drawn that very scene," I said softly. "Not six months ago."

"May I see it?" he asked.

I did not understand what he meant. "See what?"

"That drawing. I should like to see some of your art."

I had never shown my art to anyone, save my teachers when I was younger. I kept it in notebooks, as I preferred to work with paper and charcoal. Well, I had given a few pieces away here and there, but rarely. Such as recently, to the young lass Emmeline. Why? Perhaps because like her, I had no voice.

And yet I wanted the captain to see my work. "I shall fetch my notebook." I walked toward my room, smiling and waving at guests along the way. My heart went out to poor Lady Leahy, who was entrapped in a conversation with Mr. Morgan, but I whispered a silent prayer that she would keep him occupied long enough for me to return to Captain Dell'Acqua unmolested.

I returned and found, to my great relief, that my chair next to the captain was still unoccupied.

I tentatively opened the sketchbook to the portrait of Saint Peter crying in a doorway, alone. I flipped the page and showed the next sketch, of Saint Peter on the beach, joyously sharing a meal of roasted fish that the Lord had cooked for him, restoratively.

"'Feed my sheep,'" Dell'Acqua said, quoting the scripture passage represented within. "That is exactly what I intend to do. His Maltese sheep, at any cost."

At any cost. Edward had often said, in my presence, that every man has his price.

Dell'Acqua turned to me, tucked a piece of stray hair behind his ear, and spoke with passion. "Your art is remarkable, Miss Ashton. I do not say that lightly. It is among the best I have ever seen, and I do not flatter. You have a rare talent—your pictures move and emote. They draw feelings to the surface of the observer, in me. Such talent should not remain hidden."

"Thank you." Tears welled, and I looked away, quickly, to regain control lest they slip down my cheeks. To be affirmed in what I most loved, by someone who knew quality art, and in particular . . . by him. Captain Dell'Acqua's hand reached toward me and I thought he was about to take mine in his own. He did not. Instead, he turned the pages of the sketchbook, stopping at the last.

"This . . ." he said. His voice grew sharp. "What is this?"

I turned back to him. He'd found the sketch I'd just drawn, of myself wearing the new cap.

"A cap I found."

"It's heartening how you've taken to Maltese customs!" He smiled, but his voice shook. "First the engagement necklace; now you're wearing a marriage cap." He looked skeptical. "You have plans to marry."

I was shocked, but I kept my voice down so as not to draw attention. "A marriage cap?"

He looked at me, and, I guessed, ascertained that my bewilderment was real.

"Yes, Miss Ashton. Where did you come by this if it does not belong to you?"

He had entrusted me with his feelings about his father, so I decided to take a risk and tell him, on the condition that he kept it to himself.

"I found it in my returned laundry. Tucked in, somehow." I hoped he believed me. "How do you know it is a marriage cap?"

"Maltese ladies wear a lace bonnet, such as this, when they are married. Widows wear one style, never-married ladies another. This is for a first-married woman. It is most unusual. I have never seen one in England, but they are common, and treasured, in Malta. Perhaps if it's not yours . . ."—he looked at me for confirmation, and I nodded—"it was your mother's? Is there someone you can ask?"

He had not heard about my mother's history. I had to tell him myself, lest he find out from someone else.

"My mother died in a lunatic asylum, Captain Dell'Acqua, when I was four years old." I distanced myself from him, physically and emotionally. I did not wish to be hurt by his inevitable recoil.

He did not recoil. "I am sorry," he said, and then he did reach to take my hand in his own. "The circumstances, perhaps . . ."

I nodded, soothed by his acceptance, warmed through by his touch. "Yes. But no one speaks of her. She bore me in unusual circumstances, as you know." I expected him to nod in agreement, but he did not.

"Perhaps she was married after all," he suggested, removing his hand from mine, then running his finger over the drawing of the marriage cap. And then he ran his finger over the outline of my face. He touched my face on the paper, but somehow I felt it on my skin. "And this was hers. Now it has made its way to you."

"Caps cannot just 'make their way,'" I answered. But I allowed the possibility to bubble toward the surface, like a swimmer pushing hard from the murky bottom toward the light.

"No, they cannot," he said, troubled. "And yet . . ."

As for me, I was completely shaken, as though I had fallen over the Edge of the World and found myself sucked into somewhere unknown. Perhaps my mother had been married after all. The necklace. The cap. Why were they appearing now?

If she had been married, my mother had been wrongly maligned for many years. Why hadn't my father come after her? She'd been maltreated by him, and perhaps others—who might they be?—who knew she was married but had hidden or ignored it.

I could restore her honor.

If this were true, then I *must* restore her honor—it would be my sacred duty, something I alone could do. She would not have died insane, of moral madness. *My* mind would no longer be suspected of being of like inclination.

I would be heiress of Highcliffe.

I took back my notebook and wrote *Maltese Wedding Cap* in tiny letters along the bottom of the sketch. "Would you be able to locate the maker of the cap?" I held out a slender hope. Perhaps he or she would remember to whom it had been sold.

Dell'Acqua's face grew somber. "I'm sorry, but no. It looks to be valuable and well made, but there are many crocheted each year. It may be"—he put forward the possibility gently—"that someone simply purchased this as a souvenir, not knowing what it was."

I nodded. My distress must have shown on my face, because he said, "I will take this sketch back to the ship this afternoon, and ask if anyone recognizes the particular style."

CHAPTER THIRTEEN

HIGHCLIFFE HALL, PENNINGTON PARK
LATE JULY, 1851

After some hours of rest, the household stirred again. There was to be Mr. Morgan's entertainment—a surprise—followed by a light supper at midnight. Clementine herself came to knock on my door an hour before I was expected anywhere.

"Mr. Morgan would like to see you ahead of the guests' arrival."

"Is he not a guest?" I asked.

She nodded. "This is different. I told him he might speak with you in the conservatory. Maud will be along shortly to help you finish dressing." It was the end of July. Summer would end in a month, and the intimations had been that was when I would be given to Mr. Morgan.

One month.

"Will you accompany me to speak with him, then?" She was the only woman qualified, within the household, to chaperone me. There were times when I, not of the highest status, would not need a chaperone, but when a man wanted to meet with me alone, then, yes.

"The conservatory is glass, and we're all nearby," she said.

I agreed, for what choice did I have? It was clear, though, that I was not regarded as someone needing the same protection as other highly born ladies.

Maud insisted I wear the lavender gown, and I did not mind, as it showed off my coloring well, and it was a beautiful gown of dusk for midsummer. "You're a midsummer night's dream," she said, and I found the reference to the Shakespearean play touching.

"You've unplumbed depths, I think," I told her. "I thank you for the compliment. It gives me courage."

Neither of us spoke of why I would need courage. I suspected we both knew.

I presented myself within the conservatory, one of Highcliffe's largest rooms. Mr. Morgan waited, sitting on a large sofa that was amply padded and then buttoned down, as was Morgan himself.

"Miss Ashton," he said. I could see he'd taken pains with his grooming; there were no stains on his clothing and he'd slicked back his hair with tonic or grease. I chose a seat near him but did not sit on the sofa next to him.

"Clementine said you wished to see me?"

He nodded. "As you know, I'm here for a short while, then will return to London to attend to some affairs, and then be back again. While I am away, I would like to remain in your thoughts . . . and heart, if it were possible. As you remain firmly in mine."

"How kind." I did not know what else to say. Other than some brief encounters we had shared during my and Edward's childhood and the occasional social event, we had not known one another well. "I had no idea I remained firmly in your thoughts."

"To quote Madame Necker, I have 'worshiped you from afar.' I never stopped watching you, Miss Ashton, even when you were unaware."

I shivered. The evening was beginning to sour. "The rest of Madame Necker's quote, Mr. Morgan, instructs that those whom we worship should remain distant from us lest the contact wither our affections."

"Not in this case, Miss Ashton." He withdrew two cases. "My affections for you will never wither, I assure you." He pressed on. "I have three gifts for you. If you'd be so kind."

I put up my hand to protest; a lady could not accept anything but the smallest token from a man she was not married or engaged to. He interrupted forcefully. "Everedge said you'd be pleased to accept them and gave permission."

Edward must have promised me to Morgan. Protocol would require it.

Mr. Morgan continued. "The entertainment tonight is my first offering. I have hired a pantomime troupe to perform."

Well, that was delightful, in spite of my misgivings. "We'll all enjoy that," I responded. "Thank you."

"The story was chosen with you in mind," he said, leaning forward. I could smell the pitched scent of his piney hair tonic. He took the larger of two wrapped boxes in hand and held it toward me. "Here is the second gift."

Reluctantly, I pulled the ribbon. It was a wooden chest.

"Open it," he urged. I did.

Inside I found large chunks of amber, yellow tree resin that had once been sticky and soft and had now hardened and smoothed. I pulled one out. Inside was trapped a mosquito. I worked hard to keep the disgust from my face. The second one held a spider and the third, a small frog, who seemed to have been encased mid-stroke.

"Presumably these were trapped in the amber while still alive?" I asked, horrified.

"Yes, yes!" He was enthusiastic. "I know you love honey—does the amber resemble nothing so much as solid honey?"

I reluctantly admitted that it did.

"When you visited my townhouse in London—and I hope you felt quite at home there, and would at my more distant properties as well—I saw that you, too, were taken with original and unusual curiosities. 'Interesting' is the word you used, which is precisely my sentiment. It was at that moment I knew I must find something interesting for you."

I set the amber down. "I am touched that you exerted such effort." Regardless of the gruesome nature of his gifts, he had extended himself on my behalf. "Thank you."

He seemed to recognize the genuine note in my voice. He held out the final, third gift.

"Please."

Reluctantly, I accepted it. I lifted the lid of the black velvet box. Within was a necklace on a long chain. At the end of it was a gold cage, and within the cage a large diamond.

"A diamond . . . in a cage." I worked to steady my voice.

"Yes. A treasure placed where it could never be lost. Like the Koh-I-Noor we both so admired. Don't you see?"

I did see. Yes, indeed. "This is too costly, Mr. Morgan. I cannot accept it. It's not done to accept such a gift from a man to whom one is not married."

"Precisely. And so you must." He sat again and his voice turned insistent. "When you wear it, you'll think of me when I'm away. Until I'm back. I've asked Everedge, and he's agreed."

For what had Judas sold me?

"Thank you," I said.

"Should you put it on now?"

"I'll need my lady's maid to assist me. But thank you so very much."

He agreed, then, as he was eager to see it on me. I knew I should purposely not "find" Maud that evening. But Mr. Morgan could not be avoided forever. It was nearly August, and even if investment arrangements were not concluded by summer's end, as Edward had originally hoped, they would certainly be concluded by the Exhibition's close in October.

Within the hour, the other guests began to arrive. I stood near Clementine and Edward, and when Captain Dell'Acqua arrived he handed the notebook back to me, gently shaking his head no. He went to find a seat in the ballroom, and after he'd taken his leave Edward questioned me.

"What was that exchange with the captain about?"

"I'm sharing English ways with Captain Dell'Acqua, making him more comfortable here, as you'd intimated I should," I said by way of nonanswer. "I do believe it is having the desired effect, as he asked me today if you were leaning toward resolving matters with him, and I assured him you were keen to complete mutually satisfactory arrangements."

Edward grinned and squeezed my shoulder, so happy with the fatted calf that was about to be slaughtered that he did not realize I'd neatly sidestepped his question. I should have to be circumspect in my dealings with the captain henceforth. I did not want to call Edward's—or Mr. Morgan's—attention to my growing affections for the blond Maltese, or to my plans to restore my mother's reputation, if not her fortune.

Clementine had seated me by Lady Leahy. "Do call me Elizabeth," she said, and while I was pleased to have a real friend and happily surprised by her refreshing intimacy, reluctance overcame me.

I did not want to make a true friend, a heart friend, which I felt she might become, only to lose her when I abruptly moved away, as I felt must be my future. I'd lost my Winchester friends so quickly. Highcliffe would soon be sold. I'd be off somewhere new, most probably with Mr. Morgan. I'd learnt at a young age that the heart did not easily mend after abrupt tearings away.

But Elizabeth's smile and cheerful conversation, her invitation to ride and to visit her mother, soon won me over, and I agreed to show her how to draw landscapes in the following month. She reached over and pressed my hand in affection, and I responded in like manner. My spirit soared until the pantomime started.

Mr. Morgan looked at me and offered a personal smile. I waved back and as I did, saw Dell'Acqua catch the exchange from across the room. Pantomimes based on fairy tales were fashionable in London, and Mr. Morgan had chosen a rendition of *Sleeping Beauty* to be performed.

The narrator began by recounting that a beautiful child was born, unattended by many as her parents were away, but given the gifts of beauty, grace, wit, intelligence, charm, and art. One fairy wished her ill, though, and through malice, wanted her to die. A last fairy amended that so only the kiss of the son of a king, a man who loved her in full, could waken her to life. Who could that man be?

The actors then began the story, searching for her rescuer, her true love. I felt his eyes upon me, and though I willed myself not to look in his direction, after some time, I capitulated and turned my head.

Mr. Morgan was staring at me, as I knew he would be. He grinned, and nodded, knowing I would understand, and I did.

*　*　*

In the morning, a gift arrived for Clementine, a bouquet thank-ing her for the previous day and evening's hospitality. Surprisingly, one was also sent to me.

Mine was a beautiful wreath of red roses. Clementine wrin-kled her nose. "Slightly large and vulgar," she said. "I suppose that's to be expected. Gifts after the event are not done, but a foreigner wouldn't know that."

I treasured those roses up in my heart, though, which was filling with welcome, uncharted affections because I knew exactly what the sender, Captain Dell'Acqua, had meant though no card was at-tached. *Rosarium*, in Latin, a wreath of roses. A rosary. A gift only a Catholic man would think to send. He'd figured out why red roses were a favorite, and in so doing, had become highly favored. Both he and Mr. Morgan had conveyed unspoken sentiments; Mr. Morgan's had been for his purposes, while Captain Dell'Acqua's had me in mind.

The following week, Maud helped me to dress in my riding outfit. The early August day was already beginning to sweat, and the thought of my velvet-lined outfit did not bring good cheer, but I could not arrive at Pennington less stylish. I packed my drawing things in a satchel and Edward's driver brought me to Elizabeth's home.

Their footman opened the door, and Elizabeth stood just inside, waiting. A lesser woman would not have shown how eager she was to meet with me, but I appreciated that Elizabeth did without the artifice of cool reserve and took her by the hand as we made our way to the stables.

"I've ordered the bays and light saddles," she told me. "We'll ride through the woods as a means to cool off, and then I thought perhaps might draw by the seaside paths?"

I readily agreed, and we set out riding through the New Forest, past acres of golden fields, recently harvested; with left-behind stubble they looked like nothing so much as old rugs with stubborn nibs and nobs of pulled wool sticking out here and there after having been swept. There were then miles of sturdy English oak. The sun darted in and out of the shadows and though the hooves steadily pattered, I was able to hear the call and response of the few birds willing to bear the afternoon heat to peck those newly mown fields for insects. After a pleasant hour Elizabeth brought us round to the land that lay between her property and Highcliffe, facing the sea, lashed with sheep trails and those used by smugglers in times not long past.

"Janes had someone bring out chairs and easels," she said. "I trust that is all we require?"

"Perfectly suitable." I looked at the arrangement, and the land where it sloped down to the sea, thinking there could not have been a more ideal setting to begin with. I showed her how to begin with the large set pieces, and as she sketched, and I guided her, we talked as young women do. She was quite good. Without a doubt, a lady in her position would have had instruction in art previously, but it was something she'd known we could share.

"Do you like being married?" I finally brought the conversation round to something more personal, to her, and for me.

"Very much so," she said. "I miss my husband, Paul, Viscount Leahy, but I shall return to him shortly after Mother is feeling better. I hope that someday you will come to see what I mean."

"About your mother?"

She tilted her head. "It would cheer her to have a visitor before you take your leave. I meant, though, you'll understand how it feels to miss one's husband, and look forward to being reunited." She set her charcoal stick down.

I said nothing.

"You do plan to marry?" She crumpled into the chair next to me; the day had grown even hotter.

"Perhaps." I leaned over again and showed her how to shade some margins. "For us marriage is not so simple, is it? Other girls I've known, why, if their fathers make an arrangement with a man from a good family who has prospects, then they're told to capitulate and enjoy. But for us . . ."—I looked toward the sea—"marriage is a sacrament."

She leaned over and put her arm round me. "You are such a dear. The man who claims you will be fortunate indeed."

I blinked back a tear. I had never had such a friend. I would be sorry when she left.

Eventually, though, they all left. Didn't they?

An hour later, after having ridden back and taken tea, Elizabeth asked if I'd like to visit her mother for a moment. "It will do her good," she insisted. We made our way up the twisting staircase, and as we did, the house grew darker by increments; with each level we reached the shadows blackened, deepened, lengthened. When we reached Lady Somerford's expansive rooms, quiet enveloped us and her daughter knocked. "Mama?"

"Come in, my dear," came a listless voice. A woman I presumed to be her lady's maid opened the door, and Elizabeth led the way into the large room. Lady Somerford looked much older than the last time I'd visited with her. Her skin was white and taut, pulled across her cheekbones like thin linen across a wooden bed frame.

"You're wondering why I keep my rooms so far up in the house," she said.

I grinned. I had been wondering that very thing, but I would never ask.

"I'm an old woman," she teased. "I know what everyone is thinking. There, go over there." She pointed to the window. It opened upon a stunning view of the grounds, the sea, and the drive from the main road to the house.

"It's lovely," I said.

"Some years ago, when my father was young, we held Eucharist in this room. Not only for the beauty"—she wagged her finger at me—"because our minds were not upon that. But the view allowed us to see if the King's men were coming and if so, we could hide the priest before he was apprehended. This room brings me comfort. Highcliffe has such a room, too, you know."

I was taken aback. "I did not know. I did not know that there was a need for such, either, at my home, as I had understood the family to be firmly rooted in the Church of England."

"They are all Church of England now," Lady Somerford said. "It's expedient. But it has not always been so. Remember, for most of England's history, Roman Catholicism was the established church."

I had not thought about that. "So you kept a priest anyway, in spite of the risks?"

She laughed, and when she did, she seemed well and young again. "Of course! There is no gain without risk, my dear, and it made rather good sport to outfox the authorities. Our priest, Father Antoine, was also our chef. One moment, chef's cap. The next hour, vestments. All of the priests had occupations as well as callings. Should the king's men appear we could simply say, 'But he is only our chef.'"

I smiled and laughed with her. "Much was risked, and everything gained."

She nodded. "You understand." Her face grew thoughtful again. "I suspect you're the kind of young woman who would take those very risks if required—and perhaps enjoy them. Your mother was . . ." She closed her eyes for a moment. "The thought occurs to me that perhaps Father Antoine had known your mother."

She brought up something I had wanted to ask, but hadn't had the courage to do so. With the Somerfords I'd found, I thought, a place to belong, and didn't now want to despoil the nest.

"Did you know my mother, Lady Somerford?" *Please do not speak ill of her or look at me askance.*

She spoke gently. "Not well. She returned from Malta a Catholic, but your grandfather was ill, and then Judith was married, and we were often in the north, as that is Lord Somerford's preference. But she did celebrate Mass with us when she could. Father Antoine was here. Should we ask him?"

I stood up. "He is here?" Excitement flushed through me. "Now?" Perhaps he could verify that she'd been married!

She nodded. "He came when he heard I was ill." She leaned back wearily into her pillows. "I'm becoming tired—I'm so sorry, my dear Miss Ashton. Thank you for calling, and for lightening Elizabeth's day. I hope I shall see you again soon."

I leaned over and took her frail hand in my own. "I shall pray for you each day until you are fully restored to health," I said. She nodded at that, and I set her hand down upon the coverlet, gently, and followed Elizabeth from the room.

"I shall ask Father Antoine to meet you in the chapel," she whispered to me. "You know the way there?"

I nodded and made my way down the stairs and toward the chapel, where I waited for Father Antoine to find me.

CHAPTER FOURTEEN

W hen he arrived, I stood up, but he motioned that I should sit back down. "Hello, daughter." He sat next to me, in a fatherly manner. "You are very much Julianna Ashton's girl."

An indescribable burst of emotion exploded at my center: love, fear, affection, wonder, trepidation, and yes, hope. Instead of offering the sophisticated response I'd wished to, I began to cry.

"There now, it is not unusual at all, is it? Difficult circumstances lead to tears."

After a moment, and using Father's clean but well-worn handkerchief, I finally said, "It's just that I have never talked about my mother with anyone who had seen her in person. Aside from myself, that is." *Oh. Now he'd think I was often talking to myself.*

He nodded and took the damp handkerchief back, not dissuaded at all by the moist touch of it. "I did not know her well, as I was the only priest hereabouts for some time, *n'est-ce pas?*"

I nodded, and he continued.

"I did know her some."

"She was Catholic." I seemed to be stating the obvious, but that, too, had never been confirmed by someone who'd known her.

"*Oui*," he agreed. "Devoted. It would have been much easier for her to deny the faith once she returned to England, pregnant with you, and her family opposing her religion. But she did not. Some who are born into Catholic families, well"—he shrugged— "it seems as though the choice was made for them. But Julianna was not only baptized, she was truly converted. She'd had you baptized, too, you understand, secretly."

I smiled at that. Then I closed my eyes, relishing each drop of new knowledge of my mother, whom I had held at arm's length even in my own mind for fear of . . . what, exactly? Being tainted by her memory? I swallowed my shame. Perhaps. I whispered the one question I had wanted to ask since Lady Somerford told me he might be here. "Was she . . . married?"

Father Antoine looked at me steadily. "I was, of course, not there. But she was devout, and I confessed her. She would never have lied to her confessor and thereby lie to God." He took my hand in his again. "I believed her."

I held my breath. It was true. I knew it. It was true! But could anything be proved, and be proved before Edward had me married to Morgan, as threatened, in a few weeks' time?

"I do not believe she was mentally unwell," Father finished. "In fact, she'd come to me because she was considering marrying again."

I shook my head in wonder. "Her sister . . ."

"Yes," he answered. "Her sister." But he was a priest, and he speculated no more. I did, however. If my mother had married again and borne a child within wedlock, that child, and not Edward, would have inherited all.

I made my way back down the hall, and Elizabeth accompanied me for the carriage ride back to Highcliffe, which was splendid of her. Since she'd been so good to me, I divulged a secret.

"I've been thinking if I did not undertake the sacrament of marriage, or become a governess, I would consider taking holy vows." Better that than marry Morgan! And yet, my conscience would not let me lie about having a sacred call.

Elizabeth's eyes enlarged to reflect her surprise, but she did not dissuade me.

"God will show you what to do," she said just as we arrived. I did not know if I believed her. I should, I knew. But I'd been asking Him, and nothing had become clear except Mr. Morgan's insistence and the quick slippage of time toward the bottom of summer's hourglass.

Later that evening, when the household was quiet, I asked Mrs. Watts, the housekeeper, if I might speak with her privately for a moment. She looked wary but agreed.

"Lady Somerford has told me that there is a room at Highcliffe in which Catholic services were once held," I said. "Do you know of such a room?"

She nodded. "Yes . . . the quarantine room, I believe. Not only used for scouting those coming after the priests, but looking for revenue men, in more recent times."

I had not heard of this room. "Where would I find it?"

"At the top of the back stairs," she said. "Near the attic storage rooms."

Far from the family. Yes! I remembered seeing it, from the outside, from the lawn. The stained-glass window. I had never been in the room, of course. We children were not allowed up the back stairs, and I'd had no cause to visit when I'd returned now and then to Highcliffe as an adult. But I'd seen the stained-glass window from the lawn, and had wondered at it.

Mrs. Watts turned to leave and then turned back to me once more. "I believe it was the last room where your mother stayed before she was . . . taken away. Now, if you'll excuse me."

I nodded, shocked by yet another revelation about my mother.

She'd been quarantined. But why? Her supposed insanity could not have been transmitted to anyone else.

I waited until near midnight, and then I lifted a taper from my drawer and a brass holder, and lit the candle. It threw off little light compared to the lamps, and I wanted to remain undetected. The wick sputtered as I made my way up the vestibule and then quietly opened the door to the back hallway, the one staff used. I walked past the first floor and then past the second, where the maids used to sleep, when they'd lived at Highcliffe. Those rooms were all empty now, and the hallway held the eerie silence of that which had once bustled with activity but had been evacuated, impressions and silent expressions of lives that had passed through.

It seemed I could sense them. I shivered.

Wait. I thought I heard a low whine, a quiet voice, and stopped.

Highcliffe creaked and moaned at night, like an old woman, as the evenings grew cool and caused the boards to contract. That must have been what I'd heard. After some moments of near silence, I moved up the stairwell again.

The floorboards were finely filmed with dust; it was quite clear that no one had trod upon them for some time. Why would anyone? Highcliffe had been mostly abandoned for London, and there was no one ill enough to be detained. A person could be trapped up here and never be found. Who would think to look for her?

I shook the fancies of my entrapment from my mind and climbed the final stairs, cupping my right hand around the candle to concentrate the wan light. The air was stale and still and I was enveloped by darkness and, in fact, a smothering sort of fear that squeezed me tighter than any corset. The silence hurt my ears and accentuated the only sound present—that of my heart pounding in my ears. The situation reminded me, in the entirety of its sensory deprivation, of the time fifteen years gone by that Edward had locked me in the linen closet so he could eat my pudding and then forgot me there.

I put my hand upon the brass doorknob, and it slipped as though it had been greased. I looked down and saw it was the sweat of my own palm that had slicked it, so I wiped my hand on my dressing gown and tried again. And again! But it would not open. I hoped to find something, some clue, about my mother's disappearance in there.

Another noise. Another quiet call. Feet falling on the risers. I did not imagine it this time. Someone was coming!

I wedged myself close to the door and pushed back my damp hair. The footsteps came closer, and closer. Finally a voice.

"Who's there?" I called out.

"It is I, Lillian, Miss Ashton," came a harsh whisper. I sighed, and my shoulders fell in relief.

Lillian came round the corner, lamp in hand, peering at me curiously. "What are you doing, miss?"

She did not come too close. And she had that look . . . the look that indicated she was, inwardly, at least, questioning my stability.

"Looking for a room I'd just learned about."

"It's midnight, miss." She remained at the bottom of the stairs. "A most peculiar time for people to be wandering about. Regular people, that is."

"Yes, it is. Why are you up and about?" I tried a turnaround tactic. But Lillian was too savvy.

"I was wakened by young Albert and heard a noise, miss. I followed it to you. It's not always wise to let him wander to his mother's room."

I wondered why not. Green fairies, perhaps. "Lillian," I began. It was important that she not tell anyone about my midnight wanderings. "I would like to keep this a secret between us, if we may."

She nodded tentatively. "I'll help you, miss."

"Thank you, Lillian." I hoped my voice conveyed my true gratitude. I would need all the assistance I could find.

The next evening, dinner was to be held *en famille* plus the Maltese and Mr. Morgan. It would be the last time for a week or two that we'd all eat together, as the men were returning to London for a brief visit followed by, I worried, Mr. Morgan's proposal of marriage. Maud came to help me dress and I slipped into a deep red gown that, by rights, would have been better suited to autumn, but I wanted to wear my mother's hair combs and, in a way, send a message of thanks to Captain Dell'Acqua for his red roses.

Maud rolled my hair up and, unusually, after pulling out some loose tendrils, wound them round an iron she'd heated in the fireplace. The look was softer, subtler, and much more feminine. She smiled at me, and I smiled in return. "Let's arrange it this way each day," I said. "If we may?"

She nodded, and then reached into my jewelry box to extract the diamond necklace that Mr. Morgan had gifted me. *Slightly large and vulgar*, I thought, echoing Clementine's sentiments over my red rose wreath. Then I repented of the unkind thought.

"I should prefer to wear something plainer, tonight."

She shook her head at me. "Mr. Everedge told Mrs. Everedge to ensure that you wore this." Without waiting for a response, she reached round me; I humbly tilted my neck forward like a calf to the slaughter. What choice did I have?

When we made our way downstairs, the men awaited in the smoking room and as Clementine and I arrived, they joined us. Edward took Clementine's arm and Captain Dell'Acqua stepped in a lively manner to take mine. Mr. Morgan was not pleased with that, but he was pleased when he saw the trinket round my neck.

"You look ravishing, Miss Ashton, not that it would be unexpected. And you're wearing my gift, the necklace, which is so fitting." He sat directly across from me. "I'm honored."

The room grew quiet. His intimate comments were quite out of place. Gentlemen did not speak of ravishing and everyone knew that such a necklace was a sign of an approved claim.

"Thank you, Mr. Morgan," I said. I left unsaid, *I had no choice.* Even Edward appeared a bit uncomfortable at the familiarity with which Mr. Morgan spoke.

Captain Dell'Acqua, whom Clementine had thoughtfully seated to my right, looked at the enormously expensive bauble encased in gold and lying flat at the base of my collarbone. He then looked at me and I back at him but, of course, I could say nothing. What was there to say? It was the kind of gift a man gave to his wife . . . or fiancée. I wondered if Dell'Acqua was thinking back to our conversation about the Maltese marriage cap and necklace.

"You're beautiful," the captain said simply, and I tilted my head down in acknowledgment, not trusting myself to speak. It meant more to me than the florid, gin-fueled compliments Mr. Morgan had paid.

Dinner was brought out, and the conversation flowed superficially and quickly. I glanced at Edward, so young to be sitting at the head of the table, and did not envy him the task of saving the family fortune. His father had not done well by him, but perhaps would have been able to turn the tides for us had illness not taken his life early.

Be careful not to misplace sympathy on Edward, I told myself. It made me vulnerable to unexpected malice.

Perhaps the tides would be turned anyway. Lord Somerford was to meet them in London, as was Elizabeth's husband, Lord Leahy. Investments were being discussed and stitched together. Edward summoned Watts, at least twice his age, and seemed to relish doing so.

"Chef has prepared a surprise for us." Clementine sipped her water before continuing. "We'd decided upon a menu, and then at the last moment, he sent word that there would be a change. I'm sure it will be splendid."

I turned my face away from her but toward the back of the room, where footmen emerged with silver serving platters. Behind them, nearly hidden, stood Chef. He caught my eye and I his, in return, offering but the smallest smile.

The lids were lifted, and a delightful aroma filled the room—rich, savory chicken, velvety red wine, and the fresh green of thyme. "Coq au vin!" Clementine said. "It has been too long. Why had I not thought of this?"

It was served, and as it was, I felt Captain Dell'Acqua's hand on my elbow to the side of the table. The touch of his hand sent a frisson of excitement through me. He leaned over.

"Did you like the roses?" he spoke softly.

"I did. I sent a note round to your ship. Did it not arrive?"

He nodded. "I saved it. But I wanted to hear it from your lips. The dress . . ."

"Rose red," I said. I could feel Mr. Morgan's stare from across the table but I did not care. I was completely engrossed with the heady mixture of the brandy in the dish, Captain Dell'Acqua's musky cologne, and the enchanting feeling of him being so near.

"You asked Chef to make coq au vin, did you not?" he asked. "Rooster in wine?"

"As an honor, yes." I sipped my water to cool off and looked at him sideways, from under my lashes, speaking sweetly. "By your gift of the *rosarium*, I understood that you appreciated the subtlety of unspoken sentiments, Captain Dell'Acqua."

"I do indeed." He let his hand caress my arm ever so slightly as he released my elbow; my skin rippled beneath his touch. Morgan glared at us. The captain nodded, tipped his glass to him, and switched to Italian, a fine tenor in his voice. *"Alla fine andrà tutto bene se non andrà bene, non e le fine."*

All will be well in the end; if it's not well, then it's not the end.

"I hope you are right, Captain Dell'Acqua," I said shakily before turning my head back to my plate, but I could still hear him whisper, a teasing playfulness in his voice that tangled in my heart.

"I am always right, Miss Ashton."

CHAPTER FIFTEEN

⁓⁓

AUGUST, 1851

The next morning, Clementine was still abed at a late hour. I knew she would be; Edward had left for London and after an evening's entertaining, she rarely dislodged herself before noon. I sent Maud to her, with a question.

"Tell her that it's a glorious summer day, and one Albert should enjoy. Would she like to come along for a carriage ride to Lymington, with Lillian, of course, so the lad can enjoy watching the yachts departing and take in the fresh air?"

Maud returned with the message I'd expected. "Mrs. Everedge says she is not well enough for a trip into town, but that is no reason to deprive Albert. You and Lillian may take him."

"Thank you, Maud. I can attend to my dressing today so you may assist Clementine."

She nodded and then left. I pushed Mr. Morgan's necklace to the bottom of my jewel box, using a stick, as one would to force away an insect. Then I put what I believed to be my mother's fish necklace on instead, though keeping it placed under my gown. I made my way to Albert's rooms to speak with Lillian.

"Mrs. Everedge has indicated that you and I might take this young lad to watch the yachts this morning . . . that is, if he'd like to."

Albert ran headlong into my arms and, as I bent toward him, took my face in his hands, kissing each cheek. I laughed aloud and kissed each cheek in return.

"Well, then, let's be off." Lillian seemed happy to be getting out, too.

"I wonder if . . . that white cotton dress I've seen you in, the one with the pink roses scattered on it," I said. "Perhaps I might remain with Albert whilst you change, if you wish to?"

She tilted her head; it was her best dress and set off her fair complexion. She did not question me, however. Instead, she went to change and was back shortly. She'd affixed little crystal earrings into her earlobes, too.

Please, dear Lord, do not let Clementine see us dressed like this or she will certainly understand something is afoot.

We set off toward the door; Watts had ordered the carriage to be at the front entrance. While we waited, Albert and I made our way to the lawn, where I showed him how to blow the seedy white down from spent dandelions; he puffed up his cheeks and then exhaled with glee, and I plucked some strays from his neatly combed hair. After settling into the carriage, young Albert on my lap, we made off, rattling down the drive. His face was pressed to the window; a cool breeze found its way to us from the open front, as did the driver's jaunty tune. It was not noon, and yet the August day was so hot that even the dust lay listlessly on the ground beside us as the carriage wheels churned. I pulled my bonnet strings to loosen them, as did Lillian.

Shortly, we arrived in Lymington. First, we had the driver pull up to the harbor wall so Albert could view the yachts; I let him climb down from the carriage, and we stood nearby it as he watched them slip in and out of port. I hastily scanned those that were anchored; no ship had *Poseidon* scrolled upon it. Captain Dell'Acqua had already sailed to London, apparently, or wherever he'd gone to conduct his affairs.

After half an hour, I tucked Albert back into the carriage, and we clop-clopped our way to Mr. Galpine's lending library. There were plenty of books in our own library, but books were not the reason for our journey. I took Albert by the hand but insisted that Lillian should accompany us inside.

The tinkling bells on the door chimed our arrival, and Mr. Galpine raised his hat in acknowledgment of me, but his eyes were on Lillian.

"I've come to check on my newspaper advertisement," I said. Lillian looked at me, shocked, and I grinned at her. Taking charge of one's own life had been her idea, after all. "I've been faithfully reviewing Mr. Everedge's papers but I've yet to spot my enquiry for a governess situation. Is there a possibility it was not sent?"

Galpine shook his head. "No. I posted it myself, Miss Ashton. Along with the advertisement for the gentleman keen to engage a secretary, and he's had several responses. I assume if one correspondence arrived at the paper safely, the other did as well."

Now that he mentioned it, I had seen that very advertisement in the paper, the one the man ahead of me had placed.

I twisted my cameo ring. "What could have gone wrong?"

Mr. Galpine shook his head. "I'm sure I don't know. I'm sorry, Miss Ashton. Would you like to place another ad?"

I had to conserve my resources. Before I placed another ad, I should find out what had happened to the first one. "Not just yet, thank you. But I would like to peruse your lending books, as would our nanny, Miss Lillian Miller." I introduced them and then added, "Miss Miller is a fine nanny but has mentioned a talent with sums and an earnest interest in shop-keeping. I thought perhaps you might have some periodicals or books that could assist her as she considers this new avenue."

He readily abandoned me to display potential reading materials to Lillian. I smiled at them, and after locating a few books of interest, Lillian and I left. I would review Edward's newspapers again.

When we returned home, Clementine was in the drawing room, reading. Albert ran to her and told her about the ships, and she fussed over him. As they talked, I paged through Edward's papers, left untouched as he was in London.

"What are you looking for?" Clementine asked as I quickly paged through.

"Nothing of importance," I replied, wrongly, and noted that I would need to admit that at my next confession. The business at hand was most important indeed.

Edward returned from London on August 8; I remembered the date on that day's paper, which he found me searching through in the library. He was in high spirits.

"Your matters are proceeding well?" I asked.

He nodded. "It may yet be that the Maltese, who have rained trouble upon the houses of Ashton and Everedge, shall save us in the end!"

I did not point out that the Maltese man who was my father had, unknowingly, gifted the family fortunes to Edward's mother and father through my illegitimacy. It would not help matters at this point, and I needed to think how I could seek to prove my claim if it were true.

"Your friendship with Captain Dell'Acqua, and, indeed, with Lady Somerford and Lady Leahy, has proved fortuitous indeed." He sat down in a chair near me. "Put the newspapers down, Annabel, and take a seat near me."

Dread forced my heart into spitting out extra beats, and I closed the paper, wiping my hands on a handkerchief so I did not stain my gown with ink, and sat near him.

"You're searching for the advertisement you placed seeking a governess situation." He was blunt, and his face held no concern for me. I, on the other hand, was flooded with unease.

"Yes . . . how did you know?"

"Clementine told me you were looking through the paper, as did Watts. An enquiry arrived for you a week or two ago."

"Addressed to me? Enquiring as to my availability for the position?"

Edward rang for a cup of tea, nodded to the maid serving it, and then finally turned to answer me, at his leisure.

"The letter was addressed to me," he said. "How dare you accuse me of opening your mail! The writer sought reassurance about your availability, suitability, and references. I returned with a letter of my own saying that you were most unsuitable."

"Most unsuitable!" I stood, not caring now who heard me. "I am entirely suitable. I am of good education, an experienced teacher, and the Rogers school would give me excellent references—of that I am certain."

"I know the family in question," Edward said, quietly setting down his half-drained cup of tea. "They would not want a papist governess surreptitiously steering their children in a misguided direction. Governesses are charged with the moral welfare of the children, and in that, you are most unsuitable on several fronts. I responded to their enquiry in this way and have not heard another word. Upon learning that you had placed such an advertisement, without consultation with me, I spoke with the newspaper in question and had it removed."

"Then I shall place another, this time specifying that I seek a situation in a Catholic household!" I sat down and held his gaze.

He was not to be challenged.

He drew near to me, his eyes the cold gray of the stones that could be found sweating inside the dark, abandoned abbey behind Highcliffe. "I warned the man that should any further advertisements be submitted, he should alert me. There will be no more, Catholic family or not."

I sat back, and as I did, I felt my mother's necklace move, quietly, under my gown. I drew quiet strength from it.

"Then another solution shall be found."

He nodded. "I've already found it. You're to be married."

My anxiety tempered, slowly, drifting from the fast beating in my chest to the slow sickness settling in the hollow of my stomach. "I have no dowry."

His eyes widened, and he sipped his nearly empty cup, to regain the high ground, I suspected. *Ah. You didn't know that I knew that, did you?*

"You won't require one," he said. "I've found a man who is willing, eager, even, to marry you anyway. I've told him that foreign blood is only good for horse breeding." He smiled a little self-satisfied smile to himself. "He's smitten with you, Annabel, and only God knows why."

I sat back down in my chair. I could hear servants rustling about in the vestibule. I could not blame their eavesdropping. But I did not have time to worry about it at that moment, either.

"Mr. Morgan."

He nodded. "Just so. I had thought to have this business with the Maltese wrapped up by summer's end, but alas. However, when our affairs are concluded, in no more than a few weeks' time, Morgan and I will come to a formal agreement. But, as you've said, you have an education and given the circumstances regarding your birth, are not unwise to the ways of the world, so I assumed you would have guessed something was afoot. It's all but settled."

I steadied my voice. "And if I refuse?"

"What shall you do then? You cannot return to the Rogers school with no stipend. There is, as you have somehow discovered"—he looked at me angrily—"no dowry." He motioned for Watts. "Bring me a Scotch whiskey." He'd moved from tea to whiskey, so perhaps everything was not as neatly settled as he hoped to convey.

"Then why not allow me to become a governess?" I asked. "It will cost you nothing."

"I've already made arrangements; they're good for you, they're good for the family." He grimaced as he swallowed half his glassful. "Your marriage to him will satisfy certain obligations as well as please him . . . and me. You'll be well taken care of," he said, reassuringly, slipping back into his faux fatherly voice. "I've ensured that. You must trust me."

"Must I?" I let a full minute tick by. The commotion in the vestibule had quieted, but, I suspected, the servants remained, listening like tentative mice waiting to see which way the cat would move next. He smiled menacingly with his prematurely yellowed teeth, which looked like tea-stained porcelain but had, in fact, been tarnished by smoke.

I found myself in a stony place. "And if I refuse?"

"Then it's the workhouse for you."

I recoiled. The workhouse would scrub away the last vestige of my gentility.

"If there was someone else who would have me . . . a good man?" For the first time, I spoke the thought that was only half formed, half desired, in my own heart and mind.

"Dell'Acqua?" He laughed. "Oh, Annabel. You are not so wise in the ways of the world after all. To quote an Italian, which the captain is so fond of doing, 'There is nothing more important than appearing to be religious.' If I may add to Machiavelli's sentiments, 'or more important than appearing to be besotted, if one wishes one's way with a woman, or well-intentioned and well-connected, if one purposes to make investment arrangements with her family.'

"And now, dear cousin, I must be about my affairs," Edward continued. "Fear not—Morgan will treat you well or hear from me, and we need say nothing more of this till matters are concluded. But"—he raised a firm finger to me—"no more advertisements in the paper. Promise."

I nodded. "I promise not to place any more advertisements."

"You're good to your word, I know." He dismissed me with a wave of his hand. I stepped up the stairs to my room, past the silent servants, who scattered like the blown dandelion fluff when I walked past them. I wanted nothing so much as to fall upon my bed and cry. Mr. Morgan! So it had been settled? I saw no way out of this. I had to find another position, and with only a few weeks in which to do so!

However, my tears should have to wait. Surprisingly, the door to my room was open, and Clementine waited for me within. My surprise must have shown on my face.

"I didn't mean to startle you," she said.

"Are you well?" She had never, to my knowledge, been to my rooms. But perhaps she had visited when I was not there.

"I am," she said. She sat on the little sofa near the fireplace, which was, of course, cold, and indicated I should sit near her. I moved my book of saints and angels as well as my Bible, which had been placed right where I needed to sit, and joined her.

"Those books . . ." she began, looking at my beloved religious volumes.

"Yes?"

She did not continue with her earlier thoughts but moved on to why she'd come. "I did need to tell Edward about the advertisement," she said, "that you were looking through the papers for it. If I didn't tell him, and one of the staff overheard and mentioned . . . Well, you understand."

"Not quite."

"I know Edward has not always been kind to you throughout your life. And it would not go well for me, or for you, if I chaperone you but things go amiss. But that is not the purpose of my visit." She looked down at her hands. "You had mentioned that you were considering taking vows to become a nun."

I blinked. "I did?"

She put her hand over mine, "Yes, Annabel, you did. Do you not remember?"

I did not remember. Had I told her? How else could she have known? Certainly Father Gregory would not have shared our personal conversations. Nor would Elizabeth, Lady Leahy. Would she have?

"You do not care to marry Mr. Morgan," Clementine stated.

I shook my head. "Would you?"

"That is not the question, Annabel. We women are not, generally, at liberty to marry whom we wish. These things are arranged by our fathers—or our betters—in our best interests." Her voice softened, and she put her hand on my arm. I looked into her eyes, and they reflected genuine concern.

"You have a choice that I did not have, however." She lowered her voice. "You could take those vows, become a nun. Is that your intention, Annabel? I'll keep your answer confidential."

I did not answer her, though I could feel her silent insistence pressing me to respond. The vows were holy, but that was something she would not understand. Was I called? The heady scent of Dell'Acqua's cologne somehow presented itself in my memory.

"It is an option." She was no longer willing to abide the silence. "I'm here to tell you, as your friend, and as Edward's wife who hears him speak and knows his thoughts. Other than Mr. Morgan . . . it is your only option." She drew near the door. "I can see you are distressed, so Edward has excused you from joining us at dinner this evening. I'll have a tray sent to your room. Good evening, dearest Annabel." She left, pulling the door closed behind her.

Edward would not have had time to speak with her between my conversation with him and the one I'd just had with her. He must have predetermined my dismissal from dinner.

The room grew stifling. I could not open my window—it was one of those that had been sealed shut; why? Because many of the windows were old and needed expensive repair? Or had it been sealed as long ago as when my mother had occupied these very rooms . . . to protect her or to restrain her?

I put on a light cotton gown and cooled off as the day grew darker by degree. A carriage drove up; I watched as Dell'Acqua and his friends arrived for dinner. A tray of plain food was delivered to me, silently. I lifted the tray top. Macaroni with mashed calves'-head.

Some hours later, in dark punctuated only by seaside starlight, quiet disturbed only by the faint sound, through glass, of a relentless, high-tide sea, the Maltese sailors left, laughing as they departed.

For all purposes, for this evening, Edward had me quarantined.

CHAPTER SIXTEEN

Later that night, when all were abed, Mrs. Watts herself came to collect my tray. She peered at me with *that look*, and I tried to reassure her through my natural mannerisms and unaffected speech that I was quite well—physically and emotionally. Maud was, no doubt, tending to Clementine after the evening's entertainment.

Mrs. Watts left, and I counted the hours in my bed with an eye on the Chinese dragon clock, which ticked by the minutes with a clicking that sounded like nails tapping on my windowpane. Ten o'clock; the guests had departed. Eleven; staff were quiet. When midnight rolled over, Albert would be settled, certainly, and therefore Lillian would not need to be about. I'd leave for my search then.

In spite of my best efforts, I nodded into sleep and passed my midnight deadline. I woke sharply at four a.m. I slipped out of bed. I had to search for something, anything, that could help me prove my legitimacy before the household woke and saw me prowling where no others, obviously, went. I did not want to call attention to myself and have the room searched before I might find anything that remained.

I quietly picked my way up the back steps to the quarantine room. When I had last tried to enter, I felt that the door handle would, indeed, have twisted had Lillian not stumbled upon me at precisely the wrong moment. I needed to try again.

I did not light my candle but made my way in the dark, which cloaked me. Once I reached the top of the long, narrow staircase, I wiped the sweat from my palm off on my gown and reached for the knob. It was loose and did not seem to catch, but after quiet persistence I felt the knob turn and, with a little push, the door opened. I slipped into the room as quietly as I could, then pulled the door shut behind me.

Once in the room, I lit my candle. It threw off enough light that I could see a few feet ahead. The room swam with the dust my movements kicked up; motes drifted lifelessly this way and that in front of the flame. I extended the candle to the left and saw a window, a lovely stained-glass scene of angels tending the Lord Jesus after he'd been tested by Satan in the wilderness.

A wave of recognition came over me.

The window.

I had seen it in my memory of the fish necklace, and seeing it now unlocked another remembrance.

"Sit here with me, sweetness." Mummy patted a spot on the floor where the sun puddled the reflection from the stained glass all around and indeed over the top of us. She handed a note-book to me, then wrapped her long fingers around my stubby ones. I did not care if we drew anything, as long as we held hands. But soon, she guided me, and we drew one, two, three little flowers.

"Well done!" She clapped her hands, and I flushed with pleasure.

"I'm like you!" I pointed to the sketch, so like her own.

Mummy's eyes grew sad. "In some ways," she answered. *"In only the best ways, I hope."*

My chest tightened, constricted by grief. Here I was now, in this same room, alone. Alone. Always and ever alone!

As was she, in the end, at least as I'd imagined it. I would never know.

I stared at that stained-glass window, now mute in the darkness. *That's how you sometimes seem to me, God,* I whispered hotly. *Mute in the darkness.*

After some minutes I steadied my spirit and peered out the window; a rusted old spyglass, perhaps from our seagoing past, rested on the window ledge, perhaps to view a coming government official or revenue man in days past. In the distance, I saw ships at anchor in the harbor, in Lymington. Was Dell'Acqua's among them? It was too dark to tell.

I put the spyglass down and turned to look at the room. A small cot stood bereft in the corner, bare; it had no linens and was made of metal rather than the more usual wood. None of the furniture in the room had been covered with dust sheets as had the other rooms in Highcliffe, in preparation for the sale. Had it been forgotten? Or was everyone fearful to enter this room?

There were beliefs that insanity hung in the miasma; one should have a care not to breathe it in lest one be similarly afflicted.

On one wall was inserted a cylinder, a speaking tube, which Grandfather had installed throughout the house. I knew he'd drawn his inspiration from ships, which had voice pipes placed so orders could be given from the captain and heard throughout the ship. Here, it was used to convey the needs of the unwell to those who would tend her from a distance.

Far in the corner of the room squatted a heavy desk. Not just any desk. A cabinet of wonder! The most remarkable piece of furniture in the room, perhaps one of the most remarkable in the entire house.

I tiptoed over, then ran my hands across it, removing the filmy residue of decades of neglect. I quickly shook the dust from my hand and pinched my nose tightly to silence an oncoming sneeze. Once I'd forestalled that, I used the hem of my gown to wipe down the cabinet, which was perhaps four feet tall and as wide. In all likelihood, this was the reason it had not been removed from the room; it would have posed an enormous challenge to either disassemble it for removal or to try to force it down the narrow stairway that had to be climbed to reach the room.

It had perhaps two dozen drawers and doors, all overlaid with jewel tones and baroque gold. I tried one door and found it false. Another stuck; I pulled a little harder, and to my surprise it opened. I reached my hand in and leaned my dripping candle over it—the short taper was quickly burning itself to the quick and I should soon be in the dark—and spied a charcoal stick. I turned it over in my hand.

Had this belonged to my mother? It may have. It probably had, or at least, she'd used it. I caressed it. This was as dear to me as the necklace.

A small noise. A hum, really, but then the hum began to take shape into words that buzzed through the speaking tube. Staff were beginning to stir. I heard a man's voice, whispering. "We cannot risk it for his sake." Someone was up and about, and therefore I must quickly return to my room.

Risk what? For whose sake? I blew out the candle, promising myself that I would return to search the cabinet drawers when I deemed it safe to do so, and sneaked back to my room.

Once there, I took my writing materials from the bureau drawers and bringing my desk to my bed, began to compose a set of letters by the light of the rising dawn.

I must try to find a situation with a Catholic family. I could only pray that this approach would work and that those I hoped would assist me would not, in the end, betray me instead.

Although I had the letters written—and sealed—I held on to them for a short time. I left them unaddressed in case someone should be filtering through my things. I could not very well clip them to my corset, as they would crease and become dog-eared, giving entirely the wrong impression upon receipt.

The house was quieted by the stifling end of the summer heat. Albert fussed despite Lillian's best efforts and the blackberry ices I'd cajoled Chef to make for him—and for Oliver and Emmeline. I admitted to pinching one or two for myself as well. The men had all departed for London, and I did not attend Mass because Lady Somerford had been ill. One day, Elizabeth sent word that her mother was feeling much better, and could she fetch me on Sunday? I sent a note, immediately, that I would be delighted.

Saturday evening, I cornered Clementine as she rested quietly on her fainting couch. She was often found there. At first I thought she might be ill, but over time and with observation I had come to understand she actually was heartsick. Edward treated her poorly, and she had no family nearby and few friends.

"Lady Leahy will collect me for Mass tomorrow. I should return about the time the household returns from its own divine services."

"I'm too unwell to attend church," she said, waving at me as one might swat at an insect. "Dinner will be served on trays in our rooms tonight."

Again. I thought she and I might have made pleasant company whilst it was just us two at home these weeks, as she had once extended her hand in friendship and seemed in need of companionship.

"Will your mother be coming to visit?" I hoped to cheer her. I knew she'd looked forward to her mother's summer holiday at Highcliffe with great anticipation.

She clutched her watch necklace, then shook her head. "She prefers the country."

This is *the country*, I wanted to say, but perhaps not when compared to Dorset.

"You and Albert might visit her," I suggested. "Lillian could assist."

She sighed. "Edward needs me here to help him entertain. I write to her weekly. I keep checking the post, daily, but no response as yet. I expect she's consumed with my brothers." She sat up a little and looked at me, her eyes too young to be deeply rimmed. "Is there anything else, Annabel?"

I kept myself from tugging on my ring so I would not reveal my discomfort.

"Lady Somerford is recovered, and she has asked me to attend Mass tomorrow."

"You've said that."

"I thought perhaps I should bring a gift—from all of us, of course—to cheer her and celebrate her recovery."

At that, she perked up. "Yes, that is quite a good idea. The Somerfords have been good to us, all of us, and seemingly from out of nowhere. I want to maintain that affection. Flowers?"

I hesitated. "I thought perhaps a silver salver, a small one, from Grandfather's collection of Maltese items. She might use it for anointing oil."

"Very well, then, it's more impressive than flowers. Whatever pagan thing she chooses to do with it is out of my hands."

In spite of Clementine's rudeness, I felt sorry for her. I collected some ladies' periodicals from a foyer shelf, those that had not yet been brought to the library, and handed them to her. "To better pass the hours?"

Her face softened, and she looked like a young woman again. "Thank you, Annabel. You're a good friend." She held my hand a moment longer than strictly required, and I squeezed it affectionately before leaving.

I went to where the silver was kept, but couldn't decide on just the right piece. I did find something eminently suitable on the sideboard, however. A little pitcher, already in use as an oil cruet for salads, but I was sure that would be easy for Mrs. Watts to replace. I lifted the lid on the beehive honey container I used. The Maltese honey was almost finished.

I headed belowstairs, where nearly all staff were gathered by the tradesman's door, letting the cool air circulate through the kitchens. I asked Mrs. Watts about the cruet and also mentioned that the honey was nearly all gone. She said she'd attend to both.

The next morning, Elizabeth came to collect me, and after Mass I told her I had a gift for her mother. We made our way up the twisting stairway again. Father Antoine had celebrated Mass with Lady Somerford in her rooms, but she looked bright and healthy again; for that, I was grateful and relieved. I handed her the silver salver and told her its history.

"In spite of it all," she said after thanking me, "your grandfather was a good man. He made every effort, as the landowner should, to care for the local people, to ensure they were properly employed. That's more than I can say for his successor . . . and, of course, we were mainly in the north. By the time we'd returned,

BRIDE OF A DISTANT ISLE 149

there was not much Lord Somerford could do without stepping on others' toes. As to your grandmother, I didn't know her well."

"Did you know her at all?"

She nodded. "A little. Lord Somerford did enjoy your grandfather's company."

"So you had occasion to speak with my grandmother, then?"

She nodded reluctantly, and looked at her priest. "I did know her well enough to know she preferred your mother to Judith."

I tilted my head questioningly.

"Fitting to each girl's manner, because that's when I knew them, when they were young girls. Now, if I do not want to have to confess gossip," she glanced with a smile at Father once more, "I should stop talking."

I reached over and hugged her, and she hugged me back, not at arm's length, as a friend would, but pulled to the heart, as a mother might. I melted into it.

Elizabeth took me home in the carriage. "I shall be returning to my husband soon, now Mother is well."

I knew this day would come. "I shall miss you. Perhaps we can ride out once or twice more before you leave. Wednesday?"

She took my hand in her own. "Most certainly. And we will return for Christmas. I've asked Mama to promise me that we can celebrate it at Pennington this year, as it's my favorite home."

I opened my leather wallet and withdrew three letters. "I wonder if I might beg a favor."

She turned her face toward me. "Of course."

"I've been seeking a position as a governess."

She nodded slowly, but her face reflected confusion. Had she, too, heard about the plans for Mr. Morgan and me?

"I placed advertisements in the local newspapers, but Edward had them removed," I continued, hoping she would keep my secret. "It's imperative that I keep my search confidential, but also that I find a placement with a Catholic family, and soon. I wonder if I might prevail upon you to deliver these to any good Catholic family you may have an acquaintance with who would welcome me?"

Elizabeth took a deep breath and smiled, but her eyes reflected sorrow. *Over my situation? Because our friendship would be so very different, perhaps impossible, should I take on a governess position?* I did not know. I had no other option but vows, and I was not convinced I could take them in good conscience.

"I will do what I can," she promised.

I stepped out of the carriage and returned to my rooms, hoping desperately that she could locate someone, and that her husband or someone in her household would not let my pursuit be made known to Edward.

CHAPTER SEVENTEEN

———— ⚜ ————

THE *POSEIDON*

EARLY SEPTEMBER, 1851

I opened the door to my rooms one evening the following week to find Mrs. Watts and not the expected Maud. I needed help preparing for our evening aboard Captain Dell'Acqua's ship. "Maud . . ."

"She's rather preoccupied, I think, with Mrs. Everedge," Mrs. Watts said. "I thought I might lend a hand. It's difficult to be a lady's maid to two women at once."

I nodded slowly. She seemed so assured. We were running out of time; I had just been about to dress myself. I did not want to seem ungrateful for her offered assistance, but I'd hoped to shine this evening above all others. "Of course," I said. "Do come in."

I'd already placed the hair iron on my fire grate, the coals of which had considerably heated up the already stifling room. "The price of beauty, *non*?" Mrs. Watts said, an odd lilt to her voice. "Have you already selected a gown?"

I nodded. It was awkward, having a housekeeper assist. "Perhaps the silver one," I offered. "My selection is limited."

"It will be perfect by the surf and starlight."

I turned and looked at her, remembering to close my mouth from its ungainly gape. "I had not expected such a romantic notion from you."

At that, she laughed aloud, and her face softened. She was lovely. "I was young once, too, difficult as it may be to believe."

"Not difficult at all!"

She helped center me in my many layers. I kept the Maltese cap carefully tucked in one of the dressing drawers, far in the back. I would not be pinning it in tonight; I did not, in fact, want Mrs. Watts to know that it existed.

There was something oddly comforting about having her do up my hair; I closed my eyes and relaxed for a moment, something I never did when Maud was tending to me. After having perfectly curled my hair and pinned it in my usual roll, she picked up the found hair combs wired with tiny white crystals.

"With your permission," she said, "I would like to break apart the crystals and lightly stitch them onto your hair. I am handy with the needle, as you may imagine, and can sew and affix them back onto the combs at a later date."

"How wonderful!" I sat back in awe as she worked her magic. When she was done, they did indeed catch the light perfectly, this way and that, nestled in the deep folds of my dark hair.

"Mr. Everedge has just had a telegram stating that Mr. Morgan will be delayed until tomorrow," she confided. Upon hearing such glad tidings, I tossed the diamond cage necklace back into the jewel case.

I then plucked out the Maltese fish necklace instead. I dabbed on some of the neroli oil, deeply inhaling its musky citrus, and as Mrs. Watts stood to take her leave, Maud came to the door.

"Just what is going on here?" she demanded. Had Maud not known? Had she not, indeed, sent Mrs. Watts to assist me?

"I believed you over busy and thought to assist," Mrs. Watts said. As housekeeper, she and Maud were of nearly the same standing, but it would not be appropriate for her to have taken over Maud's responsibilities without direction.

"If I require the assistance of a housekeeper, I'll ask for it," Maud said. "Until then, kindly leave my charges be."

Mrs. Watts opened her mouth as if to utter a rebuke, then looked at me, bowed her head, and left. I felt rather sorry for her; I imagined doing hair and talking of gowns was more amusing than inventorying what remained in the butter larder. I didn't exactly relish a future as a governess, truth be told. But there was a place for everything, and order must rule. I sought to soothe Maud.

"She filled in nicely, but I shall be glad to have your assistance after we return this evening. If Clementine can spare you, that is."

She seemed calmed. "Of course. Do you require anything else?"

I shook my head no, and she left, pulling the door closed behind her. I took one last peek in the mirror before following her downstairs.

Mrs. Watts was a genius. My hair had never looked more alluring!

Our carriage pulled up at the yacht club just ahead of the Somerfords and the Leahys. I had not known that Elizabeth would be joining us, and my feelings were mixed. I was delighted to have her company, but I hoped that she would remain discreet about my letter mission.

"Miss Ashton, my husband, Lord Leahy. Lord Leahy, Miss Ashton."

"How do you do?" Lord Leahy's eyes were warm and twinkly. "My wife has said you've become a dear friend to her. Captain Dell'Acqua had mentioned that we might be able to do some good for the local men, joint investments, and kindly invited us to his ship."

"How do you do?" I responded. Edward, standing next to me, looked pleased and smug. He was never happier with me than when I'd presented him with something of value, and this friendship certainly hit the mark.

Elizabeth leaned over toward me and whispered, "I sent the letters straightaway, on my own letterhead. One holds especial promise." I squeezed her hand in return.

We made our way along the harbor toward a fine ship in the distance. It was not large, as it was not meant to hold a numbered crew; larger ships would follow when the investment arrangements were completed.

As promised, commanding the ship's bow was the Greek god Poseidon. Carved on the prow, all sinew and flex, his body was *somewhat* draped for modesty, which just barely did the job. His hair was a tangle of twists, and his beard appeared to be made of snakes. In his hand was a trident, and his look conveyed that he ruled the sea. I was so occupied staring at him that I didn't see the captain approach.

"Everedge, Mrs. Everedge, welcome aboard my ship," he said smoothly, and then I took him in. His clothing was a combination of the finest gentleman's wear and the rough garb of the sea; he did not mind appearing different from the others present. It occurred to me that the unlikely blend in both attire and manner might be just what I found so compelling about the man.

I'd admitted it. He was compelling.

Dell'Acqua greeted Lord Leahy next and then led us onto the ship. The top deck had been carefully swabbed, and the sails were neatly furled. Long stretches of rope were tightly coiled, and about eight men stood at the ready. We ducked down the first narrow stairway to the first deck below. Men tended to the neatly aligned quarters and storerooms. Forward was the captain's quarters, and that was where he led us.

Perhaps a half dozen other guests socialized and when Dell'Acqua entered, all took a seat. The cabin was larger than I'd expected, painted yellow with gold gilt on the chair rails. There was a deep window seat—which had been covered in ivory silk, smooth and taut as the skin stretched across a young woman's collarbone—beneath the stern gallery windows, which had been opened to inhale the night breeze and exhale our spent breath. The room was well lit with lamps, and the oil used to fuel them had been scented with something exotic and earthy. The effect was enchanting. In a display case, in pride of place, rested a perfectly rendered model of his ship.

Marvelous.

Dell'Acqua had placed my name card to his right, a place of honor. I noted that others had remarked upon it, too. Should that place have been reserved for Lord Somerford? I looked at Lady Somerford, who smiled at me, offering both encouragement and approval. At the foot of the table, next to Edward, remained an unfilled chair. Morgan's. His delay must have been at the last minute.

The meal was splendid, all meat courses, naturally, because when the men were at sea it was fish and fish alone. I had never had meat prepared quite so, basted with oils I had not tasted and roasted herbs I could not remember but savored, all delightfully moist and washed down with fine Italian wine. Dell'Acqua conversed as comfortably with the Englishmen present as Edward did, and perhaps more confidently. We made pleasant, superficial conversation as was appropriate, and I mentioned that my Maltese honey had run dry.

"I shall have some sent to you," he promised. The courses changed and with that, I was now required to speak with the person seated to my other side.

Dell'Acqua stood after dinner. "I should like to introduce you to the *Poseidon*. Because ships have narrow passages, I've divided us into groups to view different parts at different times. Then, I've arranged for musical entertainment on the beach nearby."

He separated us into groups with officers as guides. Edward tensed when he realized that I would not be joining the group that he and Clementine were in. He relaxed, though, when he saw Lady Leahy was to accompany me, along with Dell'Acqua.

The captain bragged from stem to stern, and Elizabeth and I were appropriately admiring. Once, he ordered his men, in English, to move some crates out of the way. I saw the way one looked at him, half obeying, half smirking, until he barked his order in rough Maltese, which caused immediate compliance.

It was not easy for Dell'Acqua—son of Malta, son of England, son of no one—to bridge two cultures, either.

We progressed to the nearby beach, which had been smoothed. The heels of our slippers pushed into the sand, nearly causing Elizabeth to twist her ankle.

"Why not be Maltese!" the captain asked. "Bare feet!"

We looked at each other and giggled. Could we, would we, do it? We would! I took one slipper off and so she then dared, and we both took the other off and stepped toward the water's edge, laughing like young girls on our way to build seashell castles.

Some yards away, a string quartet played softly, and there were perhaps two dozen chairs scattered along the long stretch of beach. Torches dotted the landscape here and there, and waiters circulated with cooled water and cooled wine.

"Let's put our toes in," Elizabeth encouraged me. She walked near where the water met the land, salt lightly drifting across the sand like a thin shimmer of summer snow.

"What?" It would not be done to remove our stockings, but they were already wet.

"You insisted on taking off the slippers . . ." she challenged me. I could not let such a challenge go unmet. Captain Dell'Acqua turned his head as we rolled down our stockings and let the cold water lap at our toes. After the confines of the captain's quarters, that cool refreshed me all the way up. Within a minute or two, we made our way back to a set of three chairs near the edge of the water.

"I believe I should like to be back from the water a bit more," Elizabeth said.

"*Ecco*, we can move then," Dell'Acqua offered.

"No." She held up a hand. "You two remain here and I'll be there in a moment." She sat some yards away, within sight but not within hearing distance, thoughtfully taking the third chair with her so no one could join us. My chilled toes reminded me of the pleasures of spontaneity, and her friendship.

Dell'Acqua spoke first, and when he did, the distantly genteel tone he'd used at dinner was replaced by a softer, more intimate tone. "I was disappointed, when I was last at Highcliffe, to hear that you were unwell and unable to join us for dinner."

"It was a disappointment to me as well," I replied, matching his warm voice, but I did not elaborate. The others had not arrived at the beach, and I wondered if he'd instructed his men to take them on a more elaborate and lengthy tour than he'd taken us on.

I pointed toward the exterior of his ship. "What am I to make of the devilish pitchfork, Captain Dell'Acqua, which your figure-head has in hand? An indication of your character?"

He smiled wickedly, and my heart and breath quickened. "A trident, Miss Ashton, not a pitchfork but a trident."

The captain reached over and impulsively touched one of the crystals in my hair. It was unexpected and personal, intimate. The feel of his touch traveled down the strands of hair to my scalp, causing it to prickle, and then that prickle rolled like the surf upon my whole body. "Like the stars," he said, "but more beautiful. And when I lean near you, I catch the scent of ash and honey and or-anges, the orange trees of Malta."

"It's neroli," I said softly. "From Italy."

"So unlike the English girls," he said, "who wear frivolous vio-lets."

"I am an English girl," I reminded him.

"I stand corrected." He moved his chair as close to me as, I imagined, he dared.

I did not chide him. Very soon, I should enter service as a governess, or perhaps would have to marry Mr. Morgan, unless . . . I looked at him but dared not hope. I would snatch bits of life and liberty here and now to treasure in my heart, later. "Your cologne. Likewise not English. Italian? Maltese?"

"Ah." His eyebrows raised. "You've noticed the thieves!"

"Have I been introduced to thieves and not realized? Pray tell!"

He grinned. "In the Middle Ages, there were three thieves who robbed dead victims, those who had died of the plague. It couldn't hurt, isn't that so? They were dead and did not need their worldly goods any longer."

I raised my eyebrows. "Maltese thieves?"

"Of course not," he said. "They were perhaps French, or more likely English."

I swatted at him with my fan. "Go on."

"They were caught, and in exchange for their freedom, they shared the formula for a blend of oils that protected them from the plague, which then helped many others. A mix of herbs and cloves, camphor and musk. Thieves' oil. It's healing and aromatic. Do you like it?"

I nodded, not trusting myself to say more. Healing indeed—to my spirit, but endangering to my heart! He laughed. "Then it has done more good for me than keeping away illness. As my story proves, even thieves may do good."

"Is that a confession, Captain?" I waved my fan in a delicate circle.

He grinned and shrugged; his eyes remained guarded. A long pause held with only the lapping surf and the lament of the cello strings to break it. Finally, he spoke. "Do you know any thieves, Miss Ashton? Perhaps smugglers?"

I caught and held his glance. Was he asking after Edward? Was Edward still smuggling? "I shall answer you by way of an English tale, Captain Dell'Acqua."

"Please," he said, leaning near me so our arms merged. Mine prickled again, at his touch. "Use my name. Marc Antonio. Marco."

"I cannot call you Marco!" I exclaimed.

"And I shall call you Annabella."

"You shall not!"

"Then even better . . . Bella."

Bella. In Italian, *beautiful.* It was a most promising corruption of my name, and I adored him for speaking it.

"What will Clementine think?" I asked. "Or Lady Leahy?"

"I care not."

"But I do!" He did not realize how carefully a woman like me, born out of wedlock, must protect her reputation.

"I shall refer to them as Clemmy and Liz," he said. "And they shall blame the foreigner for my poor manners." At that, I grinned. *This is what comes of allowing myself to walk slipperless. Self-restraint has fled!*

I rather enjoyed it.

"My story, Captain," I said.

"Marco," he whispered, his dark eyes holding my gaze.

Dare I?

"Marco," I whispered back and his face flushed with pleasure. "My story!" I redirected. "You are half English, you know; it's time you come to know our history, as well as exercise some English self-control."

He nodded compliantly but with a wink. At that moment, the others began to filter onto the beach.

"There is a tale of the Moonrakers," I began, looking out upon the beach, which grew wider as the tide receded. "Poor, hungry villagers, eager and desperate, as many of our English people are, had buried barrels of brandy under the sand near the beach, waiting to 'harvest' them at low tide. All of a sudden, the revenue men came upon them as they dragged the rakes against the sand. 'What are you doing?' they demanded."

"And?" Marco leaned forward.

"The men said, 'Oh, wise sirs, we're raking the ground to harvest the moonlight, don'cha know. We can use it instead of costly candles.' The king's men laughed at them for being simple country fools, but left them be. They then 'harvested' their barrels and sold them as planned—so they could eat! 'Twas a time not too long ago when the poor had to help smuggle salt just so they could have some for themselves, to preserve meat and fish, or they'd eat neither for half the year."

Marco smiled. "So thieves can do well by themselves and others."

"Some thieves," I said, glancing involuntarily at Edward, who had now made it to the beach and had a glass in hand. Marco followed my glance.

Then, hoping I had not said or implied too much about our family, or smuggling, I reached down and picked up an oyster.

"Perhaps there is a pearl within," I said hopefully.

"You should not eat it, Bella." He took the shell and tried to crack it open, but could not.

"I shan't eat it, don't worry," I said with a laugh.

"It's tightly sealed." Marco held it in his hand. "Which is as it should be. It protects what is inside it. Like my ship." He reached his hand out expansively. "The hull is tight; nothing shall breach it. 'Secret, and self-contained, and solitary as an oyster,' as your Mr. Dickens has written."

"*Our* Mr. Dickens," I corrected. "Was that a confession, Captain? Are you secret and safely self-contained?"

He blushed, and tipped his head down, used, perhaps, to being in control of the banter. "Touché, Miss Ashton." To soften the barb, I reached over and took the shell from him, brushing the sand from his hand as I did. At the touch of my finger on his palm, he half closed his eyes, and I forced myself to remove my fingers rather than impulsively entwine them in his.

"With your blond, English hair," I teased, "your beard rather looks like sand."

"Will you please brush that off, too, then?" He turned his jaw-line to me, and I looked toward the ground to regain control of my feelings. I wanted to. I wanted, most inappropriately, to reach out and caress his face.

"The heart is very like the hull of a ship, isn't it?" I fingered the rough, ridged shell, which held its soft treasure inside. "If it's tightly closed, like this"—I handed the shell back to him—"all is protected, but then you can never find if there is, or is not, a trea-sure within. Solitary is not a manner in which to live. Unless one is an oyster. And now"—I grinned—"Clemmy approaches."

At that, he roared with laughter, startling Clementine, who was just upon us, looking stern and a decade older than she was.

"*Pari Corajisima*," Marco whispered in Italian. *She looks like Lent.*

I held back a smile.

"What amuses you so, Captain Dell'Acqua?" Clementine asked.

"Oh . . ." He looked at me and I pleaded with my eyes for him to use her proper name. "Mrs. Everedge, Miss Ashton was implor-ing me to be English, as I am half English. I said I shall, for the re-mainder of my time here, if she uses her teaching skills to instruct me as I visit with your husband at Highcliffe now and again. With your permission, of course," he said. "I plan to spend some time in the next few weeks concluding the affairs Mr. Everedge, Lord Somerford, and I have arranged."

And then you shall leave, I thought, steadying myself and hiding, I hoped, my despair. A few months earlier I'd told Clemen-tine that if I could, I'd marry a good man and have children. It had seemed theoretical then. Now I wished it to become a reality.

"Of course she may," Clementine answered him. She glanced at Elizabeth, now sitting with Lord Leahy, but still chaperoning me. "My husband wishes to speak with you," she said. "If you have time."

"*Ecco*, I always have time for Mr. Everedge."

Later that night Captain Dell'Acqua saw us to our carriages by starlight. He shook the men's hands and helped each woman into the carriage. Before he took my hand, I slipped, and he reached to catch me. His face drew close to mine, and as I turned one way, in modesty, he turned that same way. We each adjusted, but as we did, our faces turned in unison, close, nearly touching. By his intention? By happenstance? I cared not. His rough beard brushed against my soft skin, then his mouth hovered over mine as I regained my footing and pulled back. Before I did, I felt his lips on mine though they had not actually met. It was bliss.

"I'm sorry," I said. "I lost my footing."

"It happens to many women," he teased. "I catch them." His eyes were soft, but I wondered if they were soft for all women.

"Good night, Bella," he whispered. "I've not lost my footing, but perhaps I've lost my bearings."

I held his gaze and the moment was caught in time. "Good night," I finally responded, though I barely had breath enough to speak. He lifted me up to my seat. The carriage driver snapped his reins, and we lurched forward. As we drove away, I turned and looked out the window, and I saw him standing there, still, on the pier watching us leave.

Marco.

He caught my eye and lifted a hand, but from within the crowded carriage, I dared not lift one in return.

CHAPTER EIGHTEEN

Elizabeth had told me she had a promising lead for a governess position, and it had now been long enough for me to make a hopeful enquiry. So one morning, after Clementine had left for the day with Edward, to Winchester, I asked Lillian if she and Albert would like to accompany me to Lymington again. She wasn't exactly qualified to be a chaperone, but I wasn't exactly required to have one, and Albert added to the layer of social safety.

"I like my situation here, caring for Albert," Lillian said tentatively.

"Clementine had said we may go, earlier. So why not now?" I answered.

She looked wary, but in the end, as I expected, she was delighted. When we met in the foyer, she had dressed in a light lawn dress the color of ivory piano keys that showed off her strawberry-blond hair to its finest advantage. Albert was cute as mice in a shorts suit, though he was beginning to look girlish in his long curls. Clementine was loath to cut them, I knew.

We took the second-best carriage and a footman drove us as Edward's driver was in use, of course. The season had tilted forward, the weight of the year behind us. The mid-September sun did not bear down quite so firmly, and the skies were the brilliant azure blue peculiar to autumn by the sea. The driver stopped in front of Mr. Galpine's, and I instructed him to return in perhaps a half hour's time.

Mr. Galpine finished assisting the woman ahead of him, a woman I recognized as a distant acquaintance of Clementine's. She had called on Clementine once since I'd been home, and I hoped she should not visit again and share news of seeing me and Lillian in town.

"Miss Ashton." Mr. Galpine nodded and bowed toward me and then toward Lillian. "And Miss Miller."

Her face brightened at the use of her proper name. I imagined few used it.

"How may I help?" he asked.

"I came to enquire if I have any letters," I said. "I had been expecting some."

"There were two last week," he said, and I nodded. They had been from friends in Winchester; Watts had brought them to me.

"Any more since then?"

He stroked his beard. "Well, the one I sent to Highcliffe in the packet of other mail, when your young shepherdess came to collect the mail."

Emmeline? Came to collect mail? I thought Oliver did, if not a footman or Edward himself. "You're certain there was one for me, then."

"Not certain. But I believe so. So many pass through my hands . . ." He made a gesture of his busyness, and Lillian giggled rewardingly.

I had not seen any new letter. If it had existed, where had it gone? "Do you remember who the sender was?"

"No, Miss Ashton, I'm sorry. There are too many things going through the post for me to keep track." His chest puffed out again, and he turned toward Lillian. "My father started this shop, and the library and post many years ago. Back in those days the recipient had to pay post, of course, so we kept better track of senders in case they needed to be returned."

Lillian smiled obligingly, and I had a sudden burst of inspiration. Divine, as Lady Somerford would have said. "What year did you stop keeping track?"

He stroked his beard once more and focused his gaze on the ceiling for a moment. "Perhaps the late twenties. My father was keen to collect the postal markings, too, so he kept some of those when allowed. Would you care to see the record books? They are really quite extraordinary."

I nodded. "I would like that very much."

He went into the back and then brought out a large stack of leather-strapped books. "Have a look. Perhaps I could assist Miss Miller with some additional library loans, and for you"—he looked down at Albert—"perhaps a lollipop?"

"Yes, please, and thank you, sir," Albert said. Mr. Galpine handed the boy a tinted, boiled sweet on a stick and the rest of us went about our business.

I quickly paged back through the first volume, looking for a year when my mother would have, could have, received mail. I found something.

1827. A letter addressed to Signora Alessandru . . . something . . . at Highcliffe Hall. The surname was blotted out.

Mrs. Alexander . . . something. My heart soared. Could that have been my mother? I looked at the signature next to the postmark, *Malte*. Someone had signed for it. Someone had paid for it.

Yes. I put my finger on the thin page, so thin that the light pressure from my fingertip almost tore it. It had been signed for by Judith.

Judith! Edward's mother. Had the mail been directed to my mother and Judith taken it, with or without my mother's knowledge? Or had the letter been directed to Judith? Whoever it had been directed to was assumed by the sender to be married. *Signora.* Mrs. If only the last name had not been blurred and blotted. Had Judith been married before she'd married Everedge?

I looked up, and Lillian caught my eye. We needed to return to Highcliffe. The footman idled with the carriage. I quickly flipped through the pages looking for *Malte*, and some years later, in 1831, there was another letter received, and this time, it had been noted that one had been sent as well.

My mother died that year. I'd always wished I'd known if she died in peace. Concern for her final loneliness and anguish haunted me.

"Thank you, Mr. Galpine."

As we drove back to Highcliffe, Lillian and Albert chattered, his lips stained blue from the lollipop. In their mutual bliss, they did not notice my quiet introspection.

When we arrived, I saw that Edward and Clementine were home already.

Early.

Lillian and Albert crept up the stairs, but Edward caught me by the arm. There were quite a few people in the hallway as he directed me forward. Clementine looked up at me; she had been going over the menu with Mrs. Watts. Watts himself was tending to paperwork and Maud had an armful of Clementine's gowns in her hand. Edward brought me to the library but left the door open for all to hear us.

"You were out? With my son?"

I nodded and smiled cheerfully. "He so enjoys his carriage rides and visits to town. I know how you favor him, and I do, too."

Edward knew this to be true; I did favor Albert, as did everyone.

"Where did you go?"

"To the yacht club," I said. "Lady Somerford said I might call by as she is often there. And to the lending library for books. I thought I might check and see if we had anything in the post." Edward looked above and up, over my head. Apparently someone was signaling to him, as he nodded slightly.

"It would be best if you arranged future outings with Clementine before leaving Highcliffe," he said. "Morgan will arrive tomorrow. He's keen to spend time with you. I gave my permission."

The trap was closing. I decided to gamble because I had little to lose.

"Of course." I pretended to acquiesce meekly. "This may interest you, as it did me. Mr. Galpine showed me his postmark collection. Knowing our Maltese connection"—I emphasized the word *our*—"I paged through looking for letters posted to and from Malta. Surprisingly, I found some had been received, and then mailed out, around the time of my mother's death. I think your mother signed for them. Had she ever mentioned it?"

He glanced up at the portrait of his revered mother. "No, Annabel, of course she would have responded to correspondence. Grandfather had interests in Malta, but Malta was not discussed, to my knowledge, for years." He did not ask if I'd been enquiring about letters mailed to me. Did he not know of the missing letters? Or did they not even exist?

I returned to my room to consider my next move, and to apply some glycerin and rosewater cream in an attempt to fade my freckles and make me less exotic, and therefore less appealing, to Mr. Morgan.

Then next morning broke beautifully, and I dressed myself and took a late breakfast. Maud and Mrs. Watts were having a heated discussion near the sideboard. It seemed Maud was rearranging items before taking a tray to Clementine, and Mrs. Watts told her that she did not appreciate interference in the household running—she would restock the condiments herself. At that, Maud let the lid drop heavily on the silver sugar-cube container.

"Good morning." I helped myself to a crumpet and a poached egg resting in a silver steamer. Mrs. Watts nodded toward me before flouncing from the room, and Maud smiled.

"Good morning." She held Clementine's tray in one hand. "Or, nearly afternoon."

"I thought I might take Albert for a walk around the grounds," I said. "I'd like to teach him to draw. Would you ask Clementine to send word if that does not meet with her approval?"

She agreed. "I am certain it will be fine. Do not forget Mr. Morgan arrives today."

I sighed. I had remembered, of course. I wondered if she was reminding me to warn me for my sake or because someone had put her up to it.

Within an hour, I went to Albert's rooms. I told Lillian I would spend some time with the boy to give her a respite and handed over two notebooks I'd had in my trunks at school, the ones that had been returned.

"Latest systems for keeping track of accounts," I said. "Some friends who were to start a school had begun to organize using them, and I thought they might be of interest to you . . . as a future shopgirl."

She smiled softly and held them to her chest. "They certainly will. Thank you, Miss Ashton."

I collected Albert, and we wandered out onto the lawn. There was a sturdy clump of trees to one side, beneath which seemed like an ideal place to draw.

I set down our blanket. "Just do not leave my side." I pointed out the Edge of the World in the distance. "There is a steep drop-off, and you must promise me you will not wander off."

"I promise." He bobbed his little head and took a charcoal stick in his fat hand. "Pretty!" He pointed to a cluster of hosta plants, late bloomers. *Like me*, I thought, with a grin.

I pointed at a wide leaf. "What does it look like to you?" He sat back, thinking.

"This!" He stuck his tongue out as far as he could.

"Yes, that's just so!" I was delighted that such a wee child already had artistic insight. "Except your tongue isn't green, or blue, or streaky, except when you've been eating sweets."

We sat sketching for about ten minutes, when all of a sudden Edward came racing across the lawn. He drew near to us and in an angry voice asked, "What are you doing out here with Albert?"

He scooped the boy into his arms.

I was bewildered. "We're drawing, of course. He's got natural talent," I teased, showed him Albert's little drawing of a circle.

"Then do it inside," he said, almost shaking. "Where there is no danger."

Ah. I understood. "I warned him about the drop and it's quite far away. I would never let him from my sight or even from my reach." Never. The quicksand at the foot of the cliffs would swallow a boy whole.

Edward did not cool off. "I'm not concerned about that," he

answered. "Well, I am. But there are dangers right here, at ground level. Bees!"

"Bees?" I did not understand.

At that, he rolled up the cuff of his left sleeve and showed me his wrist, which whitened with his pull and seemed to be pricked and pocked with light scars, perhaps a dozen or more, all clustered at the wrist and toward his palm.

"Bee stings," I whispered. "From long ago?"

"Yes." He set the boy down and rolled down his sleeve, linking it again at the cuff. Unexpectedly, I saw tears fill his eyes.

We did not keep hives any longer, but I understood his horror.

He blinked a few times, and his tears receded. "Mr. Morgan will be here shortly."

"I'll continue to draw," I said quietly. "Perhaps he and I can take a walk. It's a lovely afternoon."

Edward took a deep breath and composed himself. My answer had satisfied him. "Fine idea. I'll tell him where to find you, and Clementine can sit on a chaise on the lawn, nearby, as you stroll."

I nodded my agreement, and he took Albert's hand and walked back toward the house.

I took my sketchbook to another part of the lawn, nearer to the sheep, where young Emmeline tended her charges. Her presence and the merry, bleating sheep comforted me somehow.

I sat on a stump near her, but I could not make myself draw. I looked toward the back of the estate, toward the abbey—crumbling, ruined, with rooms and nooks and crannies that had been used once to hide the gin barrels and other smuggled stuffs. The hives had been nearby, too. A memory pressed in, one I had forgotten.

"No, Papa, no!" I heard Edward crying. "Please. I'm sorry."

"You're sorry, you are. I'm certain of it. But lessons learnt with pain are seared into the memory and will preclude poor future choices. You, young lad, will someday be responsible for all of this. I mean for you to carry on well. I'll see to it this is one mistake you do not forget. A father who loves his son is one who disciplines him."

Edward's father drove him down the hallway and out the door. I tiptoed after them and watched as Edward was force-marched toward the abbey ruins and the bee colonies.

I brought myself back into the present moment. Bees would not have cluster-stung Edward like that unless his hand had been held immobile near where they swarmed. I looked at mute Emmeline in the distance and knew what had happened to my cousin: something very like that which Emmeline and Oliver had witnessed.

An hour or so later, Emmeline had enclosed her flock for the night and made her way to greet me. "Are you well?" I asked her, and she nodded. "I trust my supply of sweets and ices has met with your approval." She grinned at that and nodded again.

I patted her hand. My heart ached for her. I wanted to encourage her, to lift her up, to free what had long been held back by fear.

"No more lost sheep?"

She shook her head no.

"I trust that if they wander or are confused you shall find them straightaway!" I continued. "I hear you've been entrusted with collecting the mail from Mr. Galpine's. That's a lovely responsibility and one not given lightly."

She beamed and indicated that she'd like to take my charcoal and paper in hand.

"By all means." I handed them toward her.

Quickly, and with great skill, she sketched a face. The likeness was remarkable. "This is who you collect the mail for?"

She nodded, proud, again, to be doing something important for the mistress of Highcliffe.

"Well done!" I hid my concern. She'd taken the mail, including the letter addressed to me, one assumed, to Clementine. Had Clementine actually received a letter for me or had one not come at all, and Mr. Galpine had been mistaken? Maybe Clementine had withheld the letter knowing Edward's wrath. Perhaps Emmeline was helping Clementine with whatever she was up to, and realized it. She was mute, not unintelligent.

I did not have time to muse on that thought because Mr. Morgan arrived in a cloud of dust and sought me out. At the sight of him Emmeline curtseyed a little, charmingly, and ran off.

Morgan brought two chairs. "Miss Ashton, I'm delighted to find you enjoying the autumn weather."

"So much more peaceful than London." I tried to make light conversation. His shadow fell upon me, rendering me in near darkness.

"Will you walk closer to the sea?" he asked, voice rumbling. In a moment, my mind flashed back to the spider he'd given me, trapped in amber, twinned with the memory of Mrs. Howlitt's poem, which we'd once taught at the Rogers school.

> "Will you walk into my parlour?" said the Spider to the
>   Fly,
> "'Tis the prettiest little parlour that ever you did spy;
> The way into my parlour is up a winding stair,
> And I've many curious things to shew when you are
>   there."
> "Oh no, no," said the little Fly, "to ask me is in vain,

For who goes up your winding stair can ne'er come down
   again."

"Miss Ashton?" Morgan's voice pressed into my mind.

"I'm sorry, Mr. Morgan. A poem came drifting back to me just
then. Yes, let's walk."

He set the chairs down, braced against a tree, and offered his
arm to me. Reluctantly, I took it. I could see Clementine in the
distance, relaxing, face shaded by her bonnet, in a chair on the
lawn.

"I have not forgotten that you like books," he said. "Which is
why I purchased that Poe volume for you. Perhaps I could purchase the poem for you? I would be delighted."

"You've already been far too generous," I said. "But thank you
for that kind thought."

"I enjoy purchasing gifts for you; it's my pleasure and I hope
to do it for a long while. Different kinds of gifts, novelties, which
are easily acquired when one imports." He looked at me, and
though his sinister nature did not diminish I saw some earnest-
ness in him and remembered that he had once been a boy, too,
like Albert, like Edward. A child, like I once was. He glanced at my
neck and frowned. I was not wearing the caged diamond.

"I've always been a bit peculiar," he continued. "My mother
said so, pointed it out to others, but I've come to terms with that.
You are unusual, too, Miss Ashton. But that makes us *interesting*,
does it not?"

Goodness above, I would never use the word *interesting*
again; it had lost any novelty and charm and had, instead, taken
on disturbing overtones.

He licked his fat lips until they glistened like slug trails. "It's
one reason I've always known we belong together . . ."

The terminus of that thought nauseated me.

"Happily, your cousin agrees," he finished. "He's . . . promised me."

"Promised you what?" I insisted. It might as well come out now.

Mr. Morgan would say no more. I looked out at the sea, not knowing what to say. What dark debts were owed by Edward that could not be satisfied by my simply becoming a governess, but instead, required I be given to Morgan?

"Perhaps I might purchase some rosary beads?" Morgan asked. "I want you to know that your religious leanings do not trouble me in the least. I find them . . ."

Interesting, I expected him to say.

"Acceptable," he finished, his voice growing more authoritative, his grip on my arm tightening. "Just so you understand, I would never forbid someone practicing their faith."

He had taken a leap in his mind. He believed he would soon be able to allow, or forbid, me at will. "Rosary beads are rather private and personal," I said. "They are not like jewelry. But thank you."

I changed the topic. "Look, what a charming bird. They are so small and vulnerable; they are among my favorites. I love to hear them sing."

"You love them, these particular ones?" His voice pitched in eagerness. I should quickly dissuade him from following that path lest I end up gifted with several of these birds after they'd been shot and had a brisk visit to the taxidermist.

"Just in the wild, Mr. Morgan. Just as they are," I said. We walked and talked uncomfortably for another thirty minutes, about his life in London, and his country houses—though he didn't quite say where they were located—until I guided us back to Clementine. "I should like to rest before dinner."

"I shall look forward to seeing you then," he said, and remained to talk with Clementine, who looked at me affectionately as I rounded the steps. I went to my rooms and firmly closed the door.

I removed the caged diamond necklace from the jewelry box; I would be expected to wear it at dinner. I closed the box and opened the drawer with the amber pieces, looking once more at the spider ensnared within. I glanced out of my window and saw Emmeline in the distance.

Perhaps the young woman I needed to lift up, to rescue, and to free from the sticky trap of a fearsome past and threatening future was myself, and not that young lass. But how? Every step I'd taken webbed me further in distress.

CHAPTER NINETEEN

———— ❧ ————

I spent the week helping Albert draw the simplest things, pinching sweets for Oliver and Emmeline with a few thrown in for myself, and paging through ladies' periodicals with Clementine. Edward had decided, now that the investments with the Maltese and the Somerfords were almost settled, that a few more dresses appropriate for our station were in order. It brought such joy to be true friends, almost equals, with Clementine, and she herself ran to fetch me the moment the post arrived with the latest fashion magazines.

We drank tea together and made our fabric choices; our coloring was so different that we would never overlap. She had Maud arrange for the dressmaker to visit. I noticed that Clementine had cheered. Now that those arrangements seemed securely in place it seemed Highcliffe might be saved; Clementine had therefore taken an even firmer interest in its housekeeping. She'd had Chef tint sugar cubes to match the china, and had little roses pipetted upon them. One afternoon while fetching some caramels I tarried in the stillroom—what fun!—and tinted some cubes myself, pink with strawberry essence, orange with neroli. Neroli, I thought, would make an especially pleasant addition to Earl Grey tea, with its bergamot notes.

It was a pleasant time, and this week held a particular pleasure of its own.

The *Poseidon* had docked.

The Chinese dragon clock on the mantel in my room ticked by the quarter hour, then the half hour. I was still in my dressing robes. With less than an hour to go, I left my rooms and began to make my way down the vestibule. Maud had not come to attend to me. I hoped I should not meet anyone in the hallway, especially Mr. Morgan, who was staying in the west wing for a day or two, and I drew my robe more tightly around me.

As I approached Clementine's door, I heard Edward's voice, raised, through the heavy oak. "You mean to greet my guests dressed like that? This isn't Dorset, Clementine. Our negotiations are coming down to the final few weeks, and I want to project an air of competence and worldliness. That's why the whole world has gathered in London for the Exhibition. To see what we English can do, and for my part, I mean to show them."

Come now, Edward. I freely rolled my eyes as no one was about. *The whole world?* Dorset was lovely, and his dealings seemed secure.

His voice continued. "Mother was right. I'd prefer our guests see my wife, and their hostess, as the town mouse, not the country mouse, if a mouse she must be."

That was unfair. Clementine was a fine hostess, and had come up with the St. James celebration ideas on her own. Why didn't she speak up for herself?

I felt shame blush from my scalp to my toes. *Why indeed, Miss Ashton. If it's so simple, speak up and refuse Mr. Morgan.*

I heard high-pitched pleading and then silence from Clementine, and quickly returned down the hallway lest Edward find me eavesdropping. I should, I gathered, have to prepare myself for the evening.

I thought about summoning Mrs. Watts and then changed my mind. A few of my things had been rearranged in my absence. Someone had been minding my business.

Dinner went smoothly, and although I did not exchange lengthy conversations with Captain Dell'Acqua, I glanced his way several times; each time I did I found him glancing my way, smiling widely with a look I knew somehow, as a woman will, had been reserved for me. Had Mr. Morgan observed this? If he had, he did not disclose it as he was deep in conversation with Lord Somerford, who in turn seemed more reserved this evening than I'd seen him before. I hoped all was progressing smoothly. Perhaps Edward was right to be worried.

After dinner, I spoke lightly with Captain Dell'Acqua about his "England lessons" and he promised he would soon agree to be lectured on customs and concerns. I smiled; we'd kept everything proper and superficial, but the feelings ran deeper. Mine did, anyway, though perhaps I should not have let them. And then we ladies withdrew to the drawing room to take tea, and the men retired to the smoking room for cigars and port.

Lady Somerford and Elizabeth took the sofa, two other ladies, wives of men who had come for the evening, seated themselves in the chairs near the window, and Clementine and I sat across a small table from one another. I lifted the lid to the honey container, brought in on a tray, and saw it was nearly empty. How odd, and unlike Mrs. Watts. Captain Dell'Acqua had not yet had time to send more round, I guessed, but local honey could have done.

Next to Clementine's saucer was a small plate of sugar cubes, the ones lightly tinted green with, I thought, mint, to match the china. I should have brought up some of the neroli-tinted ones. I dropped three into my tea and hoped that would be enough. Then I dropped in one more.

Clementine looked at me strangely but said nothing, turning back to focus her attention on our guests. She looked overdressed in the multitiered creation Edward had insisted she wear, like an elaborate wedding cake set out for simple afternoon tea.

The tea tasted very odd indeed. Within five minutes my head started to feel light and a strange, tingling sensation burned in my lips, almost as when one's hand tingles if it's been laid upon all night. The words around me began to run together a little, like a hum from which no distinct word could be parsed. I gripped the chair's arm and finished the rest of the cup of tea, hoping it would help. It did not. Five more minutes brought a sense of pressure to my chest, a swimming sensation in my mind. I hoped that my heaving efforts to breathe deeply were not noted.

I stood, but as I did my legs buckled some and I began to sway. I heard Elizabeth speak to me, but I could not make out what she'd said. Lady Somerford stood then, too, and I found, somehow, the presence to speak. "Please, be seated—I'm well."

Had I slurred my words? Clementine looked truly alarmed, and though I felt ill, I could imagine the thought running through her mind was, *What will Edward think?*

I heard someone, I could not see who, whisper, *"Her mother."*

Had someone really whispered that? Or had I imagined it? In my present state, I could not be certain.

I excused myself politely and raced unsteadily down the hall. Unfortunately, I had to pass the smoking room in order to get to the stairway. Captain Dell'Acqua was speaking with Mr. Morgan and Edward, whose backs were toward me. Dell'Acqua saw me sway, I think, and looked alarmed. Mr. Morgan turned around just as I tilted toward the wall. He seemed to be walking toward me. I could not allow that.

I disappeared into the servant's staircase and as I did, saw Father Gregory and Chef speaking at the foot of the stairs. What was the priest doing here? Or had I imagined that, too?

"Are you all right?" Chef called up to me. I hoped from that distance he would not be able to see the panic and confusion I felt.

"Yes, just a little unwell," I said, offering no reason for my being on the back stairs. I climbed up and out of their sight. I did not wish to be found until I could come to an understanding of what was happening to me. Instead of stopping at the floor where my rooms were located, I made my way to the top of the narrow passage and slipped into the blessedly quiet quarantine room.

I closed the door behind me. Clementine would find it difficult to excuse herself from her guests for some time. I went to the window, which was chilled from the night air. The stained glass brought me comfort, and pressing my face against the panes cleared my mind.

What had happened? The confusion was, thankfully, receding, but I remained frightened. Was it the first vestiges of the madness I always feared?

I thought back over the evening. I'd felt fine until . . . the tea. The tea in which I'd dropped sugar cubes that had been tinted green, but did not taste of mint but rather, licorice.

Absinthe!

I breathed a deep sigh. I had not gone mad. I was *not* mad. In fact, I had imbibed of three—no, four—doses of Clementine's green fairy. So this was how she took her spirits when she wanted no one to know. In sugar cubes. And that was, perhaps, why Maud had been so keen to tend the condiments.

I nearly cried with relief that it all made sense. I'd always disbelieved those who said I must be inclined toward instability because my mother was, but this night, this hour . . . I had worried. I admitted it. And why shouldn't I have? They'd been so apprehensive about my mother's madness contaminating us all that they'd left her to be buried, unrecognized, in the asylum grounds. At that moment, I was overwhelmed by that truth, her left alone and unrecognized, unmarked and unremarked. It was not fresh news but now, understanding what she must have felt, I pitied and loved her the more for their thoughtless gesture, one that had left her bereft and alone at the end.

I let my spirits settle and then with my head clear decided to take a moment and look through that magnificent desk once more because, perhaps, it may have been hers or at least used by her during her enforced isolation. I pulled open one drawer after another, only to find them all empty. I ran my hands down the sides of the desk and my palm caught, on one side, on a tiny hinge. I ran my finger round that whole side and found a perfectly crafted little lock. When I flipped it, a door swung open. I pressed hard, and when I did, something fell out.

A miniature sketchbook.

I sank to the floor, hard crinoline crunching round me, picked up the book, and then opened it. *Julianna Ashton* was scrawled on the inside of it, and nearly every page was filled with sketches—glorious renderings, I had no doubt, drawn by my mother. I quickly flipped through them, promising myself I would savor them, as they deserved, later. The very last sketch was done in a child's hand, but it showed promise. Underneath the small trio of feebly stemmed tulips my mother had written, *Annabel drew this. Isn't it lovely?*

A sob caught in my throat. My first drawing, with my mother. Together. I wanted to keep the notebook but dared not, not yet. Not until I could find a safe place to keep it. I could hardly clip it to my garter; it was too heavy. I had never owned anything of my mother's and now, within the span of the four months since I'd returned from Winchester, I'd been gifted with many things. I could not bear to lose any of them.

I took a deep breath, then slipped the notebook back inside the concealed side panel. I had not easily noticed it and hoped no one else would, either. The dust in the room had not been disturbed since my last visit. I heard a little buzz and leaned near the speaking tube. The guests were preparing to depart. The tube sent up voices, men's voices, from the first-floor hallway. One man made a comment about the ends justifying the means and that it would be well and profitable for all involved. It sounded conclusive and somehow wrong. What ends? What means? I opened the door to the room and started walking down the steps, then turned down the hallway toward my rooms. As I did, I noticed Mrs. Watts coming from the area just outside my door.

I looked at her quizzically.

"Are you quite well?" she asked, noting I had come from the servants' stairway. Was her brusque question to distract me from the fact that she'd been in my rooms—if she had been—or was the question due to my "episode"?

"Yes." I took the offensive. "I'm surprised to see you about at this hour."

"The household is my responsibility," she said smoothly. "Mrs. Everedge is looking for you."

"She may find me in my rooms," I said, and then nodded a dismissal.

I was not in my rooms long before Clementine knocked.

"What happened?" Her face reflected genuine apprehension and confusion. "Mr. Morgan was most concerned."

If only I could act insane long enough for Mr. Morgan's interest to move on, I would do it. I knew what the consequences of *that* would be, however, better than most. And he'd likely find it "interesting."

"I was unwell, but for a short while," I said. "After the tea." I could hardly accuse her of saturating her sugar cubes with spirits. I knew it was probable, but it was also probable that she'd deny it.

Clementine did not venture farther into the room, keeping a distance between us. "But you've recovered."

"I have." Had Mr. Morgan alone asked after me? I was afraid I'd shamed myself in front of Captain Dell'Acqua. To his knowledge, I had already bowed out of dinner once due to being unwell. "I hope I did not disturb your guests," was all I could say, and hoped she would shade in the outline.

"The ladies thought you had . . . taken ill," she said. "Lady Leahy did ask me to offer departing greetings; she returns to London on the morrow. She'll be back for Christmas, so there's that to look forward to."

I nodded.

"None of the gentlemen save Mr. Morgan seemed to notice your sudden and unusual flight," she continued. She backed to the door. "Good night, Annabel. I truly hope the morning finds you recovered. The gentlemen plan to spend the day at the ropewalk, but will return the day after next."

After she had closed the door behind her, I wondered why she had not had a similar response if she, too, had eaten the sugars. A terror of anxiety ran through me like an undisciplined child: *Perhaps it was true after all?* I caught, held, and soothed the thought. Clementine had taken but one cube, perhaps, or had grown accustomed to the effects. Her body had accommodated itself to the physic by habit.

That was all.

CHAPTER TWENTY

The next afternoon found me recovering in the conservatory, reading books I'd taken down from the library shelves. I'd left a small watercolor I'd done of Pennington, wrapped in brown paper, near the door; it was one I had hoped to give to Elizabeth the night before but then, due to the circumstances, had been unable. Watts would see it sent along to her.

I had fully recovered from the inconveniences of the previous night and was enjoying the afternoon sun slanting through the freshly cleaned windows. Mrs. Watts had hired additional staff to tend to Highcliffe now that it looked as though the house would not be sold; dust sheets were being removed rather than added, and the packing of rooms had stopped.

Shortly after tea, Watts came into the room and announced that Captain Dell'Acqua had come to call.

Clementine stood up. "He is not expected."

"Shall I tell him you are not in?" Watts asked.

"No, I shall speak with him." Clementine straightened her dress and made her way to the hall. Within five minutes she returned—Captain Dell'Acqua in tow!

"The captain says his man had confused the days and hours he was to meet at Winchester and then the ropewalks."

Dell'Acqua, beside her, lifted up his hands as if to gesture, what to do? But I saw the glint in his eye. There had been no mix-up.

"I wondered, therefore, if Mrs. Everedge would allow you to progress with a lesson on English culture," he said, looking at me. Then he turned toward her. "Your husband thought it was a splendid idea for me to become more comfortable with local ideas."

Clementine was fighting fatigue, I knew. This was normally the time when she would take a short afternoon nap, but she could not afford to put off the captain and she could not leave me unchaperoned.

"Perhaps we could stroll outside," I offered. "We could make our way toward the ropewalks, where we're sure to meet up with Edward. Watts might set up a chaise lounge for you to recline upon and watch as the captain and I walk."

She reluctantly agreed and we made our way down the path and toward the ropewalks, which were not far away.

"It was good of Clemmy to allow this," Marco offered with a tease.

I grinned. "It was not considerate of you to show up unannounced. I would have prepared differently . . ." Oh dear. Now he'd know I would have preened for him. I expected him to make a tease of that, but he did not.

"You are perfect as you are," he said. "Always." He did not seem to be trifling with me. His simple pronouncements, in stark contrast to the ornate offerings of other men, never failed to move me. "Are you quite well today?" Concern showed on his face. "I was most anxious all evening."

"I am not certain what happened," I began, because it was true that I was not certain, and I could not make unfounded accusations, nor was I sure that, even if I were certain, I should tell him. "Perhaps something I ate." We had all eaten exactly the same thing . . . except for the sugar. "But I am quite recovered. Thank you for asking."

"I was very concerned," he said. "I wanted to ride back this morning, but I thought perhaps it would be unsuitable and remarked upon and then I would not have this time alone with you. I understand from your cousin that Mr. Morgan prefers you not be left alone in my company."

Was that why he had not spoken of anything more personal, a commitment of some kind, to me? He had been told I was engaged to Morgan? "Mr. Morgan has no rule over me," I said. *Yet.* After a long pause, I added, "I look forward to our companionship. But the ropewalks? Were you not supposed to meet Edward and Lord Somerford there today?"

"I shall tell them that you accompanied me to show me where they were, when I arrived, unexpectedly, at Highcliffe," he said. "I am hoping to soon make my decision as to the ropewalks, perhaps finalizing with your cousin for our mutual arrangements. They will be good for the people of Malta, and they will be good for the people of Lymington—Lord Somerford has confirmed that. Everedge assures us that he has ample men to apply to the task." He grinned. "There is one other man who is most interested in partnering together. I am still speaking with him as well. I must decide between the two. And then there will be some weeks of negotiations for terms before we'll finally come to a mutually satisfactory arrangement. But things are moving quickly toward a conclusion."

"And you will return home soon?" I asked quietly.

"Yes, within a month or so," he said. "To Malta. Is that my home?" He turned from me and looked out over the sea. "My home is the *Poseidon*. I have a family, I have friends and . . . others in Malta. But it doesn't ever quite seem like home."

I knew that feeling. Highcliffe seemed to be home, but it could never be home because I was always there at someone's mercy.

"You have 'others' to return to?" I asked, heart heavy. "Perhaps a lady?"

"Now, Miss Ashton," he began, "Bella. What kind of man would I be if I spoke of things like that?"

In spite of myself, I grinned. "Like most other men."

"You've known rogues, then." He had neatly sidestepped my question.

I thought of the men in my family, and the men who had courted me in years past, and Mr. Morgan. "Yes," I agreed. "I have. Did you always know you were to be a sailor?" I looked out at the peaceful sea to the right, across the Solent toward the Isle of Wight.

"I'll answer that by way of a story," he said, teasingly reminding me of our last conversation. "And to tutor you, too, in the ways of Malta."

I leaned forward, and he leaned toward me. Our shoulders touched, and I did not move away, nor did he. He smelled of sand and salt and the sea, with the tiniest remnant of his Arabian-tinged cologne. I could barely concentrate on what he might say for the touch of him; I felt his muscles move beneath his linen shirt. I sent up a silent prayer that Clementine had fallen asleep in the sun and would not come after us.

"When a Maltese baby has his or her first birthday, there is a party, of course. There is always a party in Malta!"

I laughed with him. "Of course."

"At the baby's birthday, the parents, or in my case, my mother, arrange for a game called *il-quċċija*, in which a good number of objects are placed in front of the child. There might be a hard-boiled egg, a coin, a book, a rosary or a crucifix, a ring of gold, a charcoal pencil. Whatever the child reaches for and holds on to, that is said to be his or her destiny."

I was certain he'd been a beautiful child. That he would have beautiful children himself, someday.

"What did you reach for, Captain Dell'Acqua?" I asked.

"Marco, please. Call me Marco."

"Se insiste, Marco." It rolled over my tongue in Italian and not English.

"I do insist," he said. "You speak beautiful Italian. You should learn Maltese."

"What did you reach for?" I asked, gliding over that comment. He did not look at me as we strolled, but he took my hand in his own and I did not withdraw it. If only that could be true—that he'd reached for my hand, and that was his destiny.

"I reached for a rope knot," he said, simply. He let go of my hand to show me, with his hands, the shape of one. "All took that to mean I'd be at sea, and as our family was in shipping, it seemed fortuitous. When, some years later, my mother married and my brother was born, and he reached for the crucifix, we knew he would not be able to support us all." He smiled. "More children followed, and yet, here I am. My destiny has proved true."

By then we'd reached the area where the ropewalk began, and it was empty. "Where are Edward, Mr. Morgan, and the others?" I asked.

"Perhaps they have already left," he said. In front of us stretched long, narrow paths of three hundred feet or more; they had cement guidelines where the rope had been manufactured in

times past, and where it would be made again, once the arrangements had been completed.

"We'll build a shelter atop this, of course," Marco said. "So the
men are out of the elements."

"That's kind," I said.

He bent down and plucked a piece of rope, several feet long,
from the ground. It showed some signs of wear; it may have laid
there for a dozen years or more.

"Shall I make a knot for you? Like the one I chose?" he asked.

I nodded and he made a quick knot. "A traditional sailor's
knot," he said. He kept hold of one side of the rope and handed the
other side to me. "You try."

"Oh dear, I am not proficient at that," I said. But I gamely
twisted the rope until it was a loose jumble. "I do not recommend
that anyone try to secure his ship with that." I was about to drop
my end of the rope but he indicated that I should hold on to it.

He quickly made another knot, one that resembled one heart
slipped through another, circles with no end. "Lover's knots," he
said, and as he did, he made another one and another until he was
pulling me, clutching the far end of the rope, closer to himself.

"You seem well practiced at lover's knots," I teased, but my
voice had grown rough with emotions: affection for this man,
desire for a future I wished could be mine, fear that Edward and
Mr. Morgan would return, a wish that the afternoon would never
end.

"No, no, that is not true," he said, and with one final, quick tug
on the rope drew me close in front of him. "I have always thought
they resembled nothing so much as a noose. Until now, Bella,
until now."

His face was within an inch of mine, and my breath caught.
He pulled back.

"My name is Dell'Acqua, 'of the water,' and not De'Angelis, 'of the angels.' But I do not want to be numbered among the rogues you have known." With that, he pulled back from me, but the look on his face let me know that he wished he did not have to.

I wondered what he read upon my face. I let the rope fall to the ground. "We should return," I said. "They will be wondering where I am." I certainly did not want Edward to quarantine me. "And I shall tell you a story of England, as I promised Clemmy I would."

He laughed, then, a sound as rich as the sea, a laugh I imagined could be Poseidon's himself, and placed my hand inside the crook of his arm. "Teach me—I am your most devoted pupil."

"I shall tell you a story of Hampshire," I said, "as we are here. In fact, of Winchester, where I used to teach, as you know. That is also where the Benedictine sisters still teach and serve. I had thought, perhaps, to join them."

He looked at me with great, but silent, surprise, probably happily reaffirming his decision not to kiss me just minutes before. We walked along the seaside path. "My father lives near Winchester," he said. "It's one reason I decided to make connections locally rather than on other English coasts."

Now I looked at him in surprise. "Do I know your father? I know many families hereabouts."

He gently waved away the question, not willing to divulge the name yet, apparently. I wondered why. "Go on," he encouraged me. "We have not much time before we return to Highcliffe and I should like to hear your story."

"Winchester Cathedral used to belong to *us*, of course," I said, and risked a daring wink that earned me a deep laugh and his pulling me a bit closer as we walked. 'Twas worth it. "Before the Reformers stole it. Saint Swithin was one of its most beloved saints. Perhaps one hundred years after his death, in the mid-ninth century, he was chosen patron saint for the Benedictine Monastery. He was known for wisdom, and kindness and holiness, but what he is most renowned for is the simple kindness with which he treated the poor. One day as he was crossing a bridge he met a pitiable woman who had only a basket of eggs to sell."

We approached Highcliffe; Clementine remained in the distance. Marco slowed his gait.

"Go on," he urged me.

"The woman was somehow jostled by a passerby, and she dropped her basket and the eggs broke; she was completely bereft, and the saint, seeing her distress, took the basket and miraculously made her eggs whole again. Sometimes the simplest acts reveal the most about a person's character. He was known more for that kindness than for any other. Swithin reminds me of you, Marco."

He stopped. "Me? A saint? No, my dearest Bella. No."

"His care for the poor, for the underserved," I said.

He took my hand again and caressed it slightly before placing it, properly, in the crook of his arm once more as we approached Highcliffe.

There is another way he is like St. Swithin, I thought. *Perhaps, somehow, he could make me whole again.*

"You make me laugh," Marco said. "And blush. And question things. And see myself differently."

"That is good?" I didn't truly know.

He nodded.

"Then your 'English' lesson was profitable today," I said softly. Clementine quickly approached, rather than waiting for us to greet her.

"It's been a lovely day, Captain Dell'Acqua, and I'm glad you enjoyed your stroll, which I was able to supervise."

She could not possibly have seen us all the way to the rope-walk.

"And we shall be very pleased to entertain you and your men tomorrow evening for cards, and supper. Until then!"

It was an abrupt send-off but he bowed politely, and I saw that Watts had already called for his carriage.

We rounded up the steps, and Clementine took my arm rather less gently than Marco had.

"We shall say nothing of the walk," she hissed. "He need not know."

I nodded and returned to my rooms.

Who was the *he* that was not to know: Edward or Mr. Morgan?

CHAPTER TWENTY-ONE

Late the following evening, while an autumn storm threw rain against the house, we played cribbage at round tables in the ballroom. Clementine had invited a number of neighbors, now returned from the London season that had been foregone on our end due to lack of resources, so I was able to greet people I hadn't seen in years. The ballroom had been completely undraped; it was now assumed we would keep Highcliffe. I should ask Mr. Galpine, if I had cause to see him, if the advertisements or enquiries about its sale had ceased.

Edward had allowed Clementine to hire extra staff, who circulated around the room under the careful eye of Mr. and Mrs. Watts. Their son, Jack, had come from London to act as valet for Edward until they all returned to London in a few weeks' time. I saw the special look of pride that Mrs. Watts had when her son attended the master of the house; it was the look I'd seen in Clementine's eye when young Albert had scampered down for cuddles before bed to the delight of the visitors, announcing that he'd been named after the prince and demanding of his mother, "Come and tuck me up!" It was, I imagine, the look Edward's mother,

Judith, would have given Edward. It was the look my mother, I recalled just then, had for me. I blinked back a tear.

"Have a care with the candle, Annabel." Mummy and I sat on her bed, turning the pages of a book of fairy tales.

"I'm careful. I'm not a small child," I insisted. I put my head too near the candle; Mother reached forward and took the candle from me. "It throws light, but it can cause fire as well," she said.

"It smells good. Like honey."

She laughed. "Oh, Annabel. My papa always said that the reason he kept bees at Highcliffe was because they brought us two great things: sweetness, in the honey, and light, in the beeswax. You love sweetness, and you bring light. Hereafter, I dub you Princess Sweetness and Light."

"A princess, a princess!" I jumped on her bed and she put that to a quick stop with a stern look.

"A lady, a lady," she insisted, patting the bed again. I obliged and sat down whilst she started another story.

I should like to have a child look upon me that way, someday, and have that child respond with unconditional love and affection.

"Miss Ashton?" Lady Somerford rested her hand gently on my arm, bringing me back to the present. "Elizabeth has asked after you," she said, a strange tone coloring her voice.

"Tell her I am well," I responded. "And I am looking forward to seeing her at Christmas. I hope she received the watercolor of Pennington I painted and had sent to her?"

Lady Somerford shook her head. "She has not mentioned it. I am certain she would have."

Edward invited us to the dining room.

Edward and Lord Somerford led the way, unaccountably leaving Lady Somerford quite alone. Marco, a true gentleman, took her arm.

Mr. Morgan took mine. "Henceforth," he said, "please call me Nigel. And I always shall refer to you as . . . Annabel."

By the time we sat down, Clementine already looked slightly overwrought and emotional. It might have been her predinner drinks, but it probably was also due to the enormous strain put upon her entertaining week after week, knowing that the family's financial well-being depended upon the successful conclusion of Edward's negotiation. For his part, he seemed to be ignorant and unappreciative of her efforts on his behalf.

The first course was brought to the table, a little nest of potato sticks upon which rested a single quail's egg, whole. We were to break the eggs open to eat. I had never seen Chef serve such a thing. I saw a glance exchanged between Marco and Chef—had he talked to Chef?

Marco looked at me, and I saw the slightest smile on his lips. Of course. St. Swithin's eggs, restored. A sweet and unspoken message, one greatly welcomed. I did not eat my egg and allowed it to be removed whole and intact.

The Maltese men admired the art in the dining room; Edward had our most notable pieces hung there, as it was where guests were most likely to join us. I looked up at the beautifully carved plaster molded ceiling, flecked with gilt, cherubs serving baskets of fruit. "Such a fine collection—some masters, of course," Lieutenant Bosco observed, pointing toward a large portrait behind Clementine's seat, "but also some I have not seen before." He then pointed to one of a Maltese urn overflowing with Mediterranean flowers.

"Thank you," I said. "My mother painted that."

Edward opened his mouth to protest, and then closed it. He'd forgotten that was my mother's work! Bosco tugged on his collar, his face reddening. "There are others, too, which are beautiful." He followed Edward's eye and landed upon an English landscape. "Such as that one."

"Painted by *my* mother," Edward spoke up. The frame was, of course, much richer and more detailed than the one surrounding my mother's simple art. "My mother was quite an artist; she's been hung at many galleries and I intend to have more of her work placed about the house, now we're staying."

We were staying! Highcliffe was not lost. If Highcliffe could be saved then perhaps so could I.

"I should very much like to show you some of her work before you leave, but I'm afraid it will not be hung before you return to Malta," Edward continued. "Perhaps . . . perhaps a visit to the attic after dinner. I've been having it removed from storage, taken from the dust covers and wraps, and with some lamps . . ." He looked toward Watts, who nodded.

Lieutenant Bosco tried to smooth over the path by mentioning that English art could not compare in beauty to English women: Mrs. Everedge, Miss Ashton, and of course, Miss Baker.

"Ah yes, Emily Baker," Edward said. Clementine's face went sour. I looked at Marco, who smiled lightly at Bosco's mention of Miss Baker.

"Miss Baker?" I asked. "I do not think I have made her acquaintance."

"You should," Lieutenant Bosco said, but then Marco shifted the conversation toward the ropewalks, and Edward eagerly jumped in with ideas.

Who was Miss Baker?

After the final course was removed, and before the brandy and port, Edward led a few of us up the attic stairs; Lord and Lady Somerford, as well as many other guests, pleaded age and withdrew to the drawing room. The stairs creaked and moaned with the weight of so many replete-with-supper feet, each of us holding a lantern, as though Edward were leading a search party, indoors.

Perhaps he was.

When we reached the top of the stairs we spread out; several stacks of paintings leaned up against load-bearing attic beams. Most had their dust sheets removed. We looked at the first stack—some pretty pictures of Highcliffe, and some of the seascapes nearby. Lovely, but nondescript. There was a little murmuring, but no exclamations of genius. Edward looked eager to find something that would truly impress.

He led us toward the back, to another stack, and one that seemed to have just had the cover removed, judging by the disarray of dust. "Let's try these," Edward said aloud. With that, he set down his lantern and lifted a portrait toward us.

I gasped. I could not help but display my shock, though I knew it would not help me. In fact, this portrait, of all things, made my position both more hopeful and ever direr.

Clementine's eyes widened, and she signaled to Edward that he should set the portrait down. He looked at her and, instead, turned it round to view it for himself.

"That bonnet," one of the Maltese officers spoke up. "That is the traditional Maltese wedding bonnet that the captain"—he looked at Marco—"showed us a picture of. The drawing of it on her head," he added, pointing to me. "He was trying to learn from where in Malta such a bonnet might come. *Ecco*, there it is again—what a coincidence."

Mr. Morgan looked confused, though presumably he knew what my mother looked like, as he'd seen her portrait in the ballroom, with the hair combs.

Marco looked at me. The woman in the portrait was most certainly my mother, side by side with a raven-haired man, a man who looked, somehow, like me. My mother wore the cap. The marriage cap.

She'd been married, and I was legitimate.

CHAPTER TWENTY-TWO

"If your mother painted this, she was a fine artist," Marco told Edward, but I barely paid attention to any conversation as my mind swirled with the implications. Had Judith painted my mother's marriage portrait—if that was, indeed, what this was—while they were in Malta? If she had, she'd known all along that my mother was married, and that I was legitimate. Or was this a rendering done, perhaps, by my own mother? Was it real? Or had she been duped into a sham marriage?

My father had soft, kind eyes and his hand rested against my mother's jaw, tenderly. This did not appear to be a man duping a young lady or a man with no scruples. I was undone by seeing my father, perhaps, for the first time, but I did not have time to gawk and founder. *He looked like me.* "My mother," I said. "And . . . my father?"

Edward did not answer, but his face had turned to gray. His mind apparently swirled with implications, too. "This painting—it was not here, nor placed here, when I was last up in the attic. I think I could use a sherry," he said, leading us in parade back down the stairway, to the music room, where he had arranged for someone to play for our entertainment.

Even I took a sherry that night. What could this mean? Mr. Morgan stayed even more closely by my side after the attic discovery. He understood, surely, that if I were to be somehow proved legitimate, I would be the owner of Highcliffe and all the family investments.

If Morgan and I were married, it would all convey to him. I shuddered at the thought. Edward must certainly recognize that as well. Would it affect his rush to see me married to Morgan once investment matters with the Maltese were concluded?

I could hope.

But he would not want me to marry anyone else, then, either.

The other guests rejoined us and we listened to a few, final songs on the pianoforte. Clementine and Edward exchanged worried glances all evening as the multitude of domestics swirled about in silent pirouettes of service.

I stood with Edward and Clementine and said good-bye to our guests.

After Edward had closed the door on the last of them, he turned to me.

"Did you have something to do with that portrait in the attic?"

"By my faith," I said honestly, "I had no idea such a thing existed until you showed it to us all."

Clementine did not look at either of us; instead, she turned to leave instructions with the servants. Edward ran his fingers through his hair and dismissed me.

I went to my rooms, hurriedly undressed, draping my clothing across the dressing table chair, and climbed into my bed. A fire had been thoughtfully prepared for me, and it forestalled, somewhat, the early autumn cool.

It was true. I knew it was true, and so did, with all probability, everyone present in that room. My mother *had* been married unless my father had deceived her. She was a clever woman; could she have been tricked?

Perhaps.

If she'd been married, and the even more weighty consideration, if I could somehow prove that, Highcliffe and everything else would be mine and she would have been momentously wronged. Edward knew what was at stake now, too, and he, more even than Lady Somerford, was too clever by half.

I awoke the next morning aware that something felt different. Was it my circumstances? Dark premonition and presentiment closed around me like the curtains tightly drawn around my bed.

I sat up in bed, threw those curtains aside, and looked toward my dressing table. Somehow, in the night, my clothing had been rearranged.

I picked up my garters and to my dismay found that the Maltese wedding bonnet was no longer clipped to them. It had disappeared.

The others were up early, too, odd for a morning after late entertainment. Clementine and Edward had served themselves breakfast from the sideboard and were at the table. Maud, Watts, and Mrs. Watts bustled about in the background. Jack Watts passed me, going out as I was going in, and nodded.

I took a slice of toast and some marmalade and sat down.

A minute or two ticked by, then Clementine spoke up. "You had mentioned a bonnet, or cap, some time ago, hadn't you, Annabel?"

I nodded. "Yes, I had."

"Whatever gave you that idea?"

I had nothing to lose by being honest at this point. "I found one in my rooms."

Clementine finished her cup. "May I see it?"

I looked at her directly. "I'm afraid not. As of this morning, it seems to have disappeared."

Edward folded his paper. "Really, Annabel. You expect us to believe that? The night after we see an odd sort of portrait of someone, wearing something, this mysterious cap disappears."

"Believe as you may," I said, "but that is what has happened."

"Has anyone other than you seen this cap?" he asked. "Not a sketch of it, but the actual cap itself?"

I put down my toast, the reality of what he was insinuating crumbling in my mouth. Was he helping me find that which had gone missing, or, more likely, questioning whether or not such a thing may have existed?

"No. Not that I am aware of," I said.

"So perhaps . . . you had seen a portrait of this kind of cap somewhere, and then fancied a drawing of yourself with it on your head. Imitating the first portrait. Might that be true?"

"No, it is not. I did not imagine the cap; I've touched and held it. And I told you, I had not seen that portrait of my mother, wearing a cap, until last night."

"Perhaps after remembering the painting from somewhere you wanted to imagine yourself married to someone Maltese and sketched it in some hope . . ." Clementine offered me an exit, quietly.

I shook my head. "This is not true. I'm very sorry, but it's not. I held the cap; I saw it repeatedly, many times. It is now missing."

"All right," Edward said soothingly. "All right. It's gone now, so we shan't worry about it any longer. I've some accounts to tend to; then, later this afternoon, I would like to see you in my study if I may. You'll be here?"

Where else would I be? "Of course," I answered. "I'm at your command."

As I left the room, I heard Watts mention the name Lillywhite to him.

Edward was planning to visit Grandfather's solicitor. To see if there was further evidence of my mother's marriage?

I spent the morning reading in my room and thinking. Had I really seen and touched the cap? Had I placed it on my garter, each day, as I clearly remembered doing? And had I never really viewed that portrait of my mother—and perhaps my father— before? Maybe my mother had had it in her rooms, and I had remembered it so deeply that it came to my unconscious mind but no farther. The implications frightened me. Was I, truly, a lunatic? Or was someone trying to help me by placing some of my mother's things where I must see them and take heart . . . and action?

I wanted nothing so much as to visit the quarantine room to see if my mother's sketchbook was still in place, but I could not risk drawing attention to myself just then. Edward called me down to his study later on that afternoon and to my surprise he had rather good news.

I sat across from him, just he and I, while one of the day maids served us tea and small cakes, lavender scented and lightly iced, one of Chef's specialties.

"Mr. Morgan will not be joining us for a month or so," Edward began. "He had been planning to speak with you on a singular, personal matter today—"

"Marriage," I interjected.

Edward nodded. "But given the state of your health I suggested that a month of rest might be a good idea. It will allow him to tend to his other concerns, and for you to recuperate. Matrimonial matters can still be settled well before Christmas if we wish that to be so."

I did not wish that to be so, and he knew it. I took a moment and looked at Edward, who appeared to be truly befuddled. He was a shrewd card player, though; I'd partnered him at whist many times. Deep down, I knew that he was not giving me time to "recover." He was going to try to see if he could sort out whether I was legitimate, and if so, if it could be proven.

For if it could be he would not want me to marry Mr. Morgan, because then his "friend" and investment partner would, in many ways, own Edward. Should I prove legitimate, I, and not Edward, would own all. Should I marry Morgan and have children, they, not Albert, would inherit all. Mr. Morgan would control the family interests in any case. This, then, was why my engagement and subsequent marriage to Morgan had been delayed.

For now.

My relief was temporary, and replaced with a new fear. Ten minutes later, as I returned to my rooms, I started up the stairs but found that I had a hard time placing my foot down just right. My feet felt heavy, as though I had sat upon one of them, and now it tingled and did not work properly. I became aware that the day maid was watching me, and I tried to smile at her but felt that only one half of my mouth worked properly.

I was about to say something to reassure her, but the words would not form correctly. What was her name? Was she wearing my mother's Maltese cap? I think that she was. How had this happened?

"Are you quite all right, miss?" she asked.

I nodded but did not answer.

It was happening again, only stronger this time, and quite different. But I'd not taken any absinthe!

I steadied myself and reached my room, where I lay down on

my bed. My lips tingled now, too, as well as my feet. I looked at the window, and then quickly closed my eyes. The rays of sunlight had turned into swirling vortexes; then they resembled ship's masts, rushing toward me, waiting to impale me.

A knock on the door. I opened my eyes, and the masts had blessedly disappeared. "Yes?"

"It's me, Maud," came a voice. "May I come in?"

"Not fine, now. I, er, not now. I'm fine." I could barely force the words out in a sensible order. My mouth felt as though it were filled with toast crumbs once more. "I have not eaten any sugar cubes!" Why had I shouted that? I'd thought it, I knew why I'd thought it, but it needn't have been said.

"Yes, miss," she answered, her voice quietly alarmed. I heard her quick steps down the hallway.

An hour later, another knock. "Miss Ashton, Annabel. It is Father Gregory."

My confessor! I sat up, and blessedly, felt a little better. I checked my reflection in the looking glass; my eyes were rimmed with dark circles, as though I'd been hit. Perhaps it was just the dusk that made them appear so. I opened the door, and Father Gregory came in. Mrs. Watts lit the lamps in the room and then left us.

"Your cousin's wife sent for me," he said, sitting near me on one of the chairs near my fireplace, which was cold.

"I'm sorry," I said, my mouth sticky and dry. "She needn't have."

"She said you were unwell, overwrought. It's most unusual for anyone at Highcliffe to send for me."

"Perhaps because I am the only Catholic here," I said.

"I'm sorry you were troubled."

"It is no trouble, daughter. No matter what anyone has ever said or implied to you, you are no trouble, anywhere, at any time."

He took my hand in his, and I sensed how icy mine was only when enfolded in his warmth.

"Is there anything you'd like to discuss?" he asked.

I shook my head. "No, Father."

"No more thoughts of taking vows?" he finally asked. Had he remembered that on his own or had Clementine suggested that again? It would make a neat solution to their current tribulations.

Oh dear. Now I was questioning a priest!

"No, Father. I will speak to you first about anything of import."

He patted my hand and said nothing further about it. "*This* is of import and I'm happy I came. You look tired, daughter," Father said. "Would you like me to hear your confession? And then bless and anoint you?"

"Am I ill?" That would be the reason for anointing.

"I don't know," he said. "But it cannot hurt."

I nodded. "Yes, Father, I would like that. I truly would."

Later, Clementine thoughtfully sent a servant to start a fire for me; a cold dinner tray of buttered macaroni—child's food, not too excitable—was sent to my room; for this I was happy. I had no desire to face the family or the domestic staff until I was fully recovered.

When would that be? I had no idea what had overcome me. It was very like the earlier event, but also different, stronger, more confusing. I had hallucinated, or had I begun to tip into the insanity that had beset my mother at nearly my age?

A wisp of the memory of us in the quarantine room came back.

"I'm like you!" I pointed to the sketch.

Her eyes grew sad. "In some ways," she answered. "In only the best ways, I hope."

I hoped so, too.

That one memory seemed to pry loose another, this one less welcome. That sense of foreboding, like curtains closing, drew tight around me again. I could not breathe. *Edward. I'm cold! Edward, let me out."* I banged my little fist against the door of the cold pantry. The handle was too high up for me to reach.

"Edward!" There was no answer. I turned a crate upside down and sat on it, and let tears roll down my face, their hot trails the only warmth to be found. I stood up and jumped up and down, and then I opened a box of berries from the shelf and ate a few before sitting down again.

After what seemed a long time, Chef opened the door.

"Qu'est-ce que c'est?" he asked, picking me up and taking me into his arms. "What is this?"

"I got locked in," I said.

"By whom?" His voice rose. I did not tell. I could not tell. If I told, it would be worse next time.

"Come, I will create for you a warm custard, non?"

"Oui!" I said, and he laughed. I sat in the kitchen and let the others fuss over me. The next time I visited the kitchen, the handle had been lowered.

It struck me now, in the deep darkness of my rooms, that no adult from the family had come to look for me: not my aunt nor uncle, nor Edward's governess, who was to look after me, too, when we were home on holiday. It was time to admit, and face head on, the truth. No matter how much I wished otherwise, I truly had no family. No, not even Edward. Then, as now, I had to care for myself.

And I would.

At midnight, I pulled my robe on but left my feet bare and determined to do without a candle. I needed to reach the quarantine room and return to my rooms without being detected.

CHAPTER TWENTY-THREE

The macaroni twisted itself into fresh loops in my stomach as I placed my hand on the door handle to my room, deciding, *Should I risk it?* I knew I must.

I tiptoed down the silent, dark corridor. Long tables fronted each side of the hallway, some with oriental vases newly filled with fresh flowers, a sign of the loosening of Edward's purse strings. I was careful to walk right in the middle, so I did not brush anything to either side; as well, the floors were less likely to squeak in the center.

It did put me more at risk of being seen, however. I could not duck into a wall should someone open a bedroom door.

The back staircase beckoned; I gently pushed the door into it, and it gave way easily. I made my way up a flight and then two.

Someone caught and held me! I was pinned in place!

I stopped and steadied myself. My head was still not quite right yet. I turned and looked behind me. No one. I exhaled slowly, and then looked down. *Ah.* My bare foot had stepped on the hem of my dressing gown. I lifted the foot and the gown and continued up the narrow stairway to the isolation room. I opened the door, familiar to me now even in the dark, and slipped inside.

Once in, I sat on the hard bed to allow my eyes to adjust to the room's light. The moonlight shone through the stained glass once more, and I felt comforted in a very palpable way, a way I had not felt comforted before in this room. I felt at peace for the first time that day. I smelled incense, faintly. It reminded me of incense I had smelt already, dark and smoky but with a bright undertone. I had not smelt it in this room before. Had someone been here?

Or was I still hallucinating? Maybe mad.

I stood and walked over to the window where the rusting spyglass rested. I used it to peer out of the window toward the harbor, some distance away. The *Poseidon* was docked; I recognized her magnificent bowsprit in the moonlight. He was still here. There was still hope.

Now, eyes adjusted, I quickly got to the task for which I'd come. I put my ear to the speaking tube. Nothing. No one was up and about, or at least no one that I could hear.

I quietly walked to the desk and felt for the little latch on the side. I flipped it and to my great delight, the sketchbook was still in place.

I took it and then walked to the window. I wanted to view every sketch here, in the moonlight, in case the book should be taken from me on my way back to my rooms.

I flipped through the pages. There was a picture of my mother, a self-portrait. She looked happy and smiling and so young—my age. She did not look ill in any manner. There were many sketches of the streets and homes of Malta, their black iron lanterns and soapstone-smooth buildings. A gentle ocean kissing a seawall. A lighthouse.

A sketch of a man in a naval uniform. I brought that picture close. His eyes were warm, his hair black as the tar that protected ships from rot. I held his gaze, and he seemed to hold mine.

"Father." I had not meant to speak, but I could not hold it back. It was the same man as the one in the attic portrait. I touched his face on the paper. Had he left us? Had he left my mother? I was currently trapped in this unconscionable position due to his actions or lack thereof, and yet looking at his face he did not seem capable of such a callous act.

Or maybe I was incapable of judging character. I did not know.

There were several pictures of Judith; the sisters had apparently drawn one another as well as painted each other. One portrait of Judith had a man in the background—my father?—and beneath Judith my mother had written an Italian proverb, *Invidia non prende nessuna vacanza.* Envy takes no holiday. There were flowers in the garden in which Judith stood. Mother had written *belladonna.* In English, that signified poison. In Italian, beautiful lady.

Which had she meant?

I closed the notebook. I was certain, now, that my mother had been married. I did not know if she had been mad or not; perhaps that was a convenient lie others told to gain what she'd held. "I should show this to Marco," I whispered aloud. "Perhaps it may be of some help."

I did not know yet if he could be trusted with a treasure like this. What were his true intentions, in England, and with me? He'd spoken of England. He had not spoken of me.

Minutes later, safely inside my rooms, I exhaled relief. Now, where to hide the book? I knew my rooms had been searched and would be searched again. I had lost the cap *if it had ever really existed*; the unwelcome thought presented itself, and I pushed it away.

I looked around. Nowhere was safe. As I walked toward my bed, an idea came.

I knelt on the floor and lifted the porcelain chamber pot from the box, turned upside down, upon which it rested underneath my bed.

If I did not use the chamber pot, no one would have cause to move it. I would put the small sketchbook under the box, and forestall from drinking in the evenings so the pot would never need to be used.

Shivering, I climbed into my bed. I whispered my prayer. "There is no one left save me to clear her name. I will do whatever it takes . . . if You will help me."

A verse of scripture threaded through my mind. *And Jesus answering, said: You know not what you ask. Can you drink the chalice that I shall drink?*

"I can," I whispered into the dark.

It was now early October, and it seemed as though all arrangements, weighty as they were, were to be finalized between the Maltese and Edward. I had played my part, though it had lasted longer than I'd expected. I had done well by Edward, as usual. As usual, Edward had not done well by me.

One afternoon I saw Captain Dell'Acqua ride up on a horse he had leased for his stay in England. He dismounted, and I heard Watts welcome him in as a footman ran from the stables to take the horse. I quickly rolled my hair and clasped it with the ruby hair combs; straightened my dress, which was, thankfully, one of my better ones; and made my way downstairs to the library, which communicated with the study, next door.

I stood at the library shelves, looking for a book, and could hear Dell'Acqua and Edward finalizing plans.

"But the barracks can be used, I'm certain, to house others if we bring them in," Edward said.

Barracks? There were run-down barracks in Lymington, remnants of the last war with Napoleon. French prisoners of war had been held in them, but they were crumbling and unused at the moment.

"Will we need the others?" Marco's voice sounded displeased.

"For better profit, yes." Edward sounded insistent.

Marco hesitated, and then said he would take the papers to his solicitors in London as well as speak with some local lads.

Edward grew silent for a moment and then consented. They'd plan to bring things to a close by mid-October. The Exhibition's final day was October 11, there were to be a number of social events commemorating the experience, and then the waters around England would be filled with ships setting sail back to many nations. I hurried back to my chair.

The door to the study opened, and Marco and Edward came into the library, where I sat with my tea and book.

"Miss Ashton," Marco said. "I'm delighted to see you. In fact, I was hoping you would be at home. I have brought a memento for you. A book of Malta. May I?" He turned to Edward.

Edward could not very well say no with his contract in the captain's hand. "Clementine is not here to supervise," he offered.

"Where has she gone?" I asked.

"She took Albert and Lillian to Lymington to see the yachts. And return books to Mr. Galpine's lending library."

I had never seen Clementine with any reading material other than ladies' periodicals. Perhaps she was collecting the post herself these days. That which had been addressed to her, and maybe, to me.

"You could remain in the study, nearby?" I suggested to Edward. He finally agreed with a curt nod. He turned and left, and the captain came and sat near me.

"Bella," he said. He looked at me with the same wide-eyed concern as that displayed by the African masks hung on the nearest wall. We had dropped the pretenses of his visiting with me to facilitate his arrangements with Edward.

"I am well," I said. I would say no more and taint his view of my health.

"I was concerned, after the *confusione* in the attic, about the wedding portrait."

So he'd thought it a *confusione*. Or at least recognized that something odd was underfoot. "It was my mother in that picture," I said simply. "And most probably my father."

"*Ecco.* A Maltese man, for sure."

"You did not recognize him?" I held out a slender hope.

He shook his head. "I'm sorry. Perhaps if I saw the portrait again."

I could not take him up to the attic now, and if I left his company for a moment Edward would find a way to make him leave. "I shall think upon that," I said. I nodded toward the book. "It was too kind of you to bring this."

"I want you to see," he said, opening it. Inside were a dozen or more woodcuts of Malta. The first picture was of a beautiful palace, built of neatly placed stones, each window framed by ornate stone carvings. "The Auberge de Castille in Valletta," he said. "One of the inns built for the Knights of Saint John. We have been entrusted through the ages with defending the faith." He drew his chest up.

"That might come as a surprise to Queen Victoria," I teased, "who considers herself defender of the faith."

"Ah!" He held his hands up and shrugged. "What faith, I ask you. What faith? Christianity, Catholicism, has been in Malta nearly two thousand years, brought by Saint Paul himself!"

I laughed. "Show me more."

"Our art galleries are second to none. Rich in talent and treasure." He paged through. "Here is a spread of the simple but honest people of Malta. Here, a goatherd." In the engraving, a man with a neatly trimmed beard paced his goats with a stick. "Our women work, too, just as the women here." He pointed to a day maid shuffling by in the hallway. That page held wood engravings of proud, but poor, egg sellers, choristers, an onion seller—her papery wares spilling from a basket—a bran seller and a water seller, side by side, each woman balancing a heavy jar upon her head.

"A cheese man," I said, delighted with the open, honest face in front of me.

"We have the best cheese," Marco said. "I promise that. But they earn very little." He turned the page. "They often cannot eat the wares they sell."

"Lymington has many poor as well. We no longer have salterns; smuggling, for better or worse, has gone or is reduced now that revenues are restructured. It's good that you're bringing back the ropewalk. It will deliver real hope." I smiled, but he did not smile in return. Instead, he oddly pressed on with his book.

"Now here"—he put his finger on another wood-carved stamp—"is the governor's palace."

"I believe my mother was there," I said, staring at it. "I know Aunt Judith was."

"And they probably met your father there. I imagine they were of the same social station."

The final pages showed horse-drawn carriages, their beautifully turned-out passengers enclosed in lightly knit netting rather than behind door and panels, to better let through the Mediterranean breezes.

"It is Eden, is it not?" He closed the book and took my hand in his and looked into my eyes, unflinching. I hoped Edward would not come into the room just then.

Was he asking me that question, directly, or something else? I sensed something deeper. Was he asking me to . . . leave? I did not know him well enough for that and truthfully, he had not offered me anything . . . official. Perhaps this was the very kind of proposition my mother had fallen for. I remembered what his friends, who knew him so well and whom he seemed to trust implicitly, had said, the very first day I'd met him, at the Exhibition.

If he breaks an English girl's heart to avenge his poor mother along the way, why, so much the better. He'd say so himself." Was he still angry with his father?

"I should like to visit sometime," I said. "It would make a beautiful holiday, a change of place from home."

"Home?" he asked.

"As Mr. Blake has said, 'England's green and pleasant land.' Do you not care for England?"

"I like some English, of course. I like your Prince Albert, I like your berries and horses, I like Somerford, an honest man. And then, Bella, well, then, there's you." He kissed the back of my hand. I had left it ungloved and his lips lingered a moment longer than they had the time before. "Perhaps the blue and agreeable seaside of Malta would be pleasant as well?"

I laughed. Then I lowered my voice so it was barely audible, and tilted my head toward his. Our foreheads touched, tête-à-tête, head to head. I thrilled at the unexpected intimacy but continued whispering. "I must find out what happened to my mother, Marco, clear her name if I can, find out what happened to her in the end. It's a sacred duty to me. I want to set her name right. I must bide my time here whilst I look for documents or contact a solicitor or . . . Edward said Mr. Morgan will not return for a month or more."

"He may change his mind and return sooner."

I acknowledged this possibility. "He may."

Did Marco understand that if I could prove my legitimacy, I would not only reclaim my mother's honor for her, but would be heir? I could say none of that aloud, of course, with Edward in the next room. If I left England and Edward found proof regarding my parents, he would destroy it.

Marco set the book down and then pulled aside his jacket to reveal his waistcoat, this one a brilliant blue, upon which had been embroidered, of course, a rooster. "You will not fail those who depend on you at the moment of need. I admire you for that, Bella. You are more a man than most men."

I arched one eyebrow.

"Not in all ways, of course," he said, blushing, "which is obvious to all." I relished that I had caught him out once as he had caught me out when we first met. As much as I loved the tease, I did not wish to be indiscreet, so I pressed ahead to a fresh subject.

"Were you able to contact your father? I know it was important to you."

His eyes quickly grew cold. "I sent several letters. None was responded to. I cannot say I am surprised."

He tried to withdraw his hands from mine, a gesture I well knew. Retreating was safest when the heart was at risk.

"What is his name?"

He shrugged. "Mansfield."

"Oh! Lord Mansfield," I said. The Mansfields were definitely in attendance at the social events held round Winchester. "I know him—rather, I know his wife, Lady Sophia. She's quite a lovely person, an American. Their daughter took harpsichord lessons at the school I taught at. They have a young son, too." Lord Mansfield's Christian name, I knew, was Mark.

Use my name, he'd said. *Marc Antonio. Marco.*

"How wonderful." Marco's voice spilled out, decanting bitterness.

Oh dear, what a mishap! My face bloomed to the tips of my ears, and I felt real remorse constrict my heart. Just what the man needed—another reminder that he'd been cast aside. I drew close. "That was ill-considered, and I repent having spoken in haste. Please forgive me." Of course, he would not want to hear about how beloved were Mansfield's legitimate children when he and his mother had been ignored. No wonder he hadn't wanted to share his father's name. He'd been turned away.

"All is forgiven, Miss Ashton," Marco said softly. "It is good to know they are well cared for."

Miss Ashton. Not Bella.

At that moment, I heard a carriage arrive and Watts step into the hall. It was Clementine arriving, of that I was certain. I quickly spoke.

"Our time together draws to a close. I hope it will not be our last."

He smiled and took my hand between his own once more; I felt enfolded within them, both safe and emboldened somehow. "I, too, Bella. I, too." Did his voice reflect resignation, wistfulness?

Lillian, Albert, and Clementine blew into the hall like leaves on the autumn wind. Lillian bustled Albert upstairs, against his whimpering protests, and Clementine stood in the hallway.

"Good day, Annabel, Captain Dell'Acqua. Are you here together alone?"

"No, my dear, I am here." Edward quickly came through the study door and made his way to his wife, kissing her on the cheek. Had he overheard us? "Did Albert enjoy the yachts?"

She nodded. "He did. We also spoke with Mr. Galpine." Her face turned to me, then from angry red to white. Why?

"I was leaving," Captain Dell'Acqua said. He bowed to me, and to Clementine. He looked at Edward. "I shall be in touch after my solicitor has reviewed the contracts."

Edward nodded, and Watts showed the captain to the door.

I excused myself and returned to my room, from where I watched the stable boy bring Marco's horse to him. Marco placed the Maltese book and Edward's papers into his saddlebag and then rode off, his blond queue bobbing between his shoulder blades. I did not turn from the window until I could see him no more.

I walked to my bed and bent down, lifting the ruffle. I lifted the dry chamber pot and checked on my sketchbook. I closed my eyes in relief. It was still there.

What had Galpine said to upset Clementine so? I had little time with which to complete my mission. That night, when all were abed, I would continue my midnight wanderings. This time, I intended to reclaim the portrait of my parents. Where I should store it, I did not know.

The larder? The abbey ruins? Deliver it to Lady Somerford somehow?

CHAPTER TWENTY-FOUR

OCTOBER, 1851

I was becoming very much like those nocturnal animals I had so despaired of in London, scratching about in the dark whilst all others were, I hoped, abed. Like them, my very life might depend upon going unnoticed. So I took care.

I could not climb the back stairs this time, as it did not communicate with the storage attic. I went to the main staircase and very carefully took each tread silently, slowly. Once there, I tugged on the rope that dropped the attic door and stairway. It fell with a quiet whoosh, a testimony to clever craftsmanship. Then I walked up the stairway, holding my wavering candle before me.

I turned to the left first and looked at a stack of paintings leaning against a beam. There was a dust sheet over the top of them, and I reached out and lifted it, carefully, perhaps somewhat fearfully, as a person might lift a cloth before identifying a dead body.

The cunning face grinning back at me was Aunt Judith's, her eyes hard, marble blue. Somehow, although she'd been dead for some years, she came alive there in front of me and dared me, I thought, not to drop the cloth.

I covered her face and a wave of nausea passed. I then uncovered a second stack and was able to view it simply by thrusting my candle forward. The front painting was a landscape of Highcliffe, and I pulled it forward to view those behind it. Grandfather and my grandmother. Behind that, one of my mother as a child, with her spaniel. I had not seen this before. I delighted in it. In spite of her fairness, and my darkness, she looked like me, here, or I like her.

I should return for this later.

The piece just behind it was, surprisingly, one of my own. It was the unframed painting I'd just done for Elizabeth, of Pennington, and had asked to be sent to her as a gift when she returned to London.

How had it been intercepted, and by whom? She would think I had allowed her leave-taking to go unremarked, when she'd been so kind to me. I could not carry it down now, but I would see, I hoped, that she received it.

Next was a likeness of Edward with old Mr. Everedge, his father. I had never referred to him as Uncle, and he'd not encouraged it. Edward looked stiff in his young man's suit.

I could not afford to dawdle. I turned toward another stack. I held my breath and loosened the pall tightly roped round it. When I was able to lift the cloth, I saw that it was, indeed, the frame that had so recently held the portrait of my parents, my mother in her Maltese wedding cap.

But the portrait had been cut from the frame and removed. I held back the tears, for the moment, and mourned the loss of one of my few family treasures.

Edward was scared, I knew it. And rightly so; that's why the portrait had been removed.

The net was rapidly tightening round me now. My throat constricted in sympathy with my narrowing circumstances.

I walked down the attic stairs and then turned around to push the door quietly back up. When I turned again, someone was standing behind me.

My knees buckled and, with nothing to hold on to, I nearly dropped my candle on my dressing gown.

"Oh," I sighed when I recognized my stalker. "Oliver. What are you doing here?"

"I sleep on a bench in the hallway, miss, as you'll remember," he whispered. He somehow knew we should not draw attention to this interchange. "To be at the ready should I be called. I heard something. I thought if I could catch an intruder then Mr. Everedge would be most proud of me. Might even promote me. He did that for Jack, you know."

Jack, the Wattses' son. I nodded. "Yes, I remember that. But, as you see, I am no intruder." I kept my voice low.

Oliver looked rather disappointed, and I wished to reach out and gently chuck his young cheek in encouragement. But I did not.

"It would be better," I said, "if we said nothing of our meeting this night. Or of my being here."

Would he be questioned?

He nodded. "I understand, miss."

He looked understandably anxious. I was understandably anxious for him . . . and for myself. Could Oliver be trusted?

Days passed. I could think of no way to further help myself. How long would it take Edward to regain his confidence and recall Morgan, or Morgan to press his claim to me against the debts Edward owed him? Not long, I was sure. Weeks, at best. The winds turned wicked, and as I walked the grounds, I watched Edward's head gardener take down a heavy branch that had been damaged but had not completely fallen. It hung there, suspended, waiting to drop upon an innocent passerby.

I felt that branch hanging over my head. I was, in a sense, the helpless passerby. And yet I could not avoid the path I had been given to walk.

One afternoon Lillian indicated that I should follow her into the nursery. "Mr. Galpine has asked to call on me," she said. "My father has given his permission, and he shall collect me on my day out this week, from my home. Wednesday. Clementine will tend to Albert herself after I'm gone. I think she means to take him to a friend's house in Winchester."

"Wednesday . . . that's tomorrow. Marvelous!" I said. "I'm so pleased. Galpine seems like a good man."

"I believe him to be so," she said, reaching out for my hand. "And good to look upon, too." She winked. "I'll tell him about the new account-keeping books you gave to me, and how effective they are at keeping track of invoices and receipts."

I laughed with her. "He's certain to be impressed. You may live above the shop yet."

She dipped a little bow of happiness and then twirled. "I've you to credit for this. Thank you for taking me with you that very first time."

"I had my own agenda as well," I reminded her.

"I know that." I admired her forthrightness. "But it did us both a bit of good . . ." Her voice grew sad and trailed off.

In the end, we both knew, it had done me no good at all.

I returned to my room and looked over my books, my art, my mother's things, my writing desk. I could pen a letter to my friends in Winchester. I could write to Marco, but what would I say? *I've changed my mind, and I'll accompany you to Malta, in a most unsuitable irregular union though you haven't even asked me for such.* No, no.

He was nursing his wound over his father's snub. Yet, Lady Mansfield was so kind. How had she married such a man?

An idea presented itself. I should write to Lady Mansfield—what was there to lose? Perhaps she would invite me to call on her; Clementine could certainly not object to a social call to a woman so highly placed. While there, it might be that I could find some delicate way to raise the situation and Marco's concerns with her. He wanted nothing from her, from his father, after all, but an acquaintance, perhaps a friendship. Then all would be well, Marco might be content to tarry in England, and my options could open.

I would also send a note to Mr. Lillywhite, asking if he could refer me to someone who might be able to offer some forensic examination of any documents pertaining to my legitimacy, my grandfather's will, and the notations in Galpine's journals, and perhaps validate a claim to Highcliffe.

I had nothing to lose and possibly everything, and everyone, to gain.

I carefully penned the letters and quickly headed back to the nursery. Perhaps Lillian could be cajoled into giving the letters to Mr. Galpine.

Alas, she had already left. I tucked them back inside my book and started toward my room. I passed Oliver in the hallway.

Of course! The reason Clementine used Emmeline to pick up and deliver her posts was because Emmeline would not, could not, say to whom letters were posted or from whom they were received.

"Oliver, does Emmeline still deliver letters for Mrs. Everedge?"

He had letters in his hand. "Yes, miss. Or I do."

He looked as if he was about to say more, so I did not speak.

"Thank you for the boiled caramels, miss," he continued. "Em and me, we share them with all the family. You're the first person from the big house who gives to us and does not ask anything in return."

I swallowed hard. I could not now, of course, ask him or Emmeline to undertake the delivery of my letter. In fact, I grew even more aware of how the others in my family used the staff, lovingly, but carelessly, for their own ends. I had proved to be not very different.

"As long as I am here," I said, "there shall be never-ending sweets. On your way, now!"

The lad was quick. He returned to his duties, and as he did, I slipped out of the door. I knew it was dangerous but it was worth risking, and fortune was with me; because Mr. Galpine would be courting Lillian today his associate would post the letters. He was someone, I was certain, Clementine did not often speak with. I was quick, too, walking down the drive, which had been freshly laid with expensive wheat-colored gravel. I scared up a flock of ravens and they scattered, like thrown confetti, into the sky as I passed.

I arrived at Lymington and slipped one letter underneath Mr. Lillywhite's closed door before making my way to Mr. Galpine's. Once there, I posted the other letter. Before leaving, I spied a familiar person through the window.

Marco! As I was about to leave and greet him, I saw him slip his hand underneath the elbow of a woman, perhaps a year younger than I and very attractive, to help her across the street. She appeared to be laughing, as was the man next to her, and Marco engaged and reengaged her in conversation.

"Who are those people?" I asked Mr. Galpine's assistant.

"Oh, that's the Maltese captain," he said.

I nodded. "Whom is he with?"

"Mr. Robert Baker and his sister, Miss Emily," he said. He glanced at Miss Emily and then glanced again. She was lovely, and I imagined that second glance was a typical response. The beautiful Miss Baker Lieutenant Bosco had mentioned.

"They are acquaintances?" I pressed.

He looked at me oddly, but answered anyway. "It's my understanding that Mr. Baker and the captain are discussing investment arrangements. At least that's what's been said around town. The Bakers are quite . . . prosperous." He blushed, perhaps realizing he was caught gossiping, and said no more.

I paged through some books in the lending library till Marco and the Bakers left, remembering what Marco's friend had said months past. *Passing time with a pretty girl will help him attain what he wants.*

Miss Baker? And, perhaps, me.

After I was certain they had left, I returned, quickly, to Highcliffe.

The October light slanted so beautifully through the windows of the great hall connected to the foyer in that golden hour. Autumn light was, for its scarcity, perhaps more valuable than that which spilled bountifully in the summer, and its beauty drew me from my melancholy over having seen Marco flirt with Miss Baker and all that it implied. I looked up at the beautiful painting on the great hall's ceiling; the word was drawn from *cielo*, heaven, in Italian.

I got down on my knees, and then lay on my back so I could take in, fully, the painting from all angles in the afternoon light. The cherubs edged the outline; the saints rested just inside them.

An angel pointed a finger to someplace on a map; it was too small to see from this distance, but I dearly wished to know where he was telling us to go.

I closed my eyes. If I knew, I'd go.

Just then, the door opened. I opened my eyes as Watts rushed by. He looked at me with visible alarm. "Miss? Miss Ashton, are you well?"

I opened my eyes. "Yes, Watts." He shook his head and made it to the door just as Edward, Clementine, and Albert came in.

They stood stock-still and stared at me. I sat up, then stood and shook out my voluminous dress.

"Whatever are you doing, Annabel?" Clementine's voice quivered with unease.

"Losing myself in the painting." I pointed to the ceiling.

"As you lie on the floor?" she asked. Even Watts had removed himself to what, I assumed, he felt to be a safe distance in case a fit of some kind overtook me.

Albert plopped down on the floor, took my hand, and, looking up, smiled with glee. His father had done that, once. "Edward," I said, "do you not recall when we were children and would do this very same thing? Have you lost your sense of childish wonder?"

In spite of himself, I thought, Edward smiled genuinely, though briefly. We had once lain for an hour or more on that same floor, giggling at the bared breasts of the women in the portrait, wondering if his mother had noticed and, if so, why she had not demanded they be covered up.

"We're no longer *children*," he answered quietly, then pulled the roll of ginger chews from his pocket. "If you ladies will forgive me, I need to prepare for my meeting tonight, with Lord Somerford and Captain Dell'Acqua."

I kissed Albert's cheek, then nodded and made some light,

pleasant conversation with Clementine until I could escape to my rooms. She'd purchased some new slippers for me, she said, and would have them sent up.

I waited by my window, looking for Somerford's carriage to arrive, and then Captain Dell'Acqua either by hired carriage or horse. Hours ticked by on the Chinese dragon clock, but neither man arrived.

About seven p.m. there came a knock at my door. It was Mrs. Watts.

"Dinner will be served in rooms tonight," she said, "on trays. I'll ensure it's not macaroni."

"Thank you." That was kind. "Just my dinner?" I asked.

She shook her head.

"Then Edward's expected guests didn't arrive. Did they send word?"

"No," she answered softly. "Not that I know of. Nor that Mr. Watts knows of." Jack had returned to London. Mrs. Watts nodded a grim farewell in the setting darkness.

Edward must be livid. *And afraid.* Had something happened to their arrangements?

Perhaps I'd said too much.

CHAPTER TWENTY-FIVE

Some days later, I was in the library, sketching by the window as Clementine read quietly, when Emmeline brought the post. She handed it to Clementine and curtseyed slightly before Clementine shooed her back to her duties outside.

"The young lass collects the post now?" I asked as though I didn't already know.

"Why not?" Clementine riffled through the letters. One was in an especially fine envelope, sealed with red wax. "Mansfield," she said as she broke the seal.

Clementine slid an invitation from the envelope and from within that a short handwritten letter. "Lord and Lady Mansfield request our presence at a ball and charity auction donation being held four days hence." She scanned the letter. "She apologizes for the late invitation but has been very occupied." She grew quiet again and then looked up at me.

"She says you are to attend if you would care to." She closed the envelope. "I had no idea you'd made acquaintance or that she was aware you existed. Even Edward and I have only occasionally attended their events."

"Her daughter attended the Rogers Day School for Young Ladies," I said as a way of reply, hoping she would not press it. Blessedly, she did not.

My heart tried to push its way out of my chest. But would I have a chance to speak with her, privately, at such a large event?

Clementine smiled. "Edward will be very glad indeed to see this. And, it seems the entire county will be in attendance." She motioned for Watts to ask Edward to come into the drawing room when he was at liberty to do so. Edward soon arrived, and Clementine shared the news with him, which seemed to cheer him.

"Perhaps another avenue to further our interests," he said, taking the invitation. "The entire county is certain to be invited. It bodes well for us."

Perhaps Marco would be invited. That was unlikely, though, considering the reception his father had given, or rather had not given, him.

Edward continued to scan the letter. "It says we're to bring something clever and English, to celebrate Prince Albert's advancement of such. What shall we take?"

Clementine said nothing, and I didn't have anything to offer. Watts cleared his throat. "If I may suggest, sir, one of your many fine clocks?"

Edward smiled with relief. "Yes, Watts, that's exactly right. How about . . ." He thought for a moment. "The one in my study."

Watts tilted his head. "The one with Hercules fighting the lion?" He glanced toward Clementine. "Made of Derbyshire black marble?"

Edward nodded impatiently. "Yes, yes, that's the one." He looked at Clementine, who was looking at the floor. The clock, I knew, had been her father's and had been a wedding gift to Clementine.

"Respond in the affirmative, immediately."

We arrived at Hebering four nights later. It was located on the outskirts of Romsey and had been crafted from the ruins of a medieval priory. The building itself was Tudor at heart, more modern in its wings, but entirely imposing upon arrival. Even Edward looked nervous, twiddling with his white tie and flicking invisible bits of dust from his black top hat. He'd ingested half his roll of ginger chews before we arrived, I knew; I'd counted. He offered one to me and Clementine, and we both accepted.

The long drive was lined with lit torches and there appeared to be open-aired marquees set up by the lake. The house was ablaze with color, and there were perhaps two dozen carriages near the stable yard and carriage house. Our driver stopped for us to alight near the entrance; Edward carried the box with the clock in both hands, releasing it only to Lord Mansfield's man once at the door.

"Mr. and Mrs. Edward Everedge, and Miss Annabel Ashton," Mansfield's butler announced us. Lord and Lady Mansfield greeted us. I looked at Lord Mansfield straight on. With the exception of his long mustaches, which resembled the bristly fronds of a chimney broom, he was Marco, dead on. Lady Mansfield greeted me warmly, and I knew at that moment I should hold my tongue and say nothing to her of Marco. After all, she might feel him to be a threat to her own children, and their inheritance, though he was, of course, illegitimate and well provided for. Why had I thought this a good idea?

I thanked her for her hospitality, and then walked down the hallway, looking for a familiar face, adrift, out of my league. Marco caught my eye and raised an eyebrow, so I headed toward him. He was but a few feet from Clementine, who nodded her approval.

When I met with him, he took my elbow in his hand, gently, protectively, but perhaps with a tint of ownership as well.

"I couldn't be more delighted to see you here. I had hoped . . . You said you knew the Mansfields."

"I was not certain you'd come," I said. "She knew to invite you?"

"Lord Somerford sent me in his stead," he replied. "As they've gone north. He thought it would be good for Mansfield and me to talk. I'm not certain it's a sound idea, though, now I'm here. Mansfield would not meet my eye when I arrived."

Marco had certainly made his way into Lord Somerford's favor, and Somerford was a good enough man to want the family knitted together again, somehow, if it were possible.

Marco indicated the table set up in the center of the drawing room behind him. "I brought an offering." His voice was earnest. "I hope it impresses."

I did not have to look long to find which was his. "Your ship? The model of your ship?"

He grinned like a little boy. "Do you think he will like it? It says so much—about me, about my family, about our craftsmanship. And I'm English, too, correct?"

"How could Lord Mansfield not like it?" I asked. "You should speak with him tonight, as Lord Somerford suggested. Perhaps it is fate . . . or divine intervention . . . that you are here."

Marco shook his head no. "I've already determined not to."

"I think you should," I insisted. "It may go better than you think it will."

And then, you can stay in England.

He said nothing more.

We danced; my card was filled, and I enjoyed every man I danced with: the banter, the camaraderie, the sense of being equal with others and not looked down upon. I danced twice with Marco, and when he entwined his fingers through mine once he formed a lover's knot shape with his middle finger and thumb and slipped it over my wedding ring finger.

I did not look up at him to confirm his intention. I knew what he'd meant, or I thought I did. I did not withdraw my hand, and he pulled me closer.

After supper, Lady Mansfield had arranged for a casual display of fireworks over the lake. The weather cooperated, and I walked out with Clementine. We milled about the marquees and bonfires, waiting for the display to begin. When it did, the colors were splendid.

"They look rather like jewels falling from the sky, don't you think?" I asked Clementine.

She, rather melancholically, responded, "To me, they look like tears."

I put my arm around her shoulder, and she did not pull away. "Have Edward's discussions gone poorly?"

She shrugged. "I do not know. Captain Dell'Acqua said he would return with papers within the week. But it did not seem promising to me." She glanced at him then, standing nearby. "We should leave soon. Albert was unwell when we left."

I nodded, but my mind was not on the young boy. Perhaps I might intervene with Marco, for Edward, though as each day passed I loathed more and more being caught between them and their investment arrangements. However, I feared if I did not, Highcliffe would be lost. I excused myself and walked near enough to Marco to see he was with Lord Mansfield. He had decided to approach his father!

They did not notice me and I allowed myself to eavesdrop. They were, after all, in public.

". . . at your age I couldn't keep my hands off of anything in a dress." Lord Mansfield spoke boldly, his face rosy with drink. "Not sure I remember her, Carlotta. Yes, yes. Nice girl, wealthy Maltese shipping family. Yes, that's good. Good to know she's well. Now, lad, if there is nothing further I must return to my guests."

Marco stood, speechless, fists balled by his side. I didn't know whether or not I should approach him, but in the end, I decided I should. I walked next to him and slipped my hand over one of his fists, not caring if anyone saw or not. He was crushed; that was clear.

"I should not have come," he said. "And further, I should not have spoken to him. It would have been wise to regard that he did not return my correspondence. I cannot wait to leave this cold island."

I remonstrated with myself. I should not have intervened, selfishly hoping it would keep him near. "I'm sorry. He was thoughtless. Perhaps he was surprised."

Marco shook his head. "No. He just did not want me. I am, as you've said of yourself, *filius nullius.*"

"You are the son of our God," I whispered, hoping my voice would soothe and calm. "You are . . . beloved of many. Of *one.*" I emphasized the last word, hoping he understood that I meant myself.

He was not to be soothed.

"I'm sorry, Miss Ashton, but I must take my leave." He took off his hat and bowed toward me. "I hope the remainder of your evening is pleasant."

With that, he stalked off and, finding his colleagues, walked toward the carriage house while I watched. I heard him speak to one of the men in Maltese.

"I had two objectives when I arrived in this country and I achieved neither. Let's leave this place in our wake."

White fireworks shot into the black sky, the grand finale.

Gravity pulled them to earth like the teardrops coursing down my cheeks.

It took the carriage a silent hour until we three returned, worn and worried, wearied, to Highcliffe. I was ever so grateful that Edward and Clementine did not know that I had arranged for the evening. Edward went directly to his study upon arrival; Clementine raced up the stairway to Albert's rooms. I went to my own, and within minutes of having changed into my dressing gown heard a knock.

I opened the door. "Lillian."

She put her finger to her lips to shush me. "May I come in?"

I nodded and shut the door behind her. A fire had been lit when we were gone, and carefully tended. Unusual, but welcome. "Come, let's sit." I indicated the small sofa near the fire.

"I can't stay," she said. "Mrs. Everedge is with Albert, so I slipped away. I wanted you to know that, well, when Mrs. Everedge last called at the lending library, she asked Mr. Galpine about the letters to and from Malta, and examined the dates and postmarks. She asked him if she might tear the pages from the book, as a memento. When he said no . . ." She frowned. "She was most unhappy, and made that known to him. She said she'd soon send Mr. Everedge around. Mr. Galpine has stored the books with a friend for now."

Edward was concerned about those letters. As well he might be!

"Thank you," I said to her as she stood to leave. As she passed by my dressing table, she cast a reflexive glance toward it, one I might not have even noticed had I not been looking directly at her.

After letting her out and locking the door behind her, I returned to my dressing table. Everything was in place except for my mother's expensive ruby hair clips. They were gone. Someone must have taken them while we were at Hebering, because I had considered wearing them and had Maud try them on me that very evening.

Why had Lillian glanced toward the table, almost imperceptibly? Had she stolen the combs on Clementine's order? And if so, had Clementine sent her to speak with me about Galpine? The postmarks were now officially removed, although supposedly at Galpine's request, and could remain "gone" if need be.

I like my situation here, Lillian had once told me.

I lifted the chamber pot box and peeked underneath it, relieved to find the sketchbook present and untouched.

I still twitched with nerves all night. Marco blamed me for the disastrous meeting with his father. My combs and cap had been stolen. The postmarks had been "sent away." Mr. Morgan was soon to return, and, shortly, marry me and take me away to his house of plaster busts. I was utterly bereft of hope.

The next afternoon I was bothered by the strangest sensation, something that felt and sounded very much like an insect buzzing, and then I felt as though I would swoon. My tongue grew thick and heavy in my mouth, and I patted the back of my neck in a motherly action, perhaps to reassure myself, though I tried to keep it discreet and, eventually, seemed unable to stop the odd action.

Perhaps nervous energy was the cause of this growing discomfort?

"I'm sorry," I said, standing up unsteadily as Edward read the paper. Clementine came to her feet to steady me. "I'm unwell, um, er, not quite right."

"Can I help?" Clementine offered.

I shook my head, not trusting that the maze of letters formed in my mind could be uttered without confusion.

"Perhaps a doctor?" Edward's voice sounded far away, and deep. I thought I heard a dog bark in warning, though we had no such creature. And then I turned my head abruptly at the sound of Marco's sweet laughter.

"What is it?" Clementine asked, fanning herself.

I could not tell her. The captain, I knew, was nowhere near.

Clementine kindly, but knowingly, excused me for the evening; Mrs. Watts would bring a tray.

I returned to my rooms in a haze of strange misperception and nausea, voices drifting in and out of the room though no one was present. I thought of China, for some reason, but no reason at all. I could think of nothing but China: silks, opium, tea, fans—over and over the images from the Great Exhibition presented themselves. Why? I had not thought of them in months.

My stomach clenched and cold chills of fear ran through me as my thoughts raced without control no matter what I tried.

Next I heard people speaking Chinese, or what I thought was Chinese. Was it? Was it in my head? Aloud in the room? I did not know. I put my hands over my ears but the Chinese chatter did not stop.

I had never been to China, nor heard Chinese spoken. Yet I could not rid myself of the fixation! I wondered if I should try to travel there. I shook my head in horror at the thought. Why ever would I have that thought?

I washed my face in cool water from the basin again and again, but it did not help. The constant presence of unwanted, intrusive thoughts troubled me, then disturbed me, then scared me. I felt unremitting pressure inside my skull. I could not blink or shake away the voices or the images. Dread took command when I realized my inability to control my thoughts and my tongue grew too thick for me to swallow easily.

I could not bring myself to look at my Chinese dragon clock for fear of what it might provoke, and then the madness of such a thought filled me with further dread. When, after an hour, perhaps two or more, the sensations receded but would not disappear, I could no longer deny the truth.

I was nearly the age my mother had been when hers had started.

And now, my madness had begun.

CHAPTER TWENTY-SIX

MID-OCTOBER, 1851

A day or two later I heard Edward speaking to Clementine as they left the breakfast room; he mentioned that he'd sent a note, as she'd insisted, and that they should hear back soon.

His voice sounded distressed. Hers sounded pleased.

I passed him in the hall as he mentioned he was off to see his solicitor in Winchester, to potentially list Highcliffe for sale again, just in case. Clementine nodded sadly and then left to meet with Mrs. Watts; the packing might commence once more.

Marco had not returned, and, perhaps with the way things had unfolded at Hebering, he would not. If I saw him, maybe I could convince him that even were I to prove heiress, his dealings would be safe, because I was unwell and could not, therefore, inherit. By such an admission, perhaps I could save Highcliffe.

I could tell him that I had signs of madness. I worried night and day that the persistent Chinese images and sounds would reassert themselves. I had not slept well. I avoided tea, as it reminded me of China. Why China?

Such an admission, to madness, would be self-sacrificial for my family, and our home.

I could not bring myself to do it.

One other thing I did not think I could bring myself to do, but I found that I must, was ask Oliver to deliver a note for me, in confidence. I'd written to Marco and asked him to meet with me, privately, at the abbey ruins, two nights hence, when Clementine and Edward would be at a neighbor's supper party.

Oliver looked at me doubtfully but took the note. "I know you would not ask me to do this, miss, if it were not of utmost importance. I should not like Mr. Everedge to learn we have kept a second secret from him."

My heart broke. But if Highcliffe were saved, then Oliver and Emmeline's positions would be, too. Unless he was already in Edward's confidence.

"With all speed," I whispered. "To the *Poseidon*."

Although I was still a little tired and wan from my latest fit, I was feeling stronger by the hour. A letter had arrived, one that Clementine apparently had been waiting for with great impatience because she, not Watts, met Emmeline at the front door. She glanced at me, and then tucked it into her periodical. Perhaps she'd forget it . . . leave it there . . . and I could filch it later.

She paged through her magazines and returned to her room to get dressed for that afternoon's calls. I picked up and flipped through everything she had read.

No letter. She'd remembered.

Later that evening the carriage took off for the neighbors; I had pretended to eat dinner in my room, but I was too excited to do so. I remained in my room, which was lit only by the smallest fire as we were back to rationing coal. I watched the dragon clock tick by the required hours and then slipped my fur-lined cloak on.

I pulled the hood up and walked down the stairs. No one stopped me.

The fog rising from the ground enveloped me in its warm breath; I was grateful for the cover it provided. An owl cried sadly in the distance and then his call traveled up the treble clef to become more shrill. Was he preparing to kill? Or warning me? I shook the fanciful thought from my head and pushed opened the rotting door of the abbey.

It was hard to believe that one time, centuries ago, holy sisters had lived, prayed, worshiped, and served in here. The ceiling still showed the flying buttress design of the era, and the stones glowed, eerily, where my candle threw light. But the rooms were empty save for leftover barrels and lids and scraps of wood from the family's smuggling days that had, it seemed, come to a close.

Perhaps it was the weakness of my mind, or maybe it was the strength of my spirit, but I felt as though a spiritual presence was nearby, comforting me. I could, if I focused, detect the faintest bit of incense, perhaps from decades of worship, now smoked into the pocks and rivets of the very stones themselves.

A noise. Hoof steps and the sound of someone dismounting. My heart raced and I stood to the side of the door, just in case it was someone other than my expected.

The door opened creakily, its hinges protesting, and as Marco walked in, I stepped forth.

"You came," I said.

He smiled—warm, loving, tender, mine. "I came. Of course I came."

I nearly cried with relief. "I thought perhaps you were angry with me. You left so abruptly—your father, I'm so sorry." My words spilled forth in an undirected stream, but he seemed to know just what to do.

He took me in his arms, and his warm brown eyes, which tilted down at the corners like almonds, held my gaze. "Bella, that man is responsible for his own coldness."

That man. I understood. A different *that man* had abandoned my mother to her fate.

"I must apologize for the manner in which I handled my disappointment. I hurt you. I'm sorry. You reached out on my behalf, and I shan't forget that."

"I want to apologize for something, too," I said. "I . . . I fear I may have given you the wrong impression about Edward. He's not a bad man at heart, really. You can trust him in contractual arrangements."

He took my hand and led me to a corner where two empty gin barrels had been discarded and sat us down.

"Dearest Bella, that is not why I must cancel our arrangement."

I inhaled sharply. So he planned to cancel it.

"Should it be found that I am the heiress of the estate," I said, "I would certainly honor any arrangements he had made that were, well, legal. In moral standing."

He caressed the back of my hand; although he was a captain, his fingers were still callused from handling rope. "You shan't be found to be the heiress. After seeing the portrait with the marriage cap, I asked the solicitor in Lymington, under the guise of investing with Edward, if Edward had full legal rights to negotiate, or if, perhaps, there may be another claim to the estate."

I nodded, but couldn't swallow my fear.

"Lillywhite said he'd looked into it as recently as this very week and could find nothing to substantiate another claim. He did not mention you by name."

"Oh." My hopes and dreams disintegrated under the weight of reality. Mr. Lillywhite had at least given heed to my letter.

Marco put his hand under my chin and lifted it. "You are a good woman, a beautiful woman, Bella." He switched to Maltese. "I don't want to leave you."

"Then don't go," I answered reflexively in the same language before realizing I had not told him I could speak Maltese.

His eyes widened, his face flushed, and he stood up. "You speak Maltese!" His voice conveyed anger. Perhaps he had not meant me to understand what he'd said.

"I do," I admitted. "I'm sorry, perhaps you did not mean for me to understand your sentiments."

"Why did you not tell me this? To deceive me? To learn secrets to share with your cousin?"

I shook my head. "No. And please do not pretend you were not enjoying the information I provided to you whilst negotiating with Edward."

He nodded. It was true. I continued in a softer voice. "When I was in Winchester, many years as a student, and then as a teacher, I wanted to know something, anything, of my parents. It was then that I found the church, and a kind, elderly Maltese nun named Sister Rita who found me sitting in the back. She'd offered to teach Maltese to me, after hearing my tale. I loved the tangle of Italian, which I already knew, of course, and Arabic. She alone knew I could speak it. I told no one else because . . . it was one thing I could keep for myself."

No one could shame me for it or trade upon it, or steal it, I wanted to say. *Like my combs. Like my cap. Like my dignity.*

"Ah. I understand." He took both my hands in his own. "I'm sorry, lovely Bella. And while I did not have the courage to say it in English, to risk my affections, now I'm very glad that you know how I feel about you. Come with me. Come to Malta. Leave the cold English behind."

"You could remain here," I said.

"And be English like Lord Mansfield?" He flushed in anger again.

"You could be English like me," I said.

He laughed, but then shook his head. "I must sail on the tide day after next. My men, my cargo, my new investment arrangements."

So he'd replaced Edward. Would he so easily replace me?

"You will like it there." He reached up with the hand that had been cupping my chin to trace the outline of my face. "The art, the statues. You are almost like one of them, the dark, glossy hair, your sea-blue eyes, but you are not cold marble. You are a woman, and," he teased, "marble does not have freckles."

Far from breaking the moment, that light jest drew me to him. "It is not good to point out a woman's imperfections," I said with a grin.

"I would not, I have not," he said, his voice somber. "There is no imperfection." He drew close to me, our faces nearly touching.

"Come with me," he said again. "I feel I cannot leave you. My thoughts, my heart, they are drawn to you."

And yet I had promised Father Gregory that I would make or take no vow without discussing it with him first. If my mother had done that, I might not be in this difficult predicament.

He spoke in Maltese—rough, guttural, emotional, longing. "If you allow me to kiss you just once, I promise I won't ask again."

"You expect it to be a disagreeable experience, then?" I teased lightly in the same language, but my mind was swirling again, this time in the best possible manner. I was upended, I was warm, I was vibrantly alive. Was it true, was there no way that my mother's claim could be proved? Then why should I remain in England?

"By no means, Bella." His voice was thick.

I leaned toward him, nearly touching his lips, and he understood it to be the permission he'd sought.

He put his hand on the back of my hair and gently drew me toward him. His lips touched mine lightly, then they kissed each cheek, as a man claiming the woman he loves. He kissed my eyelids as someone only does for someone he cherishes. He kissed my mouth once, softly, lightly. I lost myself completely in the moment.

I was about to pull away, for the sake of propriety, when the door to the abbey was flung open.

"What is going on here?" Clementine stood, hands on her hips, with two large stable boys by her side. "One of the men saw a light and came to fetch Watts. I insisted on going myself."

There was no answer to be given. She'd caught his lips on mine.

Marco stood and tried to speak.

"You, sir, did my husband wrong and now you're tainting his cousin's good name and honor. Depart immediately!"

Marco turned and looked at me, held my gaze for a moment. He started to walk back toward me, striding, actually, but the two stable books quickly blocked his way. He began to speak, and as he did, Clementine took me by the arm, and the stable hands now moved to stand in front of us.

"It will go worse for her if you do not leave immediately," she said to Marco. I caught his eye and nodded. He said nothing more, but somehow, in some way, I believed he conveyed to me that he would return. Clementine kept my arm firmly in hers and led me toward the house.

"And you! Just as we'd feared. Moral madness is manifesting itself here in my home. I should have thought you'd have known better, but clearly, some things cannot be forestalled. Insanity. Immorality."

"*You* dare to remonstrate with *me* about that?"

She flinched at the reminder that Albert had been born but seven months from her marriage, but said nothing more, still hustling me toward the house.

My emotions whirled from the night—the declaration of love, the kiss, the apprehension, the send-off, the fear that bloomed inside me.

"'Tis a good thing I stayed home with Albert and Edward went on his own. No telling how far things might have got. Or had they already?" She threw an accusing glance at me.

"No, of course, nothing like that," I said.

"Good." She hurried me up the stairs. "We wouldn't want history repeating itself. Edward will be home soon, and we'll deal with this matter tomorrow."

Shortly thereafter I heard a noise like a heavy piece of furniture being placed in front of my door.

A tray was brought up for me for breakfast, but I was so shaken I couldn't eat any of it. I drank nothing because I did not want to have to use the chamber pot. Later, I watched out of my window as the Somerfords' carriage pulled up at teatime. I could not hear what was said, but about twenty minutes later I saw Edward walk to the carriage with Lady Somerford, waving in a friendly manner. Had she come to speak with me and been turned away? Or had her visit had nothing at all to do with me? Even from the distance I could see that Edward looked wan and distressed. He stumbled on the lower step before catching himself. His face looked pained. Perhaps he felt remorse at having locked me away and kept my friend from me.

He should.

Another hour ticked past and Marco came riding in. I quickly dressed, hoping that he would insist on seeing me and that we could, somehow, talk reasonably with Edward. Perhaps if we could settle the investment arrangements once more, Edward would be appeased.

A half hour ticked by on the dragon clock. I tried to open my door, but was still blocked in.

Shortly after that I heard loud voices downstairs. I heard Watts close the door and ran back to my window. Marco rode off, not having been escorted out by Edward. I didn't have to wonder too long what had happened. Edward appeared at my door very shortly thereafter, with Clementine quivering like aspic behind him.

"May I come in?" He stood at the door once I'd opened it.

"Of course," I said, glad that I had taken time to dress properly. Maud had not tended to my needs for some days.

"I believe you saw our guest leave," he began. He did not sit down, as I did, as Clementine had. Instead, he paced like one of the lions at London's zoological park, which I had visited with the Rogers school. He rubbed his temple over and over.

"Lady Somerford," I began smoothly. "I wondered at her visit."

"She came to call upon Clementine, as lady of the house." Edward's voice was snide. "To deliver a letter from Lady Leahy. They've become friends."

I looked sharply at Clementine. "I had no idea." Perhaps this was why my painting had not been given to Elizabeth. To sever my ties with her and replace them with ties to Clementine.

Clementine shrugged. Her face was drawn, and she looked as though she'd had little more sleep than I had.

"I meant Captain Dell'Acqua. His visit was, I'm certain, related to the unfortunate and compromising situation my wife found you in last evening. I told him to leave, to sail away, and never to return. He seems to have agreed."

"Your investments together . . ."

"He's terminated those arrangements, Annabel. Decided to do it late last night, apparently, as I had not had definite word before then. Due, in all likelihood, to the manner in which you conducted yourself with him. I asked you to do *one thing*, Annabel, to help the family, which was to smooth the path with the Maltese. You could not do that."

"Family? You are not family to me, Edward, not in the ways that count, no matter how long I'd wished that otherwise. It is certainly not my fault that your dealings went wrong. Marco told me . . ."

Clementine inhaled. "Marco?"

Edward looked self-satisfied, catlike contentment spreading across his face. "How intimate! What did Marco tell you?"

"He'd already decided to terminate the agreement before yesterday."

Edward seemed startled, but not shaken. "No doubt he had a sword up his sleeve the entire time, the foreigner. Once he found he couldn't have his way with you . . . thanks to Clementine's intervention . . . he'd concluded all he came for. Too late, I might add, for me to pursue other interests who were in attendance at the Great Exhibition. I shall, I promise, find better, more satisfactory arrangements."

"It wasn't like that." I stood up. "He . . . he asked me to marry him."

"He *asked you to marry him*? Unbelievable."

"He said . . ." My spirit fell. In actuality, he had not asked me to marry him. He'd asked me to come away with him.

"He said?" Clementine prompted.

"It was a private conversation."

"Like the other ones inside your head," Edward threw at me. Then he indicated that Clementine should stand up and motioned for her to join him by the door.

I closed my eyes. There was nothing I could say that would change his mind. He was angry and I was lost.

"When will Mr. Morgan return?" I asked, my voice heavy with shades of gray.

Edward nearly pushed Clementine through the door and then looked back to me. "Given the circumstances, Morgan will not be returning. Instead, I've sent a note to the doctor, asking him to send a nurse to help care for women in your . . . circumstances. She'll arrive this afternoon."

Of course. There may not have been proof—yet—of my legitimacy, but the proof was steadily stacking up. Edward could not allow me to be thought of as sane, nor to marry. When my legitimacy was proved, I, and my child, would take all.

He pulled the door shut, and I sank into my bed.

He'd like me to believe that the circumstance he referred to meant my mental well-being. But I knew what circumstance truly concerned him: my legitimacy and his likely loss of legacy.

Two hours later, the nurse arrived.

CHAPTER TWENTY-SEVEN

Clementine brought her to my door. I let them into my rooms, and we three sat in the small sitting area.

She looked to be about thirty years old; I had been expecting someone much older. Her face was unlined, and her hair was pulled back rather severely in a nurse's cap. She had a medical bag with her. I wondered what kinds of instruments and elixirs were hidden within; horror stories I'd read and heard about pressed into my mind, and I grew cold at the core.

"My name is Mrs. Strange." She leaned toward me. I almost laughed out loud at her name; did it not strike any of them as ironic? If Clementine were to laugh, it would be taken as poor manners, but for me to laugh aloud would be to call my sanity further into question. Once people are predisposed to believe something about you, proof offered or not, it was difficult to dissuade them from that position. In their minds, every action, word, or insight only added weight to their already foregone conclusion.

I was well accustomed to deflecting unspoken accusations. I would handle this one well.

"And I am Miss Annabel Ashcroft," I said. "How do you do? Thank you for journeying out here from . . ."

"Other parts," she said, offering nothing, which won a nod of approval from Clementine.

"I am certain I do not need your administrations," I said.

"But Mr. Everedge is certain you do," Clementine pressed softly.

"I'm here to help," Mrs. Strange said, her voice soothing.

"Edward wrote to the doctor, the doctor wrote to a specialist, and he sent Mrs. Strange," Clementine said. "I am certain you'll be well cared for upstairs."

"Upstairs?" I stood up and looked for a way to the door; I'd bolt outside and run toward Pennington if need be, though I did not know if anyone was still in residence there.

Clementine stood also, then blocked my way and closed the door.

"I am not going upstairs!" I shouted toward her, toward the door. I repeated it, shouting ever more loudly. "There is no reason to quarantine me, as you well know!"

Perhaps someone in the hallway would hear me. Clementine understood my intentions.

"It's not likely any will hear you," she said. "And if they do, your ravings will only confirm what most of us, staff included, have come to believe. You've inherited your mother's . . . condition. It's well known to be passed in families. It comes upon people at similar ages. You're very close in age, aren't you, to when your mother was locked away?"

I looked around the room for any way out. Mrs. Strange stood, too. Would the two of them physically restrain me if need be?

"I. Am. Not. Mad," I said. "There is no reason to confine me."

A memory slammed into my consciousness.

"Judith! Judith, you cannot separate me from Annabel. There is no reason for this, as you well know."

I cowered behind my mother whilst servants packed her things in this very room. A woman, in the corner of the room, looked like, looked like . . . I could not see her clearly.

"Annabel?" Clementine's voice snapped me back to the present. "I've just said that Mrs. Strange will pack your things and deliver them upstairs for you."

"I can pack my own things, thank you very much." I did not want Mrs. Strange or anyone else touching my belongings. "Several of my things have gone missing and I'd like to see to what remains myself."

Clementine sighed, and Mrs. Strange looked, patiently, at the floor. "You've said that a cap has gone missing, a cap no one else has seen. You've said you had a proposal from a man, but cannot remember the words. What else is missing?" Disbelief colored her voice. "More wild accusations are not going to help you. Next thing you'll be accusing us of poisoning your food."

"That, in particular, is a common concern many of the . . . that many of those who are mentally unstable voice." Mrs. Strange, unhelpfully, added her experience to Clementine's allegation. "Poisoning, that is."

I could not speak of the missing hair clips and add to her litany of doubt. So I said nothing. Had they, somehow, poisoned my food? Perhaps my convalescent trays? It would have to have been done without Chef's knowledge. Added afterward.

Or perhaps this, too, was the fevered imagination of a person under exceptional nervous tension.

Someone had heard me shout. Suddenly, I heard footsteps; Clementine opened the door, and two footmen and a stable boy stood there. Each averted his eyes.

"Come along." Clementine took my arm. "Quietly and on your own is better, but I can have assistance if need be."

I was very glad, then, that the hallway had been cleared of those I knew and loved so they would not witness my shame.

Realizing, now, there was no way out, I walked of my own accord, scrimping together whatever dignity remained. She brought me to the quarantine room and locked it from the outside. I hadn't even known it could be locked. Had a lock been newly added?

The cot was now made up, and I sat upon it. Then I lay down. I noticed, for the first time, that the paint was peeling from the plastered ceiling, where it blistered and boiled like burnt flesh; black mold bled out from within the gaps between paint and wall. For the first time, I noticed that the room smelt both damp and stale, like a drained pond.

I closed my eyes and thought about my mother and how distraught she must have been when separated from me. When I'd been old enough to enquire, I'd simply been told that she'd died, away, of a broken heart. Later, Edward told me the truth. I could remember no more of that time; perhaps that was a blessing. Had she known she would never leave this room except to be taken to the asylum?

I sat upright in a cold sweat. Was that what Edward intended for me?

Shortly, there was a knock on the door. Mrs. Strange appeared, Oliver behind her, carrying my trunk. He, too, would not meet my gaze, and his eyes looked as though he may have been crying.

"Thank you, Oliver." I hoped to reassure him with a quiet voice, but he only nodded.

"I've packed all your belongings," Mrs. Strange said, her voice almost hypnotizing. I supposed that was helpful in her profession. "Your room will now be packed and cleaned. The house is to be sold within the month or so."

"I . . . I had no idea," I said. That soon. She stood nearby while I looked through my trunks.

The sketchbook was not in there. But if I did not say something to her now I might never get it back. With the exception of the necklace tucked underneath my dress, it was the only thing of my parents left to me. I had to speak up.

"I know this might seem odd," I began, realizing, perhaps for the first time, how peculiar it would look to others. "But I hid my sketchbook, something very dear to me, under the box that held the chamber pot, underneath my bed. Could you fetch it?"

Mrs. Strange smiled, well, strangely, before answering. "I'm very used to thoroughly looking in every nook and cranny for my patients," she said. "I did find it. But I decided you would be better off without it."

"What?" I nearly shouted. She remained calm in the face of my angry vent. "Why would you decide that? You've no right."

"It's my sacred duty to do what is best for you," she answered serenely, and at that moment an intense burst of lava-like hatred coursed through me: toward this nurse, toward Edward, toward Clementine and my father, and even toward Marco, who had abandoned me. "Will that be all?"

I nodded, not trusting myself to speak. I could not even bring it up with Clementine—she'd believe it to be another imagined misdoing. Mrs. Strange pulled the door closed behind her.

I, Annabel Ashton, was the last evidence of my mother and father's love, their marriage, and the legacy that rightly belonged to my mother, and, therefore, to me! I had the forbidding feeling that I would soon, like the other evidence, be destroyed as well.

I ate little that night, not trusting the food, but was ill rewarded for my temperance anyway with a mild hallucination: my head pounded and I heard bits and pieces of conversations between teachers I'd once known, urging me to act, though they could not possibly know of my present situation. A dog again, in my mind's eye; I'd never owned a dog. I pushed the thought away. Perhaps it was true; I was insane. Thoughts of China still troubled my mind now and again. I'd told no one.

There would be no reason for them to continue to poison my food anymore, if there ever had been. I drank more tea; it did not matter now, for I could use the chamber pot as I needed to and Mrs. Strange would empty it. As the sun set, my life was darkened by hopelessness.

Before I went to bed, I looked out of the window. I did my level best not to notice the stained glass; I did not care to see the angels tending the Lord in His time of need when He had left me utterly alone in mine. Through the spyglass I observed Marco's ship still in the harbor.

Perhaps there was a chance. I humbled myself, knelt by my bed, and asked God to send Marco to save me.

When I awoke early the next morning, I slipped out of my cot and into the icy room. I ran to the window and what I saw made me cry. My prayer had not been favorably answered, but why blame God? The man himself had not returned for me. I tried to push away an image of the beautiful Miss Emily Baker. Perhaps Marco had finalized arrangements with her brother instead of with Edward.

The *Poseidon* had sailed. In the end, perhaps, it had been as Edward had said. When Marco no longer needed me as a comfortable and social go-between, and I would not run off with him, he shrugged and left.

Had my father done that, too?

Marco's—no, Captain Dell'Acqua's—friends had predicted that he would insinuate himself into my life and then avenge his mother. That must have felt like ointment on the wounding burn his father had made. Now, he'd left me. Wooed and abandoned. In the time-honored manner of rogues.

And yet . . . I closed my eyes, remembering his lips upon my cheeks, my eyelids, his hand steady against the back of my head, his beard rough on my jawline.

That kiss.

I dressed myself; I was well able to take care of myself, as I had for years. My mind had remained clear, and for that I was grateful—and curious, truth be told. I was sitting on my bed with a book when a knock came. I expected it to be Nurse Strange, who I understood was taking my old room, but no, it was Edward.

He opened the door. "May I come in?"

I did not rise to greet him. "What choice do I have?"

He did not offer a false smile and at that point, I did not expect one.

"I expect you'll have watched the *Poseidon* sail," he said.

"You've many faults to answer for, Edward, as do we all. But taking pleasure in someone else's misfortune is not one I would have ascribed to you."

He looked properly shamed. *Good.*

He sat on the small chair near the cot and poured two cups of tea. Only after he drank some did I.

"You could have taken vows," he said, glancing at my rosary, which rested near my cot. "Clementine said that was under consideration. The driver overheard you telling Lady Leahy. He passed it along to my driver. He shared it with one of the maids. She told Clementine." He finished his tea and poured himself another cup.

Yes. I had told Lady Leahy in the carriage.

"Even the priest was sent to enquire."

"My confessor? You pressured him into asking me?" I did not care how shrill my voice was.

"No, nothing of the sort—he couldn't be pressed," Edward admitted. "We just wondered aloud, in his presence, if the decision had perhaps weighed too heavily on your mind."

"I have no calling to take holy vows." I finished my tea and set the cup down with a clatter.

"That became eminently clear with the frolicking with Dell'Acqua."

"It was hardly frolicking, Edward." I could have, but did not, point out that Albert had arrived early, two months shy of Edward's nine-month wedding anniversary. My cousin had hastily married a girl he'd barely known and who had not been his mother's choice.

"Whatever it was, it was irregular, and as much as we wish this kind of thing was not passed through the generations, it often is." He stood; and as he did, he wobbled. He didn't look alarmed in the least. And then the cabinet behind him wobbled and I realized that neither was wobbling—I was seeing them, instead, in waves.

"The doctor is downstairs," he said. "That is what I've come to tell you. He will accompany Mrs. Strange upstairs to examine you for . . . lunacy."

I stood up in shock. "No. Edward. No. I will not be examined!"

"But I say you shall." He took my arm to both stead and restrain me, and once he set me down on the cot again he used the speaking tube to ask Oliver to send up the nurse and the doctor.

They arrived shortly.

The doctor examined me and I did my best to appear clear and level-headed, but I felt my focus go in and out and thoughts seem to pass from my left ear to my right and back. I wasn't sure if I spoke them aloud.

"Let me ask you a few simple questions, Miss Ashton," he said. "If I may."

I nodded.

"I understand from your family that you believe people are trying to defraud you."

"It's not what I believe, Doctor, it's what is, indeed, happening right here. Any number of people will tell you this is true!"

He stroked his mustache. "I've made some enquiries. Unfortunately, your concerns have not been validated."

He made some notes in a book. "So it would seem to be that others are conspiring against you?"

I nodded. But this did not seem to be the right answer, as he made more notes and grunted.

"Have you caused your loved ones to suffer apprehension and alarm because of your actions?"

"No," I said.

"Yes," Edward amended that firmly.

"Is there a family history of mental imbalance?"

He made notes before I could answer, though, so it was clear he knew that my mother had been declared insane.

He then stepped just outside my door, on the small landing at the top of the stairs, to confer with Mrs. Strange and Edward. Of course I could hear them. We were but feet away.

"I think it would do her good to have a restful stay somewhere . . . else." He seemed to address this comment to Edward. "If you feel it's best."

"I do," he said. "It pains me to admit this is the course of her life, but it is. I cannot allow it to interfere in my household, with my young son. And most important, she could become a danger to herself."

A danger to myself? I was about to march out of there, but then someone might insist on restraining me henceforth. With ties or straps.

"Could it be a long stay?" Edward's voice was tentative.

"As long as you deem it necessary," the doctor said. "We normally leave these decisions in the hands of the family, who know the patients best. Now, to where should she be sent?"

"My wife has assembled a short list of suitable institutions." Edward's voice again.

Mrs. Strange spoke up. "Perhaps Medstone would do?"

Medstone! My mother had been committed there and had not returned. Did Edward even recall the name?

"It's nearby, and I know the staff there quite well . . ." She let the insinuation hang. "I've worked there quite often. I would have quite a bit of autonomy to help manage her affairs, as it were, until matters were fully settled."

"I will not go. I do not agree!" I shouted toward the door.

Apparently, Edward did agree with Mrs. Strange's implication. He completely ignored me, as did they all. "Yes, that will be fine. You'll submit your receipts at the conclusion of your duties?"

She must have nodded because I heard nothing but, shortly, she returned to check on me before going to my rooms to pack my remaining items.

I was to be committed to the insane asylum. My greatest fear was coming to pass.

"Don't be afraid," she said soothingly. "I will accompany you."

I did not answer. I could not be expected to be happy that

someone in Edward's employ was to escort me cheerfully to and through the gates of hell.

My mind was still unclear. "I must lie down. Go away."

She nodded and patted the back of my hand. "We will leave on the morrow." After leaving me, she locked the door behind her.

A few hours later I was rested though I still felt worn, and I did not know if it was due to illness or the desperation of the situation I found myself in. I decided to call down, through the speaking tube, and have someone deliver a carafe of water or wine and some food, as I was hungry. Mrs. Watts told me she'd send someone up straightaway.

Quite soon afterward, Mrs. Strange knocked on my door. "Dinner tray," she said, setting the tray on the small table. "Medstone may bring you unexpected peace."

"My mother was committed to Medstone twenty years ago."

"Yes," she said. "I'm very well aware of that."

I waited for her to say more on the matter, but she did not. "Would you like me to give you something to sleep? A tincture?"

"No, thank you."

"It might help. But you should be careful not to take too much. It could make you comatose, or worse."

Was she suggesting something morbid? "I shan't need anything, thank you," I said firmly.

"I shall fetch you at eight, then," she said. "Sleep sweetly."

Indeed.

She pulled the door shut behind her. I drank the water and ate the meal, which was beautifully plated, all my favorites. I saw Chef's hand behind it and squeezed back tears.

My last meal at Highcliffe. I was too hungry and thirsty to forego food and drink, but I did not take tea and did not touch the honey pot. Why did I recoil at them?

My mind, clear now, could see.

More wild accusations are not going to help you. Next thing you'll be accusing us of poisoning your food, Clementine had said.

I had never liked partnering her at cards. She could not stop herself from prematurely revealing what she held in her hand.

But poisoning me with what? Perhaps . . . perhaps the tea, the Chinese tea, was what had provoked my mind. The disturbing hallucinations were related to China. Chinese tea.

The tea? We all drank it. Of course. I was the only person in the household who took honey with her tea, and Edward had found some way to corrupt it. Well, Edward took honey as well. But he, better than anyone, would know when to use it and when not to.

Edward had been poisoning me.

CHAPTER TWENTY-EIGHT

MEDSTONE, A PRIVATE HOSPITAL AND LUNATIC ASYLUM
LATE OCTOBER TO EARLY NOVEMBER, 1851

I was ready early; I could not sleep and had very little to prepare. Mrs. Strange arrived to escort me to the main foyer. We stopped at the second floor for just a moment, and she allowed me a glimpse into my old rooms, my mother's old rooms.

They were packed again; Mrs. Watts had been busy. The Chinese dragon clock, which did not provoke unsettled feelings, blessedly, remained on the mantel but had not been wound.

Time had completely stopped for me, too. What could I do? There was nowhere, and no way, to escape.

The staff lined up in the vestibule leading to the hallway and nodded or said good-bye. Some looked nervous. Perhaps they truly believed me mad. Chef hugged me like a child, which caused me to cry a little. I steadied myself to take the small box he held out to me.

"*Les bon bons* for the long journey," he whispered, his voice hoarse.

Clementine and Edward were waiting by the door, without Albert, of course. They would not want to subject him to a fuss.

Clementine kissed my cheek. "Good-bye, dearest Annabel. We shall visit."

Edward kissed both cheeks, too. "I'm sorry," he said. "There is no other way."

Oliver lifted my bag, and as he and I followed Mrs. Strange down the steps and toward the carriage that had been sent from the asylum, he tugged on my arm. We were of a height, and he leaned over.

"I put a pouch in your bag," he said. "When I was collecting your things to carry down. It's from the foreign captain. He tried to speak with you, but Mr. Everedge would not let him. He slipped it to me, and I said I would try to pass it along."

My spirits lifted, if just a little. What could be in the pouch? A note? Evidence of something important? I dared not look now and call attention to it.

"Thank you, Oliver," I said, keeping my voice low. "Please, if you can, let Lady Leahy or Lady Somerford know where I have been taken. Ask them to assist in any way possible, and with all haste."

He nodded. We reached the carriage, which was not dilapidated but not exactly one of quality, either. The driver held the door for me. I refused to step up and so, with firmness, a footman took my arm and lifted me in, forcibly. Mrs. Strange was helped in and then closed and locked the door behind us.

I had never been locked in a carriage before. We were off to the lunatic asylum.

Our journey took nearly an hour through deep and isolated countryside, and then we reached Medstone.

It was an imposing building; I knew from my earlier enquiries, when trying to know something of my mother, that it was a private institution and hospital. I was grateful for that; it meant that I should not have to suffer from the sometimes squalid and rougher conditions of the public asylums. But it also meant that, in practicality, my cousin had more control over my stay here. Perhaps that was why he was willing to brook the extra expense. The changes in the Lunacy Act six years earlier mostly affected the poor and the criminally insane. The doctors at Medstone would be in his pay.

"It's large . . ." I shivered and peered out the window. The lawns were dead brown with the season; the clouds hung low over the building that sprawled in many directions like spider legs extending from a gorged abdomen in the middle. There were no fences. There would be no place to go if someone were able to escape anyway.

"Seven hundred patients," Mrs. Strange said. "Some worse off than others."

"So many." I had no idea.

"'Tis been said that one in four hundred of Her Majesty's English subjects resides in an insane asylum."

"Now I'm to be one of them."

She nodded.

"They surely cannot all be mad, not that many."

"Some are, and some are not," Mrs. Strange said. She sat serenely, not fidgeting with her gloves as I was tempted to do.

A clutch of cottages appeared to the right of the drive.

"Where the attendants live," she said.

We pulled up to a side door, and I felt myself begin to perspire.

We alighted from the carriage; Mrs. Strange took my arm. I did not know if it was to steady me or to keep me from bolting. We made our way up the stairs; the air was crisp and cold and

smelt of wood smoke. I half expected to hear howling and scream-
ing but as we opened the door, a pleasant hum of distant conversation filtered through the halls. She spoke briefly with an
attendant, and then we walked a few feet to the medical supervi-
sor's office.

It was clear he was expecting us. His eyes never left me; instead, they traveled, most inappropriately, up and down my
person.

"Nurse Strange, how nice to see you again," he said. "Miss
Ashton, we're delighted to be of service."

"Thank you," I responded. "Though I am certain it is quite un-
necessary."

He nodded. "That's a frequently expressed sentiment.
Please . . ." He motioned toward two seats across from his desk.
"Have a seat. As the medical officer has already sent me his report
with the correspondence package Mr. Everedge conveyed, I have
but a few questions to ask you before preparing a report for the
Justice of the Peace, who will finalize the decision on your stay
with us." He pulled a book from the case behind him, *The Physiog-
nomy of Mental Diseases*, and stared at my face as he turned
pages. Finally, he spoke again.

"When did you start to feel . . . unusual?"

"I don't feel unusual," I said, but then I remembered the first fit
I'd had, after having taken Clementine's sugar.

"Come now, Miss Ashton. Mistruths are hardly the way the
mentally well handle difficult situations."

"I suppose I felt a little dizzy after having taken some of my
cousin's sugar cubes with tea. I suspect they had a *substance* in
them."

He made notes. "Did anyone else partake of these cubes?"

"My cousin's wife, I suppose."

"Did she have similar symptoms?"

I shook my head.

"It's common for our patients to feel that someone is poisoning their food. You are not alone in this concern." He made some notes.

"Often, people are made to feel, well, unbalanced when their situation changes. I understand you had recently moved back to Highcliffe?"

"I was forced to," I said.

"Physically?" His eyebrows raised.

"By circumstance."

He nodded quietly. Nurse Strange rested her hand upon my arm, which was a comfort.

"Mrs. Everedge said that there was a romantic attachment that went wrong?"

"Certainly not. It would not have gone wrong without her direct intervention, in any case," I retorted.

"She mentioned that she had chanced upon an inappropriate situation."

"It was not like that," I protested. "She's only saying that because my cousin wants to steal my property."

He sighed. *Yes, I know, another common delusion among the insane.*

"Her claim is false but she was believed, due to my mother being a patient here, decades ago."

The doctor gently bobbed his head. "Mr. Everedge had written a note relaying that he felt perhaps your symptoms first began to show when you took over your mother's rooms at Highcliffe. That memories of her may have triggered your flights and figments. Would that be correct?"

"I cannot say that is the cause of anything," I said. I now understood why Mrs. Strange had removed the sketchbook. She thought, wrongly, that it gave further rise to my imbalance. I suspected I would not have been allowed to keep it, in any case, here.

"That is all," he said, writing the word *delusional* on my chart. "You'll have a private room, of course, and Mrs. Strange is familiar with our procedures. You could not have asked for a better nurse." He smiled brightly at her, and she looked at her hands, modestly.

He stood, and so did we. "How long shall I expect to stay?" I asked.

"Our goal is the restoration of your health, of course," the doctor said, his manner cold and slippery, like a just-caught fish. "But we find that fewer than one in ten of our patients ever leave. You may, like they, find it so comfortable that all desire to leave will flee, after time."

I thought not.

He bid us good day and a woman came to deliver a packet of information to Mrs. Strange, including which room should be mine.

"It's on a good ward," she said. "Not too close to the infirmary, where the ill are treated. Not always successfully."

"Do . . . do a lot of people pass on?"

Sorrow crossed her face. "I cannot lie to you. Perhaps one in five patients admitted here each year die. Young and old."

"My mother . . ." I began.

"Consumption took her," she said knowingly.

We passed a bench in the hallway where a woman sat, silent but straining forward, crowded on both sides by two young women in uniform who pressed into her; it looked painful. Tears rolled down the woman's face but she did not stop them. The attendants to her side nodded at Mrs. Strange as we passed by. Once we were clear of them, I asked, "What are they doing?"

"It's a gentler form of restraint," she answered. "Their tight presence calms the patient, and once she is settled they will allow her freedom to move about again. They will use ties to restrain, if need be. Knowing that, the patient is more likely to comply."

Sweat trickled down my spine, and I dabbed my hairline, under my bonnet, with a linen kerchief I'd tucked into my pocket. Soon we reached Room 204. My new home.

My forever home? I swallowed hard and turned the knob. The doors had no locks. The medical superintendent's lewd appraisal flitted worryingly through my mind.

We entered the room, which was small, a false hearth on one wall. There was a wooden bed and a dressing table, along with a tiny wardrobe. On the dressing table was a book of prayers and a Bible.

"Might I have Catholic materials?" I asked.

The nurse nodded. "I shall ask for a priest to visit you, as most patients attend services that the chaplain holds."

"He's Anglican," I said.

She nodded. "I shan't enquire for a week or more, as we won't want them to believe you to be tipping into religious mania."

My eyes widened. "No, indeed."

There were two chairs, which she said meant she could spend time with me often. "I will be with you occasionally throughout the day, but you shall also have time to yourself."

She explained how the days would proceed. Waking early, toilette, bathing once per week, hair washing an additional day if I so desired. Meals, time spent industriously at tasks assigned, leisure, meals, and bed.

Day after day. Month after month, until I became the one in five who mercifully died.

"May I send letters?" I asked. "Or receive them?"

"They are under no requirement to pass along any mail,

coming or going, except to the Lunacy Commission. I suspect your cousin has left strict instructions that there is to be no correspondence, except from him."

I expected so.

"I'll return this evening after your tea, before bed," she said as she left. "Be at peace."

Be at peace? I had been wrongly committed to an asylum!

I sat on the narrow bed, and after a time, a knock came on the door. "Miss Ashton?" I stood and opened it.

"I'm Mrs. Brown." An older woman with a large scar across her face angled her considerable self into my room. "I'm here to go through your things."

CHAPTER TWENTY-NINE

"Go through my things?"

"Yes. Are you deaf?" Her face was suffused with malice and I trembled with fear. "To remove anything that might be a danger."

"To myself?"

"And to others. Sewing needles and the like."

"I'm not allowed to do needlework?" Not that it was an activity I particularly enjoyed, but I would like to be able to mend my things if need be.

"After some months you may, if considered worthy, join with the patients who are allowed to sew."

She looked through my few belongings; I had been allowed only one small bag and it did not take her long. She came across the pouch Marco had given me. "What is this?"

"A gift from a friend," I said. I hoped she would not ask me what was inside; if I said I did not know, it would surely confirm my diagnosis more securely. She opened the velvet pouch and reached in.

"An oyster shell?" She looked at me quizzically.

"Er, yes, he's a sailor." I was puzzled as well. *An oyster shell?*

She took it, opened it, and shook it. "Empty."

I nodded, as if I expected that. But I hadn't. What did it mean? That he'd opened himself up to our love and, in the end, found it empty?

"The shells would be sharp if broken." She tucked it into her pocket. "Jewelry?" she asked.

"One necklace, my mother's, which I constantly wear," I said.

"May I see it?"

I tentatively pulled it from under my gown.

"It has a sharp end," she said.

"It's rather blunt," I disagreed. I softened my voice and pled, all pride gone. "Please let me keep this. It's all I have left."

She hesitated and then nodded. "You'll hear the meal bells," she said. "Don't dawdle." She pulled the door shut behind her.

Why had Marco sent the empty shell? It had been so important that he'd given it to Oliver to pass along. To hurt me? I did not believe so, though he may not have been the man I hoped him to be.

Or he may have been. I would never know now, as I would not even be allowed to write to him.

I began arranging the items she'd unpacked. I'd been allowed two gowns, two pairs of shoes, some grooming items, and what was this? Oh dear!

I took Mr. Poe's vile volume in hand. The book's tone was dark and hopeless. The very fact that it had been a gift from Mr. Morgan made it worse.

I laughed aloud. I had escaped Mr. Morgan! I laughed again and then I began to cry. I quieted my sobs; I did not wish to be restrained between two burly women. Stifling my sobs caused me to heave, and I curled up on my bed and, eventually, cried myself to sleep.

I awoke to a knock at the door. "Miss?"

I sat up and rubbed my eyes to clear them. "Yes?"

"It's Mrs. Wickstrom, Josephine. I'm your near neighbor. I know you're new, and the dinner bell has rung."

It was dark outside my window. In my exhaustion, I'd slept away the day.

I stood and shook out my gown; I'd expressly chosen one that would not require much fuss as I would likely not have much help beyond Mrs. Strange, and I was not sure what her duties required.

"I'll be along," I called out.

"I'll wait for you," she said, her voice firm. A frisson of fear traveled through me. Was she well? Could she harm me?

When I opened the door I found a woman perhaps five years older than I, rather thin and plainly dressed, but with the exception of the dark rings round her eyes, she looked completely well.

"I thought you might like me to show you where the dining room is," she said. "The pleasant part of a private asylum is that we have more autonomy," she continued. "But less oversight means much less assistance as well."

"I'm grateful for your help," I said. We walked down the vestibule in silence, then down the stairs.

"I heard you crying," she said matter-of-factly. "You will soon reconcile yourself to being here. We all do. I have not cried in some time, though there is no saying what might trigger a relapse."

"How long . . . ?" I began, not sure if the question was impertinent or not.

"It's all right; there are no secrets at Medstone." We joined a stream of others walking toward the dining hall. "My husband had me committed here two years past for nursing our child overlong."

Horror rose within me. "Surely not!"

She nodded. "Luckily for him, he had a younger woman waiting to take over my . . . duties. He divorced me. He still pays for
my keep. I'm certain he will forever, though I have no doubts
about living long enough to do him real damage."

My spirits fell for her, for me. "I'm so sorry."

"They bring my Emily to visit." Her voice was blunt. "On her
birthday. Here we are now. As it's dinner, there shall be meat, if
you're kind to the server. If not, it's potatoes only, and they may
even spit in them when you cannot see."

I swallowed my gorge and followed her into the dining room,
which was filled with tables seating four or six, light flowered
paper covering the wall, gas lamps burning, their flames leaving
circles of black residue on the ceilings. A flat piece of brown
rested on the plates of those who had been served.

"There is no meat at other meals?" I asked.

She shook her head. "It's said to make us excitable."

I took a chair at the dining table she led me to, and she made
pleasant introductions to all; she called me her friend, which
meant they were open to me. I was so grateful for a friend. Although men and women lived on different wings, we were allowed to dine and socialize together. A man of perhaps forty
made conversation with another woman at our table until he put
his head in his hands and said, "Cooper! Cooper, mate. Cooper,
move out!" He clutched his head as though suffering intense pain.
The woman with whom he'd been conversing leaned over and
patted his shoulders. "There, now, Lieutenant, Cooper heard you,
and he's moved. He's safe now."

The lieutenant lifted his head and looked at her. "Truly?"

She nodded, and he dropped his hands and grinned, expression completely transformed, eager for the plate about to be set
before him.

The woman introduced herself as Miss Trulean, a wealthy draper's daughter. "I live here permanently," she said, but did not say why she had been committed. Her eyes were shiny and her gaze relentless and intense.

Another man, who remained silent but rocked himself in his chair the entire time, joined us, as did an elderly woman. I noticed there were few elderly people in the room.

One in five die each year.

At the end of the meal, Miss Trulean left the table to look for a fresh pitcher of water. The lieutenant began to whimper about Cooper again, and I leaned over and patted him as Miss Trulean had done. "The lad is fine, now, do not worry," I said.

He looked at me. "Thank you, young lady." When pudding was served, he ate heartily.

Josephine and I made our way back to our rooms. Mrs. Strange awaited me there, to help me prepare for the night. Josephine spotted her down the hall.

"I recognize her," she said. "She's not been here for a while, but she was kind to her last patient and stayed with her until she passed on. My husband only paid for a nurse to attend me until all my paperwork was finalized, knowing I could not then leave. Ever."

Alarm coursed through me. Mrs. Strange's last patient had died? Once the paperwork was completed, there was no likelihood of leaving?

We said good night, and I opened the door and let us into my room.

"Why are you here?" I asked as she brushed out my hair.

"Why, to help you, of course."

"Did you suggest I come here?" I asked, knowing the answer already.

"Yes," she said.

"For what cause?"

"For your protection," she said.

I had given no indication I would harm myself.

"Perhaps I may learn something of my mother," I said.

"That has long been my very thought," Nurse Strange replied. "I shall make gentle enquiries." She blew out my lamp and left me for the evening.

For an hour or so I lay stock-still and stiff in my bed, wondering if someone could come in through the unlocked door.

It could not have been inexpensive, a private asylum. But it would not cost Edward nearly as much as losing what was left of his fortune, to me, would. We would likely not qualify for a publicly funded stay. And they'd be prone to ask more questions of him.

The hallucinations had grown stronger after my mother's things started being returned. And after I became increasingly attached to Marco. *Could it be true?*

There was perhaps in all of us a fine line between that which disoriented but could be overcome or managed and that which eventually caused our inner scaffolding to collapse. None of us were masters of our own minds, or our own fate.

One in five died each year. There were few old people at Medstone.

I awoke in the night. Josephine, next door, was crying. I pulled on my robe and went into her room, sitting next to her on her bed, my arm round her, for some time.

One afternoon I sat at a table with the others I dined with, playing draughts. A stern woman passed, and as she did, the others put their heads down.

"Mistress Malmstead," the lieutenant said.

"I have not met her," I said.

"The odds of that are extraordinary!" a man sitting with us named Mr. Dabney said. At that, the table burst out in sharp peals of laughter, which frightened me. Others around the room quieted.

"He's got math mania," Josephine whispered to me.

"Who is Mistress Malmstead?" I asked.

"She's responsible for overseeing our tasks. They feel it's important to occupy irrational minds. You haven't been assigned a task yet?"

I shook my head.

"That is not good." Josephine's face darkened.

"Perhaps my cousin paid them enough that I need not participate," I said.

She capitulated her game and took me aside, near a window. We watched a flock of black birds, startled by the wind in the twiggy trees, fly from their barren branches. "If you live idly, it's an indication that you will not adapt to life on the outside again. Even though I've little chance of leaving, I still participate on the off chance that I may be released someday. If you ever hope to leave this place, you cannot be idle."

Why hadn't Mrs. Strange told this to me?

"What can I do?"

"Help in the kitchens?" she offered.

"I'm afraid I'm not a very good cook."

"I paint the blackened marks from the chair rails and the ceilings," she said. "But we're full up."

"Teach?" I asked. That I could do!

She shook her head. "The chaplain does the teaching, to ensure that we don't stray from light moral and improving lessons. How about entertainments? We're allowed an entertainment at least once per week, especially now it's growing close to Christmas."

I hadn't thought of that. I was used to being rather alone at Christmas, but not locked in an asylum!

"Could you contribute to the entertainments?" she asked anxiously as Mistress Malmstead walked by again.

I pressed my memory. What could I do? Mr. Morgan's recent pantomime came to mind. At least it was fresh. "How about a pantomime?"

"Splendid!" Josephine looked as relieved as I felt. "Let's speak with her"—she nodded toward Mistress Malmstead—"now."

We did, and after hearing my suggestion Mistress Malmstead turned to me, eyes brimming with contempt. "So, Miss High and Mighty wants to put on parlor entertainment." She burst out laughing but it held no joy, only sharp edges. "No, I think not. But it's turning to the season of illness, and the infirmary can always put idle hands to work. That's the place for you."

I opened my mouth to protest, but Josephine shook her head no and led me away. Once we were clear of Mistress Malmstead, she squeezed my hand. "I'm terribly sorry," she said. I was, too.

Those who worked with the unwell often became unwell themselves. Sick unto death, in fact.

CHAPTER THIRTY

MID TO LATE NOVEMBER, 1851

My job was to help wash filthy rags. The rank smell of disease still rose from them. My hands grew raw and cracked and all day the ravings of the ill, those ill in mind and in body, assaulted my sensibilities. I felt their sufferings and prayed for them, in silence, while I worked. I had seen others working in the infirmary become ill and not return. I monitored my own health most closely. Perhaps too closely. My imagination had begun to take over.

One afternoon I was excused early. A priest had arrived at the request of Mrs. Strange. I was allowed to walk the frozen grounds with him. It was a pleasure and a rare privilege to be outside on a dry day, and I knew I'd only been allowed it as I was in his care. Patients were not normally permitted to walk outside unescorted; I'd learned that if anyone escaped and was not returned within fourteen days their admitting paperwork would have to be resubmitted, proving them mad again.

The priest tucked my arm through his crooked elbow. We walked, scaring up a flock of irritated birds that had chosen to brave the bare English winter rather than fly away to warm Mediterranean quarters for the season.

"Thank you," I said to him.

"For what, daughter?" He was perhaps ten years older than I was.

"Treating me as you would treat any parishioner, not as someone who is mad."

"We are all subject to the distress and vagaries of this world, and every soul here is as much a parishioner as any in my church."

I nodded. He was leading me to the very back of the property, away from the side that held the attendants' cottages, and toward an open field.

"Mrs. Strange said you wanted information about your mother. As you know, Catholics in the past were allowed even less freedom of worship than they are now. But we keep secret parish records, and the Medstone staff have always readily granted access to any who wished to meet with their clergy."

The grass beneath our feet was frosted as though it had been encased in glass; it shattered into wicked brown shards as we moved forward. I was grateful that I'd been allowed to bring and keep my fur-lined cloak and muff against the chill. Soon we arrived at a section of the field where small iron markers with numbers upon them dotted the ground.

"Grave markers," I whispered.

He nodded.

"And my mother is here."

He tightened his grip on my arm. "Yes, I thought you would want to see. After Mrs. Strange let us know you were interested, I went through the records and found the notes the priest had left at the time of her death."

He stopped in front of marker 256. I stood there for a

moment, uneasy, not knowing where to step. Was I stepping on her? Stepping on someone else?

The priest seemed to understand. "Do not worry, daughter. You do no disrespect standing on the field and, as you know, your mother is not there in the truest sense of the word. No one can see you. You can cry if you like."

I shook my head no. Perhaps later, perhaps alone. Not here. I had always wanted to know how her life had ended, but no one would say. Had I not come to Medstone, had the priest not brought me here, I'd never have truly understood.

My face began to freeze. My heart began to bleed. "I just . . . I suppose I'd hoped until now that she really hadn't died. That she was waiting somewhere for me. I knew she'd find me if she could, but still, one hopes."

He smiled softly. "She did die. The notes state that she was given the last rites, died in peace with her priest and a friend by her side, and mentioned Annabel and an Alessandru Bellini."

"Bellini! Alessandru Bellini!" He looked at me rather firmly, and I quieted down. I did not want to give the wrong impression to any who might be about.

My father's name was Bellini. Perhaps I could locate him. Had Judith known his name? Certainly. And yet she'd erased all trace. Had Edward known, too?

I looked down at the ground, which gave no indication of ever having been disturbed. The grass grew as an unbroken blanket over her final resting place. She'd died in peace, which quieted a tremor my heart had always known, and with a friend. "Why was she buried here? Not returned to her family?"

"That was their request," he said. "That was allowed many years ago, but now, not as often. We have run out of room in the ground, so the earthly remains are always returned to families unless they refuse to take them. Then, as often as not, their final resting place is in a pauper's field."

I was relieved that had not happened to my mother.

"I wish I'd have been old enough to help. I wish I would have known more, and sooner. I wish there was something I could do to honor her."

"Do what you think you should do," he said. "Be who you hope and pray you could be. Be kind. Be courageous. That is what will honor her. Any good mother."

He nodded toward Medstone. "Ready?"

I nodded. "Will you come back?" I asked.

"I shall visit when I can. But an outbreak of influenza has just taken hold in one of the attendants' cottages and visitors are not likely to be allowed soon, I'm sorry to say. The risk . . ."

I nodded. I understood the risk. I saw, I heard, I feared it all afternoon, every afternoon, at the infirmary. It spread like flame to pitch. There were no quarantine rooms here.

Late that night, after a dinner of mutton stew, I returned to my room and sat thinking in the silence while the night grew quiet but for the coughs of the newly ill.

My mother, Julianna. My father, Alessandru Bellini. My mother's name was Julianna Bellini, and she had named me, I'd just realized, for the contraction and conjoining of their names. The last portion of her Christian name and the first portion of her surname.

Annabel.

My mother had risked all for my father—and had paid the final, permanent price for their love and for bearing me. And yet as I looked back on the few memories I had of her, I could not imagine that she would have foregone those risks. The pictures of her and my father glowed with love and affection.

They had risked; they had lost, that was true, but they had also gained.

I had already grieved the loss of my mother, so that was not a fresh wound. It brought me comfort to have her remains nearby. Instead, I sought to think carefully about what I might do to help reclaim her life, her name, and if in any way achievable, my fortune.

It would not be easy, if it were even possible. And I had so little time before being permanently admitted.

Late that night, Mrs. Strange came to visit and to see if I needed some sleeping medication after my difficult day. I had always foregone her suggestion of it, not trusting much in substances after my recent encounters with the poison-stirred honey at Highcliffe.

But wait! Perhaps it had not been poisoned. It was foreign. Greek honey.

Mad honey!

She must have seen my startled, agitated expression. I sat upright, and then back again. "Would you like a draught?" she asked again. "It may help. You won't hear the nighttime . . . screams."

The screams. I hated them. Were they due to illness? Or was someone harming someone else? I shuddered, and was tempted. "No, thank you," I finally said. "But can you stay and sit with me for a moment?"

"Of course," she said, plumping herself on the small chair in the corner of the room.

"You say you are here to help me, and the priest said you were trustworthy. But I must know: Are you here working on Edward's behalf?"

"No," she said. "Certainly not."

"And yet you were sent in response to his letter to the specialist."

"Yes." She looked at her hands for a moment. "I know Father Gregory at the Earl of Somerford's as well."

Understanding expanded from the center of my being outward. I now understood. Father Gregory had somehow been involved, perhaps even sent her to me. I decided to take a chance.

"I suspect that my cousin's wife saw my reaction to her absinthe, told her husband, and then my cousin arranged for his import partners to provide me with foreign honey, and began to dose me with it in my tea; my cousin's wife had heard the Maltese captain speak of such a thing when she was with me. It was within his means."

"*His* meaning the captain?"

I nodded slowly. "That is possible. But my family also imports many goods from Turkey and Greece. So Edward could have acquired some of their 'mad' honey quite easily, given prompting from Clementine as a way to solve their problems. If I were found mad, even though I might be legitimate, I could not inherit our property or resources. My cousin would not have wanted me married—and bearing a child."

A thought occurred to me. Mr. Morgan could also have acquired the crazy honey, to bend me to his will. The stone he'd given me was from Turkey, certainly acquired through those same importers.

"That would certainly explain things," Mrs. Strange said.

"You cannot liberate me from here?"

She shook her head. "I'm sorry, Miss Ashton. I do not have leave to do that. There are limits on what I may do."

Money again. It always bought, or denied, power.

She bid me good night and took the lamp with her, as always. A light impression of sweet, ashy incense remained in the room as she left. Most probably from church, which is how she must know the priests.

I did not hear Josephine cry that night, which was happy news, but the coughs up and down the corridor, which had started out as an occasional punctuation of the silence, had now grown to an insistent chorus. I found myself in the awkward, somewhat shameful position of hoping that the woman who screamed almost every night had been taken ill, temporarily, so we would not be subject to her shrieking.

The next evening, oddly, none of my tablemates were present for the evening meal. Mrs. Strange came to help me ready for bed that night and her face soon showed concern.

"What is it?" I slipped into my nightgown.

"The lieutenant passed away."

I sat on the bed. "Oh no."

She nodded. "And yet, in a way . . ."

"It's a comfort for him."

"I think it is," she said. "He no longer suffers."

I said nothing for a long moment. "I do not want to look forward to death as a blessing and a comfort," I said. "I am young, and I am not insane. I want to live."

A long silence. What more could be said? "I shall leave a candle tonight if you promise not to share the secret, so you may read and take pleasure in that if you like."

"Thank you," I answered. Mr. Poe's melancholic musings were unlikely to bring me cheer, but perhaps they would help pass the long evening hours.

She shut the door behind her, and in boredom I began to turn his pages. I quickly passed "Annabel Lee"; I was tempted to tear out the pages but imagined what kind of hullabaloo that would cause should the discarded pages be found. Defacing a book would no doubt be seen as another symptom of madness. There were other short selections in the volume.

I came to his story of premature burial.

Like many of my own countrymen, Mr. Poe shared a fear of being interred into the ground before he was fully dead. Stories had gone round my school about crypts being opened many years later only to find someone previously thought dead leaning against the doorway, outside of her coffin. Poe had, apparently, made a pact with his friends that they would ensure he was not buried alive. Friends of my own had, indeed, joined the Winchester Society for the Prevention of People Being Buried Alive. Yes, they'd told me, one could have a bell attached to a coffin, but what if no one is around to hear it being rung after it's been interred? Yes, it was true that coffins no longer were screwed shut, but what if one did not possess the strength to push the lid open?

I had scoffed at that, but they had not. Several had spent their few pennies to join, and one assumed that Mr. Poe would have gladly joined them. I opened his story again and read, but one phrase stuck in my mind, and I could not push beyond it.

The boundaries which divide Life from Death are at best shadowy and vague. Who shall say where the one ends, and where the other begins?

I blew out the candle and lay back. A thought came to me, a wisp at first, like the smoke curling away in the dark.

Would it be possible for me to be prematurely buried? Sent home as dead? Could I feign death as an escape, and then remain free for those necessary fourteen days? It was possible. To stay here was to die—that much was certain. Perhaps soon.

I thought back to my discussion with Lady Somerford about the rooms in which priests had once held secret divine services. She'd told me, *"There is no gain without risk, my dear, and it made rather good sport to outfox the authorities."* I'd smiled and laughed with her before affirming, *"Much was risked, and everything gained."*

Yes. It was possible.

So much must be risked. So much might be gained.

CHAPTER THIRTY-ONE

LATE NOVEMBER, 1851

The next day marked nearly a month since my arrival; Mrs. Strange came to sit with me as she did each morning. I firmly shut the door behind her. "I need to take you into my confidence. Can I trust you?"

"I've said that you can," she replied. What choice did I have? There was nothing she could do to me, nothing even she could relay to Edward, that would make my situation any more precarious than it currently was. If I did not leave the asylum soon I would be permanently admitted.

"What I'm wondering is . . . are the bodies of those dying of influenza subject to a postmortem?"

She shook her head no. "Too many right now, and there's the risk that those who are alive might catch it from them. Even the doctors do not want to come too close. We nurses are being asked to make judgments."

I nodded. "Do you recall when you said I must be careful with the sleeping preparations or I should be comatose?"

She nodded. "Yes, of course."

"Could I take enough so that I would be thought to be dead, but actually just near death? Enough time to have my body sent back to Highcliffe?"

Mrs. Strange did not answer me right away. Instead, she rested her head in her hands for a moment in a most peculiar manner. Was she praying? I hoped I had not suggested anything sinful. Finally, she spoke.

"The dispensary here uses morphine, chloral hydrate, or Indian hemp for the treatment of mania. I could procure enough to make you appear dead for perhaps six to eight hours."

That would be time enough. "Would it be safe?"

"If the right dosage was given."

"Otherwise?"

She shrugged. "I would need to ascertain the exact dosage, a dosage that would keep one asleep for a few hours. The coffins used here are of poor quality, so they would allow air in."

Did I trust her? She could do Edward a very large service by ensuring that I took the dose required never to wake up.

I'd seen how it happened in the infirmary. "You would examine the body; the doctor could give his signature."

She nodded. "Normally we hold a lock of wool under the nostrils for but a moment; your breaths would be so slow that would suffice. Lucky for you, Miss Ashton, it's not like ages back with the Greeks. They cut the fingers off just to make certain a person was truly dead."

My eyes widened. The Greeks again!

"I'd see that the coffin was sent to Highcliffe."

Of course, there was a real risk they'd dispose of me quickly, and I'd be buried alive before I came to!

I calmed my breathing and tried to quell my twitching nerves by forcing myself to sit still.

"It's not likely any staff here would suspect. I'm not aware of it having been attempted at Medstone before, and I would know. Once you get to your Highcliffe, what will you do?" Mrs. Strange asked.

I'd already thought this through. I'd recalled one time as children when Edward wanted to jump over a ditch to the other side, which was faced by a large stone wall. He'd had to take a running leap in order to clear the water, but had not thought how he would return with no land for a running leap on the other side. His father had one of the stable boys wade over to fetch him and Edward got a good hiding for his efforts. It taught me, observing, to think through my entire course of action.

I'd sometimes wished, though, for Edward's childhood daring, now safely quenched. That I had more often taken a *saltus fidei*, a leap of faith. Perhaps I should have with Marco. I would not brook regret over inaction here.

"Is it true that if I am not returned to confinement within fourteen days my madness will have to be proved anew?" I asked.

She nodded.

And that I could avoid, because now I understood about the honey. "I shall walk to Pennington and seek sanctuary for two weeks," I said. "While I have the constable search for the honey, and perhaps even have them make enquiries, if necessary, from our importers."

"When?" she asked me. I heard Josephine stirring next door and thought what sorrow news of my death would bring her. It was entirely possible if I stayed too long that news would be real: I might die of influenza. I would find a way to send word to her, to help her in some way. I promised this to myself.

The staff were at their busiest in the late afternoon. "In three days. It will give me long enough to feign illness and, sadly, there will by then be more truly ill for the staff to attend to. But there will still be enough daylight hours for them to send me on to Highcliffe."

I dressed in my sleeping gown and robe because that is what would have been most appropriate. My feet were bare but for thin cotton stockings. Nurse Strange was to meet me here at two o'clock that afternoon.

Did I trust her? She did know the priests, who trusted her, and I them. She had been kind to me. But she had also removed my sketchbook, she was clearly in Edward's employ, and she seemed to be just a bit eager to discuss large doses of sleeping medications.

I had no choice. If I stayed here, I would be forcibly contained, unable to clear my mother's name, and powerless to contact Marco, though I did not know if he would wish me to contact him. If I stayed here, I was quite likely to die young of disease.

I closed my eyes to pray. What came to me was a remembrance of Marco sitting at the table, by my side, his face warm and full of life as he glanced across the table at the nuisance that was Nigel Morgan. Then Marco had whispered, *"Alla fine andrà tutto bene se non andrà bene, non e le fine."*

All will be well in the end; if it's not well, then it's not the end.

I chose to believe that.

Mrs. Strange knocked on the door. I let her in and closed the door behind her. I had not said good-bye to my friends because I did not want to involve them in any manner in case things went awry.

A holy but unsettled hush filled the room. Somber. Serious. A gamble of immense magnitude.

"I have the medication," she said. "I will dose you properly, then call the doctor to come and do a brief test—it's likely he will send an orderly as I am here anyway. I will request a rough-hewn coffin, and you will have sufficient air from between the cracks. The driver will take you, your things, and notice of your death with all haste to your family's estate. Patients are being sent home quickly."

"The coach house," I said. "That's where they'll put me. I am sure Clementine will not want my body in the house, putting them at risk."

"From the moment you fade into the unconscious you will not be aware of what is transpiring around you. I will protect you, though."

Yes, but no one would be there to protect me at the other end. No matter. My course was irrevocably determined. I could not be left to rot my way toward death here.

I sat on the bed, and she handed a cup to me partly filled with liquid. "Do not fear," she encouraged me, and I drank the liquid. "All will be well." She brushed her hands lightly over my face and prayed in a language I did not understand. Then I lay back on my bed.

For a moment, nothing happened, but then a sleepy darkness began to course throughout my body. My eyes grew heavy, and I could no longer feel my feet. I did not feel the agitation that the honey had brought on; instead I felt blanketed in peace, as if I were being ushered to the very border of heaven and I was not certain I wished to return. Soon my breathing slowed down. Slowed down. Slowed down . . . slowed down . . . slowed down. My heart kept rhythm with the breaths.

The blackness carried me away.

. . .

I awoke with a start. It was dark and cold. My breathing was still labored, and my jaw would not open. Had I been paralyzed? Had the medication damaged me, or was it still in effect?

I lay in the box and reached my hands, slowly, up from my sides and touched my jaw. I tried to open my eyes, but something was on them. I reached up and plucked a coin off of each; they had been placed there so my eyes would remain closed after death. Likewise, my jaw had been wrapped with a cloth strap, to support it. I reached atop my head and undid the tie. I moved slowly because I did not know where I was, and if the coffin had been balanced upon something in a precarious manner, I did not want to tumble off.

I blinked and took quiet, deep pulls of air through my nostrils and my mouth, to regain a clear head. The air smelt of horse dung and men's sweat, of earth and of leather. The coach house, as I had suspected.

The inside of my coffin had but the lightest linen lining, and my bones ached. I had been, I was sure, jostled against the knobby country roads for the hour the journey had taken and would likely be blotched with bruises. I breathed in deeply again. Incense.

Had I been given last rites?

I did not hear anyone moving about, so I guessed it was past the hour when the stable boys worked. I blinked repeatedly to clear the sepia haze from my eyesight. After I had steadied myself, I gently pushed on the coffin lid; it did not give easily, as Mrs. Strange had assured me it would. She'd promised it would not be nailed down, as most families wished to bury their loved ones in better coffins on the family property. Had she been wrong? Was I stuck? To be buried alive? Perhaps I was already buried in the family mausoleum.

No. The air was not stale.

Finally, the lid lifted a bit, and I used both hands to then push it up. Nothing. I pushed further, and all of a sudden a loud clatter could be heard. First sliding, and then a loud clank of metal hitting the ground. I sat up, and when I did I saw a man's face looking directly back at me.

CHAPTER THIRTY-TWO

He screamed, and I screamed in response. Our screams brought another man, who grew as white as the ghost I expected he thought I was.

"I am not dead!" I said, and the men said nothing.

One pointed to the chain on the ground. "I set that on top of the coffin after using it on the carriage and then when I heard some noise . . . she's back from the dead. She knows she was done wrong and has come back to avenge herself!"

If I had been a woman who gambled with money, and I was not, I should have bet that this was the craven man who had passed along the information about my interest in taking sacred vows from the Somerfords' driver.

"There was a mistake made," I claimed. "I was not dead." My head still whirled from the mania medication, and my tongue stuck to the roof of my mouth.

"I'll watch her," the young man said. "You fetch the master."

"I mean to go to Pennington," I said. This had gone wrong. I had not counted upon a chain. "Perhaps you could drive me there."

"You'll go nowhere without the master's permission," he said. "And his Lordship is long gone up north. Pennington is empty." He still looked ill, but he was well able to contain me—my being flesh and blood and not simply spirit as he had first feared—should I now try to break away.

Within five minutes, Edward and Watts ran into the carriage house. Edward looked as sick as his driver; Watts looked likewise.

"Annabel?" Edward whispered. "Have you come back from the dead to hold me to account?"

"I am certainly here to hold you to account," I said. "But I am not dead."

"Undead . . ." he whispered.

In spite of the dire situation, I wanted to roll my eyes. Had he been reading Clementine's sensational magazines? "No, Edward. I am not dead, was never dead. I shall speak more of this to you in the drawing room, with the others present."

He willingly agreed, then seemed to regain some strength and sent Watts ahead of me, to clear the house, I assumed. Watts had looked at me as if I were well and truly mad. Edward took hold of my arm, and now that he, too, knew it to be flesh and not spirit he marched me angrily forward. My feet were nearly bare on the frozen grass; the blades sliced into me. The garden statues had been covered up for the season, so it seemed to me that they, too, were blinded from seeing what transpired around them.

I could not allow myself to cry at this setback. I had to stay ready to act, though I did not know what those actions might be.

We did not, as I would have thought, stop in the silent drawing room.

"Where are we going? I wish to speak to this in front of everyone!"

Edward force-marched me straight toward the quarantine

room. "You'll not be speaking to anyone in the drawing room. You'll be quarantined and silenced!"

I shouted loudly, hoping someone would hear and come to assist. "There is no reason to quarantine me and you know it!" I tried to twist out of his grasp, but could not. He took my arm and twisted it behind my back, jacking it higher till I winced and had no choice but to comply. "I've been poisoned by honey!"

The house was eerily silent, the tempo of life stilled like the clocks within; now all their hands were rendered immobile, too.

I shouted as I was forced forward. "Hello? Can anyone hear me? Please, if you will, come to my aid. I'm well, I'm home, and I need assistance!" I turned to Edward. "The staff will surely hear," I said loudly, hoping that my shouts would break that silence, that someone would actually hear me as we wound our way up through the back and to the top floor.

"Aside from Watts and Mrs. Watts, no staff is domiciled at the house any longer," Edward said. "We leave soon for London, for Christmas. Highcliffe has been sold. Or had you forgotten?"

I had lost track of the days while in the asylum. And I could not have known, of course, what day they were leaving. He hurried me ever faster up the steps.

"We thought to ask that priest at Pennington to help bury you tomorrow and then we were to leave within days."

"I suppose I should thank you for thinking of that," I said. A sudden idea. I stopped, and he pushed me forward while I spoke. "Could Father Gregory be brought to me now?"

Edward snorted. "When you're dead, I'll call for him." He turned me toward him and looked at my face; it must have been wan from the cold, the journey, and the syrup I'd taken. "Apparently your stay at Medstone was not improving. You don't look well."

"It may not have been physically improving, but while there I learned much."

Edward moved me firmly into the room and closed the door. "Some neat tricks, apparently," he said. "Was the institution staffed with a complement of Morgan's magicians? Someone told you how to escape. Morgan would be very pleased."

"I came to understand, whilst there, that I'd been poisoned," I said. "With foreign honey that you procured."

He looked at me with contempt. "The only honey brought to this house was by your *friend*, Dell'Acqua. He delivered honey. Foreign honey. However, he was a clear double-dealer, and it would not surprise me if he was trying to taint you with honey. Turkish honey, for example, is well known for its aphrodisiac effect. Perhaps that is what he was after."

I sharply inhaled, which proved that I had not known that. I did, however, know Edward well enough to know, as I searched his face, that he was truthful. He had no knowledge of any foreign honey. Could it have been Marco, after all?

I pressed on. Edward's sense of justice, warped as it was, would insist that he address the truth once it was spoken. "My mother was properly married and was not mentally unwell. Your mother, knowing this full well, had her placed in Medstone so she could steal her fortune. The Somerfords' priest told me that my mother was about to marry someone else. Your mother may have thought I was illegitimate, but she'd known that any child from a new marriage would most certainly not be. She acted quickly."

Blood suffused his face. "How dare you accuse my mother of this!"

"I believe, in any case, that my parents were married." I spoke loudly and hoped and prayed that Watts was at the speaking tube, listening, willing to call for help. "Plenty of people do. I had her wedding cap. *Your* mother painted the portrait while my mother wore it. Difficult to believe your mother did not know my mother had been married. Perhaps she'd even attended the ceremony. Maybe as a witness."

"There is no cap."

"Perhaps not any longer, but there was." His candle had burned three-quarters of the way down. It flickered, beckoning me, *hurry, hurry*. But what else could I do?

"Where is that portrait, the one your mother painted?"

"In the attic, I suppose." Edward did not appear to be dissembling. Could he not know that it had been cut from the frame and removed?

"There was her engagement necklace."

"Who knows how that came to you?"

"I don't know," I admitted. "But given time, I will find out. There were letters sent from Malta that came to the old Mr. Galpine but apparently never reached my mother. They were sent, and recorded in Lymington, to her married name—which I now know was Julianna Bellini. Wife of Alessandru Bellini. With help, I can pursue that lead and find someone who knew my father. Perhaps still knows my father. Someone who will help me prove my claim. Others, at Medstone, know now, too. So the secret is out."

Edward's face grew waxlike, his skin more pallid than it had been at that moment when he first saw me and believed me to be a venging apparition. "How did you learn his name? The man who fathered you?"

I flinched at his choice of words. "It was recorded at Medstone." I did not need to tell him it was parish records.

"You're mad. These are the ravings of a lunatic, and honestly,

Annabel, if anyone had any doubts about you being mad when I first had you put away they won't now. Escaping in a coffin in the middle of an epidemic, having word sent that you'd died of influenza. Coming back to life in the coach house."

I did not let him change the subject. "My mother was married and I will be able to prove it. I'm certain of this."

He said nothing for a long moment, still blocking the door, as I shivered in my dressing gown and robe that were wet with sweat and dew.

"It may be that they were married . . . in a manner of speaking," he admitted.

A flush ran through me, and I stopped shaking.

"There are men of the sea, men of the world, who have wives in many ports and lands."

Marco had mentioned something similar. Could it be true? Was it common in Malta? Had Marco done this? Had my father? Lied to and left wives who were not wives and baseborn children across the world? My left eye twitched.

Edward fed off my discontent and went back for second helpings. "The men are bigamists, of course, adulterers if we look at it honestly. The women, for the most part, don't know about the others, each believing herself to be the real wife when they are nothing more than a—"

"How dare you?" I interrupted. Calling my mother a . . . something. I held my breath. Edward's candle spluttered. We were in nearly utter darkness.

"My father was not such a man," I said. "My mother would not have told her priest that she was married if she were not."

"She didn't know, Annabel. She was duped into thinking the man loved her. Just like you've been duped by the man who delivered the honey you say you were poisoned with. I'm sorry."

I had nothing to say. He might have been right. I needed to think what to do next.

"How did you get out? Who helped you?"

A lick of moonlight flickered through the stained-glass window, and I earnestly prayed for a solution to present itself.

"It was that nurse, wasn't it?" Edward continued. "That private nurse. Once I've taken care of you, I shall ensure she is severely dealt with."

Oh. I had not thought what I might wreak upon Mrs. Strange.

I heard Albert crying in the distance. "Where is Lillian?"

"Dismissed," he said.

"Why? Albert loved her so."

"She'd been apparently working behind Clementine's back. Refusing to carry out her duties properly. Perhaps you taught her that it was fine to mislead and deceive, with your unauthorized journeys to Galpine's."

Had I been responsible for Lillian's dismissal?

"And . . . the rest of the staff?"

"Jack's in London, and the others will apply to Highcliffe's new owner," he said. "After you are properly secured. If you'll excuse me, I mean to begin to make arrangements this very night. You will remain in this room, alone. I do not want the influenza you brought with you to run rampant in my house."

Or for others to help me. But who would help me? Who *could* help me at this juncture? There was no way around him.

He locked the door behind me, though five minutes later he returned with a pillow and a blanket. As he handed them over to me I glimpsed real sorrow of some kind in his eyes. The hardness softened for just a minute.

"It doesn't have to be like this," I said to him. "We were like brother and sister. Things were not perfect, but I trusted you."

He held my gaze for a moment, but didn't answer.

I saw the truth then. I had considered him to be as a brother to me, but he had never considered me as a sister. I had placed good intentions and hopes on the only person I could consider family, choosing not to see what was plainly true; terribly, but plainly true.

What would my naivety cost me?

Edward shook his head and then left.

After he was gone, I heard a commotion downstairs and put my ear to the speaking tube.

CHAPTER THIRTY-THREE

—————— ❦ ——————

Edward was talking with Watts. He told him he would arrange for me to be taken the very next day or night to another asylum; Clementine had made a short list of some she'd had investigated. They'd find one where the security was stringent and not one with a private nurse, and Watts should have everything prepared for a journey. Clementine, he said, would pack a trunk.

A trunk filled with my meager belongings from the asylum. For what else was left? Clementine, I knew now, understood that I was home and isolated.

I stood there a moment longer after Edward left, and then I heard Mrs. Watts. She was apparently not close to the speaking tube; she mumbled something I could not make out, but I could hear her sniff. Had she been crying? On my behalf?

Watts sought to soothe her. She said something insistently, and he answered, "Can't be done."

The tube! If I could hear them, then they could hear me! "Hello!" I spoke into the tube, as loudly as possible. "Mrs. Watts? Watts? Can either of you hear me, and if so, please come to the quarantine room. For but a moment only."

No one answered. I could hear as they pattered away. Had they heard and ignored me, or not heard at all?

With nothing left to try, I went to the bed, so familiar, in a house that seemed forebodingly quiet.

Who had purchased Highcliffe? Would they love it as I did?

I did not want to sleep away my last hours at home, and so I paged through the Bible, which didn't hold my attention, but I prayed, mightily. I stood again and looked out at the village in the distance. Chef dwelled in a small house there; the Wattses had a little cottage as well to which they would return. I hoped Mr. Galpine would make an offer of marriage to Lillian. I looked toward the land that lies between Highcliffe and Pennington. The cottage where Oliver and Emmeline's parents lived sat someplace in between, near the sea, near the trails that the sheep and the girl knew so well. Would she still tend them . . . or would the sheep be perhaps sold off?

The waves roiled relentlessly against the shuddering cliffs, then smoothed like a shaken blanket would farther out to sea. That water had carried Marco off. Had he learned of my confinement? Perhaps he did not care.

On the morrow, Edward would have me interred in an institution that was not likely to be as welcoming as Medstone had been.

I'd stay there forever.

I'd be buried alive.

An hour later I was nearly asleep, unable to fight off the growing drowsiness brought on by the residual effects of the medications. I heard noises. Someone was stepping on the treads up to my room. It was a light step . . . a woman.

I held my breath. The door handle turned. Then it stopped. Finally, I could wait no longer. "Who is there?"

Nothing. Slow breathing. And then, light steps leading back downstairs.

Edward himself brought my breakfast. I should have laughed if, months earlier, someone had told me that Edward would be playing housekeeper to me, bringing my bedding and delivering my food, but he was. The tea was tepid, and the eggs not quite done. Who had cooked breakfast? Certainly not Chef.

After a time, I watched Edward ride off, returning about three hours later. He brought me a late-afternoon meal, and this time, he sat down with me. His face was troubled.

"What troubles you?" I asked, not wanting to right it, of course, but thinking it might offer a clue as to what his plans were.

"I did not send you there to be poorly treated," he said. "To the madhouse. I was assured it was a good place, that the staff were kind and that you would be well cared for. Not like the horrors I've heard of in other, public asylums. Screams, medications, restraints, and such."

"Well, there were those," I said. "Sometimes they are needed. It would be a fine establishment within which to reside *if I were insane*. Which I am not."

"I wanted you treated well, Annabel. But, you must understand, I can't leave the family fortune at odds. Especially now that things have gone wrong with your Maltese friend and he's likely tainted Lord Somerford's opinion of me, too."

I tilted my head.

"I . . . I think you to be as baseborn as I always suspected you were," he said. "As we've always known. But you're clearly also unwell, and somehow strangely able to cajole or deceive people into cooperating with you. Staff. Nurses. Foreign sailors. Who knows what or who shall be next?" He ran his hand through his hair, releasing a slight scent of pomade and stale cigar smoke.

"Maybe you, Edward. You shall be next. Perhaps this madness runs in your veins, too. We're cousins, you know."

The blood drained from his face, and by his frightened expression I knew it was something he had considered. Then he reached his right hand into his trouser pocket and took out a roll of ginger chews.

"Have you had symptoms?"

He did not answer me, which was, in itself, an answer. Terror, then anger, flickered across his face, then he stilled it.

Ever and always acutely aware of good breeding, he offered one of the chews to me. I politely declined. I caught a glimpse of myself in the mirror. My eyes were rimmed with dark circles, my face pale. I looked unwell, perhaps physically and mentally. But who would not be given my circumstances and situation?

"The truth is, Annabel," Edward continued, "you've proven to be a loose cannon. I cannot risk Albert's future in any way." He stood and the floorboard creaked. He reached out to brace himself on the wall and painted, peeling plaster loosened and fell to the floor.

"Albert's future is not at risk," I said.

He looked at me wryly. *Oh, I understand. You mean to take what is mine and give it to Albert.*

I recalled the conversation I'd overheard him having with Morgan and Dell'Acqua. *The ends justify the means.* Then, and now, too.

"And now, apparently, there is the new complication of your casting aspersions on my mother's reputation." He stood next to the window. He picked the old spyglass up, rubbed a bit of rust from the lens rim, and looked out. He scanned the horizon for a moment and then set it down on the window ledge once more.

"You don't know what she lived through, who she really was, what she suffered. I simply cannot have you denigrating her name to anyone who will listen. I understand you are desperate—some would say delusional—and have a manic desire to right your own mother's name. But it can't be done, and I simply cannot allow it to happen at the expense of my own mother's reputation. 'If thy hand offend thee, cut it off.'"

It seemed the only portions of the Bible Edward had managed to memorize were hurled like stones at those who blocked his way.

He was planning to cut me off, then, for the sin of speaking honestly and pursuing what was rightly mine. "So you're willing to rewrite the truth, then," I said.

"What truth? Stamps? Post markings? Caps? Priests? It's all hearsay, Annabel. Nothing a judge would take seriously, and yet you have somehow managed to undermine people's sense of reason." He barked out a laugh. "Perhaps it's true that insanity is in the miasma. It's certainly true it can be passed from mother to child."

"And in your case?" I taunted, tired of this game.

He grew close to me. "I'm warning you. I shall not brook discussion of my mother in that manner."

Suddenly, I knew.

"Then how about your wife?" I asked. "She saw the reaction I had to the green fairy—the sugar cubes she had dipped in absinthe—and how it unsettled and upset me. And the idea came to her—yes, right then. *All have seen Annabel appear unstable. Unsettled. How can I ensure this continues?*"

Suddenly Edward's face was convulsed by shock and understanding, which affirmed my suspicions. He recoiled from me and shook his head. "No. That did not happen."

I nodded. "Yes it did. When Captain Dell'Acqua escorted Clementine and me at the Exhibition, he made a great jest of the 'crazy Greek honey' and how it had been used for centuries as a truth serum unless it provoked madness. Clementine knew I was disoriented over the discovery of the necklace, and when she heard that, Edward, her idea began to jell. Then she brought you into it. And you bought Greek honey and made sure I took it, publicly, when my 'madness' would be in full view of the others."

"I did no such thing!" He was telling the truth. I could see it in the shocked pink of his cheeks and the alarm registering in his eyes. "Clementine, why, I won't believe she would or could do such a thing. And I would never harm you."

"But you'll send me to the madhouse, where I shall die of an epidemic or a broken heart."

"Both are risks whether one is in the madhouse or not," he said. "At least there you'll not be a danger to others or yourself."

"You do not want to see the truth of your mother nor of your wife. I can understand that it would be a bitter gall to swallow. But it is the truth, Edward."

"The truth is you're mad—clever, but mad. And you're illegitimate, and not fit in any way to inherit. Perhaps you're actually French, too?" He laughed sharply. "You'd be disqualified in three of three categories, Annabel. Because we do not know who your father was. All so-called evidence is either *circumstantial or missing*, and the parties are either deceased or disqualified. I have had enough of this discussion."

I was right, and I knew it. But he was right, too. It was all hearsay and anecdotal.

"Care of Highcliffe, and all the family legacy, was a responsibility left to me. I've let my mother down in marrying Clementine. At all cost, I shall not let my father down once more as well. I cannot risk you, Annabel." Edward walked back to the window, picked up the spyglass once more, and nodded. "Yes. That is good."

I did not know what he was looking for in the deepening dusk. But he'd found it. He took me by the arm and opened the door. I wriggled free and he grabbed my arm again, twisting it behind me, and shoving me forward.

"We're leaving now." We took the servants' stair to the floor below, then went on to the second floor. Perhaps because the family were hidden away and would not see me. Clementine was with Albert, probably in her rooms. I did not know where the Wattses were. I shouted for help once or twice but no one came. Too, I was aware that everything about my shocking reappearance and constant crying out only made me seem more mad.

He set me in the front of the carriage, and then after the young man had hefted my trunk onto the back, Edward climbed in himself. "You're driving?" I asked.

"I know how to drive a carriage, Annabel."

But why was he driving? The only answer could be that he wanted no one save himself and me to know where we were going.

CHAPTER THIRTY-FOUR

We started down the drive. Edward drove, but unsteadily. The horses must have sensed his insecurities because they kept looking left and right, and the reins were too slack to control them confidently. Even I could see that.

It was now dark.

Instead of turning left, as we would if we were going to town and which would be natural if he were bringing me to another madhouse, he turned right.

"Where are we going?" I asked. I looked off the side of the cart. I could jump, but where would I go if I could even escape a moving carriage without hurting myself?

"You're going home," he said. "And then I'm going home, too, to set things right."

He made no sense. Perhaps he was mad after all.

The clouds clotted into a dark and pregnant gray. About a half mile along the road he stopped the carriage and secured it. He helped me down and then kept a firm hand on my arm. We walked around the back of the carriage and he took my trunk; it was too heavy for him to manage with one arm, wobbling this way and that like a drunk in an alleyway, so he let go of me.

"Follow me or things will go much worse for you," Edward said, and I did, all the time looking for a possible escape. My cloak stiffened as shards of ice, which the sky had begun to spit, burrowed their way into its fabric, like worms.

I knew just where I was, and it did not bode well for me. In the far distance was the stone cottage where Emmeline and Oliver's family lived, halfway between our estate and Pennington Park. Just ahead was the Edge of the World. To the left were the trails leading down to the Keyhole, where smaller boats and skiffs could slip in, take on contraband, and slip out into the dark waters, unseen, like sprats. Why had Edward brought me here now? If he was going to push me off, over into the abyss, why bring my trunk?

We stood there for a moment. Nothing happened, and he did not move, but the water crashed into the hillside just below us, making it nearly impossible to hear what Edward was saying. I drew a little nearer so I could hear, though his close presence repelled me. He smelt of the sour odor a body exudes when it's anxious.

"There is no insane asylum here, Edward," I spoke loudly. "Why are we here?"

He scanned the water. "I have a better plan, Annabel. You'll be put away, but it will be somewhere much more pleasant. Somewhere you'll be treasured as well as kept. And kept well. I've ensured that. He knows he's to answer to me."

I looked just over the edge of the slope, where the trails began to ribbon up the hillside. A boat skimmed the water, coming ever closer to us.

I thought I recognized, even at this distance, the skiff and the beard of the man piloting it by lamplight. I could not be sure because the man on board was dressed for the wet and cold, but it seemed he held himself in a certain way that I recognized.

"Nigel Morgan!"

Edward grinned. "I could not take a chance that you would find some overly sympathetic nurse at the next lunatic asylum. This is the best for everyone. Morgan will treat you well. He loves you."

"I do not love him! He frightens me."

The wind picked up and blew my hair round me. Edward shifted my trunk to his other shoulder. It had not been well tied and locked; the top burst open, and the lid gaped like the mouth of a ghost's jaw, freed in the afterlife from its rag support.

"Even if I am forced to marry, I will continue looking for documentation of my parents' marriage from Morgan's home in London."

"He plans to keep you in Ireland. Way beyond the pale. It's an arrangement we came upon. There will be no escape from Ireland, Annabel. His estate is back in the bogs where few Englishmen venture, and the Irish are all in his family's employ."

My rib cage hurt. "If we have children, they will become heir to the Ashton legacy."

He grinned and licked his lips, his tongue darting as he did so, and he looked as if he were about to enjoy a particularly favored pudding. "No, Annabel. Do you remember I told you I'd learned some men have 'wives' in every port? I've come across documents showing that Morgan has 'married' women in Sicily and perhaps the West Indies. Surely you understand that women and trade have gone together like wind and sail since the beginning of time? I've shown the documents to him. If ever a claim is made on behalf of a child of yours, or any child he begets, I will be able to prove he is a bigamist and your child illegitimate."

Had "Mrs. Wemberly" been a false wife? Or simply someone

he'd used and then set aside? In either case, he was not to be trusted. The ice turned to snow, which drifted down upon me like bleached wood ash. Edward lifted his lamp toward the Keyhole, where the skiff waited. A signal of some sort.

"Morgan will want my money if I prove myself legitimate."

"There will be little left after Highcliffe is sold and my debts paid. He is uninterested in your money, but you, my dear, will be partial payment for those debts. I'll build it back up over time, and he's better off than I. He simply wants a beautiful woman for pride of place. He wants you. I shall give you to him—he will treat you well, he's assured me—and I will keep his many secrets."

I was trapped. There was no way out of this. I prayed silently for any divine intervention that might save me from this cruel and bleak fate. I blinked away snowflakes from my eyelashes; they melted and coursed down my cheeks.

"Come along." Edward tried to take my hand but could not reach it while still carrying my trunk. He pushed me in front of him and then nudged me onward, down the winding sheep's path that led to the water.

I stopped and turned and tried to make my way up the path again, but it was narrow, and I could not edge past Edward. One side led to a fairly steep drop-off toward the water: a few scrubby trees anchored the land, but lightly.

The other led to the green where the sheep grazed. I should try to dart around him on that side.

He blocked me. We were perhaps one hundred feet from the sea, the rolling tide of which echoed back and forth in my ears. I saw the bobbing boat waiting for us. "There is no escaping fate, Annabel," Edward said. "Your mother sealed yours when she decided to become the doxy of some Maltese."

"Doxy?" I shouted, though none should hear me but Edward over the pounding surf to one side and the echo of the walls around the Keyhole to the other. "You mean wife. And even if she'd been a doxy . . . and she had not . . . that's a far better thing than being a murderess. Your mother was a murderess, Edward. And you're following right along behind her, as is your murdering wife. Judith Everedge killed my mother by sending her to her death. Julianna Ashton was not mad. She died of consumption, and a broken heart, so your mother could plunder her estate like the cold-blooded thief that she was!"

Edward's face, also red with the cold, detonated with fury. His eyes widened, his jaw clenched, and then his mouth opened. "You *will not slander* my mother!" He did not defend his wife. In his anger, he shifted on the wet trail, and as he did he lost the balance of the trunk. He quickly moved his weight to try to accommodate and regain his balance, but the trunk shifted mightily to the left, the water side, pulling him down with it. His feet went out from under him, and he slipped, his trousers hitting the hard ground as he groaned and shouted in pain.

The trunk disgorged its contents all along the side of the scrubby slope, and the lid narrowly missed hitting Edward in the head. My fine dresses, my silk slippers, my precious book of saints and angels were all launched into the air like the ivory rods thrown into the air in a game of pick-up-sticks. Strangely enough, when everything had landed, I spied my mother's lace wedding cap hooked upon a shrub.

Who had stolen and kept that? Who had placed it in my trunk, and why? When?

A slice of the ground fell away at Edward's feet, and his expression changed from one of anger to one of panic. He grabbed hold of a relatively thin tree trunk, a sapling, which had grown to tilt landward away from the wicked sea winds.

He caught himself, just, from falling over the side of the cliff and into the sticky quicksand a hundred or more feet below. I jumped back so I should not slide, too.

I well understood the horror on his face. We'd always known that the land at the bottom of the Edge of the World would swallow whatever was dumped into it, whole. It was one reason I'd heard that smugglers wouldn't bury anything seaside hereabouts like the Moonrakers famously had by their lake. Not only would their booty be fully ingested, but the smugglers foolish enough to walk out upon the land to bury it would soon find themselves firmly trapped mid-stride, like the frog in Mr. Morgan's amber.

"Annabel. Help me!" Edward clutched the small tree. The slope was such that he could not pull himself up onto the path again without risking losing his balance altogether. "Even I was not willing that you should die, and you are a much more religious person than I am. Can you live with my death on your soul?"

"I cannot help you!" I shouted. If I were to step near him, I could slip myself. The effort required to pull him up could unbalance us both and send us hurtling over the cliff.

Or he might push me to save himself.

The skiff loitered. Surely the man on board could see that we were in need of assistance. Why didn't he come?

And . . . perhaps this was my chance. Maybe I could simply leave Edward to his fate—why not? Scripture promises, *Whoso diggeth a pit shall fall therein, and he that rolleth a stone, it will return upon him.* Would this not be justice? It would not be on my soul in spite of Edward's ludicrous and desperate accusations.

I started to walk up the hill. "I shall not help you help me to a life of misery!"

"Annabel! I would not have left you to die. Clementine would have."

Ah! An admission!

"Pleeeease!" The effort required for him to scream above the surf caused the ground to slip a little, and he looked at me, silently pleading.

Albert, he mouthed. *For Albert.*

I turned my back and ran up the hill, and once at the top I stopped.

Did I want my freedom? Certainly. Did I want to leave Edward to his death?

I could not leave him to his death; it would make me complicit. I admitted that. But I would not risk myself and my own life.

"I'll go for help!" I ran as fast as I could, slipping twice on the path that muddied my gown, to the stone cottage, perhaps ten minutes away. The home of Oliver and Emmeline.

I banged on the door, and after a moment or two it was opened by an older man.

"Hello, I am Miss Ashton of Highcliffe," I said.

"Do come in." The man opened the door wider.

"I cannot! I cannot. There has been an accident. My cousin, Mr. Everedge, has tumbled over the side of the sheep's trails, and I wondered if there was some way you could assist me in rescuing him."

The man's children gathered behind him, including Emmeline and Oliver.

"Certainly. Let me get my boots." The man pulled his boots on and called for Oliver and another of his sons to come along with him. Emmeline pulled her boots on, too. Her father shook his head no.

She nodded and somehow made him understand she should come with us.

"She best knows the trails, Father," Oliver interpreted for her.

At that, her father nodded, and we started back toward the Edge of the World.

It took us perhaps another ten minutes walking quickly in the lightly falling snow on wet ground to return to the spot I'd shown them.

When we arrived, Edward was gone.

"It's clear he was here, miss." Oliver pointed to my trunk with its widely scattered contents. "But Mr. Everedge is not."

It was true. Edward had disappeared completely, and there were no footsteps leading from where he'd slipped to the path we now stood upon. We walked down the trail just a little farther until Emmeline made a warning wave with both hands, and we stopped. According to her counsel, Edward and I had not been wise to be even as far down this trail as we had gone.

I looked down at the water, toward the Keyhole. The skiff was no longer present. Morgan had either made a hasty retreat with his rower or had hidden in one of the coves along the shore.

None of us were willing to venture down the path any farther and check for footprints, but we shouted, all of us, for Edward.

"Do you hear anything?" Oliver's father asked.

We shook our heads. No call for help, just the crash of the surf, the shudder of the land it punished, the sigh of the winter wind. That was all.

"We'll return to the house, and I'll send someone to fetch the constable," their father said. "Quickly, in case Mr. Everedge is to be found alive at the foot of the hill."

We each agreed in turn, but I knew, and so did they by the somber looks they passed between them, that Edward was unlikely to be found alive after such a fall.

"I'd prefer to return to Pennington," I said.

"There's no one there, miss," Oliver said. "They've all gone north and the house is shut. Even the priest went with them this time."

The air was fogged with our exhaled breaths and snowflakes so small they were nearly dust. The children's father looked at me as he drew his shivering daughter near. "There is no choice, miss. It's back to Highcliffe."

I shivered, too. Would that someone could protect me as he did little Emmeline.

Oliver and Emmeline's father drove our carriage, still roped by the wayside when we returned to it, back to Highcliffe. I was cold and tired and shaken, and in spite of it all wished for Edward to get his just desserts but not be dead.

We pulled in front of the house. "Would you like me to go in with ye?" the older man asked.

I shook my head, though I truly did not wish to face Clementine on my own. "No, you'd best fetch some men to search the beach for Mr. Everedge." He clearly thought this was wise, nodded, and then clucked to the horses. He did not need to ask permission to take them; no one would deny that looking for Edward was the most important task before us.

I quickly walked up the front steps, and Watts opened the door. As I headed inside, he looked behind me, for Edward, I presumed.

"Mr. Everedge is not with me," I said. "There has been an accident. Please call Mrs. Watts and Maud and Mrs. Everedge to the drawing room. I would like you to stay while I explain the situation to Mrs. Everedge."

"Maud is no longer in service," he said. "But I will ask Mrs. Watts to bring Mrs. Everedge."

When Mrs. Watts returned with Clementine she had a blanket and gave it to me to wrap myself in, which I was thankful for. Watts stoked the evening fire, and we sat near it. Clementine could no longer contain herself. She was frightened, I thought, to see me returned to Highcliffe.

"Where is Edward?" She gripped my arm, and I recoiled. My heart coursed between sympathy for her situation—she was most probably a widow, now—and utter revulsion that she had wished me poisoned, mad, and perhaps married to Mr. Morgan.

"There has been an accident," I said. "Edward was taking me to be escorted somewhere."

"The asylum," she put in. I held her gaze, which was intense and upset but gave no indication that she had any idea I had been on my way to Morgan. Perhaps she hadn't known, but then she had been able to hide her true intentions regarding the honey and her false friendship for months. So she was more capable of deceit than I had first thought.

"No," I said. "He was sending me to Ireland to be married."

Mrs. Watts gasped.

"To Mr. Morgan."

"I never," Mrs. Watts said. "He said you were unwell like your mother, and that he needed to find you a more secure institution."

"Gabrielle," Mr. Watts warned. His face looked tired and concerned. Surely, he knew what kind of man he had served. I could not hold that against him, though, if he did not know what had been undertaken against me. And I'd appeared somewhat mad, due to the influence of the honey.

"Edward!" Clementine cried. "Annabel! Where is he?"

The clock in the corner marked five ticks.

"He was taking me via the Keyhole," I said, "and he slipped on the trail. There is some indication he fell, and I ran to get help."

"You abandoned him!" Clementine stood and shrieked. "Or pushed him!"

Mrs. Watts stepped protectively in front of me.

"I barely had the strength to walk the trail," I shouted in return, "after having just escaped from Medstone whilst medicated for a mania I do not have, because I am not insane in any manner!"

"To Medstone you shall return," Clementine promised. "We must summon help!"

"The constable and men have already been sent for," I said. "We must wait patiently as they conclude their findings."

She grew nearly hysterical, wringing her hand and clutching a chair cushion until her fingertips were white. How long had it been since Maud left . . . Had she, too, been dismissed? I thought it unlikely she'd left Clementine, to whom she'd seemed devoted, voluntarily.

Mr. Watts brought a small, steadying port to Clementine. I changed into something Mrs. Watts found for me and brought to the nearby study, and two hours later the constable and his men arrived.

They were shown into the drawing room; Emmeline and Oliver's father followed them, and the children, who had arrived about thirty minutes earlier to wait for their father in spite of the late hour, sat in the hallway, listening. Oliver had, I reminded myself, spent much later nights than this when he slept on a hall bed waiting to be summoned to service.

"I'm sorry," the constable said to Clementine. "Mr. Everedge has passed away. Died from the fall, you'll want to know, and I hope you'll take comfort that we were able to extract him from the sand in time. He's been cleaned up, and we've laid him to rest in the coffin in the coach house."

My coffin first, it was now Edward's.

Clementine sat weeping softly in her chair, and we let her weep for about ten minutes. Mrs. Watts brought her a second handkerchief to dry her eyes.

"I'll see to the stable boys, who will then see Mr. Everedge brought into the study for the night," Watts said. He looked discomfited and sad, too. "Then I'll call the vicar." He turned to me. "We've sent for someone to gather as many of your belongings as possible from the spilt trunk."

I nodded.

"I shall want him buried quickly," Clementine finally spoke. "A small funeral, as we have so little family, and we cannot remain long at Highcliffe."

She turned and looked at me, her eyes dry and hard now, her mouth firmed into a slash, before speaking to the constable. "I believe Miss Ashton is responsible for his death."

CHAPTER THIRTY-FIVE

I shrank from her as I would have from a black beetle scuttling toward me. "I've already said I had nothing to do with this."

The constable asked me some questions. I told him exactly what had happened, and he seemed satisfied that the facts as presented lined up with what he had observed.

"Did you see the face of the person in the boat?"

I shook my head. "There were two people. I could not see exactly who they were. I thought one of them might have been Mr. Nigel Morgan, but I cannot be certain."

He wrote that down. "I shall call upon him, but if you cannot identify him without a doubt . . ."

In truth, I could not. Edward had not even said it was Morgan himself who was coming to pick me up.

"Perhaps she should be escorted to the asylum from which she has escaped?"

For a grieving widow, Clementine seemed rather insistent upon ridding herself of me.

"What is this, then?" The constable turned back to me; his face looked both bewildered—how could he have expected both a death and an escaped lunatic in one evening?—and at the same time, stern. He was a man of responsibility, of course. "An escape from a madhouse?"

Could he return me to Medstone? I explained that my paperwork had not been completed and that most around me had not found me to be insane. "I have, however, been acting strangely," I admitted. "The cause of which was I'd been poisoned, I believe, with foreign honey."

"Poisoned?" The men stepped closer to me. "Are you certain?"

I nodded. "Yes. Poisoned and then accused of lunacy, both in this very house."

The officer turned to Clementine. "Do you mind if we search the estate?"

She shrugged, but a tremor of dread quivered across her face. "Not at all." She'd never expected me to return. She'd not have thought to remove the evidence.

We waited in the drawing room and within ten minutes one of the constable's men appeared with a jar he said he'd found concealed in a corner underneath the breakfast sideboard.

It was a jar of honey with what looked to be Turkish writing upon it.

"Have you seen this before?" he asked me.

I shook my head. "But that could have been what was used."

"Have you seen this?" He held it out to Clementine.

"Never," she said firmly.

He turned to Mrs. Watts. "You?"

"No," she responded. "Which is most irregular, because as housekeeper I would have overseen all inventory. It was not purchased by me and it must have been well hidden."

At that moment, Emmeline entered the room from where she'd waited, listening, one thought, from the hallway. She smiled at me, and then looked at the officer's notepad and indicated she'd like to take it. He gave her the pad and his writing implement. She turned the page and started drawing, quickly. We each looked to one another in the room, and I wondered, as I'm sure the others did, what she was drawing while her father stood protectively close behind her.

Clementine sobbed quietly into her handkerchief, mumbling Edward's name, but pulled herself together when Emmeline handed the notepad back to the constable.

He stared at it for a moment before questioning her. "You picked up the post from Mr. Galpine's and amongst the letters there was a box?"

She nodded.

"And you saw this box opened, and this jar of honey pulled from it?"

She nodded again.

"Who opened the box?"

She backed into her father for safety and then pointed at Clementine.

"Mrs. Everedge pulled the jar from the box?"

She nodded again, confirming. The constable turned to Clementine. "Is this true?"

"May I see the jar close up?" she asked quietly. "My vision is blurred, you understand, from weeping."

The jar was brought to her. "Yes . . . yes, now I remember. You understand, in the stress of the evening, I did not recall it right away. I did open it with the rest of the post, as I always do. But the box was addressed to my late husband, Edward."

The constable turned back to Emmeline. "Young lass, do you remember who the box was addressed to? Was it addressed to Mr. Everedge?"

Emmeline closed her eyes for a moment and then she nodded her agreement. The constable closed his notebook.

Each of us in the room knew it was entirely possible, and I believed probable, that Clementine had ordered that honey in Edward's name. If it were to come from his importing partners, and Clementine always took the post, she could order as she may with impunity. I knew she had ordered the Turkish honey and had dosed me to send me mad. I think the others knew it, too.

"I'll investigate," the constable said. I believed we all knew it would be found to be hallucinogenic. "Until then, Miss Ashton will remain here. Under my care."

Clementine turned to me. "Annabel, I am so sorry. I had no idea Edward had planned anything of this sort, or I would have intervened. Goodness me! His mind had grown unsteady—I'd noticed things. More and more things, actually. Strange behavior. Odd thoughts and the inability to control them. But I thought, well, things do run in families. Don't they?"

She locked eyes with me and then I knew.

She'd been poisoning Edward, too.

He *had* had symptoms, and was frightened because of it. I remembered his stumble on the stair after teatime, seeing Lady Somerford out. And his fear when I suggested that he, too, might be prone to insanity. After having me put away, Clementine had intended to have him committed to a madhouse as well. It was perhaps why she hadn't disposed of the honey. She still had need of it. Edward knew it, too, in the end. He died knowing his wife was sending him off next. Commit me to the lunatic asylum, show it was a family trait, commit Edward for life, then death.

Clementine's eyes did not soften though her voice did, and she turned toward the constable. "It may have been a terrible accident in every sense. I don't take honey in my tea, of course. Annabel must stay with me for a short visit until another situation can be found for her."

"I assure you a solution will be found, and it will not be to your liking," I said.

She held my gaze, contemptuously, and then she turned back to the constable, wringing her hands as a grieving widow would. "I have so much to understand about my late husband. I love him. Loved him. But if he tried to send her off tonight via the Keyhole, well, then, one must believe he was capable of such a thing as poisoning her as well. Perhaps his mind was unwell. Perhaps that runs in the family."

Her feminine, pity-inducing plea worked. Men could be so malleable. The constable muttered some kind words about not always knowing those we thought we knew best and closed his notebook.

It's very easy for all to assign blame to a dead man. Especially a dead man with many visible faults.

The constable offered his regrets again and asked if a telegram should be sent to anyone; Clementine mentioned her mother and then sent them off for the night.

Mrs. Watts turned to me and spoke quietly. "I'll put Mrs. Everedge to bed with a sleeping draught and then I'll be around to see you. While we were waiting, I prepared your old rooms. I have something to share with you."

"Thank you," I said. "I'll await your arrival."

Clementine turned toward me, eyes red, as she left the room. She spoke softly. "This hasn't altered your situation, Annabel. Edward's estate will, of course, come to Albert, to be managed by me. We shall discuss your options once Edward's had a decent Christian burial."

Her voice was hard. All pretense of friendship had fled.

I returned to my rooms, which had fresh linens and a fire, to wait for Mrs. Watts, and, in truth, to mourn Edward. Not the one who had died this very night, but the one who might have been, had he so chosen.

A knock on the door. "Come in," I called.

Mrs. Watts entered the room. "You must be very tired. Mr. Watts and I have agreed to be domiciled here once more until the funeral has passed and Mrs. Everedge and Albert return to London. So we can speak tomorrow if you'd prefer."

I shook my head. "No. Please, take a seat."

She joined me by the fire. The dragon clock still presided over the hearth and I found its familiar presence comforting.

"I don't think you remember, but my Christian name is Gabrielle, and I was your mother's lady's maid."

I looked at her face, which somehow transformed itself in my mind into the face of a younger woman. A memory came back.

Mummy sat on the dressing stool, where Gabrielle brushed and rolled her hair.

"Do you want a turn next, Annabel?" she asked me. She caught Gabrielle's glance in the mirror, and the young woman nodded.

I sat on the stool, and Gabrielle brushed my hair. It felt so good; it prickled all the way over my head and down to my toes.

I looked at Mrs. Watts. "I do remember, just a little. I was so young . . . so much has happened in the decades since."

She nodded kindly. "I know. When your mother was sent to Medstone, I thought it terribly unfair. But there was nothing I could do. Judith had her way, and her husband was a most intimidating and insistent man. I had not been her lady's maid for long; she'd had another woman, earlier, who had just married. But I found your mother to be a lovely woman and of sound mind. And, of course, I'm French."

French lady's maids were preferred, I knew. That explained the melodic lilt in her voice. The one time she'd ended a sentence with *non*. I poked the fire in the grate for a moment and then sat down. "I found my mother's grave marker at Medstone."

"I'm sorry you had to see that," she said.

"I'm not. I have little left of her, so the bits I can collect and keep are precious to me. The few memories. The sites and the knowledge of where she rests. Her necklace." I looked up at her. "You put that into my box, didn't you?"

She nodded. "I wanted to do for you what I hoped someone might do for Jack. It was for Jack's sake, you see, that I could not speak up. He works"—her voice caught a little—"worked for Mr. Everedge in London. He was so proud, and truth be told, Mr. Everedge was good to him. There are few opportunities around here for a young man. I did not know if the items I'd saved would help you in any way, or just bring you comfort. We had no cause to cross paths in the years you lived at home and you were but a child, of course, till you left for schooling and then Winchester. I would have had to give the items to one of the Mrs. Everedges, first or last, to pass along to you.

"Watts no longer served here, of course. And, in the end, they proved nothing about your . . . your . . . circumstances of birth, and I could not risk my son's future for sentiments, treasured as they may be."

I nodded. "I truly understand. The cap?"

"I took the necklace from your things when they were packing her bags. I found the cap after she'd left the house for the institution. Her sister Judith took the combs, of course; they were of great value. I took them back and kept them with me when I

left, hoping to return them to you someday. Mrs. Everedge—
Judith, that is—never learnt of it. I made sure the cap was in your
trunk when it was packed for you. I thought you were returning
to the institution and wanted you to have it. I was going to speak
with you last night . . . I heard you call through the tube."

Ah. The light footsteps I'd heard.

"But the door was locked. There was nothing I could do once
Mr. Everedge had decided. To be clear, we weren't sure of your
mental state. None of us knew about the honey. And, of course,
we servants have our own sweeteners downstairs."

I leaned forward. "Thank you," I said. "For all you have done."

"I believe that Maud was asked to procure the cap from your
room under a pretense, and she kept it. When Mrs. Everedge
next asked her to remove the combs from your rooms, Maud refused. Perhaps that was when she decided to leave service; she
gave the cap, quietly, to me. Perhaps she knew something about
the honey. She was very particular about sweeteners for Mrs.
Everedge."

I did not reveal Clementine's absinthe addiction; no doubt
Mrs. Watts already knew about it, as I recalled the housekeeper
and Maud arguing near the sugar cubes at the breakfast sideboard.

"Maud's gone?"

Mrs. Watts nodded. "Moved to London last week. Mrs. Everedge accused her of conspiring with you, and Maud did not want
to tarry and be accused by the mister and missus of heaven knows
what . . . as you were. Mr. Everedge had been acting odd as well.
She thought, we all thought, really, that perhaps it was floating in
the miasma and any one of us might be next."

It did not do to sympathize or socialize with the mad; others
thought you might be mad, too.

"Mrs. Everedge will miss her. Good lady's maids are hard to find. Maud's mother was a scullery maid, and she worked hard to raise herself above that station."

I sat back in my chair. "Maud told me about clipping things to my crinoline, things I wanted to keep private."

Mrs. Watts grinned and wrung her hands a little. "An old lady's maid trick. 'Twas good she shared it with you, but that's most likely how she knew how to help Clementine procure your cap."

"Do you have my ruby hair combs?"

She looked surprised. "No. Are they missing? Perhaps they were removed when you were taken to Medstone."

I shook my head. "No, they went missing before I left."

"I'm sorry," she said. "I don't know. The cap I know about, and the portrait of your parents . . . I believe it was burnt. Mr. Watts saw someone from the stables lighting the burn barrels shortly after the portrait was discovered, something that gave off a greasy odor when set alight. He couldn't be sure. Neither of us could, miss. We did what we could. It was he that left the slip of paper with Mr. Lillywhite's name."

"I am most grateful for all that you both have done on my behalf."

She stood. "What will you do now, miss?"

I took a deep breath and walked to the window, looking out. Where could I go? What could I do? I exhaled, fogging the window, which had lacy frost webs in each corner, before turning back to her. "I'm not certain what I shall do."

"Mr. Everedge has answered rather sharply for his role in this matter," she said. "It does not appear Mrs. Everedge will answer for hers . . . whatever part she may have played."

"None," I said, "according to her account." I sighed again and remembered her last words to me. Nothing had changed. "With Edward dead, I need not marry Mr. Morgan. Nor be returned to the madhouse. Perhaps I'll end up in the poorhouse." I tried to keep a jesting tone, but that was not a thing to jest about.

"If I may suggest, you'd make a fine lady's maid," she said. "With some training. Maybe Lady Leahy could help."

Yes, that was just the person with whom I needed to speak— Lady Leahy. In spite of Mrs. Watts's kind encouragement, a lady's maid position was not for me, but perhaps Elizabeth's friends had contacted her about a governess position. It would not be what I would have chosen, but would be a respectable way in which to settle.

"Would you be able to bring some writing papers to me?" I asked. "And then post letters for me? I'm very sorry, but at the moment I do not even have enough money to pay for a post."

She nodded. "Certainly. I'll do better than post them. I'll ask Lillian to give them to Mr. Galpine, so they'll be sent off with all speed. She's back at her father's house now. How many sheets of paper will there be?"

I allowed myself a smile. So Lillian still held sway over Mr. Galpine.

"Two," I said. One to be sent to Elizabeth in London. One to be posted to Malta. To Marco.

Edward's funeral was held shortly after that; we all wore mourning attire, myself and little Albert included. I wore it as a matter of form, and to respect the past he and I shared, but I should not wear it long; after all, he had tried, in effect, to murder me, or at least my spirit. I thought it unlikely anyone would dare to reprove me.

Clementine had purchased a fine coffin for Edward, which was installed in the family mausoleum overlooking the sheep fields. She'd made a point of telling me she'd had the other coffin burned, even though she would have to pay Medstone for it.

The afternoon after he was buried she called me to his study, which she had taken over. She perched on the edge of a leather chair; I sat across from her. She was close enough that the licorice spirit from her breath traveled across the space and further embittered the air between us.

"I've decided to make you a generous offer," she began. "I shall have the proceeds from the sale of Highcliffe very shortly and I will fund the, er, installation fee or whatever it's called for you to take sacred vows. To become a nun, as you said you wanted to."

"It's a dowry." I looked her in the eye. "I did not tell you that I wanted to become a nun. Someone at Pennington overheard me considering it and told you, which is why you raised the subject."

"Yes, well, you're not the only one with friends at Pennington," she neatly volleyed. I knew her implication was that Elizabeth was her friend and had told her.

"I don't make a habit of befriending carriage drivers, but I do understand that one was your source."

"Do not refuse my offer, Annabel," she said. "Or rebuke me in my kindness. I shall not offer again."

"Did Edward tell you I'd learned my father's name?"

She shrugged. "Yes, and what of it? There is nothing that can be proved even if your mother was married. I've enquired of Lilly-white. I wanted nothing to complicate the sale of Highcliffe."

Yes, of course. If I were proved heir and not Edward, she would not be able to sell Highcliffe.

"The cap, the necklace, the portrait . . ." I said. She did not flinch.

"The Maltese stamps at Galpine's."

Then she did.

"Oh yes, I know you had gone looking for them. To remove them." She said nothing, and I stood. "I'm sorry, but I have no calling to take sacred vows."

"Then you'd best find another position somewhere, with someone, quickly. You will remove yourself from my home within the week."

I turned to leave the room. "If my claim had been proved, I would have taken care of you and Albert."

"I *am* taking care of you, Annabel," she said. "Consider very carefully my proposal to fund your joining the Benedictine sisters in Winchester, as it will be my only offer. I've made enquiries. It seems they would welcome you."

CHAPTER THIRTY-SIX

A note arrived two mornings later, laid on my dressing table. I assumed Mrs. Watts had placed it there. It read, *Please meet me this afternoon in the Abbey.*

My heart leapt. Could it be from Marco? But the handwriting was a woman's. Marco would not have received my letter yet in any case, would not perhaps until just before Christmas. Then, too, there was no guarantee he would even respond. Was he the man I'd thought him to be? Or was he the man Edward claimed he was? Perhaps I should never know.

Lady Leahy, Elizabeth, would not have sent me a secret note, and though I still hoped to hear from her, too, she had probably only just received my letter. Who could have written this?

I did not have to wait long to find out.

After a light, welcome luncheon of salmon patties prepared by Chef, who had come back at my pleading until Clementine concluded Edward's affairs and returned to London, I pulled my boots on and walked down the stairs.

Emmeline tended the sheep in the distance; they looked like

giant puffs of breath hanging in the winter air. She waved at me, and I waved back. I slipped my way into the abbey.

"Hello?" I called out. "Who's there?"

A moment of fear passed through me; could Morgan have had his "sister" write the note and be waiting for me? Surely I would have seen his carriage. He had not tried to contact me since the night Edward had died.

"Miss Ashton." I turned around and saw Lillian waiting behind the door.

"Lillian!" I grinned and then my face fell. "My combs!" My ruby combs, the ones that had belonged to my mother, were neatly pushed into her hair.

She laughed. "Yes, your combs." She shook her hair out a little and then handed them to me. "One night when I approached Mrs. Everedge's room, to update her as to Albert's illness, I heard her instruct Maud to take the red combs from your room. I was not eavesdropping; she had not even cared to shut her door, so bold was she. Maud refused. When you left for Winchester that night . . ."

"The night of the soirée at Lord Mansfield's," I said.

"Precisely. I went to your room and took them. I knew you could not keep them safe, but I could hide them at my father's house."

I wrapped my hands around the combs, not caring if they pinched my palm in the process. "Thank you, Lillian. How go matters between you and Mr. Galpine?" I let my eyes twinkle at her.

"Very well indeed," she said. "I expect he shall soon be speaking to my father. It is for that very reason I have not taken on another position after Mrs. Everedge let me go. She was not pleased with me; I would not speak ill of you to the nurse who came to care for you in your, er, affliction."

"You've heard, then, that I was not truly afflicted. The constable has all but determined the cause of my symptoms to be a particular honey from Turkey that induces something like madness."

She blushed. "Yes. I'm sorry to say that none of us was sure if you were well or not, and would not have expected that of Mr. Everedge."

Nor should you have, I thought. I smiled at her. "Do not remonstrate with yourself." I would not tell her, but there had been recent times when I had not been completely certain I was sound! "It may be that soon I shall have to apply for a position. I must leave Highcliffe by the end of the week. Was Mr. Galpine able to post my letters? Mrs. Watts said she would deliver them to you."

"Indeed he was," Lillian said. "He's also safely kept the postmarks from Malta from years past. He understood the true meaning of them once Mrs. Everedge asked to rip them from the book." She kept smiling broadly, in a most unexpected way. I was truly happy that she'd returned my combs to me, but that did not seem to call for this level of jollity.

"I hope to hear back soon," I said.

"Indeed you shall!" She took my arm in her own.

"When I first sent the note to you," she said, "I thought that the happiest news I would have to share with you would be the return of your mother's combs. But I was wrong."

I tilted my head. "How?"

"Mr. Galpine handed me a letter, to you, from Lady Leahy. He was most insistent that it safely make its way to you and asked if I might assist. I assured him I would place it into your hands myself!"

She handed me the letter, sealed with an "L" for Leahy.

"Now that I've delivered both the combs and the letter to you, and I've no fear of Mrs. Everedge stopping us, I'll share my most happy news."

She smiled so largely I expected to hear her laugh. What was the cause of this?

We walked around the grounds until we'd nearly reached the Edge of the World. I saw Emmeline, in this distance, keeping an eye on me.

"Can you see it?" Lillian pointed toward the harbor in Lymington, some miles away.

"No." All was so distant, and gauzed in sea haze.

"I will tell you, then. A ship has arrived. From Malta."

"The *Poseidon*!"

Lillian laughed aloud. "Didn't you just send a letter to the captain of that ship?"

I nodded. "But a few days ago. It could not possibly have arrived in Malta by now."

"Well then," she said. "As of an hour ago, he's arrived without your bidding."

Hope suffused throughout me. Why would he come back if not for me?

Perhaps for the beautiful Miss Baker. My heart twisted as I turned the cameo on my finger. I hoped not.

Perhaps it was for his investment concerns.

With whom? Someone in Winchester? He would have sailed into Southampton or Portsmouth, then.

Lord Somerford? Lord Somerford was not here; he was in the north.

He must have come for me. Had he? *Had he?*

"What shall I do?" I asked Lillian.

She laughed again. "Change out of mourning! He's sure to arrive at Highcliffe soon!"

And so I changed. Mrs. Watts helped me find my clothing, which had been placed in storage until the house sale was complete, and I plucked out the silver evening gown Marco had so admired. It did not matter to me that it was daytime, and might be viewed as somewhat inappropriate. I'd already been viewed as being most irregular much of my life and did not care to concern myself with that just then.

I placed my mother's combs in my hair. I found the bottle of neroli oil and rubbed some into my hair, into my neck, into the pulse points at my wrists. Clementine was in the library, still in widow's crepe, when I went downstairs to read, Albert by her side, quietly stacking some blocks.

"Where did you find that dress, and why are you wearing it in the middle of the afternoon?" she asked. "It's perhaps a little flamboyant when Edward is so recently buried."

"The dress is mine," I simply answered. "And I'll honor him as he deserved to be honored."

I read my letter from Elizabeth. She promised to look into a situation for me, or perhaps, even better, introduce me to a Catholic gentleman in need of a governess. She told me her mother had come calling for me once and had been turned away, but was pleased to hear I was now well and would look forward to seeing me at Christmas.

I, of course, did not know if I would still be here at Christmas. I'd rather hoped she could find a situation for me even sooner, as Clementine had given me only six more days.

A carriage rumbled up the drive and Clementine stood. "I am not expecting anyone." She did not even think to ask, of course, if I was.

I stood near a window, too, but not too close to her. I did not wish to be within striking distance when she saw who alighted from the carriage.

"Mr. Lillywhite," she said, her voice reflecting light concern, then climbing a pitch higher on the scale of desperation. "And that Captain Dell'Acqua!" She turned to face me. "He's been gone more than a month and we had expected him never to return. Did you know about this?" She looked at my fancy gown and nodded knowingly.

"Not until today," I said sweetly. She had no more time to question me further, as the men were walking toward the door; Watts appeared prepared to let them in. Watts then came into the library to announce them.

"Well, bring them in, then, I suppose." Clementine waved her hand in irritation. Albert looked at me for guidance, sensing, I suppose, something freshly amiss in his newly upended life. I gently smiled at him in reassurance.

Clementine stood as they entered the room. "Mr. Lillywhite . . . Captain Dell'Acqua. What a surprise! I did not expect visitors. I'm in mourning, as you'll"—she nodded toward Lillywhite—"remember."

Both men offered sincere condolences.

And then, Marco locked eyes with me. There he stood—his blond hair pulled back into its queue. His rough-stubbled sailor's beard. His silk clothing. I did not believe, quite yet, that this was happening; I closed my eyes and swayed for a moment, overcome by emotion. I could barely keep myself from swooning. From smiling. From running toward him. I could not keep the smile from my face, however, and in spite of the somber week he smiled broadly back.

"It is for that very reason I have come," Mr. Lillywhite said. "After having spoken with Captain Dell'Acqua." He nodded politely at me, but I caught a note of pleasure in his mostly somber face. "May I speak with you, Mrs. Everedge, in the study?"

She nodded. "I'll leave Albert with you, Annabel," she said. She made no mention of Captain Dell'Acqua.

Once they left the room, though they were just in the next room, Marco came and took my hands in his own, then pulled me to my feet and embraced me in a most intimate, most welcome way. I felt the warmth of him radiate through me, smelled his sandalwood soap and Arabian cologne; they made me heady.

"You came back," I said softly as he let go of me and led me to two soft chairs by the window, where we could still keep an eye on Albert.

"Of course I did. Was there any question?"

I raised my eyebrow. "I had no idea you would ever return."

He pulled his jacket back to reveal his rooster-embroidered waistcoat. "I could not let down the one who was most dependent upon me. You shall see. I could have stayed and said much, but, *un oceano si trova tra ciò che viene detto e ciò che è fatto.*" An ocean lies between what is said and what is done.

"You did not abandon me, then." I brushed a tear away. He lifted his hand to my other cheek, catching the tear's twin.

"No, my love, I raced the wind and mastered the sea to do the one thing that I knew could save you."

"I do not understand," I said. "Oliver made certain I received your parting gift. The empty oyster shell. I understood its meaning—that you had opened yourself to the possibilities—but, in the end, found our, er, association to be empty at heart."

He laughed lightly, though I did not think it amusing and pursed my lips to convey that.

"Bella, no. That was not the meaning. I could not risk a note but, in this case, my unspoken message went completely awry. I opened myself, the tightly closed oyster, as you'd said. I found the pearl, but the pearl was lost when I lost you. Without you, Bella, I am empty inside." He put his closed fist to his heart for emphasis.

"Oh." A little sigh escaped my mouth. "But then why did you leave? You've heard that Edward had me committed . . ."

He smiled again. "Yes."

"Why are you smiling?" I demanded, though I kept my tone lighter than the words themselves might have implied. "That was no sport."

"I'm smiling because I heard how you escaped. You see? The Maltese woman inside you broke out of her English coffin. Literally and figuratively!"

"An English girl broke out of that coffin," I sniffed. Then I laughed. Then I grew somber again. "I see you've heard Edward has died."

"I'm very sorry for that," he said. "He was not a good man, but did not perhaps deserve that death. You understand that I had returned to Highcliffe, before I went to Malta, to tell him that we could not sign a contract."

I nodded. "He told me it was because of me."

"No." He took my hands in his own again, enveloping them completely. "If anything, I considered the possibilities far too long knowing that your family home was at stake, which gave me an excuse to do what I wanted to do, though I thought it, perhaps, wrong. He was not going to use local lads for work, men who needed it, but was going to bring in outside labor cheaply. I could not abide that; it was not my intention. Somerford eventually backed out, too; he was only to invest for the good of the men hereabouts. He and I said we would consider the ropewalks together, on more moral terms and only for the benefit of local families, here and in Malta. I did not have a chance to finalize that with him, though, before I fled."

"Edward was not a good man," I said. "But it pains me to think this of him."

"I was not so very different than he was, not so very long ago." Marco looked in my eyes, searching me, seeking an answer to a question he had not yet posed. I did not turn away, though my middle weakened and my breath came quickly. "I found a new star to navigate by—you, Bella—and changed courses because you saw something good in me. When you said I was like Swithin, I knew I was not. But then, I wanted to be."

He'd just said I was his star.

"If I'd not left, perhaps your cousin would not be dead," he continued. "I feel badly about this."

I reached out and touched his face. "Edward's death was of his own making. Do not blame yourself. And though I should not care to repeat my confinement, if I had not gone to Medstone I should not have found my mother's grave, nor understood that portion of her life and learned that she died in peace, something I'd always yearned to know. I might not have developed a tender conscience toward those incarcerated within, who are much like you and me, and who became my friends. I should not have learned my father's last name. I was kept safe, for a time, while you sailed back to Malta to find proof of my parents' marriage. Had I not been confined, Edward might have sent me to Mr. Morgan much sooner. I should not have known how very much I treasure life in whatever form it is given, and how much I was willing to risk to keep it."

The winter wind rattled the sea salt–filmed panes next to us, and Watts came in to stir the fire; it was dusk now, and he began to light the lamps. He had hovered in the background, a most unusual chaperone, but the only one at hand; and it allowed us to talk in private, though now more softly.

"On one point, you are wrong," he said. I opened my mouth to ask him what he meant, but he put his finger softly to my lips to hush me. Against the gentle pressure, I obeyed.

"Why did you flee?" I said when he removed his hand.

"Because of your nurse," he said simply. "Your Sister Rita."

"Sister Rita? My nurse's name was Mrs. Strange, not Sister Rita. Sister Rita was the nun who taught me to speak Maltese, a Benedictine sister."

"Yes, I know—you'd just told me that very night, you'll recall. In the abbey. When I returned to discuss the termination of our arrangements with Edward, who would not let me speak with you, your nurse stopped me on the way out. She spoke to me in perfect Maltese. She handed me this." He withdrew something from his pocket. "And then she told me you'd be safe with her. I knew you trusted her, and so I did, too."

"My mother's sketchbook!" I snatched it from his hand, and he laughed.

"Yes. And she told me to return to Malta with all speed. So I did. You'd said she was old, though." His face looked puzzled.

"Sister Rita *was* old, at least thirty years older than Mrs. Strange, the nurse," I said. "And I did not know Mrs. Strange could speak Maltese."

"And yet . . ." Marco began.

"And yet." I looked at him strangely, and then at the sketchbook, and I smelt the faint aroma of incense once again. From where did it come?

"On the way back to Malta, I paged through the notebook, wondering why you had given it to me. And then, I suddenly knew. It was divinely appointed, I think, Bella."

"I did not send it to you," I said. "Mrs. Strange must have done that on her own."

Now it was his turn to look bewildered. He spoke on, however.

"I did not know if you intended to marry Mr. Morgan."

I could not keep the reflexive revulsion from my face, and he grinned. "Or," he continued, "if you'd intended to take sacred vows, as you'd once mentioned. I only knew that I must do what I could for you, to restore your faith in Maltese men and to rescue you if you wanted to be rescued."

I nodded. *Yes, yes, how I wanted—want—you to rescue me.*

"When you returned the quail egg, uneaten, that night, I thought that perhaps you did not feel for me as I did for you. But I pressed on for your sake, if not mine."

"I returned it uneaten so you could see that you, like Swithin, could make me whole and I did not wish to be broken any longer!"

He laughed. "Perhaps we have learnt a lesson, you and I, about unspoken messages."

I grinned. "Perhaps."

At that moment, Clementine stormed from the study and yanked Albert up, by the hand, before racing upstairs.

Mr. Lillywhite followed after, and we stared questioningly.

"I shall meet you in the hall," he said to Marco. He turned toward me. "I shall return to speak to you within days, Miss Ashton."

I nodded and then stood and faced Marco, who stood, too.

"Are you to leave, then, so soon?" My voice pleaded, I knew, but I did not care.

"Yes," he said. "But I shall return very soon. I have something for you, a gift."

I drew near to him, not caring who might see. "You are the gift."

He pulled me into his arms and embraced me for a moment. "You will see, Bella—patience. Where is the self-controlled English girl?" He held me at arm's length and squeezed both of my hands at once. Then he was gone.

Late that night, Oliver appeared at the door with a note from Marco. Watts made sure it was delivered to me. Clementine had not been seen since fleeing the study.

I went into my rooms and opened the letter.

Bella,

I sent a trusted man to the Benedictine sisters; they told him there had never been a Sister Rita who served with them, and as they were mostly Belgian and English, did not think a Maltese woman had lived among them. I sent the man to Medstone, too, to enquire after your Mrs. Strange. She has not been seen since you left, but this is not unusual. She serves as a private nurse and leaves when her charges do.

Due to some seasickness, my guest and I will not visit you until the day after next. Patience, my self-controlled English girl.

Marco

A guest? I wondered who that could be; I should learn soon enough, and should try to be patient for Marco's sake.

I took my sketchbook and quietly left for the quarantine room where I'd found it, to pray, as we had no chapel at Highcliffe.

CHAPTER THIRTY-SEVEN

DECEMBER, 1851

It was dark, of course, so I brought my lamp. There were so few servants, now, and no one who could contain me, and so I stepped heavily and with ease. It did not matter who heard me. I opened the door to the room and stepped inside.

The cot was still made up, as no one had likely visited in the days since Edward had trapped me in here. I looked at the drawers of the cabinet but found nothing else of my mother's.

Why had young Mrs. Strange given the sketchbook to Marco? Why hadn't she told me her intentions, or that she could speak Maltese? Where had old Sister Rita gone, and even more importantly, who had she been?

I said my prayers, and then after a few minutes, I stood and went to the window, picking up the old spyglass. The sea mists were thick; I could not see the *Poseidon* or, indeed, much of anything beyond the cold window. I put it down and looked once more at the stained glass.

The angels tending Jesus in his hour of need. And there, in a tiny corner, I spied something I had not seen before. Psalm 91 carefully etched on the glass.

I returned to the cot and picked up my Bible; it, too, remained from my brief and recent captivity. I turned to Psalm 91 and began to read.

> *Because thou hast made the Lord, which is my refuge, even the most High, thy habitation, there shall no evil befall thee, neither shall any plague come nigh thy dwelling. For He shall give His angels charge over thee, to keep thee in all thy ways.*

A rush of understanding. The sudden light of knowledge. The sweetness of love. I looked up once more to the stained glass and spoke.

"You are not mute in the dark, Father, though I may not always be able to see Your hand or recognize Your servants, or who they are, at work. You've never left me. You've never forsaken nor forgotten me."

Peace embraced me warmly, a faint incense filled the room once more, and I sensed the presence.

"Thank you," I whispered. And then the presence and the smoky scent were gone.

The next morning, Albert knocked on the door to my rooms. "Come in, young man," I said. "Why are you on your own?"

"Mama is crying," he said. "Because of Papa. She said I'm to call you Auntie Annabel henceforth. Isn't that lovely?"

I kissed the top of his head. "Yes, it is."

Auntie Annabel? Knitting the bonds of kinship ever more tightly after Mr. Lillywhite's visit. What had he said?

"Run along now and see if Chef has any sweets he does not know what to do with. Then I shall perhaps speak with your mama about finding a nurse. I saw Lillian, you know. She loves you so."

"As I do her," Albert said, skipping from my room.

I dressed myself and rolled my hair back, fastening it with silver hair clips. Within an hour I saw a carriage pull up; I did not recognize the driver. It was most probably a hired carriage. I peeked out through the window and saw Marco exit. Joy soared inside me, and then I watched as, curiously, he helped a man out of the carriage.

I could not be certain. The man was older and was dressed like a priest. But he looked like my father.

My stomach clenched. Surely Marco would not have kept this kind of secret from me. I was ill prepared for a reunion, and yet I knew Mrs. Watts would summon me downstairs momentarily.

I sat on my bed, caught my breath, and reapplied some lemon chalk powder and neroli oil.

A tick of the dragon clock. A knock on my doors. "Miss Ashton? Captain Dell'Acqua and another gentleman are here to see you."

I stood and then walked down the stairs, where Marco and his guest waited for me.

Could it be . . . could it be my father? He looked just like the man in the portrait.

"Miss Annabel Ashton, I'd like to introduce you to Father Giovanni Bellini. Father Giovanni, Miss Ashton. I'm sorry we could not come more quickly, but Father was recovering from the rough sea journey."

"How do you do." I held my hand out to him, and he took it,

shook it, and then did away with the pretense and embraced me. "Father?" I asked when he let go, and I caught my breath.

"Father," he said softly, "*Si*. Father as in a priest, but uncle to you."

I hoped my disappointment did not show on my face. He was not my papa.

"Shall we sit down?" Marco steered us toward a trio of chairs with a table in the center. Mrs. Watts soon appeared with a teapot and three cups.

"Honey?" Marco teased me to break the tension, and it did. I laughed and immediately was able to regain my confidence.

"You are my father's brother," I said.

Father Giovanni nodded. "His older brother."

"My father . . . ?"

"Sailed and fought the battles for Greek independence. He passed away a long time ago. In the Battle of Navarino, in 1827."

The year I was born.

Father Giovanni thanked Mrs. Watts, who smiled at me and then left the room. "I assure you, if your father had been alive he would have tracked you down without hesitation. He—we—did not know you existed."

"He died before I was born."

"It seems so," my uncle continued. "We wrote when your father died, and when the response came from your mother's sister, there was no mention of a child. We thought perhaps your mother was too grief-stricken to write herself, and then, perhaps, had immersed herself back into the English life."

Any other mail my mother might have tried to send was most probably intercepted. Perhaps when my father never answered, she gave up.

Father Giovanni continued. "Later, Judith wrote to us, to the family, to tell us your mother was dead. We were all very sorry to hear that, of course. But we did not know this treasure, this Bella Bellini, existed." He reached over and kissed my cheeks again.

Maltese, Marco mouthed to me, and I smiled.

"When Sister Rita passed your sketchbook on to me, I could not imagine why," Marco said. "I knew it must have been a treasure to you, and so cruel to keep it from you. I suspected that she thought it might be taken from you and perhaps gave it away for safekeeping. But why me? That is what I wondered."

Clementine walked down the hall but did not call by the library for introductions.

Eavesdropping.

"Partway into my two-week journey home, I looked through the pages most carefully. Missing you," he admitted openly, which brought a smile to my uncle's face. "And then I came to some pictures of houses in Valletta. There are only a few thousand people, so I know each area well. I recognized a house. There was a house number drawn on it, and bougainvillea cascading over the wrought-iron fence, which had been carefully crafted. 'Bellini!' I said to myself. 'She has been to the Palazzo Bellini.' I pushed my men and my ship to arrive with all haste. And when I did, I visited the Bellinis and, *ecco*, they knew of your mother. They did not know of you."

"Mama was so happy," my uncle said. "She is still crying, I expect. Tears of joy. We had to make her promise not to swim out after the *Poseidon*."

I had an uncle. I had a grandmother, one who would swim the sea to reach me. A father who would not have stopped pursuing me. A mother who cherished me, who dubbed me her sweetness and light.

I looked up at Marco, who smiled hopefully, tentatively. He was strong and yet willing to be vulnerable to me, did not like England and yet had returned, had guarded his heart inside a rough shell and then opened it, and told me I was the missing pearl.

This was my man.

"Your parents met when your mother was on the Grand Tour," Father Giovanni continued. "She wandered the cathedrals looking for art, good art, to draw and to paint, and *ecco*, she found it. But she also found faith, and she found love. My brother."

"They loved each other," I said. The winter wind squalled off the sea and battered the walls, chill seeping into the room, but I hardly noticed. I'd never felt warmer from the inside.

"Indeed they did," he affirmed.

I held my breath, then let the question softly escape. "They were married . . ."

He nodded. "I married them myself. I filed the paperwork with the church. The witnesses are still alive. Have no fear! Your mother was a beautiful bride . . . the bride of a distant isle; for her, Malta. And from a distant isle to us, England."

Something dropped and clattered in the hallway. I stood up and walked toward the window to gather myself and then returned to my seat and squeezed back the tears, speechless for a minute.

"I'm sorry," I said. "It's just that . . ."

Father Giovanni . . . my uncle . . . reached over and took my hand. "No need to apologize. You've done well. You're a strong Maltese woman."

I laughed. "We English are quite sturdy stock."

"Your English mother was very strong, and beautiful, and talented," he answered softly. "My brother adored her. Her sister, Judith, wanted him for herself, but he had nothing of it. It was Julianna and only Julianna for him."

Judith had wanted my father! And ended up with Everedge. It was enough to make you pity her.

Almost.

I recalled the belladonna inscription my mother had written beneath her sister's picture. Poisonous, beautiful woman indeed.

"I . . . I am legitimate," I said. And I was not insane. I need not become a lady's maid or a governess. I need not marry Mr. Morgan. Elizabeth and I could remain friends. I could not be returned to Medstone but I could use my newly found largesse, whatever it may be, to help my friends who could not leave.

"Yes," Marco said. "And that is what Mr. Lillywhite shared with Mrs. Everedge the day I first returned. I asked him not to tell you until you could meet your uncle, first. Lillywhite asked Mrs. Everedge not to say anything, either. We wanted nothing to spoil that."

"And she kept her word," I said, though I better understood Albert's new title for me now. Clementine would want us all to be family . . . intimate. Obligated.

"He had to tell her that the sale of Highcliffe would be stopped," he said. "Edward had not been the rightful owner and therefore could not legally convey it."

"I am the rightful owner?" My voice sounded high and wondering even to my own ears. All the years of hiding in the pantry or being locked in the linen cupboard, the years of keeping out of Aunt Judith's way, and most recently, of having been placed in the quarantine room came back to me. The Christmases I had not been allowed to return for.

Highcliffe was no longer to be my prison in any sense of the word. It was my home. I was its mistress. All of my Christmases had come at once.

"You are the rightful owner." Marco stood and looked at Father Giovanni, who was wavering a little on the small sofa. *Not yet used to the steady land*, I thought. *Time for him to return to rest.*

I offered my uncle rooms at Highcliffe, but he said he preferred the simple comfort of the ship. We walked to the hall, and after I kissed my uncle good-bye and promised to visit with him soon, the driver helped him to the carriage.

Marco remained in the hall with me for just a moment. "About Highcliffe. I had thought, if I were to work with Somerford, I might make an offer to its rightful owner."

"I may be persuaded to entertain an offer, Captain Dell'Acqua," I teased. "Perhaps a deal might be struck."

"What offer would you entertain?" He leaned toward me and held my gaze. I thought he was going to kiss me there in the foyer, but after a moment he asked, "Could your uncle and I collect you tomorrow, in the carriage, after he's rested? There is something I'd like you to see."

I nodded. "Of course."

"Until then, Bella." He took my ungloved hand in his own and brushed his lips and beard against it before leaving. My hand tingled to life.

I watched him until he reached the carriage, and then he turned and waved to me. This time, I waved back. In the distance, Emmeline corralled her sheep, chasing after one that had wandered away, bringing it back to the fold.

I should see Oliver reinstated as hall boy, promptly, and promote him from there.

I turned and began to walk toward the stairs, not caring who saw the wide grin on my face.

"Annabel," Clementine sang out. "If you have a moment."

She was not exactly pleasant, but she wasn't throwing icicles any longer, either.

"Of course."

This time, I took the lead. I walked to the study, which would soon become *my* study, and closed the door behind us.

She seemed flustered and did not know where to sit. I indicated the chair in front of a sturdy writing table and then I sat behind it.

"With regard to Highcliffe."

"I don't intend to sell it," I said. "I'm sure you heard that the priest Captain Dell'Acqua brought with him is my uncle. He officiated at my parents' wedding and retained the necessary documentation."

She nodded. "It's not as though one can eavesdrop in one's own home."

One certainly can. "This is no longer your home," I said.

"Annabel. Everything I did, I did for Albert's sake. Not for my sake, not for Edward's sake, but for Albert's sake. Edward did everything that was immoral, unethical, or harmful. You saw how unkind he was to me. You lived how unkind he was to you. I only went along with it. What else could I do?"

"That is the very thing I expect Judith Everedge told herself with regards to my mother." My hands were balled into fists behind the table where she could not see them. I kept my face placid and self-controlled. "But you used tainted honey to try to have me admitted, forever, to an insane asylum. And Edward was next. He died knowing it."

She had the decency to flinch.

"There is no evidence I did anything wrong," she said. "Edward ordered the honey and made every other arrangement. I was not involved."

She was right that I lacked evidence. But we both knew she had been the hand in the glove. "You will depart before Christmas. I will file an enquiry with the constable, and though they may not find proof, this time it will be on the record should any harm come to anyone in your acquaintance henceforth."

She stood up and fairly shrieked, decorum and false grief and remorse having fled. "Where am I to go? Albert! You said you would have taken care of Albert and me, and now you reverse your word?"

I said nothing for a long minute. She gathered herself, perhaps realizing that her tantrum would not bring her favor.

"I have not thought this through, of course, completely," I said. How could I have? "Perhaps you could return to Dorsetshire. 'Tis not far away. I would be able to visit you . . . and keep up with Albert, his health and well-being."

She nodded. "My mother won't have me forever. She shamed me for . . . the situation that led to my marriage with Edward and wants little to do with me or with Albert." I pitied her. She had a living mother who rejected her in favor of her sons, and though mine was dead, my mother had loved me without boundary.

"Perhaps you can marry again," I said. "Someone who loves you this time, thereby doing away with the reliance on licorice spirits. I am prepared to fund Albert's nanny and eventually schooling and a number of his other expenses. The nanny and headmaster shall report to me and me alone each and every month, regarding his well-being and the environment provided in your home. I cannot, however, in good conscience, support you. Any investments, after debts are paid, which were Edward's alone and did not derive from family funds shall, of course, be yours."

We both knew there would be little to eat from that particular pot.

"Choose wisely next time," I said, not caring if I lectured after all she had put upon me. "One cannot quarantine oneself from a husband. What he is often is what one becomes."

She nodded. It was an easier pill to swallow, I think, to believe she was good at heart and tainted by a bad man rather than that she had enjoyed the fruits of his dealings all along.

She departed, and I asked Mrs. Watts to bring a tray to my room for supper, which she gladly did, along with a return letter from Elizabeth rejoicing in my health and looking forward to a Christmas together.

I went to bed early.

I wanted to be well rested on the morrow.

CHAPTER THIRTY-EIGHT

My uncle chaperoned us the following day, a day that was filled with, fittingly, sweetness and light. It was cold outside, but the fur-lined cloak I wore kept me warm, as did my muff. Albert hugged my leg as I left the house and I promised him I'd soon return, and we'd draw pictures together by the fire in the library. If he was especially good, perhaps we might even take the covering off the billiard table and I would show him how to play.

We drove down the lane and soon arrived in Lymington, at the harbor. My uncle stayed in the carriage but could see us. We alighted from the carriage and stepped onto the quay.

"She's . . . different!" I looked at his ship. As we stood in front of the prow the men aboard scrambled out of the way, giving us privacy. The ship was well cared for as always, but what had changed was . . . "The mast!" I said.

He laughed. "Can't help but notice, can you."

Where Poseidon alone had blazoned the way across the seas on the bowsprit before, now there was a woman by his side. She was not a mermaid but a proper lady. Except for her hair. Her black hair was wild and free and flew out behind her in waves as though it were being blown by the oncoming wind.

"She has black hair," I said, looking up at Marco with a smile.

"And blue eyes." He winked and took my hand in his own.

"I thought you said a woman would distract you and your men as you sailed."

"I had thought that to be true. But I've had a change of heart. I still sail," he said, looking at me firmly, "and must always. But the men and I now can look forward to returning home to someone, someone who is guiding us there in the heart and on the ship."

"Who is she?" I asked. My voice was a husky whisper in the cold air.

"She's the Bride of Poseidon," he said. "*Jien inħobbok*, Bella," he said in Maltese. *I love you.*

"*Jien inħobbok għal dejjem*," I whispered. *I will love you forever.*

"I had asked you to be mine before I left and you did not answer."

"You had not asked me to marry you," I pointed out.

"What? Oh. Ay!" He hit his forehead with his one free hand.

"I thought perhaps your mother wouldn't allow it," I teased. "Foreign woman."

He turned to face me and caressed my face with his hand. "I told her you could speak Maltese. That you *are* Maltese. Neither convinced her. Then I told her that if I did not marry you then you would most probably take sacred vows. Now, once she understood that to you, the only sensible choice was between me and no man, she saw immediately that you were wise and gave her blessing. It does help," he said with a grin, "that she knows Mama Bellini. But no matter what she thought, I'd marry you as soon as you'd allow."

He pulled me toward him until I was warm and kissed me

again and again, as a man would when suddenly given leave to do that which he had long dreamt of.

"Please marry me, Annabel Ashton Bellini."

I remembered what his friend had said early in our acquaintance. *A loving father only chooses a man who will love and cherish his daughter.* Was this the man my father had chosen? "Will you leave me?" I asked, thinking of how the sea had swallowed my father and with him, my life.

"If you mean the sea, I must sail away from time to time, but I will always return home to you, and only you, wherever those homes may be. If you mean, will I ever leave you for another? No. Absolutely not. I promise this. There has never been another woman who has captured my heart. There is no other; there could not be. There will never be another."

A lifetime had unraveled and then been re-knit since I'd left Winchester seven months earlier, hoping for a quiet life as a teacher. I had learnt who I was, and that I was beloved, and that I could chance risk and prevail. I did not know if the sea would take him from me. But I knew that nothing else, and no one else, would. I once thought I fitted everywhere because I belonged nowhere. I now knew where I belonged. With Marco.

"Yes," I said. "I will marry you, Marc Antonio Dell'Acqua." He pulled me to him and as he did, he kissed each cheek and kissed my eyelids and caressed my face once more before he took my face in both his hands and kissed my lips.

"There is one thing I have been longing to do," he said. "Something I promised myself I would do as soon as you agreed to become my wife."

I arched an eyebrow, and he laughed. "I assured you I am not a rogue, Bella. For that, I will wait for the priest's blessing. No, what I want to do is to free you."

I nodded my approval, and he unpinned my long black hair and then ran both hands through it, which tumbled in the wind. His hands sent a shiver through me, and I grinned as I heard the roar of approval and applause that came from the ship.

I was to be the bride of a distant isle, too.

He kissed me tenderly once more and then my uncle alighted from the carriage, aware, one thought, of his chaperoning duties as uncle and priest.

"Do you remember what once you told me?" I asked Marco.

"Of what do you speak, Bella? Please, remind me, my love."

I drew near to him, and he tucked me securely and with love underneath his arm.

"*Alla fine andrà tutto bene se non andrà bene, non e le fine,*" I said.

All will be well in the end; if it's not well, then it's not the end.

EPILOGUE

―――――― ∾⦿∾ ――――――

Homer called Malta the center of the sea, and though England was and always would be my home, on this day, Malta was the center of my world.

We'd left our palazzo in a horse-drawn carriage, netting covering all round so the breezes might cool us while we remained protected from tiny flying pests or wheel-thrown rocks. I sat on one side of the carriage holding our child and twisting the long strand of pearls—Marco's wedding gift—with the other. Marco sat across from us, arms extended in case the carriage should jostle the baby.

"How will he be a courageous sailor if you're overattentive during a carriage ride?" I teased.

"Can't be too cautious," he grumbled. A rooster strutted in the center of our driveway, unafraid. I grinned. A worthy mascot, indeed. I glanced down at the sleeping bundle in my arms.

"You've heard Morgan has been sent to Australia," Marco said.

"I'd never! But I cannot say I am surprised. I am certain that it was he in the boat the night Edward died. For what was he sent to Australia?"

"A variety of offenses that may have led to hanging a man who was not as well connected. Instead, they'll ship him off for good. Hopefully he won't harm anyone else," Marco said. "In any case, my love, he shall ever be far from you, from us."

I pulled my son close, thankful he was out of reach from all who had intended to harm me.

My son. Our son. "You are not *filius nullius*," I whispered to Alessandru as I kissed my child's plump cheeks. "You are a child of Malta, a child of Hampshire, a child of God, the beloved son of Marc Antonio Dell'Acqua. Most of all . . . my son." I kissed his little cheek again and his mouth opened into a small "O" before he drifted toward sleep once more, his head falling heavily against my arm.

We made our way down the narrow lanes, the turn of the wheels echoing off the rounded cobblestone. The houses did seem to be carved in buttery stone; in fact, the entire island was alive with gold, saffron, mustard, and yellow. It was as though the sun lit everything from within and without. Doors painted in emerald or olive opened into courtyards with laughing families; turquoise balconies were lashed by wrought iron; oval Arabian windows framed the sides of the doorways.

We pulled up at Mama's palazzo, and she ran out to the carriage, greeting Marco and me as quickly as she could, and then relieved us of the baby, who woke and then laughed with her. He was, after all, given the day's pride of place. It was his *il-quċċija*.

Once inside, I saw tables groaning with food to the left and to the right. My own grandmother was already in the room, adding her offering to the copious bounty. She kissed me again and again and then returned to help Mama Dell'Acqua. I approached the table with the *il-quċċja* items on it.

A boiled egg, a gold coin. A quill, a small book, a cross.

A sailor's knot.

I reached my hand toward it; it would not be missed. I had already lost my father to the sea; each year I would risk losing Marco, too. I did not want to lose my son.

A loving hand reached round me and then enclosed my own hand, the one that held the knot.

"No, my Lady Poseidon, you shall not," Marco teased. "Alexander will rule the seas someday."

Alexander. Not Alessandru. I suppressed a grin and replaced the knot on the table. I would let my boy choose his own fate, his own destiny, guided by the hand of God.

It had turned out well for me.

AUTHOR'S NOTE

Christianity was established in England in the first or second century; of course, Christianity at that time meant, for the most part, the faith as celebrated by the Roman Catholic Church; non-Catholic worship was prohibited and dissenters, including Protestants, were often swiftly and severely punished. Although there were dissenters throughout the centuries, the Catholic Church remained the official church of England until Henry VIII famously broke with Rome in 1534 to establish the Church of England. Following this, all religious properties in England became properties of the crown. Many of them were distributed to friends and supporters of the king, and their families and heirs then inherited them throughout the ages. It is for this reason that many noble houses have names that include religious terms such as "Abbey" in them.

Henry's daughter Elizabeth tried to walk the *via media*, the middle ground between Protestantism and Catholicism, and was tolerant of Catholic worship early in her reign as long as it did not become treasonous. When it did, she acted swiftly; later in her reign that swift action became more frequent and began to reach down to middle- and lower-class Catholics. Highly born Catholics were safe, and some, such as the Dukes of Norfolk—the premier duke—retained power and influence in every age and era after that. However, the common Catholic was penalized, as were others in the intermediate social strata. According to *One Hundred and Fifty Years A-Growing: The Story of the Catholic Parish of Lymington*, "From 1577 the authorities decided to impose more severe measures for disobeying the religious laws of the land. These included a £5 fine, equivalent to £1000 today (about US $1500) for non-attendance at a Protestant Sunday service."

James I, who succeeded Elizabeth I, was even more staunchly Protestant. It was he who commissioned the King James Bible. In spite of a few ensuing years with a Catholic monarch (notably James II, 1685–1688), Britain remained strictly Protestant. "The Act of 1700, provided rewards to spies and informers against Catholics . . ." according to *One Hundred and Fifty Years A-Growing*, which also tells us, "The New Marriage Act of 1753, compelled Catholics to marry in the Protestant Parish church to legalize the marriage. This rule continued until the early days of Queen Victoria's reign." Catholic couples were often married in their own faith, and then "remarried" to comply with the law.

Change was coming, but slowly. *A-Growing* states that the "Catholic Relief Act of 1788 enabled Catholics to buy and inherit legally, and it was no longer an offense punished with life-imprisonment to exercise the functions of a Catholic Priest, or run a Catholic school."

The Catholic family upon which I loosely based the Somerfords were the generous Welds. Mr. Thomas Weld of Lulworth Castle bought Pylewell House (Milford on Sea) in 1801 for the use of his son Joseph; he was also a founding member of the Royal

Yacht Squadron. *A-Growing* confirms that "A year or so after the Welds first took over Pylewell House, a large ground-floor room at the south end of the house was converted into a chapel, where Mass and other services could be held. The chapel was available for 'all the local Catholics, both estate and employees, and others living nearby.'" Indeed, chapels were set up in private homes all across England for just such a purpose.

It was true that some priests also served as chefs, and some as butlers, to be legally present and indistinguishable in Catholic households. *A-Growing* states, "Some other Catholic landowners in this district . . . often employ(ed) a man in their household who was in reality an ordained priest, and could minister to their spiritual needs."

The Emancipation Act of 1829 brought more freedoms, including assuring Catholics the freedom to vote and hold office, and freedoms slowly returned to England's Catholic subjects. Prejudice, however, remained.

As for that honey Clementine so effectively employed! It has long been known in the ancient world. The Greeks are believed to have been the first to name the honey harvested from bees that feasted on rhododendron blossoms "mad honey." It was supposed to be a truth serum, and also an aphrodisiac. As for the effects? "This amber-hued mutant's effects range from a pleasant tingling to dizziness, blurred vision, and impaired speech. Worse, it was once used as a weapon of war. In 67 BC, King Mithridates's army left chunks of 'mad honeycomb' in the path of the Roman enemy, who gobbled it up, lost their minds and were promptly slain" (*The Guardian*, October 1, 2014).

According to the September 2014 issue of *Modern Farmer*, "The dark, reddish, 'mad honey,' known as deli bal in Turkey, contains an ingredient from rhododendron nectar called grayanotoxin—a natural neurotoxin that, even in small quantities, brings on light-headedness and sometimes, hallucinations. In the 1700s, the Black Sea region traded this potent produce with Europe, where the honey was infused with drinks to give boozers a greater high than alcohol could deliver."

The article continues, "When over-imbibed, however, the honey can cause low blood pressure and irregularities in the heartbeat that bring on nausea, numbness, blurred vision, fainting, potent hallucinations, seizures, and even death, in rare cases. Nowadays, cases of mad honey poisoning crop up every few years—oftentimes in travelers who have visited Turkey."

Turkey has long been the trading partner that connects Asia and Europe. For a family involved in import, smuggling, or both, acquiring some would have been an easy get.

So what if you didn't eat any *deli bal*? Could you still be considered mad? Of course you could. The Trans-Allegheny Lunatic Asylum, on the other side of the Atlantic held similar requirements for confinement; it listed some reasons for admission from 1864 to 1889, and they included:

Reading novels
Nursing too long
Political excitement
Time of life (perhaps related to another reason for admission, *Uterine Derangement*)
Laziness or, conversely, Hard Study
And, yes, *Immoral Life, or Moral Madness*

Having someone admitted to an insane asylum was made more difficult in England due to the Lunacy Act of 1845, but it was not impossible, especially for those with money or influence.

According to *Life in the Victorian Asylum* by Mark Stevens (which I loosely based my account upon), one in four hundred British subjects were placed in an asylum during the Victorian era. About 2 percent of them escaped, if you counted the criminally insane.

The quote about bees who fill their "hives with honey and wax; thus furnishing mankind with the two noblest of things, which are sweetness and light" was written by Jonathan Swift, and appropriate to the era, but the author would not have been remembered by Annabel at that young age, so I did not quote Swift in the book.

Finally, there truly was a deep paranoia about being buried alive. Victorians invented items such as the coffin bell to avoid such a fate, and the fear of it shows up in Poe's stories "The Fall of the House of Usher" and "The Premature Burial." There was, established in the late Victorian era, an American Society for the Prevention of People Being Buried Alive, sometime after the setting of this story, but the sentiments had prevailed throughout the era.

Too, I rather liked the idea of Annabel breaking out of her coffin, in a metaphorical sense as well as the physical sense.

It's something each of us should do.

ACKNOWLEDGMENTS

As always, I am blessed to have a number of wonderful people who graciously contributed their many talents to this book.

I am deeply indebted to Dr. Alex Naylor and Finni Golden, historical advisers and residents of Hampshire, England, both of whom continue to be instrumental in the development of this series. They not only kept my history straight (Alex is a sailor who often represents Lord Nelson; Finni is a genius polymath who had a Victorian grandmother!); they also help me keep my English English, and not American.

Danielle Egan-Miller, Joanna MacKenzie, and Abby Saul of Browne & Miller Literary Associates are among the rare agents who are also great editors. Thanks, too, to the entire hardworking team at Howard Books who help bring these books to life and to market, including my enjoyable, professional partnership with Senior Editor Beth Datlowe Adams, whose refinements made truly important contributions. Jenny Q of Historical Editorial once more brought her mighty pen and thoughtful insight to both the planning and the rough draft.

Friends Serena Chase, Dawn Kinzer, and Debbie Austin deserve a shout-out for their focused, valuable comments. My dear friend Janelle Schneider, a Catholic woman, read to ensure fidelity in my representation of the Catholic faith.

My wonderful husband, Michael, brings not only excellent research skills but great coffee-making and constant encouragement. My three children love and cheer me on at each step of what can sometimes be a daunting journey.

This book, then, is for the four of you, with love.

ALSO BY
SANDRA BYRD

PROUDLY PUBLISHED BY

HOWARD BOOKS®
A DIVISION OF SIMON & SCHUSTER, INC.
A CBS COMPANY